God's
Spy

GOD'S SPY

Juan Gómez-Jurado

Translated by James Graham

First published in Great Britain in 2007
by Orion
An imprint of the Orion Publishing Group
Orion House, 5 Upper St Martin's Lane,
London WC2H 9EA

A CIP catalogue record for this book is
available from the British Library

Typeset by Deltatype Ltd, Birkenhead, Merseyside

Printed in Great Britain by
Clays Ltd, St Ives plc

www.orionbooks.co.uk

For Katu, the light of my life

'And I will give unto thee the keys of the kingdom of heaven ...'

MATTHEW 16:19

Prologue

THE SAINT MATTHEW INSTITUTE

(CENTER FOR THE REHABILITATION OF CATHOLIC
PRIESTS WITH A HISTORY OF SEXUAL ABUSE)
SACHEM PIKE, MARYLAND

July 1999

Father Selznick awoke in the middle of the night to find a fish knife pressed against his throat. Victor Karosky had come into possession of the knife by mysterious means, and had made use of the endless nights spent in solitary confinement to sharpen it on the edge of a tile he had pried loose from the floor of his cell.

This was the second time he had successfully squeezed out of his wretched six-by-ten-foot cell, freeing himself from the chain that fastened him to the wall with the cartridge of a ball point pen.

Selznick had insulted him and he had to pay.

'Don't try to talk, Peter.'

Karosky's firm, gentle hand covered Selznick's mouth while his knife caressed the fresh stubble on the face of the other priest. Up and down it went in a macabre parody of shaving. Selznick watched him, paralysed with terror, his eyes wide open, his fingers clutching the edge of the sheet, feeling the other man's weight pressing upon him.

'You know why I'm here, don't you, Peter? Blink once for yes and twice for no.'

At first Selznick didn't react, but then he saw the fish knife stop in mid-air. He blinked twice.

'Your ignorance is the only thing I find more infuriating than your lack of manners, Peter. I have come to hear your confession.'

A faint glimmer of relief passed over Selznick's face.

'Do you repent of your abuse of innocent children?'

Selznick blinked once.

'Do you repent of the stain you laid on the ministry?'

A single blink.

'Do you repent of having caused offence to so many souls, defrauding our Holy Mother Church?'

Another blink.

'And last but not least, do you repent of having interrupted me during group therapy three weeks ago, an act that has considerably set back my social reintegration and my eventual return to the service of God?'

A strong, fervent blink.

'I am happy to see you repent. For the first three sins, your penance is six Our Fathers and six Hail Marys. For the last sin …' The expression in Karosky's cold, grey eyes was unwavering as he lifted the knife and inserted it between the lips of his terrified victim. 'You have no idea how much I'm going to enjoy this.'

Selznick took almost forty-five minutes to die, and he did so without making a single sound. Even the guards who stood only a hundred feet away never heard a thing.

Karosky let himself back into his cell and shut the door. This was where the Institute's petrified director found him sitting the next morning, covered in dried blood. But that wasn't what disturbed the elderly priest the most. What he found completely terrifying was the absolute, icy indifference with which Karosky asked for a towel and a washbasin. 'I've spilled something on myself,' was all he said.

Dramatis Personae

Priests
ANTHONY FOWLER, former intelligence officer in US Air Force
VICTOR KAROSKY, priest and serial killer
CANICE CONROY, former director of the Saint Matthew Institute
(deceased)

Senior Civilian Officials in the Vatican
JOAQUÍN BALCELLS, Vatican spokesman
GIANLUIGI VARONE, the sole judge in Vatican City

Cardinals
EDUARDO GONZÁLEZ SAMALO, the Pope's chamberlain (*camerlengo*)
FRANCIS CASEY
EMILIO ROBAYRA
ENRICO PORTINI
GERALDO CARDOSO
The 110 other cardinals present for the Conclave

Members of Religious Orders
BROTHER FRANCESCO TOMA, Carmelite. Parish of Santa Maria in Traspontina
Sister HELENA TOBINA, director of Saint Martha's House

Corpo di Vigilanza, the Vatican police
CAMILO CIRIN, Inspector General
FABIO DANTE, Superintendent

Italian Police

Unità di Analisi del Crimine Violento (UACV, or Department for the Analysis of Violent Crime)

PAOLA DICANTI, inspector and psychiatrist. Head of the Laboratorio per l'Analisi del Comportamento (LAC, or Laboratory for Behavioral Analysis)

CARLO TROI, Director General of UACV; Paola Dicanti's boss

MAURIZIO PONTIERO, detective

ANGELO BIFFI, forensic sculptor and digital image expert

Civilians

ANDREA OTERO, freelance reporter writing for *El Globo*, a Spanish daily newspaper

GIUSEPPE BASTINA, courier for Tevere Express

Some Pertinent Facts about Vatican City
(taken from *The CIA World Factbook*)

Surface area: 17 square miles (the smallest country in the world)

Borders: 1.99 miles (with Italy)

Lowest point of elevation: Saint Peter's Square, 62.34 feet above sea level

Highest point: Vatican gardens, 246.06 feet above sea level

Climate: Moderate, rainy winters from September to mid-May; hot, dry summers from May to September

Land use: 100% urban. Cultivated land, 0%

Natural resources: None

Population: 911 citizens with passport; 3,000 daily workers

System of government: Ecclesiastic, absolute monarchy

Rate of birth: 0%. No births at any time in the course of its history

Economy: Based on charitable donations and the sale of stamps, postcards, prints and the management of its banks and finances

Communications: 2,200 phone lines, 7 radio stations, 1 television channel

Annual income: $242,000,000 (US dollars)

Annual expenditure: $272,000,000 (US dollars)

Legal system: Based on the Code of Canon Law. Although it has not been officially applied since 1868, the death penalty remains in effect.

Special considerations: The Holy Father has great influence over the lives of more than 1,086,000,000 believers around the world.

$\mathcal{A}$POSTOLIC $\mathcal{P}$ALACE

Saturday, 2 April 2005, 9.37 p.m.

The man in the bed was no longer breathing. His personal secretary, Monsignor Stanislaw Dwisicz, who had spent the last thirty-six hours clinging to the dying man's right hand, burst into tears. The doctors on duty had to use force to pull Dwisicz away, then spent the next hour trying to bring the old man back to life. Their efforts went above and beyond the call of duty. As they undertook each successive attempt to preserve the man's life, the doctors knew they had to do everything in their power, if only for the sake of their consciences.

The Supreme Pontiff's private apartment would have been a surprise to the uninformed observer. The ruler before whom world leaders respectfully bowed their heads lived in conditions of utter simplicity. His private quarters were austere, the walls bare except for a crucifix, the furniture no more than a chair, a table and the hospital roll-away that, in the last few months of his illness had replaced the dark wooden bed. Stationed around it, the doctors were now doing everything they could to revive him, shedding large drops of sweat on to the immaculate white sheets, which four Polish nuns changed three times a day.

Doctor Silvio Renato, the Pope's personal physician, put an end to their futile efforts. He gestured to the nurses to cover the time-worn face with a white veil and then asked everyone to leave apart from Dwisicz. He drafted the death certificate then and there. The cause of death was obvious: the man's heart had collapsed, as had his circulatory system, both aggravated further by inflammation of the larynx. Renato hesitated for a moment when it came to filling in the elderly man's name, although in the end, to avoid confusion, he chose the one he had been given at birth.

Once he had filled out and signed the document, the doctor handed it over to Cardinal Samalo, who had just entered the room. The cardinal, dressed in his red robes, had the distressing task of officially certifying the death.

'Thank you, doctor. With your permission, I'll proceed.'

'It's all yours, Your Eminence.'

'No, doctor. From here on, God is in charge.'

Samalo slowly approached the deceased's bed. At 78 years of age he had prayed to God many times to be spared this scene. He was a calm and peaceful man, but was well aware of the heavy load, the numerous responsibilities and duties, that now descended upon his shoulders.

He examined the body carefully. The man had reached 84 years of age, in the course of which he had overcome a bullet to the chest, a tumor in his colon and a complicated case of appendicitis. Parkinson's had gradually worn him down, a little more each day, eventually leaving him so weak that his heart had given out.

From the third-floor window of the Palace, the cardinal could see nearly two hundred thousand people swelling Saint Peter's Square. The rooftops of the surrounding buildings overflowed with antennae and television cameras. 'In just a short time there will be even more,' Samalo thought to himself. 'What's coming will overwhelm us. The people adored him; they admired the sacrifices he made, his iron will. This will be a blow to them, even if we've all been expecting it since January ... and more than a few people actually wanted it to happen. And then there's the other business we must deal with ...'

A noise came from the other side of the door, and the Vatican's head of security, Camilo Cirin, walked into the room ahead of the three cardinals who were charged with certifying the Pope's death. Worry and lack of sleep were etched on their faces as they drew close to the bed.

'Let's begin,' said Samalo.

Dwisicz held a small, open case at Samalo's side.

The chamberlain lifted the white veil that covered the face of the

7

deceased and opened a tiny phial containing holy oils. He began to recite the millenniary ritual in Latin:

'*Si vives, ego te absolvo a peccatis tuis, in nomine Patris et Filii et Spiritus Sancti. Amen.*' Samalo made the sign of the cross over the man's forehead and continued. '*Per istam sanctam unctionem, indulgeat tibi Dominum quidquid ... Amen.*' With a solemn gesture, he invoked the apostolic benediction. 'By the power invested in me by the Holy See, I hereby grant you full forgiveness for and remission of all sins, and I bless you. In the name of the Father, the Son, and the Holy Ghost. Amen.'

Next, he took a silver hammer out of the case the bishop was holding. Three times he gently tapped the forehead of the dead man, asking each time, 'Karol Wojtyla, are you alive?'

There was no response. The chamberlain looked at the three cardinals who stood by the bed, all of whom nodded.

'The Pope is dead. There can be no doubt.'

With his left hand, Samalo removed the Fisherman's ring – the symbol of the Pope's authority in this world – from the dead man's right hand. Using his right hand he once again shrouded the face of John Paul II with the veil.

He took a deep breath, and looked at his three companions. 'We have a lot of work ahead of us.'

Church of Santa Maria in Traspontina

VIA DELLA CONCILIAZIONE, 14

Tuesday, 5 April 2005, 10.41 a.m.

Inspector Paola Dicanti briefly closed her eyes and waited until they were accustomed to the darkness as she stood in the entrance to the building. It had taken her almost half an hour to get to the scene of the crime. If Rome was always in a state of vehicular chaos, after the Holy Father's death it was transformed into an auto-inferno. Thousands of mourners were arriving every day in the capital of Christendom in order to bid their last farewell to the body lying in state in Saint Peter's Basilica. This Pope had gone to the next world fêted as a saint, and there were already volunteers moving around the streets collecting signatures to begin the process of beatification. Every hour, eighteen thousand people passed in front of his mortal remains.

'A huge success for forensic medicine,' Paola commented to herself with irony.

Her mother had warned her before she left the apartment they shared on the Via della Croce: 'It will take too long if you go by Cavour. Go up Regina Margherita and down Rienzo,' she said as she stirred the semolina porridge she was cooking for her daughter, just as she had done every morning for thirty-three years.

So Paola had of course gone by Cavour, and had lost a good deal of time.

The taste of semolina lingered in her mouth. It was always the first thing she ate every morning. During the year she spent studying at FBI headquarters in Quantico, Virginia, she had missed it so much that it had nearly become an obsession. She had ended up asking her mother to send her a big box of the porridge, which she used to cook in the microwave in the Behavioral Studies Unit. The taste wasn't the same, but simply having it had made it easier to be so far from home during a year that was both difficult and rewarding. Paola had grown up only two steps from Via Condotti, one of the most exclusive streets in the world, but her family was poor. She hadn't even known the meaning of the word until she went to the United States, a country with its own measure for everything. She had been overjoyed to return to the city she had hated so fervently when she was growing up.

In Italy, the Department for the Analysis of Violent Crime (the UACV, or Unità di Analisi del Crimine Violento) was created in 1995, with a specific focus on serial killers. It seems incredible that, until this date, the country ranked fifth in the world for the number of psychopaths it contained lacked a unit designed to track them down. Inside the UACV there was a special department known as the Laboratory for Behavioural Analysis (LAC, or Laboratorio per l'Analisi del Comportamento) founded by Giovanni Balta, Dicanti's teacher and mentor. Balta died at the beginning of 2004 after a sudden and massive heart attack, at which time Dottoressa Dicanti became Ispettore Dicanti, the head of the LAC's Rome office. Her FBI training and Balta's excellent reports on her work were what got her the job. On the supervisor's death, the LAC found its personnel drastically reduced: Paola became the entire staff. Even so, the department was part of the UACV, and they could count on technical support from one of the most advanced forensic units in Europe.

Nevertheless, as of that moment, they had yet to solve a single case. In Italy there were thirty serial killers running around free, all of them unidentified. Of these, nine were considered 'hot' cases, since they were connected to the most recent deaths on record. No new bodies had turned up since Dicanti had become head of the LAC, and the absence of any definitive evidence increased the pressure, so that at times her psychological profiles were the only lead the police had. 'Castles in the air', Carlo Troi called them. Troi was a physicist and mathematician by training, a man who spent more time on the phone than in the laboratory. Unfortunately, Troi was the UACV's Director and Paola's immediate boss, and every time they passed in the hallway he gave her a sarcastic look. 'My pretty little novelist' was his nickname for her when they were alone – a mocking allusion to the abundant imagination that Dicanti poured into her profiles.

Paola was desperately hoping her work would begin to bear fruit, just so she could flaunt the results in the bastard's face. She had made the mistake of sleeping with him one night in a moment of weakness. Working until late each night, her guard down, her heart overwhelmed by an emptiness she could not name ... and then the time-honoured regrets the morning after. Especially when she reminded herself that Troi was married and nearly twice her age. He'd been a gentleman – hadn't gone on about it and was careful to keep his distance; but he never let Paola forget it either, hinting at what had happened with comments that were somewhere between sexist and charming. *God*, how she hated the man.

But now finally, for the first time since her promotion, she had a case she could tackle from the outset, one in which she wouldn't have to work with shoddy evidence gathered by dim-witted agents. She took the call in the middle of breakfast, and immediately hurried to her room to change. She combed her long, dark hair, tied it up in a bun, put away the trousers and jersey she had been going to wear to the office, and instead took out an elegant suit with a black jacket. She was intrigued: the caller hadn't supplied her with a single detail, except that a crime had been committed and that it fell within her area of expertise. They had summoned her to Santa Maria in Traspontina 'with the utmost urgency'.

And that's precisely where she was now, standing in the doorway of the church. Behind her, a surging mass of people milled about in a queue that stretched for almost two and a half miles, coming to an end just short of the Vittorio Emmanuel II Bridge. Paola looked back at the scene and it worried her. The people in the queue had spent the whole night there, but anyone who might have seen something would be far away by now. As they passed, some of the pilgrims glanced over at the discreet pair of carabinieri who were preventing the occasional group of worshippers from entering the church. The police diplomatically assured them that the building was undergoing repairs.

Paola took a deep breath and crossed the threshold. The church had one nave with five chapels on each side, and the air was filled with the musty scent of old incense. The lights were dimmed, no doubt because that was how the church would have been when the body was discovered. It was one of Troi's mottos: 'Let's see it the way he did.'

She looked around, her eyes trying to pick out objects in the darkness. Two men were conversing in low tones at the rear of the church, their backs to her. A Carmelite friar, nervously praying the rosary at the foot of the baptismal font, stared at her as she surveyed the scene.

'Beautiful, isn't it, signorina? It dates from 1566. Constructed by Peruzzi, its chapels—'

Dicanti interrupted him with a firm smile: 'Sadly, brother, art is the last thing on my mind at the moment. I'm Inspector Dicanti. Are you the parish priest?'

'Indeed, ispettore. And I'm also the one who discovered the body. I'm sure that's of more interest to you. Blessed be the Lord, in days such as these ... A saint has departed and left us with devils in his stead!'

The Carmelite looked very old. He wore tortoiseshell glasses with thick lenses, and the traditional brown habit with a large scapulary knotted at the waist. A thick white beard covered his face. He walked to and fro around the font, hunched over and limping slightly. His hands nervously thumbed his prayer beads and shook uncontrollably at odd moments.

'Calm down, brother. What is your name?'

'Francesco Toma, ispettore.'

'Tell me, in your own words, what took place here today. I know you've probably been through all this six or seven times already, but it can't be helped – take my word for it.'

The friar exhaled. 'There's not much to tell. In addition to my pastoral duties, it is also my responsibility to take care of this church. I live in a small room behind the sacristy. I got up as I do every morning at six, washed my face and put on my robes. I crossed the sacristy and entered the church through a hidden door at the foot of the main altar. I went to the chapel of Our Lady of Carmen, where I say my prayers each day. I noticed that there were candles burning in front of the chapel of Saint Thomas, yet when I turned to go back to my room, they had all gone out. That's when I saw it. I started running towards the sacristy, terrified because I thought the killer could still be in the church. Then I called the emergency number 113.'

'You didn't touch anything in the crime scene?'

'No, ispettore, nothing. I was frightened out of my wits, may God forgive me.'

'And you didn't try to help the victim?'

'He was clearly beyond any earthly help.'

A figure moved towards them down the main aisle of the church. It was Detective Maurizio Pontiero from the UACV.

'Dicanti, hurry up. They're going to turn on the lights.'

'Just a second. Take this, it's my card. My mobile number is at the bottom. Call me any time if you remember anything else.'

'I will. And here's a gift for you.' The Carmelite handed her a small, brightly coloured card.

'Santa Maria del Carmen. Take it with you wherever you go. It will show you the way in these uncertain times.'

'Thank you.' Dicanti accepted the card from the old friar without giving it a second look, then slipped it into the pocket of her coat.

The inspector followed Pontiero through the church to the third chapel on the left, which was cordoned off with the UACV's classic red-and-white crime-scene tape.

'You were late,' Pontiero reproached her.

'The traffic was murder. It's a circus out there.'

'You should have taken Rienzo.'

Although Dicanti technically occupied a higher rung than Pontiero in the hierarchy of the Italian police, as the agent in charge of UACV field investigations he outranked any laboratory researcher, even someone like Paola, who was head of her department. Pontiero was 51 years old, trim and hot-tempered. He had a face like a shrivelled raisin and wore a perennial frown. It was quite clear to Paola that Pontiero adored her, but he took care not to let it show.

Dicanti was about to cross the police line but Pontiero's arm shot out to stop her. 'Hang on a second, Paola. You won't ever have seen anything like this before. It's completely sickening, I swear.' His voice was trembling.

'I'm sure I'll be able to handle it, Pontiero. But thanks.'

She walked into the chapel. An investigator from the UACV had arrived before her and was taking photographs. At the rear of the chapel, against the wall, was a small altar adorned with a painting of Saint Thomas at the moment he pressed his fingers into Jesus' wounds. The body lay beneath it.

'Holy Mother of God!'

'I warned you.'

It was a spectacle straight out of Dante. The dead man was leaning against the altar and his eyes had been torn out, leaving two gaping wounds the colour of dried blood in their place. The mouth was wide open in a horrendous, grotesque grimace, and from it hung a greyish-brown object. In a sudden flash from the camera, Dicanti saw the worst: the victim's hands had been severed and were resting one on top of the other on a strip of white linen next to his body. The hands had been cleaned of any blood and one of them was adorned with an unusually large ring.

The dead man wore the black robes with red sash and piping of the cardinals.

Paola's eyes widened. 'Pontiero, please tell me it's not a cardinal.'

'We don't know yet, Dicanti. We're investigating who it might be, though there's not much left of the face. We held things up for you so you could take a look at the place and see it the way the killer did.'

'Where's the rest of the Crime Scene Analysis team?'

The analysis team were the UACV's big shots. All of them were highly skilled pathologists, specialising in the recovery of finger-prints, hairs and anything else a criminal might leave at the scene. They worked according to the rule that in every crime there is an exchange: the killer takes something and he leaves something behind.

'They're on their way. Their van is stuck in traffic on Cavour.'

'They should have gone by Rienzo.' The photographer put in his two cents.

'No one asked for your opinion,' Dicanti snapped back.

He left the chapel muttering unpleasant things about Paola under his breath.

'You've got to get that temper of yours under control.'

'Why in God's name didn't you call me earlier, Pontiero?' Dicanti asked, completely ignoring the detective's remark. 'This case is serious. Whoever did it is really sick in the head.'

'Is that your professional opinion, Dottoressa?' Carlo Troi strolled into the chapel, directing one of his mocking glances her way. He was enamoured of surprise entrances like that. Paola now realised that he must have been one of the two men talking at the back of the church when she came in; she blamed herself for letting him catch her unprepared. The other man wasn't far behind, but he didn't utter a word, nor did he enter the chapel.

'No. My professional opinion will be on your desk as soon as it's ready. I simply put forward the observation that, whatever else we might say, the man who committed this crime clearly has a few screws loose.'

Troi was about to say something, but at that moment the lights of the church came on; and then all of them saw something that they had previously missed: written on the floor of the church, close to the body of the dead man, were letters of no great size that spelled out:

EGO TE ABSOLVO

'Looks like blood,' Pontiero said, voicing what everyone else was thinking.

A mobile phone began to ring out the first chords of Handel's Hallelujah Chorus. The three of them looked at Troi's companion as he took the phone out of his coat pocket and answered the call. He barely said a word, just a few 'Ahas' and 'Hmms'.

After he hung up, he looked at Troi and nodded. 'It's as we feared,' the UACV's director said. 'Dicanti, Pontiero, needless to say, this is a very delicate case. The body we have here is that of the Argentine Cardinal, Emilio Robayra. The assassination of a cardinal in Rome is, in itself, an unspeakable tragedy, but it is even more vexing at the present moment. The victim was one of a hundred and fifteen men who in the next few days will participate in the Conclave to choose the next Supreme Pontiff. Consequently, the situation is extraordinarily delicate. This crime cannot reach the ears of the press for any reason whatsoever. Imagine the headlines: "Serial Killer Stalks the Papal Election". I don't even want to think about it.'

'Just a minute, you said a serial killer? Is there something we don't know?'

Troi cleared his throat and looked at the mysterious person who had come in with him. 'Paola Dicanti, Maurizio Pontiero, let me introduce you to Camilo Cirin, Inspector General of the Corpo di Vigilanza of Vatican City.'

Cirin nodded as he stepped closer. When he finally spoke, it seemed an effort, as if he strongly disliked having to use words at all: 'We believe this man is the second victim.'

The Saint Matthew Institute

SACHEM PIKE, MARYLAND

August 1994

'Come in, Father Karosky, come in. Take your clothes off behind the screen, if you would be so kind.'

The priest started to remove his cassock. The technician continued to talk to him from the other side of the white screen.

'No need to worry about the test, father. It's all completely standard, OK? Standard procedure.' The technician laughed under his breath. 'Maybe you've heard the other residents talking about it, but the lion isn't as fierce as they make him out to be, as my grandmother used to say. How long have you been with us?'

'Two weeks.'

'Time enough to be acquainted with the test, yes indeed. Played any tennis yet?'

'I don't like tennis. Shall I come out now?'

'No, father, put the green gown on so you don't catch cold.' The doctor laughed again.

Karosky walked out from behind the screen wearing an oversized green shirt.

'Walk over to the examining bench and lie down. That's right. Hang on, let me adjust the back for you. You have to be able to see the image on the television screen. Is that OK?'

'Perfect.'

'Great. I just have to make some adjustments to the machine, and then we can get started. What we have here is a fine television, wouldn't you say? A thirty-two-inch screen. If I had something like this at home my other half would show me a little more respect, don't *you think?'* Once again, the technician laughed at his own joke.

'I'm not sure.'

'Ha. Of course not, father. That witch wouldn't even respect Jesus Christ himself if he popped out of a packet of crackers and slapped her on her flabby arse.'

'You shouldn't take God's name in vain, my son.'

'Right you are, father. OK, everything is ready. You've never had a penile plethysmograph before, is that correct?'

'No.'

'Of course you haven't. Did they explain to you what the test consists of?'

'In general terms.'

'OK, now I'm going to put my hands under your gown so I can attach two electrodes to your penis. Is that all right? This will help us to measure your level of sexual response to various stimuli. Good, all done.'

'You have cold hands.'

'Yes, it is a little chilly in here, isn't it? Are you comfortable?'

'I'm fine.'

'Then let's begin.'

One image after another began to appear on the screen: the Eiffel Tower. Dawn. Mist in the mountains. Chocolate ice cream. Heterosexual coitus. A forest. Trees. A woman performing oral sex on a man. Tulips in Holland. Homosexual intercourse. Las Meninas by Velázquez. Sunset on Mount Kilimanjaro. Two men engaging in oral sex. Snow on the rooftops of a Swiss village. A young boy performing oral sex on an older man, the child's sad eyes looking straight into the camera as he sucks on the adult's member.

Karosky stood up, his eyes full of rage.

'Father, you can't get up. We're not finished yet—'

The priest grabbed the man by the neck, and smashed his head against the instrument board again and again, until blood began to spill over the various buttons, soaking the doctor's white lab coat and Karosky's gown, bathing the whole world in blood.

'Do not commit impure acts like this ever again, do you understand me? Do you hear me, you dirty little piece of shit?'

CHURCH OF SANTA MARIA
IN TRASPONTINA

VIA DELLA CONCILIAZIONE, 14

Tuesday, 5 April 2005, 11.59 a.m.

The silence following Camilo Cirin's words became even more pronounced when the bells in nearby Saint Peter's Square began ringing the angelus.

'The second victim? Someone has ripped another cardinal to pieces and we're only finding out now?' Pontiero's expression made his opinion of the matter absolutely clear.

Cirin, unmoved, stared straight back at him. He was, no doubt about it, an unusual man. Of medium height, with brown eyes, of indistinguishable age, wearing a plain suit and grey overcoat – nothing about him called attention to itself, which was, in itself, extraordinary: he was the paradigm of normality. He used as few words as possible, as if in doing so he took himself out of the picture. But none of those present were fooled: all of them had heard talk about Camilo Cirin, one of the most powerful figures in the Vatican and in charge of the smallest police force in the world, the Vatican Vigilanza. A team of forty-eight agents (officially), less than half that of the Swiss Guard but infinitely more powerful. Nothing took place in his tiny country without Cirin knowing about it. In 1997 a man had tried to outshine him: Alois Siltermann, the newly chosen commander of the Swiss Guard. Two days after his appointment, Siltermann, along with his wife and a corporal with an impeccable reputation, had been found dead. They had all been shot. The blame had fallen on the corporal, who, after supposedly going mad, had shot the couple and then put his 'regulation firearm' into his mouth and squeezed the trigger. The entire explanation would have made sense had it not been for two small details: corporals in the Swiss Guard do not carry weapons, and the front teeth of the corporal in question had been knocked out, suggesting that the pistol had been brutally forced into his mouth.

A colleague in the Italian Inspectorate had told Dicanti the whole story. After the event had taken place, he and his fellow officers had set out to give the Vigilanza any assistance they might need, but they had barely set foot on the crime scene when they had been cordially invited to return to their inspectorate and close the door, without so much as a thank you for showing up. The dark legend of Camilo Cirin had travelled from mouth to mouth in police precincts right across Rome, and the UACV was no exception.

Now the three of them stood there, just outside the chapel, stupefied by Cirin's declaration.

'With all due respect, *ispettore generale*, I think that if you knew that a killer capable of committing a crime such as this was running around loose in Rome, you had a duty to report it to the UACV,' Dicanti said.

'Absolutely right, and that is exactly what my distinguished colleague did,' Troi responded. 'He communicated it to me personally, and we both agreed on the need for the strictest secrecy in this case, for everyone's benefit. And we both agreed on something else: the Vatican has no one capable of going head to head with a criminal as – how shall I say it? – idiosyncratic as this one.'

Surprisingly, Cirin interrupted. 'Let me be honest, signorina. Our work consists mainly of containment, protection and counter-espionage. In those fields I guarantee we are among the best. But with a man who has – how did you put it? – a few screws loose, we are outside our field of competency. We were thinking about asking for help when we received news of this second crime.'

'It's our feeling that this case requires a much more creative grasp of the subject, Dicanti.' Troi was speaking now. 'And that is why we don't want you to limit yourself only to producing profiles, as you've done up to now. We want you to lead the investigation.'

Paola didn't say a word. This was work for a field agent, not for a criminal psychologist. Certainly, with the training she had received in Quantico, she could do the job as well as any field agent, but the fact that the request had come from Troi, and the timing of it all, astonished her.

Cirin spun around towards a man in a leather jacket who had just joined the group. 'There you are. I'd like to introduce Fabio Dante, Superintendent of the Vigilanza. He'll be your liaison with the Vatican. He'll bring you up to speed on the first murder, and he'll work with you on this one, since it's all the same case. Anything you ask of him is the same as asking me. And the reverse holds true as well: anything he refuses you, it's as if I have refused it myself. In the Vatican we have our own rules, I hope you understand. And I hope that you catch this monster. The assassination of two princes of the Holy Mother Church cannot go unpunished.'

And without a word more, he walked out of the door.

Troi moved over to Paola, so close it made her feel uncomfortable. Their romantic interlude was still fresh in her mind.

'Well, you heard him, Dicanti. You've just met one of the most powerful men in the Vatican, and he has given you a very specific assignment. I don't know why he settled on you but he particularly mentioned your name. Do what you have to do. Give me a report every day; keep it short, sweet and to the point. Above all else, get me substantial proof. I hope your castles in the air amount to something this time. Bring me something, and soon.' Turning on his heels, he headed for the exit in pursuit of Cirin.

'What utter bastards,' Dicanti blurted out when she was sure the others couldn't hear.

'Keep going; don't hold back.' Dante, the most recent arrival, was laughing.

Paola blushed and held out her hand. 'Paola Dicanti.'

'Fabio Dante.'

'Maurizio Pontiero.'

As Pontiero and Dante shook hands, Dicante studied the latter closely. Just short of 41 years old, he was short and well built, his head of dark hair sitting on top of a thick neck that seemed barely two inches long. A mere five foot six inches in height, the superintendent was attractive, even if he wasn't classically good-looking. His eyes were olive green, characteristic of the south of the Italian peninsula.

'I take it "bastards" includes my superior, ispettore?'

'Well, yes. I believe an honour has been bestowed on me that I don't deserve.'

'We both know it isn't an honour, it's a real pain in the neck. But it isn't undeserved. Your track record so far and your CV prove that you are ready for this. It's a pity you don't have the results to go along with it, but that's about to change, isn't it?'

'You've read my CV? Isn't anything confidential around here?'

'Not for Him.'

'Listen, you pretentious little ...' Pontiero had smoke coming out of his ears.

'Basta, Maurizio. We don't need to fight. We're at the scene of the crime, and I'm in charge, so let's get down to work and we can talk later. We'll leave the field to them.'

'OK. You're in charge, Paola. The boss said so.'

Waiting prudently some distance behind the red line were two men and a woman sheathed in dark-blue overalls. They were the team from Crime Scene Analysis, specialists in the recovery of evidence. Dicanti and the two others exited the chapel and walked towards the central nave.

'Right, Dante, tell us everything you know,' Dicanti said.

'Well ... the first victim was the Italian cardinal Enrico Portini.'

'No way!' Dicanti and Pontiero exclaimed at the same time.

'Take my word for it, friends. I saw it with my very own eyes.'

'He was the reformists' great hope, a liberal candidate. What a mess it would be if the media got hold of this.'

'No, Pontiero, it would be a *catastrophe*,' said Dante. 'Yesterday morning George Bush arrived in Rome with his whole family. Another two hundred representatives and international heads of state are currently staying in your country, but they'll be in mine for the funeral on Friday. We're on maximum alert, but you know what the city is like. It's a very complex situation and the last thing we want to do is spread panic. Come outside with me. I need a cigarette.'

Dante lead them out into the street, where the crowd was constantly growing larger and more tightly packed. The Via del Conciliazione was completely swarming with citizens of every flag: French, Spanish, Polish, Italian, and countless others. Young people were playing guitars; the faithful sat with candles lit; there was even a blind man with his guide dog. Two million people would attend the funeral of the pope who had changed the map of Europe. It was the worst possible environment to work in, Dicanti thought – any scrap of evidence would be completely lost in the whirlwind of pilgrims.

'Portini was staying at the Madri Pie residence, on the Via de Gasperi,' Dante said. 'He arrived on Thursday morning since he already knew that the Pope's condition was critical. The nuns say that he seemed perfectly normal on Friday evening: he had dinner, and then he spent a long time in the chapel, praying for the Holy Father. No one saw him go to bed. There was no evidence of a struggle in his room. His bed hadn't been slept in unless the man who kidnapped him made it again perfectly. He didn't come down for breakfast on Saturday, but everyone thought he must have been praying in the Vatican. It's not clear to us what actually happened that Saturday, but the city was in complete chaos. Do you understand? He disappeared somewhere in the middle of the Vatican.'

Dante stopped, lit a cigarette and offered one to Pontiero, who turned him down and took out one of his own.

Dante went on: 'His body showed up yesterday morning in the chapel of the residence, but, just as we saw today, the lack of blood meant that the scenario was planned in advance. Luckily the man who discovered the body was an honest priest and he called us straight away. We took photographs of the crime scene, but when I suggested that we call you, Cirin told me he would take care of it. And he ordered us to clean up absolutely everything. The cardinal's body was taken to a location deep inside the Vatican, where it was incinerated.'

'What! They destroyed all the evidence? This I really can't believe.'

Dante stared at them both, defiant. 'My boss made the decision, and perhaps it wasn't the best response. But he did call your boss to explain the situation. And here you are. Are you aware of what we're dealing with here? The Vigilanza simply isn't equipped to handle something like this.'

'Which is precisely why you should have left it in the hands of professionals,' Pontiero interjected, a stony look on his face.

'You still don't get it. We can't afford to trust anybody, which is why Cirin did what he did. Don't look at me like that, Dicanti. Try to take into account the reasons for our actions. If Portini's death had been the only one, we could have invented some excuse, and

23

buried the whole subject. But it didn't turn out that way. It's nothing personal, please understand.'

'What I understand is that we've been invited to the second course of the meal – with half the evidence. Just perfect. Is there anything else we should understand?' Dicanti was furious now.

'Not at the moment, no,' said Dante, hiding behind an ironic smile.

'Shit, shit, shit. This is all a terrible mess, Dante. From now on I want you to tell me everything. And I want one thing to be very clear: I'm in charge. You've been ordered to help me as much as you can, but you must understand that, as far as I'm concerned, it matters less that the victims were both cardinals than that the crimes took place in my jurisdiction. Is that clear?'

'Crystal clear.'

'It had better be. The modus operandi was the same?'

'As far as my detective skills can deduce, yes. The body was stretched out at the foot of the altar. His eyes were gone. The hands, just like today, were cut off and placed on a piece of canvas alongside the body. It's repugnant. I was the one who put the body in a bag and carried it to the crematorium. I spent all that night in the shower, take my word for it.'

'It would have been a good idea if you'd stayed a little longer,' Pontiero muttered.

Four long hours later they finished working on Robayra's body and began the process of removing it. On the express orders of Director Troi it was the men from Analysis who put the body in a plastic bag and carried it off to the morgue, so that no one else would see the cardinal's robes. It was made clear to everyone that this was a very special case and that the identity of the dead man had to be kept a secret.

For everyone's benefit.

The Saint Matthew Institute

SACHEM PIKE, MARYLAND

September 1994

Transcript of Interview Number 5 between Patient Number 3643 and Doctor Canice Conroy

DR CONROY: Good afternoon, Victor. Welcome to my office. Feeling better?

No. 3643: Yes, doctor. Thank you.

DR CONROY: Do you want a drink?

No. 3643: No, thank you.

DR CONROY: Well, a priest who doesn't drink – that's a novelty! It won't bother you if I …

No. 3643: Go ahead, doctor.

DR CONROY: It's my understanding that you've spent some time in the infirmary.

No. 3643: I picked up a few bruises a week ago.

DR CONROY: Do you remember how these bruises came about?

No. 3643: Yes, doctor. It was during an altercation in the observation room.

DR CONROY: Tell me what happened, Victor.

No. 3643: I went there to undergo a plethysmograph, on your recommendation.

DR CONROY: Do you recall the purpose of the test, Victor?

No. 3643: To determine the causes of my problem.

DR CONROY: Exactly, Victor. You recognise that you have a problem, which no doubt shows progress.

NO. 3643: I always knew that I had a problem, doctor. I should remind you that I'm attending the centre on a voluntary basis.

DR CONROY: That's certainly a subject I want to explore with you in our next session. But for now I'd like you to keep talking about what happened the other day.

NO. 3643: I went into the room and took off my clothes.

DR CONROY: And that made you feel uncomfortable?

NO. 3643: Yes.

DR CONROY: It's medical procedure. You have to take your clothes off.

NO. 3643: I don't think it's necessary.

DR CONROY: The technician has to attach the instrument that measures your reaction to a part of your body that is normally difficult to reach. That's why you had to take your clothes off, Victor.

NO. 3643: I still don't think it's necessary.

DR CONROY: Very well, just go along with me for a moment. What happened next?

NO. 3643: He attached the electrodes, down there.

DR CONROY: Where, Victor?

NO. 3643: You know where.

DR CONROY: No, Victor, I want you to say it.

NO. 3643: On my thing.

DR CONROY: Could you be more explicit, Victor?

NO. 3643: On my ... penis.

DR CONROY: Very good, Victor. The masculine member, the male organ used for copulation and urination.

NO. 3643: In my case, only for the second function, doctor.

DR CONROY: Are you sure, Victor?

NO. 3643: Yes.

DR CONROY: It wasn't always like that in the past, was it, Victor?

NO. 3643: The past is over. I want to change all that.

DR CONROY: Why?

NO. 3643: Because it's God's will.

DR CONROY: Do you really believe that God's will has anything to do with such matters, Victor? – with your problem?

NO. 3643: God's will is part of everything.

DR CONROY: I'm a priest too, Victor, but I believe that God sometimes lets Nature run its course.

26

No. 3643: Nature is an intellectual construct that has no place in our religion, doctor.

DR CONROY: Let's go back to the observation room, Victor. Tell me how you felt when the technician attached the electrodes.

No. 3643: He had cold hands.

DR CONROY: Just cold, nothing else?

No. 3643: Nothing else.

DR CONROY: And when the images started to appear on the screen?

No. 3643: I felt nothing then, either.

DR CONROY: You know, Victor, I have the results from the plethysmograph and they show specific reactions here and here. You see ... those spikes?

No. 3643: I felt disgust when I saw certain images.

DR CONROY: Disgust, Victor?

[*The conversation pauses for more than a minute.*]

DR CONROY: Take all the time you need, Victor.

No. 3643: Sexual images disgust me.

DR CONROY: Any in particular, Victor?

No. 3643: All of them.

DR CONROY: Do you know why they disturbed you?

No. 3643: Because they offend God.

DR CONROY: Nevertheless, when you observed particular images, the apparatus registered tumescence in your masculine member.

No. 3643: It's not possible.

DR CONROY: To put it in vulgar terms, they gave you a hard-on.

No. 3643: Language like that is an offence to God and to your priesthood. I ought to ...

DR CONROY: What ought you to do, Victor?

No. 3643: Nothing.

DR CONROY: Did you just feel a violent impulse, Victor?

No. 3643: No, doctor.

DR CONROY: Did you feel a violent impulse the other day?

No. 3643: What other day?

DR CONROY: Sorry, forgive my lack of clarity. Would you say that the other day, when you were beating the head of my lab technician against the control board – that you experienced a violent impulse?

No. 3643: That man was tempting me. 'And if thy right eye offend thee, pluck it out and cast it from thee,' says the Lord.

DR CONROY: Matthew, chapter five, verse twenty-nine.

No. 3643: Precisely.

DR CONROY: And what of that eye? – the agony of that eye?

No. 3643: I don't understand.

DR CONROY: The man's name is Robert. He has a wife and a daughter. You sent him to hospital. You broke his nose, seven teeth, and gave him severe concussion. Thank God the guards managed to subdue you in time.

No. 3643: Maybe I did become a little violent.

DR CONROY: Do you think you could become violent now, if your hands weren't strapped to the sides of the chair?

No. 3643: If you want, we could find out, doctor.

DR CONROY: I think we'd better stop the interview here, Victor.

Municipal Morgue

Tuesday, 5 April 2005, 8.32 p.m.

The autopsy room was a chilly place, painted a jarring greyish mauve that did nothing to lighten the atmosphere. An overhead light with six bulbs hung over the autopsy table and lent the cadaver a few last moments of fame as the eyes of the four spectators stared down at him. It was their job to find out who was responsible for his untimely demise.

Pontiero clamped his hand over his mouth when the coroner lifted Cardinal Robayra's stomach on to the tray. A putrid odour permeated the autopsy room as the examiner proceeded to cut it open with his scalpel. The smell was so strong it even overwhelmed the formaldehyde and the cocktail of chemicals used to disinfect the instruments. Dicanti asked herself why coroners always kept their instruments so clean before the first incision – it wasn't as if the dead man was going to pick up an infection.

'Hey, Pontiero, do you know why the dead baby crossed the road?'

'Yeah, Doc. Because he was stapled to the chicken. You've told me that one at least six or seven times. Know any others?'

The coroner was humming quietly as he went about making his incisions. He was a good singer, with a hoarse, smoky voice that reminded Paola of Louis Armstrong, above all because he was humming 'What a Wonderful World'. He only interrupted his humming to torment Pontiero.

'The real joke is watching you struggle not to puke, Pontiero. Now that really *is* funny. This guy got what was coming to him.'

Paola and Dante glanced at each other over the cardinal's dead body. The coroner, a recalcitrant Communist, was an old hand at his job but sometimes he showed a certain lack of respect for the dead. He seemed to find Robayra's demise terribly funny – something Dicanti didn't find the least bit amusing.

'Doctor, could you limit yourself to an analysis of the body and just leave it at that? Both our guest, Superintendent Dante, and I find your attempts at humour both offensive and out of place.'

The coroner threw a glance in Dicanti's direction, then continued examining the contents of Robayra's stomach. He gave up the satirical jabs but gritted his teeth and cursed everyone in the room as far back as the third generation. Paola ignored him because she was more concerned about the look on Pontiero's face, which was a shade somewhere between white and green.

'Maurizio, I don't know why you torture yourself like this. You've never been able to stand the sight of blood.'

'Damn it, if this sanctimonious little shit can take it, then so can I.'

'You'd be surprised to know how many autopsies I've attended, my delicate colleague,' Dante replied.

'Really? Well, there's at least one more waiting for you, though I think I'm going to enjoy it more than you.'

For Christ's sake, here they go again, thought Paola, attempting to mediate between the two. They had carried on like this all day. Dante and Pontiero had felt a mutual repulsion from the moment they met, but, to be fair to Pontiero, anything in trousers that came within ten feet of Dicanti always wound up on the wrong side of him. She knew he treated her like a daughter but he took it too far sometimes. Fabio Dante was frivolous and he certainly wasn't the brightest bulb in the box, but he didn't deserve the venom her co-worker was lavishing on him. What she couldn't work out was how a man like Dante had come to occupy such a lofty position in the Vigilanza. His constant jokes and biting comments all stood in sharp contrast to the closely guarded, shadowy figure of Inspector General Cirin.

'Perhaps my distinguished visitors would be so kind as to lend their attention to the autopsy they've come here to watch.'

The coroner's rough voice dragged Dicanti back to reality. 'Go ahead, please.' She shot a cold look at the two policemen to get them to stop arguing.

'OK, the victim hadn't eaten anything since breakfast, and everything indicates that he ate very early, because I'm only finding a few scraps.'

'So maybe he skipped a meal, or he fell into the killer's clutches before lunch.'

'I doubt he would miss a meal … He ate well, as you can see. Alive, he would have weighed a little over fourteen stone, and he was six foot tall.'

'Which tells us the killer was physically fit. Robayra was hardly as light as a feather,' Dante interjected.

'And it's a hundred and thirty feet from the church's doorway to the chapel,' said Paola. 'Someone must have seen the killer bringing the body into the church. Pontiero, do me a favour. Send four men you trust to the area. Tell them to go in plain clothes, but take their badges. Don't tell them what happened. Say there was a robbery at the church, and you want them to find out if anyone saw anything during the night.'

'Asking any of the pilgrims would be a waste of time.'

'So don't do it. Talk to the people who live nearby, especially the elderly. They get by on very little sleep.'

Pontiero nodded and hurried out of the autopsy room, visibly pleased at not having to stay on.

Paola watched him leave and when the doors had slammed shut behind him she looked straight at Dante. 'What exactly is going on with you, Mr Vatican? Pontiero is a good man; he just can't stomach the sight of blood. I'm asking you to stop all this inane verbal jousting.'

'You said it. So there's more than one big mouth in the morgue.' The coroner was laughing to himself.

'Stick to your work, doctor. We need to get on. Do I make myself clear, Dante?'

'Calm down' – Dante raised his hands in self-defence. 'I don't think you quite understand. If tomorrow I had to go into a burning building with a pistol in my hand, shoulder to shoulder with Pontiero, don't think for one moment I wouldn't do it.'

'So why do you keep picking on him then?' Paola was utterly dismayed.

'Because it amuses me. And I'm convinced that he enjoys being angry with me, too. Why don't you ask him?'

Paola shook her head, muttering unflattering phrases about men under her breath. 'Let's get on with it, shall we? *Dottore*, do you know the time and cause of death?'

The coroner scanned his notes. 'I should remind you that this is just a preliminary report, but I'm fairly sure. The cardinal died around nine o'clock yesterday evening, Monday. The margin of error is one hour. His throat was slashed. The cut was made from behind, by someone I believe to have been around the same height. I can't tell you anything about the weapon, except that it was at least six inches long, had a straight edge and was very sharp. It could have been a razor – the kind barbers use; I don't know.'

'What about his wounds?' said Dante.

'The extraction of the eyes took place ante-mortem, as did the mutilation of the tongue.'

'He pulled out his tongue? Christ almighty.' Dante was disgusted.

'In my opinion he did it with a pair of pliers. When he was finished, he stuffed the cavity with toilet paper to staunch the bleeding. He later removed it, but there were a few traces of cellulose left behind. Dicanti, you surprise me. This really doesn't seem to be affecting you very much?'

'I've seen worse.'

'So, let me show you something I'm sure you've never seen before. I've never come across anything like it, and I've been doing this job for years. Our killer stuffed the tongue into the rectal cavity with astonishing expertise. Then he cleaned up the blood around it. I wouldn't have caught it if I hadn't looked inside.'

The coroner showed them photographs of the mangled tongue. 'I've put it on ice and sent it to the laboratory. I'd like to see a copy of the report when it comes in, ispettore. I still don't know how he did it.'

'Don't worry, I'll see to it personally,' Dicanti assured him. 'What about his hands?'

'Those were cut off post-mortem. Not a clean job. There are marks showing hesitation here and here. It was either difficult for him or he was standing in an uncomfortable position.'

'Anything under the nails?'

'Only fresh air. The hands are impeccably clean and I suspect the killer washed them with soap – my nose detects a trace of lavender.'

Paola was thinking. 'In your opinion how long did the killer need to inflict these wounds on his victim?'

'I hadn't thought about it. Let me see ...'

The coroner brushed his hands along the corpse's forearms, the sockets of the eyes and the mutilated mouth, thinking it over. He was still singing to himself quietly, this time something by the Moody Blues. Paola couldn't recall the name of the tune.

'Well, gentlemen ... He would have needed at least half an hour to remove the hands and clean them, and something like an hour to wash the rest of the body and put the clothes back on. There's no way we can tell exactly how long he tortured the victim, but it looks like he took his time. I'm certain he spent at least three hours on it, probably more.'

Some place quiet, hidden. Far away from prying eyes. Sound-proof, because Robayra would certainly have screamed. How much shouting does a man do if somebody is pulling out his eyes and his tongue? A great deal, no doubt. They had to come up with a time frame, establish how many hours the cardinal had been in the killer's possession, then subtract the time he had spent doing what he did to his victim. That way they could reduce the scope of the search, if they were lucky and the killer hadn't had all the time in the world.

'I know the boys in forensics haven't found any fingerprints. Did you come across anything out of the ordinary before you washed the body – anything you sent to be analysed?'

'Nothing much. A few fibres, a few traces of something that could be make-up on the shirt collar.'

'Make-up? Interesting. From the killer?'

'Maybe our cardinal had a few secrets, Dicanti,' Dante said.

Paola looked at him. She was caught off guard.

The pathologist gave a cynical laugh. 'No, that isn't what I meant,' Dante hurried to say. 'I'm just saying it's possible he took great care over his appearance. After all is said and done, he was getting on a bit.'

33

'Still, it's a detail worth noting. Any traces of make-up on his face?'

'No, but the killer must have cleaned it, or at least wiped the blood from the eye sockets. I'll take a closer look.'

'Doctor, could you send a sample of the make-up to the laboratory, just in case. I want to know what brand it was, and the exact shade.'

'That could take some time if they don't have a database already set up, to compare with our sample.'

'Write on the forms that they can empty an entire perfumery if they have to. It's the type of detail that really appeals to Troi. What about blood or semen? Did we get lucky?'

'No chance. The victim's clothes were spotless, and there were only a few traces of blood, the same type as the victim's, so definitely his own.'

'Anything on the skin or in the hair? Spores – anything?'

'I found small traces of adhesive on what was left of the wrists, which makes me suspect that the killer stripped the cardinal, bound him with duct tape before torturing him, and afterwards put his clothes back on. He washed the body, but not in a bath. See this?' The pathologist pointed to a thin white line of dried soap on Robayra's side. 'He used a sponge with water and soap, but the sponge didn't have much water in it or he wasn't being very careful here, because he left a lot of soap on the body.'

'What kind of soap?'

'That's easier to identify than the make-up, but I'm not sure that it's very useful. It appears to be ordinary lavender.'

Paola leaned over the body and took a deep breath. Lavender it was. 'Anything else?'

'There's some adhesive on his face too, but a minute quantity. That's it. And the deceased was very shortsighted.'

'And what does that have to do with anything?'

'Dante, pay attention. He doesn't have his glasses.'

'Of course he doesn't have his glasses. The killer tore his eyes out – what does he need his damn glasses for?'

The coroner was clearly annoyed by Dante. 'Fine. Listen, I'm not telling you how to do your job. I'm just telling you what I see.'

'That's good, doctor. Call us when you have the complete report.'

'Of course, ispettore.'

Dante and Paola left the coroner bent over the body, whistling his versions of the jazz classics, and stepped out to the hallway, where Pontiero was barking short, concise orders over his mobile phone.

As soon as he was finished, Dicanti spoke to both of them. 'OK, this is what we're going to do. Dante, you go back to the office and write out a report of everything you can remember from the scene of the crime. I'd prefer you to do it alone, which should make it easier. Include all the photos and pieces of evidence your wise and knowing leader has let you keep. And then come back to the UACV headquarters as soon as you're done. I'm afraid this is going to be a long night.'

FBI BEHAVIORAL
SCIENCES DIVISION

FINAL EXAM: VICTIMOLOGY

Student: DICANTI, Paola
Date: 19 July 1999
Grade: A+

Question: Describe in 100 words or less the importance of *time* in the creation of a criminal profile, using the Rosper method. Make a personal evaluation connecting the variables with the perpetrator's level of experience. You have two minutes from the time you turn the page.

Answer: The perpetrator has given himself the time necessary to:

a) kill the victim
b) interact with the body
c) remove any traces of himself from the victim and dispose of the body

Comment: According to my deductions, variable a) is defined by the perpetrator's fantasies, variable b) helps to reveal his hidden motivations, while c) defines his capacity for analysis and improvisation. In conclusion, if the perpetrator dedicates more time to

a) he has a moderate level of experience (3 crimes)
b) he is an expert (4 crimes or more)
c) he is a beginner (this is his first or second murder).

UACV HEADQUARTERS

Tuesday,5 April 2005, 10.32 p.m.

'Let's see. What do we have?'

'Two cardinals murdered in the most horrific way imaginable.'

Dicanti and Pontiero were eating sandwiches and drinking coffee in the laboratory's conference room. For all its modernity, it was a grey and depressing space. The only colour came from the hundreds of crime-scene photos spread out in front of them on an enormous table, with four plastic bags full of evidence piled up at one end. At that moment it was all they had. They were waiting for Dante to bring them whatever was left from the first murder scene.

'All right, Pontiero. Let's start with Robayra. What do we know about him?'

'He lived and worked in Buenos Aires. Arrived on an Aerolineas Argentinas flight on Sunday morning, with an open ticket he'd bought several weeks before. He didn't reserve his flight until one o'clock on Saturday afternoon. With the time difference, I guess that was around the time the Holy Father died.'

'A return ticket?'

'Just one way.'

'Strange ... Either the cardinal didn't plan ahead or he was coming to the Conclave with high hopes. Maurizio, you know I'm not particularly religious. What had you heard about Robayra's chances of becoming Pope?'

'Not much. I read something about him a week ago, I think in *La Stampa*. They thought he was well positioned, but not one of the favourites. In any case, you know what the Italian media are like: they only pay court to our cardinals. Portini I have read about, however, and plenty too.'

Pontiero was a family man and impeccably honest. He was, as far as Paola knew, a good husband and father who went to mass each Sunday without fail; and his invitations to Dicanti to accompany the family were just as reliable, forcing her to come up with one excuse after another. Some excuses were good, some bad, but none of them really held up. Pontiero knew that in Dicanti's heart of hearts faith didn't play a large part; it had died along with her father, ten years before.

'Something bothers me, Maurizio. We need to know what sort of frustration connects this killer to the cardinals. If he detests what the cardinals stand for, if he's a seminarist who isn't playing with a full deck, or he just hates their little red hats.'

'Their *cappellos cardenalicios*.'

'Thank you for clearing that up. I suspect there's something that links the victims together, more than just their hats. Basically, we're not going to get very far unless we can talk to a real source – someone who speaks with authority. It's Dante's job to open doors for us, so he needs to give us access to someone high up in the Curia. And when I say high up, I mean very high up.'

'Won't be easy.'

'We'll see. But for now, let's focus on what we know. For starters, Robayra didn't die in the church.'

'There wasn't much blood, so he must have been killed somewhere else.'

'Clearly the killer had the cardinal in his power for quite a while, in a secluded place that no one else knew about, somewhere he could take his time interacting with the body. We know that he had to gain his victim's trust somehow, so that the victim would go with him of his own free will. From there, he moved the body to Santa Maria in Traspontina, obviously for a reason.'

'What about the church?'

'I spoke with the parish priest. It was locked up tight when he went to sleep. Remember, he had to open it for the police when they arrived. But there's a second door, a tiny one, that leads out on to the Via dei Corridori. That's probably how the murderer got in. Have we checked it out?'

'The lock was intact; it was new and wouldn't give. But even if the door was swinging on its hinges, I don't see how the killer could have got in.'

'Because …?'

'Do you have any idea how many people were standing by the main door, on Via della Conciliazione? And on the street behind, even more. Jesus! The whole place is crammed with people here for the funeral. They're in every street, blocking the traffic. Don't tell me that our killer walked in with a body in his arms in full view of the entire world.'

Paola thought for a few seconds. Even if the tide of humanity had served as wonderful camouflage for the killer, how would he have entered the church without forcing the door?

'Pontiero, let's make it a priority to find out how he got into the building. Tomorrow we'll talk to the friar. What was his name?'

'Francesco Toma, a Carmelite.'

Pontiero nodded slowly as he jotted down notes.

'Yes, him. Then, we have all the macabre details: the message on the floor, the severed hands resting on the canvas … and these bags here. Go ahead.'

Pontiero started reading the list while Inspector Dicanti filled out the evidence report with a ballpoint pen. An ultramodern office, yet they were still using relics from the twentieth century like these antiquated forms.

'Item number one: a priest's stole. Embroidered cloth, rectangular, worn by Catholic priests during the sacrament of confession. Found hanging from the dead man's mouth, soaked in blood. Blood type is the same as that of the victim. DNA analysis in progress.'

This was the brownish object they hadn't been able to make out in the half-light of the church. The DNA analysis would take at least two days, even though the UACV had one of the world's most advanced laboratories at its disposal. Dicanti always creased up with laughter whenever she watched the American show *CSI* on television. If only evidence could be processed that quickly.

'Item number two. White canvas. Origin unknown. Material, cotton. Presence of blood, minimal. The severed hands of the victim were found sitting on top of it. The blood type is that of the victim. DNA analysis in progress.'

'One thing: Robayra is written with "ay", not an "i"?' Dicanti hesitated.

'With "ay", I'm fairly sure.'

'Good. Keep going, Maurizio.'

'Item number three: a crumpled piece of paper, approximately one and a quarter inches square. Found in the left eye socket of the victim. The type of paper, its composition, weight, and percentage of chlorine are all being investigated. Written on the paper, by hand, using a ballpoint pen, are the letters:

Mt 16

'MT 16,' Dicanti said. 'An address?'

'The paper was found covered with blood and crushed into a ball. It's clearly a message from the killer. The absence of the victim's eyes could be not so much a punishment as a sign ... as if he were telling us where to look.'

'Or that we're blind.'

'A killer who likes to play games. The first of his kind to show up in Italy. That's why I think Troi wanted you to be in charge, Paola. Not your usual detective, but someone who can think creatively.'

Dicanti reflected on Pontiero's words. If it were true, then the risks doubled. The profile of a game-player typically corresponded to an extremely intelligent person, someone who was usually much more difficult to catch, as long as they didn't trip up. Sooner or later they all tripped up, but in the meantime they filled the morgue with bodies.

'OK, let's think for a minute. What streets do we know with those initials?'

'Viale del Muro Torto.'

'No, it runs through a park and it doesn't have street numbers, Maurizio.'

'In that case Monte Tarpeo is out too. It's the street that crosses the Palazzo dei Conservatori gardens.'

'And Monte Testaccio?'

'By Parco Testaccio … That might be it.'

'Wait a minute.' Dicanti picked up the phone and dialled a number in the police department. 'Documentation? Ah, Silvio, hello. Take a look for me and see if there's a number 16 on Monte Testaccio. And could you bring a map of the city streets to the conference room? Thanks.'

While they waited, Pontiero continued with the list of evidence.

'And the last, for now: item number four: crumpled paper, one and a quarter inch square. Found in the victim's right eye socket, in identical condition to that of item number three. The kind of paper, its composition, weight and percentage of chlorine are being investigated. Written on the paper, by hand, using a ballpoint pen, the word:

'*Undeviginti*.'

'It's fucking hieroglyphics.' Dicanti was exasperated. 'I just hope it's not the continuation of a message that he left on the first victim, because that first part went up in smoke.'

'I guess we have to resign ourselves to what we have, for now.'

'Stupendous, Pontiero. Why don't you tell me what *undeviginti* means, so I can resign myself to that?'

'Your Latin's a little rusty, Dicanti. It means nineteen.'

'Damn it, that's right! I was always failing at school. And the arrow?'

At that moment one of the assistants from Documentation entered the room with the street map of Rome.

'Here you are, ispettore. I looked for the street you asked me about: number 16 Monte Testaccio doesn't exist. That street only has fourteen distinct residences.'

'Thanks, Silvio. Do me a favour: would you stay here with Pontiero and me and help us go through all the streets in Rome that begin with MT. It's a shot in the dark, but I have a hunch.'

'Let's hope you're a better psychologist than fortune-teller,

Dottoressa Dicanti. You'd do better to look in the Bible.'

Three heads spun round to the entrance of the conference room. In the doorway stood a priest dressed in dog collar and suit. He was tall and thin, a wiry frame, and noticeably bald. He seemed to be about fifty but was well preserved, and he had strong, hard features that testified to having seen many dawns in a harsh climate. Dicanti's first thought was that he looked more like a soldier than a priest.

'Who are you and what do you want? This is a restricted area. Please leave immediately,' said Pontiero.

'I am Father Anthony Fowler and I'm here to give you a hand.' His Italian was grammatically correct but slightly sing-song and hesitant.

'This is part of the police department and you've entered without authorisation. If you want to help us, find a church and pray for our souls.'

Pontiero started to walk towards the new arrival, determined to make him leave whether he wanted to or not. Dicanti had already turned back to the photographs when Fowler spoke again.

'It's from the Bible – the New Testament, to be precise.'

'What?' Pontiero was surprised.

Dicanti raised her head and looked at Fowler. 'Would you mind explaining yourself?'

'MT 16. The Gospel according to Matthew, chapter sixteen. Did he leave another note?'

Pontiero looked upset. 'Paola, you're not really going to pay any attention to this guy ...'

'We're all ears.'

Fowler stepped into the conference room. He carried a black overcoat draped on his arm, which he laid over a chair.

'As everyone knows, the Christian New Testament is made up of four principal books, one for each of the Evangelists: Matthew, Mark, Luke and John. In Christian bibliographies, the book of Matthew is abbreviated as MT and the number that follows represents the chapter. The next two numbers indicate a citation in that chapter, between two verses.'

'The killer left this.'

Paola placed item number four, wrapped in plastic, in front of him. The priest studied it closely. He gave no indication that he recognised it, nor did the blood upset him. He simply examined it thoroughly and then said:

'Nineteen. How appropriate.'

Pontiero was about to boil over. 'Are you going to tell us what you know now, or are you going to make us wait around, *padre*?'

'*Et tibi dabo claves regni coelorum,*' Fowler recited. '*Et quodcumque ligaveris super terram, erit legatum et in coelis; et quodcumque solveris super terram, erit solutum et in coelis.* "And I will give unto thee the keys of the kingdom of heaven; and whatsoever thou shalt bind on earth shall be bound in heaven; and whatever thou shalt loose on earth shall be loosed in heaven." Matthew sixteen, verse nineteen. That is to say, the words with which Jesus confirmed Peter as the leader of the apostles, and awarded him and his successors power over the whole of Christendom.'

'Holy Mother of God!' Dicanti exclaimed.

'Considering what is about to take place in this city, ladies and gentlemen, I think that you ought to be worried. Very worried.'

'Shit, some crazy vagabond slits the throat of a priest and you're ready to sound the alarm. It doesn't sound all that scary to me, Father Fowler,' said Pontiero.

'No, my friend. The killer isn't just some crazy vagabond. He's a cruel man, methodical and intelligent, and he's extremely disturbed. Take my word for it.'

'Really? Seems like you know a great deal about his motives, *padre*.' Pontiero was mocking their visitor.

The priest fixed Dicanti with a steady gaze. 'I know much more than that, gentlemen. I know who he is.'

Article from the *Maryland Gazette*, 29 July 1999, page 7

AMERICAN PRIEST ACCUSED OF
SEXUAL ABUSE COMMITS SUICIDE

Sachem Pike, Maryland – As sexual abuse scandals continue to rock the Catholic Church in North America, a Connecticut priest accused of sexually abusing minors hanged himself in his room at an institution for troubled clergy, according to a report police made to the American Press service last Friday.

Peter Selznick, 61 years old, relinquished his position as parish priest at Saint Andrews in Bridgeport, Connecticut on 27 April of last year, just one day after authorities in the Catholic Church interviewed two men who claimed Selznick had abused them over the course of several years, from the end of the 1970s to the early 1980s, according to a spokesman for the Bridgeport Diocese.

The priest was being treated at the Saint Matthew Institute in Maryland, a psychiatric centre that deals with members of the clergy who have been accused of sexual abuse or have 'problems in sexual orientation', according to a statement from the institution.

'Hospital personnel knocked on his door several times and attempted to enter his room, but something was blocking the door,' Diane Richardson, spokesperson for the Prince George police department, stated at a press conference. 'When they entered the room, they found the body hanging from one of the exposed beams in the ceiling.'

Selznick hanged himself with a bed sheet, Richardson stated, adding that his body had been taken to the mortuary for an autopsy. At the same time, she categorically denied rumours that when the body was found, it was nude and had been mutilated – rumours she characterized as 'completely unfounded'. During the press conference, reporters cited 'eyewitnesses' who stated that they had seen the mutilations. The spokeswoman replied that 'a nurse who works for the County's medical team was under the influence of marijuana and other drugs when those declarations were made'. This particular employee has been suspended from his job without pay until his case is resolved. This newspaper made contact with the nurse who started the rumour, but he refused to say anything other than a brief 'I was wrong'.

The Bishop of Bridgeport, William Lopes, stated that he was 'profoundly saddened' by Selznick's 'tragic' death, adding that the scandal presently preoccupying the North American branch of the Catholic Church has 'many victims'.

Father Selznick was born in New York in 1938, and was ordained in Bridgeport in 1965. He served in various parishes in Connecticut and for a brief time worked as a priest at the parish of San Juan Vianney in Chiclayo, Peru.

'Every person, without exception, has dignity and value in the eyes of God, and everyone needs and deserves our compassion,' Lopes stated. 'The disturbing circumstances that surround his death cannot eradicate all the good that he did in life,' the Bishop said in conclusion.

The Director of the Saint Matthew Institute, Father Canice Conroy, refused to speak to this publication. Father Anthony Fowler, director of new initiatives at the Institute, apologized for the absence of a statement from the Director, explaining that Father Conroy was presently 'in a state of shock'.

Uacv Headquarters

Tuesday, 5 April 2005, 11.14 p.m.

Fowler's declaration was like a shot to the solar plexus. Dicanti and Pontiero were frozen in their tracks. They stared at the priest.

'May I sit down?'

'There are plenty of empty seats,' Paola said. 'Take any one you like.'

She made a sign to the employee from Documentation, who quickly left the room.

Fowler laid his small black suitcase on the table, its edges scratched and frayed. The suitcase had seen its fair share of the world and its condition was a testament to the many miles it had travelled with its owner. Fowler opened the case and took out a thick stack of papers from a cardboard box, whose edges were bent and coffee-stained. He set the papers on the table and sat down across from the inspector. Dicanti watched him carefully, noting his economy of movement and the energy radiating from his green eyes. The question of where exactly this strange priest came from very much intrigued her, but she made a firm decision not to let herself be overwhelmed, particularly on her own turf.

Pontiero grabbed a seat, spun it around and sat to Fowler's left, his hands resting on the back. Dicanti made a mental note to remind him to stop imitating old Bogart movies – her second-in-command must have watched *The Maltese Falcon* at least three hundred times. If he considered someone suspicious, he inevitably sat to their left, compulsively smoking one unfiltered Pall Mall after another.

'Go ahead, *padre*. But first show us something that proves you are who you say you are.'

Fowler took his passport out of his breast pocket and handed it to Pontiero, then grimaced, showing his displeasure at the cloud of smoke billowing from Pontiero's cigarette.

'I see, I see – a diplomatic passport. So you have immunity, eh? Who the hell are you? Some sort of spy?'

'I am an official in the United States Air Force.'

'What rank?'

'Major. Would Detective Pontiero mind if I asked him to stop smoking right next to me? I gave up years ago and have no desire to start again.'

'He's addicted to tobacco, Major Fowler.'

'Father Fowler, Doctor Dicanti. I am … retired.'

'Wait a second. How do you know my name, or the inspector's?' Pontiero muttered.

The criminologist smiled. She found herself both curious and entertained. 'Maurizio, I suspect that Padre Fowler is not as retired as he says he is.'

Fowler returned Dicanti's smile, but with a hint of sadness. 'I've recently gone back into active service, it's true. And strangely enough, the reason for that is the work I did in civilian life.' He grew quiet, waving his hand to push away the smoke.

'So tell us, if you're so clever, who and where the son of a bitch is who did what you see here to a cardinal of the Holy Mother Church, so that we can all go home to bed.'

The priest remained silent, as unflappable as his white collar. Paola suspected the man was simply too hardened to fall for Pontiero's little act. There was no doubt life had thrown some terrible experiences at him, as witnessed by the creases on his skin, or that his eyes had confronted worse things than a small-time policeman and his smelly tobacco.

'Enough, Maurizio. And kill the cigarette.'

Pontiero angrily threw the butt away.

'OK, Padre Fowler,' Paola said as she shuffled the photographs on the table, her eyes bearing down on the priest. 'You've made it clear that, for now, you're in charge. You know something I don't – something I need to know. But you're in my neck of the woods,

47

on my turf. It's up to you where we go from here.'

'What about starting off with a profile?'

'Can I ask why?'

'Because in this case there's no need to create a profile in order to find out who the killer is – I can tell you that. In this case we need a profile in order to know where to find him. And those are two different things.'

'Is this an exam, *padre*? Do you want to know exactly how good the person sitting opposite you is? Are you going to be the judge of my deductive capacities, like Troi?'

'I think that at this moment the only person judging you is you yourself.'

Paola took a deep breath and mustered every bit of self-control to keep herself from shouting. Fowler had put his finger right in the wound. But just when she thought she was about to lose it, her boss showed up in the doorway. He stood there, not moving, carefully studying the priest, who looked back at him intently. Finally, the two greeted each other with nods of the head.

'Padre Fowler.'

'Direttore Troi.'

'I was informed of your arrival by – shall we say? – an unusual channel. It goes without saying your presence here is an imposition, but I recognise that you could be of some use to us, if my sources aren't lying.'

'They aren't.'

'Then please go on.'

From her earliest childhood Paola had had the discomforting sensation that she was a late arrival to a world that had already begun, and at that instant the feeling returned. She was fed up with the fact that everyone seemed to have information that she didn't. She could ask Troi for an explanation later, when she got the chance, but right now she decided to turn the situation to her advantage.

'Padre Fowler has told Pontiero and myself that he knows the identity of the killer, but it seems he wants a free psychological profile before he reveals the man's name. It's my personal opinion that we're losing precious time here, but I've decided to play along with his game.'

She leapt to her feet, surprising the three men watching her. She walked over to the blackboard that took up almost all of the back of the room and started to write.

'The killer is a white male, between the ages of 38 and 46. He's of medium height, strong and intelligent. His studies took him as far as university, and he has a gift for languages. He's left-handed; he received a strict religious education and endured difficulties or abuse in his early life. He's immature, his work subjects him to pressure that exceeds his emotional and psychological stability, and he suffers from intense sexual repression. He most likely has a history of considerable violence. This isn't the first or even second time he has killed someone and, obviously, it won't be the last. He has nothing but contempt for us – both for the police and for his victims. And now, *padre*, why don't you give our killer a name?' Dicanti spun round and tossed the chalk into the priest's hands.

Fowler watched her, a look of surprise on his face; Pontiero beamed; Troi looked sceptical. Finally it was the priest who spoke up.

'Well done, *dottoressa*. Ten out of ten. I may be a psychologist but I can't figure out how you came to your conclusions. Could you explain a little further?'

'The profile is only provisional but the conclusions should be quite close to reality. That he is a white male is shown by the profile of his victims, since it's very unusual for a serial killer to kill someone from a different race. We can tell he's of medium height, since Robayra was tall and the angle and location of the cut in his neck indicate that he was assaulted by someone about five foot nine inches tall. That he's strong is obvious; otherwise it would have been impossible for him to take the cardinal as far as the interior of the church, because even if he used a car to transport the body to the back door, there is still a distance of some one hundred and thirty feet to the chapel. His immaturity corresponds to the type of murderer who plays games: he has profound disrespect for his victims, considers them to be mere objects, and the same goes for the police. He sees us all as inferior beings.'

Fowler interrupted her by politely raising his hand. 'Two details in particular grabbed my attention. First, you said that it's not the first time he's committed murder. Did you deduce that from his handiwork at the scene of the crime?'

'Exactly. This person possesses a basic familiarity with police work. He's carried this off on more than one occasion. Experience tells us that a first murder is usually very messy and spur-of-the-moment.'

'The second thing was when you said, "His work subjects him to pressure that exceeds his emotional and psychological stability." I'm at a loss to explain how you came to that conclusion.'

Dicanti, still standing, blushed. She crossed her arms and didn't answer. Troi took the opportunity to intervene.

'Ah, good old Paola. Her great intelligence always leaves a small crack for her feminine intuition to slip in, isn't that so? *Padre*, at times Dicanti arrives at purely emotional conclusions. I don't know how. Of course, she would make a great writer.'

'Better than you know, because she's hit the bull's eye,' said Fowler, getting up from his chair and striding towards the blackboard. 'Inspector, what is the correct name for your profession? Profiler – isn't that it?'

'Yes,' Paola said, still embarrassed.

'When did you receive your qualification as a profiler?'

'Once I'd finished the course in Forensic Criminology and after a year of intensive study at the FBI's Behavioral Sciences Division. Very few candidates manage to pass the entire course.'

'Can you tell us how many qualified profilers there are in the world?'

'At present, twenty – twelve in the United States, four in Canada, two in Germany, one in Italy and one in Austria.'

'Thanks. Is everyone clear on that, gentlemen? Only twenty people in the world are capable of drawing a psychological portrait of a serial killer with any degree of certainty, and one of them is in this room. Believe me, if we want to catch this man ...'

Fowler turned round and wrote a name on the blackboard in large, thick letters:

VICTOR KAROSKY

'... we are going to need someone capable of getting into his head. Now you have the name. But before you race to the phone to bark out orders for his arrest, let me tell you everything else I know about him.'

Excerpts from the correspondence between Edward Dressler, psychiatrist, and Cardinal Francis Casey

Boston, 14 May 1991

[…]Your Eminence, we no doubt find ourselves in the presence of a born recidivist. From what I am told, this is the fifth time he has been reassigned to a new parish. The tests we carried out over the course of two weeks confirm that we cannot take the risk of sending him to live in close proximity to young children without putting them in danger. […] By no means do I doubt his desire to repent, because it is strong. But I do doubt his ability to control himself. […]We cannot permit ourselves the luxury of having him in a parish. It would be better if we clipped his wings before he loses all control. Otherwise, I cannot take responsibility for what might occur. I recommend a period of internment of at least six months in the Saint Matthew Institute.

Boston, 4 August 1993

[…] This is the third time I've had dealings with him [Karosky]. […] I have to say that the 'fresh air', as you called it when you moved him from parish to parish, hasn't helped at all; rather the opposite. He is beginning to lose control with greater frequency, and I detect traces of schizophrenia in his behavior. It's very possible that at some point he will completely cross the line and become another person. Eminence, you know my devotion to the Church, and I understand the present overwhelming lack of priests, but to lower the bar so very close to the ground … Thirty-five of these men have passed through my hands so far, Eminence, and I have seen, in some of them, the possibility that they might recover on their own. […] Karosky is definitely not one of them. Cardinal, only on rare occasions has Your Eminence followed my advice. I beg you to do so now: persuade Karosky to enter the Saint Matthew.

𝒰acv 𝐻eadquarters

VIA LAMARMORA, 3

Wednesday, 6 April 2005, 12.03 a.m.

Paola sat down, bracing herself to hear what Fowler had to say.

'Ninety ninety-five was when it all began – for me, anyway. At that time I'd retired from the Air Force and was working under the direction of my bishop. He wanted to make use of my training in psychology, so he sent me to the Saint Matthew Institute. Have any of you heard of it?'

All three answered in the negative.

'I'm not surprised. The very existence of the institution is a secret to the majority of the public in North America, even the more informed ones. It officially consists of a residential centre set up to deal with priests and nuns who have "problems", and it's located in Sachem Pike, Maryland. The reality is that ninety-five per cent of its patients have a history of sexual abuse of minors or problems with drugs. The institute's facilities are, without question, luxurious: thirty-five rooms for the patients, nine for the medical personnel (nearly all interns), a tennis court, a pool, a recreation room with billiard table ...'

'Sounds more like a health resort than a psychiatric institution,' Pontiero interjected.

'Well, the place is a mystery, in more ways than one. It is a mystery to the outside world and a mystery to those who stay there: at first, they see it as a place they can retire to for several months, somewhere they can rest; then, little by little, they discover that it is altogether different. All of you know the enormous problem the Church in my country has had with certain Catholic priests over the last few years. From the public's point of view, it wouldn't go down very well if they felt that priests accused of sexual abuse were getting paid vacations in a luxury hotel.'

'So were they?' asked Pontiero, who seemed to be very affected by the subject, perhaps on account of having two children himself, both teenagers.

'No. I'll try to sum up my experiences there succinctly. Upon my arrival I found it to be a profoundly secular place. It didn't look like a religious institution: no crucifixes on the wall, no one wearing habits or robes. I've spent many nights in the open air, on an expedition or at the front, and I never took my clerical collar off. But everyone there seemed to come and go as they pleased. Faith and self-control were obviously in short supply.'

'You didn't communicate this to anyone?' Dicanti asked.

'Of course. The first thing I did was write a letter to the bishop responsible for that parish. He accused me of being too influenced by my time in the armed forces, by the "rigidity of the military environment". He advised me to be more "adaptable". Those were tricky times for me; my career in the Air Force had been a roller-coaster ride. I don't want to get into that – it has nothing to do with the case at hand – but let's just say that I had no desire to add to my reputation for being intransigent.'

'You don't have to justify yourself.'

'I know, but what happened there does weigh on my conscience. They cured neither minds nor souls in that institution; they simply gave their patients a little push in the direction of least resistance. What took place there was exactly the opposite of what the diocese had hoped.'

'I don't follow,' said Pontiero.

'Nor do I,' Troi chimed in.

'It's complicated. To begin with, the only psychiatrist with a university degree on staff at the centre was Father Conroy, at that time the institute's director. None of the other staff had a further degree beyond nursing or a technical diploma. Yet they were allowed to make psychiatric evaluations!'

'Insane.' Dicanti was amazed.

'Completely. The only endorsement you had to have to get hired was to belong to Dignity, an organisation that promotes the ordination of women and sexual freedom for male priests. Personally, I don't agree with them about anything but it's not my place to judge. What I could do was evaluate the professional capacity of the personnel, and that was extremely lacking.'

'I don't see where all this taking us,' Pontiero said, lighting another cigarette.

'Five more minutes and you will. As I was saying, Father Conroy, a great friend of Dignity and as liberal as they come, managed the Saint Matthew in a completely erratic manner. Honest priests arrived there, men confronted with baseless accusations (which did happen), and thanks to Conroy they relinquished the priesthood that had been the light of their lives. Others he urged not to struggle against their nature but to simply get on with life. He considered it a success when a religious person gave up their vows and began a homosexual relationship.'

'And you see that as a problem?' asked Dicanti.

'No, not if the person really wanted or needed to do it. But the patient's needs didn't matter to Conroy in the slightest. First, he established his objectives and then he forged ahead, applying his plan to each person without any prior knowledge of them at all. He played God with the hearts and minds of those men and women, some of whom were deeply troubled. And then he washed it all down with a fine single malt.'

'God in heaven!' said Pontiero.

'Take my word for it, He was nowhere on the premises. But that wasn't the worst thing. Owing to several grave errors in the selection of candidates, many young men in my country who weren't fit to be the shepherds of men's souls had entered Catholic seminaries during the seventies and eighties. They weren't even fit to take care of their own souls, let alone anyone else's. With time, many of these young men gave up the cloth. They did a great deal of damage to the good name of the Catholic Church, and what's worse, to many children and younger men. Many priests accused of sexual abuse – guilty of sexual abuse – didn't go to jail. They disappeared from view and were moved from parish to parish. Some of them finally ended up at the Saint Matthew. There, and with a bit of luck, they were directed towards civilian life but, shamefully, many returned to the ministry when they should have been behind bars. Tell me,

Dottoressa Dicanti, what chances are there for the rehabilitation of a serial killer?'

'Absolutely none at all. Once he crosses the line, there's no way to bring him back.'

'It's the same for a compulsive paedophile. Sadly, the certainty you possess does not exist in our field. You know that you are dealing with a monster, someone who must be caught and caged. But it is much more difficult for the therapist working with a paedophile to know whether he has crossed the line for good. I know of only one case when I never had the slightest doubt. And that was a case where, beneath the paedophilia, there was something else.'

'Let me guess: Victor Karosky. Our killer.'

'The same.'

Troi cleared his throat before interrupting. It was an irritating habit that he repeated every so often. 'Father Fowler, would you kindly explain to us why you are so sure that this is the man who has torn Robayra and Portini to pieces?'

'Certainly. Karosky turned up at the institute in August 1994. He had been moved around various parishes, his superior shunting the problem from one place to another. In every single one there were complaints, some more serious than others, though none of an extremely violent nature. According to the testimony we collected, we believe he abused eighty-nine children in all, although the number could be higher.'

'Fuck.'

'You said it, Pontiero. But the root of Karosky's problems is located in his childhood. He was born in Katowice, Poland, in 1961. There—'

'Hold on, *padre*. He's forty-four years old now?'

'That's correct. He stands five foot eight and a half inches tall and weighs one hundred and eighty-seven pounds. He has a strong build, and testing revealed an IQ somewhere between 110 and 125, depending on when he took the test. He took seven in all at the institute. He found them entertaining.'

'That's pretty high.'

'You are a psychiatrist, while I studied psychology and wasn't an especially brilliant student. The most extreme psychopaths I encountered were revealed to me too late to read up on the subject.

So tell me: is it true that serial killers are very intelligent?'

Paola smiled, half ironically, and glanced at Pontiero, who looked at her with the same expression.

'I think that the detective here can give you a good response to that one.'

'"Hannibal Lector doesn't exist and Jodie Foster should stick to costume dramas." Dicanti says it all the time.'

Everyone laughed, not because the joke was particularly funny but simply to release some of the tension in the air.

'Thanks, Pontiero. *Padre*, the popular figure of the super-psychopath is a myth fashioned from novels and films. In real life, people like that don't exist. There have been serial killers with high IQs and others with low IQs. The big difference between the two is that the ones with the high IQs tend to carry out their crimes over a longer period of time because they are more cautious. What the academics all do agree on is the serial killer's great talent for killing.'

'And those who aren't academics?'

'Outside academia, I've noticed that some of these bastards are more clever than Satan himself. Not intelligent, but clever. And there are some, a minority, who have a high IQ, an innate aptitude for their despicable task and for dissimulation. And in one case and one case only until now, these three characteristics have coincided in a criminal who also was very cultured. I'm talking about Ted Bundy.'

'A well-known case in my country. He strangled and then sodo-mised something like thirty women with a tyre iron.'

'Thirty-six – that we know about,' Paola corrected him. She re-membered the Bundy case in great detail, in as much as it had been required reading in Quantico.

Fowler nodded sadly. 'As I was saying, Victor Karosky came into the world in 1961 in Katowice, ironically just a few miles from where Karel Wojtyla was born. In 1969 the Karosky family, composed of himself, his parents and two brothers, emigrated to the United States. His father found work with General Motors in Detroit and, accord-ing to all the records, he was a good worker if somewhat difficult. In 1972 there was a cutback owing to the gas crisis, and Karosky senior was the first worker out the door. By then, the father had received his American citizenship, so he made himself comfortable in the tiny apartment he shared with his family, drinking away his severance pay and unemployment benefit. He really went at it – gave himself over to the task completely. He became another person, and he started to sexually abuse Victor and his older brother. The brother's name was Beria. When he was fourteen years old, Beria walked out of the house one day and never came back.'

'Karosky told you all this?' Dicanti asked, intrigued and puzzled at the same time.

'Only after intense regression therapy. When he arrived at the institute, his story was that he came from a model Catholic family.'

Paola, writing everything down in tiny script, rubbed her eyes. She wanted to dislodge every speck of exhaustion before she started talking.

'What you're telling us fits perfectly with the common registers of first-level psychopaths: personal charm, absence of irrational thinking, a lack of trustworthiness and of remorse, a great talent for dissimulation. The blows from his father and the general consumption of alcohol by his parents have also been observed in more than seventy-four per cent of known violent psychopaths.'

'So it's the probable cause?' Fowler asked.

'More likely, it's one factor among many. I can cite thousands of cases of people who were brought up in households much worse than the one you've described, and they've reached a relatively normal maturity, if such a thing actually exists.'

'But we've barely scratched the surface. Karosky told us about the death of his younger brother from meningitis in 1974, and no one seemed really to care about it. I was surprised by how cool Karosky was when he related this particular episode. Two months after the child died, his father mysteriously disappeared. Victor didn't explain whether he had something to do with the disappearance, although we didn't think so, since he would only have been thirteen years old at the time. But we do know that it was about this time that he began to torture small animals. The worst thing for him was that he remained at the mercy of an overbearing mother, who was obsessed with religion and even went so far as to dress him up as a girl so they could "play together". It seems she fondled him under his skirt, and often told young Victor that she would cut his "little packages" so that

57

his disguise would be complete. The result: Karosky still wet the bed at the age of fifteen. He wore cheap, unfashionable clothes because they were poor. He was teased at school and became very isolated ... One time a friend made an unfortunate comment about Karosky's attire as they passed in the corridor. Karosky, furious, repeatedly beat the other kid in the face with a heavy textbook. The kid wore glasses and the lenses shattered into his eyes. He was left blind.'

'The eyes ... Just like the cadavers. So that was his first violent crime.'

'As far as we know, yes. Victor was sent to a reformatory outside Boston, and the last thing his mother said to him before waving goodbye was, "I should have had an abortion." A few months later she committed suicide.'

The room went utterly silent. Words seemed indequate.

'Karosky stayed at the reformatory until the end of 1979. We don't have anything on that year, but in 1980 he entered a seminary in Baltimore. His application forms stated that his record was clean and that he came from a traditional Catholic family. He was nine-teen years old by then, and it seemed that he had been reformed. We know almost nothing about his stay in the seminary, except that he studied until he almost made himself ill, and that he was profoundly sickened by the institution's openly homosexual environment. Conroy insisted that Karosky was a repressed homosexual who de-nied his true nature, but he was wrong. Karosky isn't a homosexual or a heterosexual. He doesn't have a definite orientation. The fact that sex isn't an integral part of his personality is what, in my view, has caused such grave damage to his psyche.'

'Care to explain yourself?' Pontiero asked.

'I may as well. I am a priest who has made the decision to remain celibate. But that doesn't stop me from being attracted to Doctor Dicanti,' said Fowler, gesturing towards Paola, who couldn't help turning red. 'So I know I am heterosexual, but I choose chastity of my own free will. I've integrated sexuality into my personality, although I don't exercise it. Karosky's case is very different. The profound traumas of his infancy and childhood provoked a split down the middle of his psyche. Karosky clearly rejected the part of his being that is sexual and even violent. He both hates and loves himself, simultaneously. This has resulted in outbreaks of violence, schizophrenia, and finally in the abuse of minors, duplicating his father's abuse. In 1986, during his pastoral year, Karosky had his first incident with a minor. The victim was a young boy, fourteen years old, and there were kisses and petting but nothing else. We believe the minor did not consent to it. In any case, there's no official proof that the bishop heard about this episode, and in the end he ordained Karosky as a priest. From that day on, Karosky had an unhealthy obsession with his hands. He washes them between thirty and forty times a day and takes exceptional care of them.'

Pontiero searched hurriedly among the hundreds of macabre photographs spread over the desk until he found the one he was looking for and spun it through the air to Fowler. The priest made an effortless two fingered catch, an elegant move that impressed.

'Two hands, severed and washed, placed on a white cloth. In the church, white cloth is a symbol of respect and reverence. There are many references to it in the New Testament. As you know, Christ was covered with a white shroud in his tomb.'

'Not so white now,' Troi jested.

'I'm sure you would be delighted to apply your gadgets to the shroud in question,' Pontiero commented.

'No doubt about that. Please continue, Fowler.'

'A priest's hands are sacred. With them he administers the sacraments. This fact stayed very firmly in Karosky's mind, as we'll see. In 1987 he worked at a school in Pittsburgh, where the first cases of abuse took place. His victims were young boys aged between eight and eleven. Karosky had never experienced any type of adult consensual relationship, homosexual or heterosexual. When the complaints began to reach his superiors, they did nothing at first. Later they transferred him, from parish to parish. Very soon there was a complaint of an attack on an altar boy, whom he struck in the face, but still there were no lasting consequences … Finally he arrived at the Institute.'

'Do you think that if he'd begun to receive help earlier, things would have turned out differently?'

Fowler's whole body was tense, his hands twitching. 'We never helped him in the slightest. The only thing we achieved was to liberate the killer lurking inside him. And then we made it possible for him to escape.'

'It was that bad?'

'Worse. When he arrived, he was a man overwhelmed as much by his uncontrolled emotions as by his violent outbursts. He felt remorse for his actions, though he denied them many times. He was simply unable to control himself. But with the passage of time, the wrong-headed treatments, and his close contact with the dregs of the priesthood who lived alongside him at the institute, Karosky turned into something much worse. He became cold and ironic. The remorse disappeared. As you can see, he had blocked out the most painful memories of his childhood. That alone turned him into a pederast. But then came the disastrous regression therapy ...'

'Why disastrous?'

'It would have been better if the objective of this treatment had been to give him some peace of mind. But I fear that Doctor Conroy had a morbid, almost immoral curiosity for Karosky's case. In similar cases, the person doing the regression therapy normally attempts, through hypnosis, to implant positive events in the memory of the patient, urging them to let go of the worst things that happened. Conroy prohibited this line of action. And not only did he record Karosky; he forced him to listen to the tapes in which he begged his mother, in a child's voice, to leave him in peace.'

'What sort of Mengele did they have running that place?' Paola was in shock.

'Conroy was convinced that Karosky had to accept himself. According to him, it was the only solution. He said Karosky had to recognise that he'd had a difficult childhood and that he was a homosexual. As I told you before, Conroy used to decide his diagnosis in advance and was then determined to squeeze the patient into it, with a shoehorn if necessary. To top it all off, he subjected Karosky to a cocktail of hormones, some of which were experimental, like the variant of the contraceptive Depo-Covetan. Using this drug, injected in abnormal doses, Conroy reduced Karosky's level of sexual response; but in doing so he increased his aggression. The therapy went on and on, with no positive results. There were periods in which Karosky did calm down, and Conroy interpreted this as a sign that his therapy was succeeding – but they were just that: periods. In the end it was nothing short of a chemical castration.

Karosky is now incapable of having an erection, and the frustration is destroying him.'

'When did you first come into contact with him?'

'I spoke with him frequently when I arrived at the institute in 1995. Between us we established a relationship with a certain level of trust, but it collapsed later on. I'll tell you about that in a minute, but I don't want to get ahead of myself. Fifteen days after his arrival at the institute, the powers that be decided to give Karosky a penile plethysmograph – that's a test where the penis is connected to a measuring device by means of electrodes in order to measure the sexual response to various stimuli.'

'I'm familiar with that test,' Paola said, like someone who had just heard about an outbreak of the Ebola virus.

'Anyway, he took it very badly. During the session he was shown terrible images; they really went too far.'

'Meaning …?'

'Images of paedophilia.'

'Fuck.'

'Karosky reacted violently, and seriously wounded the specialist running the machine. The attendants finally managed to restrain him; otherwise he would have killed the guy. In the wake of that episode Conroy should have recognised that Karosky was beyond treatment and sent him off to a mental hospital. But he didn't do it. Instead he hired two security guards, and ordered them not to take their eyes off Karosky; then he started subjecting him to the regression therapy. That coincided with my arrival at the institute. As the months went by, Karosky gradually withdrew into himself. His outbursts of anger disappeared. Conroy attributed this to a significant change in his personality and decided to reduce the watch on him. Then, one night, Karosky forced the lock on his room – they used to lock him in at certain times, as a precautionary measure – and he lopped off the hands of a priest who slept in the same wing. He told everyone that the priest was an impure man and that he had seen him touching another priest in an "improper" manner. While the guards ran towards the cell where the priest was howling in pain, Karosky was busy washing his victim's hands under the nozzle of the shower.'

'The same modus operandi. As far as I'm concerned, that removes the last shred of doubt,' Paola said.

'To my amazement – and fury – Conroy didn't report the incident to the police. The mutilated priest received compensation and a team of doctors in California managed to reattach his hands, although he had much less movement in them than before. In the middle of all this, Conroy ordered security to be stepped up and built a six-by-ten-foot isolation cell. This was where Karosky lived until he escaped from the institute. Session by session, Conroy was failing and Karosky was evolving into the monster he is today. I wrote several letters to the cardinal, explaining the problem. I never received an answer. In 1999 Karosky escaped from his cell and committed his first known murder: Father Peter Selznick.'

'We heard about that here, but it was said to be a suicide.'

'Not true. Karosky escaped from his cell by forcing the lock with a ballpoint pen and then he used a metal shank he had sharpened in his cell to cut out Selznick's tongue and lips. He also sliced off Selznick's penis and forced him to eat it. It took Selznick three hours to die, yet nobody knew anything about it until the next morning.'

'What did Conroy say?'

'He officially defined the episode as a "setback", and managed to cover it up by coercing the county judge and the sheriff to issue a ruling of suicide.'

'And they went along with it? – just like that?' Pontiero asked.

'They were both Catholics. I think Conroy manipulated them by appealing to their duty to protect the Church. But even if he didn't want to admit it, my boss was very much afraid. He watched as Karosky's mind slipped away from him, as if it were absorbing his will day by day. In spite of this, he refused on repeated occasions to report the incidents to a higher level, no doubt for fear of losing his position. I wrote more letters to the archdiocese, but they wouldn't listen to me. I talked with Karosky and couldn't find even a hint of remorse. Finally I realised he'd become someone completely different. That was when all contact between us broke down and it was the last time I spoke to him. I can't lie: the beast locked up in that cell scared me. And Karosky stayed right where he was, at the institute. They set up cameras, hired more guards – until one night, in June 2000, he disappeared. Just like that.'

'And Conroy? – how did he react?'

'He was traumatised. He began to drink even more. On the third week his liver gave out and he died. A pity.'

'I wouldn't go that far,' Pontiero said.

'Anyway, I ran the institution on a temporary basis while they looked for a suitable replacement. The archdiocese didn't trust me, I suppose on account of my continual complaints about my superior. I was in charge for barely a month, but I made the most of it. I restructured the staffing as quickly as I could, hired professional personnel and drew up new programmes for the patients. Many of those were never put into practice but others were, so it was worth the effort. I sent a concise report to an old contact of mine at VICAP by the name of Kelly Sanders. The suspect's profile and the unpunished murder of Selznick really disturbed her. She gave an agent the job of bringing Karosky in. Came up with nothing.'

'That's it? He just disappeared?' Paola had a hard time believing it.

'Disappeared into thin air. In 2001 it was thought he had resurfaced, after there was a murder with partial mutilation in Albany, New York. But it wasn't him. Most people gave him up for dead, but fortunately someone logged his profile into the computer. I found a spot at a soup kitchen at a charity in Spanish Harlem in New York City. I worked there for several years, until just a few days ago. Then an old boss contacted me on behalf of the service. I thought they wanted me to be a military chaplain again. I was informed that there appeared to be signs that Karosky was back on the scene again after his long silence. So here I am. I've brought you a dossier with all the pertinent documentation I pulled together on Karosky in the five years I worked with him.' Fowler let the heavy file flop onto the table. 'There are emails relating to the hormones I told you about, transcriptions of his therapy sessions, an article in a magazine that mentions him, letters from psychiatrists, reports ... It's all yours, Doctor Dicanti. Ask me anything you're not sure of.'

Paola stretched her hand across the table to pick up the thick pile of papers; even opening the dossier made her feel uneasy. Attached to the first page was a photograph of Karosky. He had pale white skin, straight brown hair, grey eyes. In the years she'd spent studying the empty husks, void of human sentiment, that made up a serial killer, she'd learned to recognise the vacant look behind the predator's eyes. These were men to whom killing came as naturally as eating a meal. There is only one thing in nature remotely similar to that look: the eyes of the white shark. They look without seeing. It is unique, and terrifying.

And there was that look again, in Father Karosky's eyes.

'Shocking, no?' said Fowler, studying Paola's reaction. 'This man has something in his bearing, in his movements – something indefinable. At first he passes unnoticed, but when – how shall I put it? – his entire personality is alight ... it's terrible.'

'And captivating, no?'

'Yes.'

Dicanti passed the photograph to Pontiero and to Troi, both of whom leaned over to get a better look at the killer's face.

'What scares you more, *padre* – physical danger or to look that man directly in the eyes and feel yourself scrutinised, stripped, as if he were a member of a superior race?'

Fowler stared at the photo a second time. His mouth was slightly open. 'My guess is that you know the answer already.'

'Over the course of my career I've had the opportunity to interview three serial killers. All three produced the sensation in me I just described, and other people better than you or I have felt it too. But it's a bogus sensation, *padre*, and we mustn't forget one thing: those men are all failures, not prophets. Human waste. They don't deserve even the least iota of compassion.'

**Report on the synthetic pro-gestational hormone 1789
(injectable progestin)**
Commercial name: Depo-Covetan
Report classification: Confidential, encrypted

To: Marcus.Bietghofer@beltzer-hogan.com
From: Lorna.Barr@beltzer-hogan.com
CC: filesys@beltzer-hogan.com
Subject: CONFIDENTIAL: Report 45 on SPH 1789
Date: 17 March 1997, 11.43 a.m.
Attachment: Inf#45_SPH1789.pdf

Dear Marcus:

Attached is an advance copy of the report you asked about.

The analysis carried out in the ALFA-area field studies has shown serious irregularities in menstrual flow, sleep disruption, vertigo, and possible internal hemorrhaging. The report describes serious cases of hypertension, thrombosis and cardiac disease. There has also been an increase in a specific minor problem: 1.3% of the patients have developed fibromyalgia, a side effect not observed in the previous version.

If you compare the report with that of version 1786, which we are currently marketing in the United States and Europe, side effects have been reduced by 3.9%. If our risk analysis is correct, we can estimate a maximum of $53 million dollars will be spent on legal damages. Therefore, we are staying within our guidelines, that is to say, an amount less than 7% of profits.

No, don't thank me … just give me a raise!

By the way, the laboratory has received test results on the use of 1789 with male patients, with the goal of repressing or eliminating their sexual response. In the practical test, dosages sufficient to effect chemical castration were administered. From the reports and analyses examined by this laboratory, increases in the volatility of the subject can be clearly seen in specific instances, as can particular anomalies in cerebral activity. Our recommendation is to extend the framework of the study in order to determine the percentage at which said side effects occur. It would be interesting to undertake tests with Omega subjects, such as patients who are psychiatrically beyond hope, or prisoners on death row.

I would be happy to be in charge of those tests.

So are we going out for lunch this Friday? I've found a great little restaurant in the Village that serves divine bass from Chile.

Regards,
Dr Lorna Barr
Research Director

Uacv Headquarters

Wednesday, 6 April 2005, 1.25 a.m.

Paola's harsh words silenced the room. No one said a thing. The long day weighed heavily on the bodies and the early hour on the minds and eyes of all concerned.

Finally it was Troi who spoke up. 'Tell us what to do, Dicanti.'

Paola took half a minute to reply. 'I know it's been a long day. Let's all go home and sleep for a few hours. We'll meet back here at 8.30 in the morning. Let's begin with the places where the victims were killed. We'll go back over the settings and hope that the agents Pontiero sent into the field come up with some new evidence, no matter how ridiculous that hope is. And Pontiero, call Dante and tell him when we're meeting.'

'It'll be a pleasure,' he answered caustically.

Acting as if she hadn't heard a thing, Dicanti walked over to Troi and touched his arm. 'I'd like to speak with you in private for a minute.'

'Let's step out to the hall.'

Paola exited the room in front of the older scientist, who, as always, played the part of the gallant, opening the door for her then closing it behind him. Dicanti detested her boss's deferential manner.

'So, tell me.'

'What exactly is Fowler's role in this investigation? I just don't understand it, and I have no faith whatsoever in his vague explanations about why he's here.'

'Dicanti, to cut to the chase, I had a call from someone high up – right near the top – in US intelligence this morning, while we were with Robayra, and we had a very long conversation. This person informed me that Fowler was flying direct from Washington to join the investigation, and he gave me no choice in the matter. It's not just a question of the fact that President Bush is in Rome himself and everyone is therefore on guard. These are the guy's exact words: "I'm sending you one of my most trusted colleagues, and we're lucky because he knows this case from top to bottom."

'How did they find out so fast?' asked Paola, staring at the ground. She was dumbfounded by the magnitude of what she was hearing.

'My dear Paola, never underestimate Camilo Cirin, not even for a moment. When the second victim turned up, he called a US intelligence chief himself. According to the person I spoke to, they didn't have the remotest idea how Cirin had got his hands on a phone number that has only existed for the last two weeks.'

'So how did they know who to send so quickly?'

'That's no mystery. Fowler's friend in VICAP interpreted Karosky's last words before he fled the Saint Matthew as an implicit threat against the Church, and as such they were communicated to the Vigilanza five years ago. When they found Robayra's body this morning, Cirin broke his own rule about washing dirty laundry at home. He made some calls and pulled the threads together. He's a well-connected son of a bitch, but I guess you're finding that out for yourself, my dear.'

'I had a vague inkling,' Dicanti said, heavy on the irony.

'He told me, over and over again, that there is a personal interest in this case at the very highest levels of government.'

'Oh, God. We're not going to have a support team this time, are we?'

'You can answer that one on your own.'

Dicanti didn't say anything. If the priority was to keep the matter secret, she would have to work with what she had – and only that.

'You don't think I'm in over my head with all this?' Dicanti was extremely tired and overwhelmed by the whole situation surrounding the case. She'd never experienced anything like it, but for a long time afterwards she regretted letting those words slip out.

Troi's fingers stroked her chin and he forced Dicanti to look at him. 'We're all in over our heads, bambina. But don't let it get to you. Just focus on the fact that there's a monster out there killing people, and spend your time hunting monsters.'

Paola smiled. She was grateful and for a moment she wanted him again – one last time, right there – even though she knew it would be a mistake and would break her heart. Luckily for her, the feeling was short-lived. She made an effort to recover her composure as quickly as she could, hoping he hadn't noticed.

'I worry that Fowler may stir things up during the investigation. He could be an obstacle.'

'Could be. And he could also be very useful. The man was enlisted in the Air Force and he's a consummate marksman – among his other … talents. Not to mention the fact that he has a thorough knowledge of our suspect and he's a priest. He'll help you move around in a world you're not accustomed to, the same way Dante will. Think about it like this: our colleague from the Vatican will open the doors for you, and Fowler, their minds.'

'Dante's an insufferable asshole.'

'I know. But he's a necessary evil. All of our suspect's potential victims are in his country. Although we're only a few feet away from him, it's his territory.'

'It's still Italy, which is ours. What they did with Portini was illegal – acting without our say so. It was an obstruction of justice.'

The cynic in Troi shrugged his shoulders. 'What would we have gained by reporting them? We'd have made a new enemy, that's all. Forget about politics and the fact that they might put their foot in it. Right now we need Dante. As you know, he's part of your team.'

'You're the boss.'

'And you're my favourite ispettore. Anyway, I'm going home to rest. Tomorrow morning I'll be in the laboratory, running tests on every last fibre they bring me. I'll let you build your castles in the air.'

Troi was already walking down the hallway when he suddenly stopped in his tracks, turned round and gave her a piercing look. 'One more thing: US intelligence wants us to catch this son of a bitch. Don't for a second doubt that I'd be overjoyed if they owed us one.'

$\mathcal{D}$ICANTI FAMILY APARTMENT

VIA DELLA CROCE, 12

Wednesday, 6 April 2005, 1.59 a.m.

'Keep the change.'

'*Molto generoso*. Thanks for the huge tip.'

Paola ignored the driver's attempt at humour. It was the kind of crap you got used to in the city, where even the taxi drivers bitched if they thought their tip wasn't big enough. In lira that would have been … enough. Definitely. And to top it off, the prick had his foot on the accelerator before she'd even got fully out of the car. A gentleman would have waited until she was safely inside the door. Two in the morning and the street was deserted, for God's sake.

It was already warm by this time of the year, but Paola shivered as she opened the front door. Was that a shadow at the end of the street? No, just her imagination.

She quickly pulled the door closed behind her, feeling ridiculous for her sudden wave of fear. She hurried up the three flights to her apartment. The wooden stairs groaned with every step, but she barely registered the noise: the blood was pounding in her ears and she was gasping for air by the time she arrived at her door. Yet once she got there, she didn't move. She stood, riveted to the spot.

The door to the apartment was half-open.

Slowly, carefully, she opened her jacket and slipped her right hand under the arm. She pulled the pistol out of its holster and went into a crouch, her elbow at a sharp angle to her body. She kicked the door open and stepped slowly into the apartment. The hallway light was on. She took one cautious step towards the interior and then moved away from the door, pointing the pistol at empty space.

Nothing.

'Paola?'

'Mamma?'

'Come on in. I'm in the kitchen.'

Paola took a deep breath and returned the gun to its holster. She'd never taken it out in a real situation before – at the FBI Academy, certainly, but … This case was definitely making her too nervous.

Lucrezia Dicanti was in the kitchen, spreading butter on digestive biscuits. The buzzer on the microwave went off and she removed two steaming cups of milk. She placed them on a small formica table. Paola took a look round the room. Her heart was still beating quickly. Everything was as it should be: the little plastic pig with the wooden spoons in its back, the brightly coloured walls they had painted themselves, the lingering odour of oregano in the air. She supposed her mother had made cannolis. She also suspected that her mother had eaten all of them, which was why she was now offering her biscuits.

'Have a few. I can put more butter on if you want.'

'Heavens, Mamma, you nearly scared me to death! Why did you leave the door open?' Paola was almost shouting.

Her mother looked at her, concern written across her face. She removed a paper towel from the pocket of her dressing gown and used it to wipe the tips of her fingers, cleaning off the last traces of butter. 'I was up, listening to the news on the terrace. All Rome is in a spin about the election of the next pope. They can talk of nothing else on the radio. I decided to wait up for you, and then I saw you get out of the taxi. I'm sorry.'

Paola instantly felt bad and apologised to her mother.

'Don't worry, young lady. Have a biscuit.'

'Thanks, Mamma.'

The younger woman sat down next to her mother, who kept her eyes firmly on her daughter. From when Paola was a little girl, Lucrezia had become adept at perceiving her trials and tribulations and knowing how best to advise her. But now it was clear that the problem engulfing her was too heavy, too complex – simply too much.

'Something's happened at work?'

'You know I can't talk about it.'

'I know, and I also know that when you have that face on, like someone's stepped on your corns, you're going to spend the whole night tossing and turning. Are you sure you don't want to tell me anything?'

Paola stared at the cup of milk on the table, ladling spoonful after spoonful of sugar into it as she spoke.

'It's just … It's another case, Mamma, but this one is crazy. I feel like this damned glass of milk that someone keeps spooning sugar into. The sugar isn't dissolving; it's just making the glass overflow.'

Lucrezia tenderly put her hand over the glass, palm up, and Paola poured a spoonful of sugar into it.

'Sometimes it helps if you talk about it.'

'I can't, Mamma. Sorry.'

'That's all right, my dove – I understand. Do you want another biscuit? I'm sure you haven't eaten anything.' Her mother knew when it was wise to change the subject.

'No, Mamma, this is more than enough. My backside is already bigger than the Coliseum.'

'My daughter happens to have a very pretty rear.'

'Right, and that's why I'm still single.'

'No, Paola. You're still single because you have a bad temper. You're pretty, you take care of yourself, you go to the gym … It's just a matter of time before you meet a man you won't scare off with your loud voice and scary faces.'

'I don't believe that's ever going to happen, Mamma.'

'And why not? What about your boss, the charming one?'

'He's married. And he's old enough to be my father.'

'You love to exaggerate. Bring him here – you'll see I don't disgust him. Besides, in today's world, being married doesn't seem to matter as much as it used to.'

If you only knew, Paola thought to herself. 'You really believe that, Mamma?'

'I'm convinced. Madonna, but he has such lovely hands! I'd like to jump between the sheets with that one …'

'Mamma! Sometimes you really shock me!'

'Since your father departed ten years ago there's not a single day goes by that I don't think of him. Still, I'm not like those Sicilian widows, dressed in black from head to toe, pouring out their hearts at their husbands' graves. Go on, have another biscuit and then we'll go to bed.'

Paola dipped the biscuit in her milk, mentally calculating the calories and feeling very guilty. Luckily for her, that feeling didn't last long.

Correspondence between Cardinal Francis Casey
and Mrs Edwina MacDougal

Boston, 23/02/1999

Dear Mrs MacDougal,

In response to your letter of February 17th of this year, I want to show you [...] that I respect and regret the pain that you and your son Harry are experiencing. I am conscious of the tremendous anguish and suffering he has gone through. I agree with you that when a man of God falls into sin, as Father Karosky did, it shakes a person's faith to its foundations. I acknowledge my error. I should never have reassigned Father Karosky [...] Perhaps on the third occasion when the faithful, such as yourself, came to me with their complaints, I ought to have taken a different road [...] I was poorly advised by the psychiatrists who reviewed his case, such as Doctor Dressler, who put his professional reputation on the line when he asserted that Karosky was fit for the ministry. I conceded [...]

I hope that the generous compensation we have agreed to with your lawyer has brought a measure of satisfaction to all parties [...] as it is more than we were able to offer[...] without, however, of course attempting to mitigate your pain with money, if I may permit myself to advise you not to speak of the case, for everyone's good [...] our Holy Mother Church has already suffered terrible calumnies at the hands of the wicked and the Satanic media [...] For the good of our small community, for that of your son and for yourself, let us go on as if this terrible thing had never occurred.

I bestow blessings upon you.

Francis Augustus Casey
Cardinal, Archdiocese of Boston

THE SAINT MATTHEW INSTITUTE

SACHEM PIKE, MARYLAND

November 1995

Transcript of Interview Number 45 between Patient Number 3643 and Doctor Canice Conroy, with the Assistance of Doctor Anthony Fowler and Salher Fanabarzra

DR CONROY: Hello, Victor. May we come in?

No. 3643: Certainly, doctor. It's your clinic.

DR CONROY: It's your room.

No. 3643: Do come in, please.

DR CONROY: I see that you are in a good mood today. Do you feel well?

No. 3643: Stupendous.

DR CONROY: I'm happy to see that there have been no violent incidents since your departure from the infirmary. You're taking your medications on schedule, you're participating in the group sessions ... You're making progress, Victor.

No. 3643: Thank you, doctor. I do what I can.

DR CONROY: Fine. As we discussed earlier, today we're beginning your regression therapy. This is Mr Fanabarzra. He is a therapist from India, a specialist in hypnosis.

No. 3643: Doctor, I don't know if I'm comfortable with the idea of participating in this experiment.

DR CONROY: It's important, Victor. We spoke about it last week, do you remember?

No. 3643: Yes, I remember.

DR CONROY: Then we've agreed. Mr Fanabarzra, where do you

want the patient to sit?

FANABARZRA: He'll be most comfortable lying down. It's important for him to be as relaxed as possible.

DR CONROY: On the bed, then. You can lie down, Victor.

No. 3643: As you wish.

FANABARZRA: Very well, Victor. I am going to show you a pendulum. Could you lower the blind a little, doctor? That's enough. Victor, watch the pendulum, if you'd be so kind.

[*Transcription omits Fanabarzra's process of hypnosis, at his request. Pauses between responses have also been eliminated for the sake of brevity.*]

FANABARZRA: All right then ... it's 1972. What do you remember from this period?

No. 3643: My father ... He was never at home. Sometimes the whole family went to wait for him at the factory on Friday afternoon. Mother said he was a good for nothing and if we found him we'd stop him spending our money in the bars. It was cold outside. One day we waited and waited. We stamped our feet on the ground to keep our toes from freezing. Emil asked me for my scarf because he was cold. I didn't give it to him. My mother rapped me on the head and told me to give it to him. Finally we got tired of waiting and we left.

DR CONROY: Ask him where his father was.

FANABARZRA: Do you know where your father was?

No. 3643: He'd been fired from his job. He came back home two days later in bad shape. Mother said he'd been drinking and sleeping with strangers. They'd given him a cheque but there wasn't much left. We'd go to Social Security to get Dad's benefit but sometimes he got there first and he drank it. Emil didn't understand how someone could drink a piece of paper.

FANABARZRA: Did you ask for help?

No. 3643: Sometimes the parish gave us clothes. Other kids got their clothes at the Salvation Army, because they had better clothes there. But Mother said that they were heretics and pagans and it was better to wear decent Christian clothes. Beria said that his decent Christian clothes were full of holes. That's why he hated them.

FANABARZRA: Were you happy when Beria left?

No. 3643: I was in bed. I saw him walk across the bedroom in the dark, carrying his boots in one hand. He gave me his key chain with a silver bear and told me I could put the keys I needed on it. In the morning, Emil was crying because he hadn't said goodbye to Beria, so I gave him the key chain. But he kept crying and threw the key chain away. He cried all day. I tore up a book of stories he was reading, just to get him to shut up. I cut it into pieces with a pair of scissors. My father locked me in his room.

FANABARZRA: Where was your mother?

No. 3643: Playing bingo at the parish hall. It was Tuesday. She always played bingo on Tuesdays. Each card cost a penny.

FANABARZRA: What happened in your father's room?

No. 3643: Nothing. I sat around.

FANABARZRA: Victor, you have to tell me.

No. 3643: Nothing happened. Do you understand, sir? *Nothing.*

FANABARZRA: Victor, you have to tell me. Your father locked you in his room and he did something to you. Correct?

No. 3643: You don't understand. I deserved it.

FANABARZA: What did you deserve?

No. 3643: To be punished. I had to be punished so many times so that I would repent for all the bad things I'd done.

FANABARZA: What bad things?

No. 3643: So many bad things. The bad person I was. The things I did to the cat. I threw a cat into a rubbish bin full of old newspapers all crumpled up and set the paper on fire. The cat howled. It sounded like a human voice. And for what I did to the book of stories.

FANABARZRA: What was the punishment, Victor?

No. 3643: Hurt. He hurt me. And he liked it, I know that. He told me that it hurt him too, but that was a lie. He said it in Polish. He didn't know how to lie in English, he got the words all mixed up. He always spoke in Polish when he was punishing me.

FANABARZRA: He touched you?

No. 3643: He gave it to me in the rear end. He didn't let me turn around. And he put something in me. Something hot that hurt.

FANABARZRA: Did these punishments happen frequently?

No. 3643: Every Tuesday. When Mother wasn't around. Sometimes, when he was finished, he just lay there, sleeping on top of me, as if he was dead. At times he couldn't punish me so he hit me instead.

FANABARZRA: How did he hit you?

No. 3643: He spanked me until he was tired. Sometimes after he hit me he could punish me and sometimes not.

FANABARZRA: And your brothers, Victor? Did your father punish them?

No. 3643: I think he punished Beria. Never Emil; Emil was the good one. That's why he died.

FANABARZRA: Only the good people die, Victor?

No. 3643: Only the good. Bad people never do.

Palazzo del Governatorato

VATICAN CITY

Wednesday, 6 April 2005, 10.34 a.m.

Pacing back and forth on the rug in the hallway with short, nervous steps, Paola waited for Dante. The day had begun badly. She'd barely slept a wink, and when she'd arrived at her office she'd run smack into a pile of insufferable paperwork and admin. The man in charge of civil defence, Guido Bertolano, was throwing a fit over the increasingly enormous number of pilgrims who were inundating the city. By now the sports stadiums, universities, and any municipal institutions with space to spare were full to the rafters. People were sleeping in the streets, in doorways, the town squares, even the vestibules of ATMs. Dicanti had got in touch with Bertolano to ask him for help in the search for a suspect, and he'd almost laughed in her face.

'My dear ispettore, even if your suspect were Osama himself, there's very little we could do. It's going to have to wait until after this whole madhouse has died down.'

'I don't know if you are aware that—'

'*Ispettore* – you said your name was Dicanti, right? Air Force One is parked at Fiumicino. There isn't a single five-star hotel that doesn't have at least one monarch ensconced in its presidential suite. Can you imagine what sort of nightmare it is to protect these people? There are reports of possible terrorist attacks and fake bomb threats every fifteen minutes. I'm in contact with the carabinieri in towns from over a two-hundred-kilometre radius. Believe me, your problem has to wait. So please stop tying up my line,' he said, hanging up without another word.

Go to hell! Why didn't anyone take her seriously? This case was an absolute killer. The silence it dictated, inherent in the nature of the beast, only contributed to the clash between what she was trying to do and the indifference she met with. She'd wasted a long time on the phone without finding out anything. Between the various calls she'd asked Pontiero to go to talk to the old Carmelite at Santa Maria in Traspontina while she headed off for her meeting with Cardinal Samalo, the Pope's chamberlain, or *il camerlengo*, as he was known in Italian. So there she was, at the doors to the *camerlengo*'s office, pacing like a tiger, with a belly full of black coffee.

Fowler, meanwhile, relaxed on an ornate bench of dark-red wood. He was reading his breviary. 'It's at moments like this that I regret having given up smoking.'

'A bit nervous yourself?'

'No, but you're making it hard not to follow in your footsteps.'

Paola took the priest's hint, stopped walking in circles and sat down next to him. She pretended to read Dante's report on the first murder, all the time thinking about the strange look that the superintendent had given Fowler when she'd introduced them at UACV headquarters that morning. Dante had taken Paola aside and said tersely, 'Don't trust him.' She was worried, intrigued. She decided that the first chance she got, she would ask Dante exactly what he'd meant.

She turned her attention back to the report. A complete disaster. It was clear that Dante didn't take assignments like this very often, which was lucky for him. They would painstakingly have to go back over the scene where Cardinal Portini died, in the hope of turning up some other piece of evidence. This afternoon, no later. The photographs weren't so bad in any case. She slammed the folder shut. She couldn't concentrate.

Paola found it difficult to admit that she was frightened. There she was, in the very heart of the Vatican, in an edifice set apart in the centre of the City – a building with more than fifteen hundred offices, including the private office of the Pope himself. To Paola, the mere profusion of statues and paintings that filled the hallways was unsettling, distracting. And, of course, for the Vatican's states-men over the course of the centuries, that was the desired result; they were well aware of the effect their city produced on visitors. Yet Paola couldn't allow herself even the slightest distraction.

'Padre Fowler?'

'Yes?'

'Can I ask you a question?'

'Of course.'

'It's the first time I'm going to see a cardinal.'

'Really.'

Paola thought for a moment. 'I mean to say, in the flesh.'

'And what is your question?'

'How do you address a cardinal?'

'Normally you would say "Your Eminence".' Fowler closed his book and looked her in the eye. 'Relax. He's only a person, like you or me. And you're the inspector running the investigation. You're a professional. Act just as you would under normal circumstances.'

Dicanti smiled gratefully.

At last Dante opened the door to the office's waiting room. 'Please come in.'

There were two desks in the waiting room, with two young priests seated by the telephone and a computer. They greeted the visitors with polite nods of the head, and the small party continued on into the chamberlain's office. It was an ascetic room, without paintings or carpets. There was a library on one side and a sofa with small tables on the other. A wooden crucifix was the only decoration on the walls.

Unlike the empty walls, the desk of Eduardo González Samalo, the man who held the reins of the Church until the election of the next Pope, was crammed with papers. Samalo, in dark-red robes, got up to greet them. Fowler kneeled and kissed the cardinal's ring as a sign of respect and obedience, something every Catholic does when meeting a cardinal. Paola hung back, hoping to be discreet. She bowed her head a little, perhaps slightly ashamed. She hadn't regarded herself as a Catholic for many years.

Samalo took Dicanti's rudeness gracefully, but exhaustion and anxiety were clearly etched on his face and in the slump of his shoulders. He was the ultimate authority in the Vatican for the next few days and he didn't seem to be enjoying the role.

'Forgive me for making you wait. I was on the phone with a delegate from Germany. He's extremely out of sorts. There are no hotel rooms to be found anywhere and the city is a veritable nightmare.

81

And the whole wide world wants to be in the front row at tomorrow morning's funeral.'

Paola nodded her head courteously. 'I imagine this whole commotion must be tremendously trying.'

Samalo merely let out a long, painful sigh in response.

'Have you been informed about the situation, Your Eminence?'

'Of course. Camilo Cirin has been diligent in keeping me abreast of events as they've taken place. It's a horrible state of affairs, all of it. I suppose that in other circumstances I would have reacted much more strongly to these nefarious crimes, but I must tell you in all sincerity, I just haven't had the time.'

'As you know, we have to think about the security of the other cardinals, Your Eminence.'

Samalo gestured in Dante's direction. 'The Vigilanza has made a special effort to gather all of them together in the Domus Sanctae Marthae ahead of time, in order to maintain the building's security.'

'La Domus Sanctae Marthae?'

Dante interrupted. 'Saint Martha's House. A building that was remodelled at the direct request of John Paul II. He wanted it to serve as the principal residence for the cardinals during the Conclave.'

'A very specific use for a whole building, wouldn't you say?'

'When it isn't hosting a Conclave, it is used to lodge prominent visitors,' said Cardinal Samalo. 'Unless I'm mistaken, Padre Fowler, even you stayed there once. Isn't that so?'

Fowler seemed very uneasy. For a few moments it looked as if there was going to be a minor confrontation, without blood, but a battle of wills nonetheless. It was Fowler who lowered his head.

'Indeed, Your Eminence. I was once invited to the Holy See.'

'I believe you had a problem with the Holy Office.'

'I was called to an inquiry regarding activities in which I had taken part; that much is true – nothing more.'

The cardinal seemed to be satisfied with the priest's visible discomfort.

'Ah, but of course, Padre Fowler … There's no need to give me any sort of explanation. Your reputation precedes you. As I was saying, Ispettore Dicanti, I am reassured with regard to the safety of my fellow cardinals, thanks to the good efforts of the Vigilanza. Nearly all of them are accounted for and are safely installed here inside the Vatican. A few have yet to arrive. In principle, residing at the Domus was optional until 15 April and many of the cardinals have been staying with various congregations or in religious residences. But we are in the process of letting them know that they should transfer to Saint Martha's House immediately.'

'How many are at the house right now?'

'Eighty-four out of one hundred and fifteen. The others will arrive in the next few hours. We've attempted to contact all of the latter and have asked for their itinerary in order to supplement security. They are the ones uppermost in our minds. But as I've told you, Inspector General Cirin is in charge of everything. So there's no need to worry, dear child.'

'Does that one hundred and fifteen include Robayra and Portini?' asked Dicanti, riled by the chamberlain's condescending tone.

'Well, I suppose that in reality I should say one hundred and thirteen cardinals,' Samalo responded resentfully. He was a proud man and took no pleasure in being corrected by a woman.

'I'm sure Your Eminence has already settled on a plan in that regard,' Fowler added, making an attempt to mediate between the two.

'Indeed. We are spreading the rumour that Portini has been taken ill at his family's country home in Corsica. The illness will unfortunately end on a tragic note. With respect to Robayra, we are saying that matters relating to his pastoral mission will prevent him from attending the Conclave, although he certainly plans to travel to Rome to render his obedience to the new Supreme Pontiff. Sadly, he will die in a tragic car accident, something that the police will be able to confirm. These stories will only be sent to the press after the Conclave, not before.'

'I see that Your Eminence has everything well in hand,' Paola said, thoroughly astonished.

The chamberlain cleared his throat before answering. 'It's one story among many. And it is one that causes no harm to anyone.'

'Except to the truth.'

'This is the Catholic Church, inspector – the inspiration and light that illuminates the way for millions of people. We cannot allow ourselves any further scandals. From that point of view, what exactly is the truth?'

Dicanti wore a sceptical look on her face, even though she recognised the logic implicit in the old man's words. She thought of the many ways she might reply to him, but understood that it wouldn't prove a thing. She preferred to return to the interview.

'I suppose that the reason for gathering earlier than planned won't be communicated to the cardinals?'

'Absolutely not. I have told them that a radical group has made threats against the Church hierarchy and that they therefore must not leave the city without being accompanied by a member of the Vigilanza or the Swiss Guard. I believe they all understand.'

'Did you know the victims personally?'

The cardinal's face darkened for a moment.

'Good heavens, yes. I had less in common with Cardinal Portini, despite the fact that he was Italian. My work has always been very centred on the internal organisation of the Vatican and he dedicated his life to doctrine. He was always writing and travelling. A great man. On a personal level, I didn't always agree with his politics, which were so open and revolutionary.'

'Revolutionary?' Fowler leaned forward.

'Very much so, *padre*. He argued for the use of condoms, for the ordination of women priests. He would have been a pope for the twenty-first century. Furthermore he still would have been relatively young for a pope, although he was nearly 59 years old. If he had sat on the throne of Peter, he would have been in charge of Vatican Council III, something many people believe the Church urgently needs. His death has been a terrible and senseless misfortune.'

'You would have voted for him?' Fowler asked.

The *camerlengo* laughed silently. 'You're not seriously asking me to reveal who I'm going to vote for, are you, *padre*?'

Paola stepped back in. 'Your Eminence, you said you had less in common with Portini. What about Robayra?'

'Another great man. Totally committed to the cause of the poor. He had defects, certainly. He was very given to imagining himself dressed in white, standing on the balcony overlooking Saint Peter's Square. Of course, he never spoke of his ambition in public. We were very close friends and wrote to each other all the time. His only sin was his pride. He always made a great show of his poverty, and signed his letters with a *beati pauperes*. Just to rile him, I used to sign mine with *beati pauperes spirito*, but he never let on that he understood my allusion. Despite his defects, he was a statesman and a man of the Church. He did so much good over the course of his lifetime. I never dreamed I'd see him wearing the fisherman's sandals, but I suppose that was because I was so close to him.'

As he spoke about his friend, the old cardinal shrank a little and turned a shade of grey, his voice became sad and his face revealed the accumulated fatigue of his seventy-eight years. In spite of the fact that she didn't share the man's ideas, Paola felt sorry for him. She knew that behind his carefully crafted homage, the old Spaniard regretted not having any time to be alone and weep for his friend. Damned dignity. As she was thinking this, she realised that she was beginning to look beyond the cardinal's cape and his red robe, to see the person wearing them. She'd have to learn to stop looking at the clergy as if they were one-dimensional. Her prejudice against the priesthood could easily jeopardise her work.

'When all is said and done, I suppose no one is a prophet in their own country. As I mentioned, we agreed on a great many things. Good old Emilio came here seven months ago. It was the last stop on his trip. One of my assistants took a photograph here in the office. I know I have it somewhere.'

The man in the dark-red robes walked over to his desk, and reached inside a drawer for an envelope that contained some photographs. He looked through them, chose one and handed the picture to his visitors.

Paola looked at the photograph without much interest. Suddenly she saw something that seized her attention and forced her eyes wide open. She grabbed Dante's arm, nearly pulling it out of its socket.

'Oh, shit. Shit!'

Church of Santa Maria in Traspontina

VIA DELLA CONCILIAZIONE, 14

Wednesday, 6 April 2005, 10.41 a.m.

Pontiero knocked on the rear door of the church – the one that led into the sacristy – again and again. Following the police instructions, Brother Francesco had placed a sign on the door, written in an unsteady hand, which indicated that the church was closed for renovations. Beyond being obedient, the friar must also have been a little deaf, because Pontiero had now spent five minutes pounding away. Behind him, thousands of people crammed the Via dei Corridori, in ever growing, ever more disorderly numbers. There were more people on that small street than on the Via della Conciliazione.

At last Pontiero heard sounds coming from the other side of the door. The bolts were drawn back and Brother Francesco's face appeared through a crack, squinting in the harsh sun.

'Yes?'

'Fratello, I'm Detective Pontiero. Remember me from yesterday?'

The monk nodded once, and then a second time. 'So, why are you here? You've come to tell me that I can reopen my church now, praise the Lord? With so many pilgrims out there ... See for yourself, look around you,' he said as he gestured towards the thousands of people in the street.

'No, brother. I need to ask you a few questions. Is it all right with you if I come in?'

'Must it be now? I was just saying my prayers.'

'I won't take much of your time. Really, just a minute or two.'

Francesco shook his head slowly from side to side. 'What times these are, what times. Death everywhere – death and people running around. I can't even finish my prayers in peace.'

The door opened slowly and then closed behind Pontiero with a loud bang.

'That's one heavy door, *padre*.'

'Yes, my son. At times it's very hard for me to open it, most of all when I come back from the supermarket. These days nobody helps an old man carry his bags. What times these are, what times.'

'You should get one of those shopping bags on wheels.'

Pontiero walked back and inspected the door from the inside, attentively checking the bolt and the heavy hinges that fastened it into the wall.

'There's no damage to the lock. It doesn't seem to have been forced at all.'

'No, my son. It's a strong lock. The door was painted about a year ago by a parishioner, a friend of mine, good old Giuseppe. He has asthma, you know, and the fumes from the paint didn't agree with him …'

'I'm sure Giuseppe is a good Christian.'

'He is, my son, he is.'

'I've come to find out how the killer was able to get into the church, especially if there are no other means of access. Inspector Dicanti thinks it's an important detail.'

'He could have come through one of the windows, if he had a ladder. But I don't think so, because none of them is broken. Madre, what a disaster; imagine if he'd broken one of the stained-glass windows …'

'Would it bother you if I took a look at those windows?'

'Not at all. Follow me.'

The friar limped from the sacristy towards the church, which was illuminated only by candles placed beneath the statues of saints and martyrs. Pontiero was surprised that so many of them were lit.

'So many offerings, Brother Francesco.'

'Ah, I lit all the candles you see here – a supplication to the saints to carry the soul of our Holy Father John Paul straight to the heart of heaven.'

Pontiero was amused by the friar's simplicity. They were standing in the central aisle, from which point the sacristy door was visible, along with the main entrance and the windows at the front of the church, which were the only ones. He slid a finger along the back of one of the pews, an involuntary gesture he had repeated during thousands of Sunday masses. This was the House of God, and it had been profaned and defiled. Today, lit by the flickering glow of candles, the church took on a very different aspect from that of the day before. Pontiero couldn't repress a chill. The interior was cold and damp, in stark contrast to the heat outside. He looked up towards the windows. Even the lowest one was some sixteen feet off the ground. The entire window was composed of intricate stained glass, and not one pane had suffered so much as a scratch.

'There's no way the killer could have come in through the windows carrying two hundred pounds on his back. He would have had to use a crane. And he would have been seen by thousands of pilgrims outside. No, it's impossible.'

Both men heard the songs the young people were singing as they stood in line to say farewell to Pope John Paul. All of them sang of love and peace.

'Ah, young people. Our hope for the future. Isn't that so, detective?'

'Right you are, brother.'

Pontiero scratched his head. He couldn't think of any entrances to the building except for the doors and the windows. He took a few steps that echoed loudly through the empty church.

'Listen, does anyone else have keys to the church? Perhaps the person who does the cleaning?'

'No, absolutely not. A few of the more devout parishioners help me clean the church early on Saturday mornings and on Monday afternoons, but I'm always here when they come. In fact, I only have one set of keys and I always carry them with me. See?' The priest put his left hand into an interior pocket of his white habit, and shook the key ring.

'OK, *padre*, I give up. I can't understand how he could have got in without being seen.'

'I'm afraid I can't tell you anything, my son. I'm sorry I haven't been of more help.'

'Thank you.'

Pontiero spun round and started to walk towards the sacristy.

'Unless ...' The Carmelite seemed to reflect for a moment, and then nodded his head. 'No, it's impossible. It can't be.'

'What is it? Tell me. Even the smallest thing could be helpful.'

The friar stroked his beard and brooded. 'Well, there is an underground access. It's an old passageway that dates from the time when the church was rebuilt.'

'There was another church here?'

'Yes, the original building was destroyed during the Sack of Rome in 1527. It was in the line of fire of the cannons that were defending Castel Sant'Angelo. And at that time this church—'

'Do you mind if we leave the history class for later? Let's take a look at the passage now.'

'Are you sure? You're wearing a nice, clean suit—'

'Sure I'm sure. Show me where it is.'

'As you wish, detective,' the friar said humbly.

He hobbled around to the entrance of the church, near the font of holy water, and pointed out a crack in between the stones in the floor. 'Do you see that crack? Stick your fingers in there and pull hard.'

Pontiero got down on his knees and followed the friar's instructions. Nothing happened.

'Try again. Pull hard, to the left.'

Pontiero did as Francesco told him to, but to no avail. Short and skinny as he was, Pontiero was nonetheless strong. He wasn't about to give up. On the third try he felt the stone shift. Then it came up easily. It was, in fact, a trapdoor. He held it up with one hand. Down below was a short, narrow stairway, some eight feet high. He found a small flashlight in his pocket and shone it into the darkness. Stone steps, and they looked solid enough.

'Very nice. Now let's see where this takes us.'

'Detective, don't go down there by yourself, I beg you.'

'Take it easy, brother. There's nothing to it. I'll be careful.'

Pontiero imagined Dante and Dicanti's faces when he told them what he'd found. He got to his feet and then took his first step down the stairway.

'Wait. Let me get a candle.'

'Don't bother. I can see all right with this torch,' Pontiero shouted.

At the bottom of the stairs was a short passageway with damp walls, which in turn gave way to a room about eighteen feet square. Pontiero ran his flashlight over every surface. It looked as if the basement stopped here. There were two truncated columns, each about six feet tall, both in the middle of the room. They looked very old. Pontiero couldn't identify what period they dated from – he'd never paid much attention in history classes – but even so, on one of them he could see pieces of something that shouldn't have been there. It looked like …

Duct tape.

This wasn't a secret passage: it was an execution chamber.

Pontiero turned round just in time for the blow, which was intended to split his skull, but hit him on the right shoulder instead. He fell to the ground, shuddering with pain. The flashlight had rolled away, its beam now illuminating the base of one of the columns. He knew intuitively that a second blow was on its way, from the right, and it struck him on the left arm. He felt around for his pistol in the space between his arm and his side and managed to nudge it out with his left hand, in spite of the pain. The pistol felt as if it was made of lead. He had no feeling in his other arm.

An iron bar. He must have an iron bar or something like that …

He tried to aim, but couldn't. He got to his feet and was hobbling towards the column when the third blow, square on the back this time, knocked him flat on the ground. He gripped the weapon even tighter, holding on for dear life.

A foot on top of his hand forced him to release the gun. The foot kept pushing down hard and the bones in his hand made a crunching noise. He heard a voice he vaguely recognised, a voice with a very distinct timbre. 'Pontiero, Pontiero. As I was saying, the original church was in the line of fire of the cannons that were defending Castel Sant'Angelo. And that church had in turn replaced a pagan temple that was torn down by Pope Alexander VI. In the Middle Ages, it was believed to be the tomb of the Romulus himself.'

The iron bar descended once again, striking Pontiero on his back as he lay on the ground, stunned.

'But its exciting history doesn't end there. The two columns you see here are the very ones to which Saints Peter and Paul were bound before being martyred by the Romans. You Romans, always so attentive to our saints.'

Once more the iron bar struck a blow, this time on his left thigh. Pontiero howled in pain.

'You would have learned all of this up there, if you hadn't interrupted me. But don't worry: you're going to get to know these columns extremely well. Yes, you will become very well acquainted with them.'

Pontiero tried to move but he discovered to his horror that he couldn't. He didn't know how badly he was hurt but he couldn't feel his extremities. He was aware only of powerful hands carrying him into the darkness, and of acute pain. He screamed in agony.

'I don't recommend you shout. No one will hear you. No one heard the other two either. I took plenty of precautions, you know? I don't like being interrupted.'

Pontiero felt his consciousness falling away into a deep black hole, like someone slipping little by little into a dream. And just as in a dream, he heard far off the sounds of young people in the street, just a few feet above him. He thought he recognised the hymn they were singing. It was a memory from when he was a child, a million years in the past: 'If you're saved and you know it, clap your hands.'

'In fact, I really can't stand it when people interrupt me,' Karosky said.

$\mathcal{P}$ALAZZO DEL $\mathcal{G}$OVERNATORATO

VATICAN CITY

Wednesday, 6 April 2005, 1.31 p.m.

Paola showed the photo of Robayra to Dante and Fowler. A close-up, the cardinal laughing affectionately, eyes glittering behind his thick tortoiseshell glasses. At first Dante just stared at the photograph. He didn't see anything special about it.

'The glasses, Dante. The ones that disappeared.'

Paola looked for her mobile, dialing frantically as she headed towards the door and flew out of the office of the astonished chamberlain.

'The glasses! The Carmelite's glasses!' she shouted from the hall-way.

Finally Dante understood. 'Let's go, *padre*!'

Dante hastily apologised to the chamberlain and left with Fowler in pursuit of Paola.

Paola was furious: Pontiero wasn't answering his phone. He must have switched it off. She raced down the stairs towards the street. She'd have to run the whole length of Via del Governatorato. At that second a small car with SCV on the licence plate appeared from the opposite direction. Three nuns were sitting inside. Paola frantically waved her arms at them and then jumped in front of the car. The bumper jerked to a stop an inch or so from her knees.

'Santa Madonna! Are you insane, miss?'

Paola hurried over to the driver's side, holding out her badge. 'Please, I don't have time to explain. I have to get to the Santa Ana Gate.'

The nuns stared at her as if she were mad. Paola climbed into the back seat on the driver's side.

'You can't get there from here; you'd have to cross the Cortile de Belvedere on foot,' the nun who was driving said. 'If you want, I can get you as close as the Piazza del Sant'Uffizio. It's the quickest way to get out of the city right now. The Swiss Guards are putting up barriers on account of the Conclave.'

'Whatever, but let's get there quickly.'

The nun put the car into gear and was accelerating quickly when the car came to a halt a second time.

'Has the entire world lost its mind?' one of the nuns blurted out.

Fowler and Dante were standing directly in front of the car, both of them with their hands on the hood. They ran around and squeezed into the rear. The nuns crossed themselves.

'Anything you say, but for Christ's sake hurry up!'

It took barely twenty seconds for the little car to cover the quarter-mile that separated them from their goal. The nun with her hands on the wheel seemed to want to get away from her strange and troublesome cargo as quickly as possible. She hadn't even hit the brakes in the Piazza de Sant'Uffizio before Paola was out and running towards the black iron gates that guarded that entrance to Vatican City, her mobile phone in her hand. She dialled the number for police headquarters. The operator came on the line.

'Inspector Paola Dicanti, security code 13897. Agent in danger, I repeat, agent in danger. Detective Pontiero is on site at 14 Via della Conciliazione – the Church of Santa Maria in Traspontina. Send as many units as you can. Possible murder suspect inside the building. Proceed with extreme caution.'

Paola was still running, her jacket flapping in the wind, the gun peeking out of its holster, as she shouted into her phone like a maniac. The two Swiss Guards at the gate took one look at her and prepared to block her escape. One of them grabbed her by her jacket and she thrust her arms out violently, losing her grip on the phone, which flew out of her hand. The Swiss Guard was left holding two empty arms on a jacket pulled inside out. He was just starting after Dicanti when Dante arrived at full speed, his Corpo di Vigilanza ID thrust out in front of him.

'Let her go. She's one of us.'

Fowler was close behind, clutching his case. He lost a few valuable seconds stooping down to retrieve Paola's phone. She'd decided on the shortest route, straight through Saint Peter's Square. The crowds were smaller there, owing to the fact that the police had set up one line crossing the square, in contrast to the incredible masses of humanity on the earlier stages of the route. Paola ran with her ID out so to avoid any further trouble if she encountered police along the way. They crossed the esplanade and passed Bernini's colonnade without too much trouble, arriving at the Via del Corridori completely out of breath. From there on, the mass of pilgrims was menacingly tight. Paola plastered her left arm across her chest to lessen the chances of her pistol being seen. She moved in close to the buildings and tried to make headway as quickly as she could. Dante was now a few steps ahead and he served as an effective battering ram, all arms and elbows. Fowler was immediately behind.

It took them ten excruciating minutes to arrive at the door that led into the sacristy. Two agents were already there waiting for them, knocking on the door non-stop. Dicanti was in a state, panting and covered in sweat; nevertheless the two police officers greeted her respectfully as soon as they saw her UACV identification.

'We received your message but there's no answer from inside. We've got four officers at the other entrance.'

'Can you tell me why the hell you haven't gone in yet? Don't you know a fellow officer could be trapped inside ...?'

The two agents stared at their shoes. 'Director Troi called. He told us to proceed with caution. There are a lot of people watching us, ispettore.'

Dicanti leaned against the wall and took five seconds to gather herself. Shit, she thought, let's hope we're not too late.

'You've brought the "master key"?'

One of the policemen pointed to his thigh, where, cleverly concealed from view in an extra pocket, he carried a steel bar with two teeth on the end. People in the street were beginning to pay attention to the drama unfolding around this group at the church door. Paola gestured to the officer who had shown her the iron bar.

'Give me your walkie-talkie.'

The policeman handed her the device, which was hooked by a cable to the holder on his belt. Paola dictated a few short, precise instructions to the team on the other side of the church: no one to make a move until she got there, and of course no one to go in or out.

'Could someone explain to me where all of this is leading?' Fowler asked, gasping for breath.

'Our best guess is that the suspect is inside. I'll go over it a little more slowly now. For a start, I want you to stay outside and wait here,' said Paola.

The priest handed her the phone she had dropped. 'This is yours.'

'Thanks, *padre*.' She gestured in the direction of the human tide surrounding them. 'Do what you can to distract them while we force the door. Let's hope we get there in time.'

Fowler nodded. He looked around for a place to perch himself above the crowd. There weren't any cars in the vicinity, as the street had been closed off, and there was no time to waste. The only thing he had at his disposal was people, so he'd have to use them to gain a little height. A tall, rugged-looking pilgrim stood out from the crowd close by. He must have been six feet tall.

Fowler went up to him and said, 'Do you think you could lift me on to your shoulders?'

The young man held up his hands to say that he didn't understand, so Fowler used the same language of gestures to indicate what he wanted. After several tries, the pilgrim understood. He put one knee on the ground and lifted the priest up, a large smile on his face. Surveying the crowd from above, Fowler began to sing the communion chant from the Requiem Mass:

> *In paradisum deducant te angeli*
> *In tuo advente*
> *Suscipiant te martyres ...*

People in the crowd began turning around to look at him. Fowler gestured to his porter to move towards the centre of the street, taking attention away from Paola and the others. Several of the faithful – friars and priests for the most part – joined in the hymn for the dead Pope.

Making use of the distraction, the two policemen were able to force open the door to the sacristy using the steel bar. They slipped in without calling attention to themselves.

'Boys, one of our own is in here. Be very careful.'

They entered one by one, Dicanti taking out her pistol. She left it to the two officers to search the sacristy, while she walked into the main part of the nave. She hurriedly searched the chapel of Saint Thomas. It was empty, still cordoned off by the UACV's crime-scene tape. She looked over at the chapels on the left, her finger poised on the trigger of her gun. She signalled to Dante, who was covering the aisle on the other side of the church, checking each one of the chapels there. The faces of the saints moved restlessly, projected on to the walls by the flickering, sickly light cast by the candles burning on every available surface. The two met up in the central aisle.

'Nothing?'

Dante shook his head. No.

They both saw it at the same time. There, written on the floor near the entrance, at the foot of the baptismal font, in large, red letters:

VEXILLA REGIS PRODEUNT INFERNI

'The banners of the King of Hell are drawing closer,' a voice behind them intoned.

Startled, the two agents turned around. Fowler was walking up behind them. He had brought the hymn to a close then slipped into the church.

'I thought I told you to stay outside.'

'That's not important,' Dante interjected. His attention was riveted to the trapdoor lying open on the floor. 'I'll call the others.'

Paola was wild with fear. Her heart told her to go down below immediately, but she didn't dare step into the darkness. Dante raced over to the front door and opened the locks. Two officers rushed in, leaving the other two standing on the threshold. One of the policemen pulled the MagLite from his belt and offered it to Dante. Dicanti grabbed it and headed down, her back against the steps, her muscles tense, her pistol pointing straight ahead. Fowler stayed above, murmuring a short prayer.

Paola's head emerged out of the darkness a short time later. As soon as she'd climbed the stairs, she raced out of the church. Dante slowly dragged himself up the steps. He looked at Fowler, and shook his head.

Paola stood on the street. She was sobbing. She got as far as she could from the doorway and threw up everything she had in her stomach. Young people who appeared to be foreigners waiting in the queue came over to see if she needed help.

'Are you OK?'

Paola waved them off. Then Fowler was there, lending her his handkerchief. She accepted it and wiped away the vomit and tears. Her head was spinning. It couldn't be: Pontiero just couldn't be that bloody pile she'd found tied to the column. Maurizio Pontiero, detective: a good man, fit, overflowing with an always surprising, pleasant and devilish sense of humour. A paterfamilias, a friend, a companion. On rainy afternoons he slunk around inside his rain-coat. He always paid for the coffee they shared; he was always there. He'd been there for many years. It just couldn't be true that he'd breathed his last, that he'd been reduced to that formless mass of flesh. She wanted to tear that image right off her retina. Her hands pressed against her eyes with terrible force.

Her phone rang. She grabbed it out of her pocket, disgusted, and stood there paralysed. On the screen the caller was identified as M. Pontiero.

Paola was trembling with fright as she took the call. Fowler studied her, intrigued.

'Yes?'

'Good afternoon, inspector. How are you?'

'Who is this?'

'Inspettore, please. You asked me to call if I remembered anything useful. And I've just remembered that I had to take your colleague out of the picture. I'm truly sorry, but he got in my way.'

'We're going to catch you, Francesco. Or should I call you Victor?' Paola was spitting the words out furiously, her eyes damp with tears. She tried to keep her cool and hit him where it hurt – so that he knew his mask had been torn off.

Silence on the other end of the line. But only for a second. She hadn't taken him by surprise in the slightest.

'So you already know who I am. Well, give my best to Father Fowler. He's lost a bit of hair since the last time we saw each other. And you look a little pale.'

Paola's eyes widened in surprise. 'Where are you, you sick bastard?'

'Don't you know? I'm right behind you.'

Paola looked out over the thousands of people crushed into the street, some wearing hats, some baseball caps, waving banners, praying, chanting.

'Why don't you come over here, *padre*? We could have a little talk.'

'No, Paola, I'm afraid I have to keep my distance from you a little while longer. But don't think for a second that you've made any progress because you've unmasked good old Francesco. His life had run its course anyway and it was time to let him go. But don't worry, you'll be hearing from me soon. There's no need to trouble yourself over the way you treated me when we met. I've forgiven you. You're very important to me.'

He hung up.

Dicanti threw herself into the crowd, pulling people aside without rhyme or reason, looking for men of a certain height, grabbing them by the arms, turning them around, tearing off their hats. People scattered and moved away. She was demented, the look in her eyes like that of a lost soul. She was ready to search every last pilgrim, one by one if she had to.

Fowler waded into the heart of the crowd and caught her by the arm. 'It won't work.'

'Take your fucking hands off me!'

'Paola. Let it go. He's not here.'

Dicanti started to sob. Fowler put his arm around her. On all sides, the gigantic human serpent moved slowly forward, pushing towards the body of John Paul II.

Somewhere inside its body, the serpent carried a killer.

$\mathcal{T}$HE $\mathcal{S}$AINT $\mathcal{M}$ATTHEW $\mathcal{I}$NSTITUTE

SACHEM PIKE, MARYLAND

January 1996

**Transcript of Interview Number 72 between Patient
Number 3643 and Doctor Canice Conroy, with the Assistance
of Doctor Fowler and Salher Fanabarzra**

DR CONROY: Good afternoon, Victor.
No. 3643: Hello again.
DR CONROY: It's regression therapy day, Victor.

[*Transcription once again omits the process of hypnosis, as in previous reports*]

FANABARZRA: It's 1973. From here on in you will listen to my voice
and no other. Are we in agreement?
No. 3643: Yes.
FANABARZRA: He cannot hear you, gentlemen.
DR CONROY: The other day we performed a Rorschach test. Victor
participated in the process in a normal fashion, pointing out the
usual birds and flowers. Only in two did he say that he saw nothing. Take note, Father Fowler: when Victor takes no interest in
something, it's because it affects him deeply. What I hope to do is
to provoke that response during the state of regression, so that we
can learn its origin.
DR FOWLER: I disagree more about the soundness of the method
than whether it is empirically possible. When he's in a state of
regression, the patient doesn't have as many defence mechanisms

at his disposal as he would in a normal state. The risk of inflicting trauma is too high.

DR CONROY: Those same defences are what's holding back his treatment and progress. You know that this patient suffers from a profound rejection of particular episodes in his life. We've got to get past the barriers to uncover the origins of his illness.

DR FOWLER: At what cost?

FANABARZRA: Gentlemen, please keep your discussion to a minimum. In any case, it is impossible to show the patient any images, as he cannot open his eyes.

DR CONROY: But we can describe them. Go ahead, Fanabarzra.

FANABARZRA: Yes, sir. Victor, it's 1973. I want us to go to a place that you like. Which one shall we choose?

No. 3643: The fire escape.

FANABARZRA: Do you spend a good deal of time on the fire escape?

No. 3643: Yes.

FANABARZRA: Tell me why.

No. 3643: The fresh air. It doesn't smell bad out there. It smells really bad inside the house.

FANABARZRA: It smells?

No. 3643: Like rotten fruit. The stench is coming from Emil's bed.

FANABARZRA: Your brother is sick?

No. 3643: He's sick. We don't know why. Nobody takes care of him. My mother says he's possessed. He can't stand light and he has shaking fits. His throat hurts.

DR CONROY: All symptoms of meningitis: photophobia, rigidity of the neck, convulsions.

FANABARZRA: No one is taking care of your brother?

No. 3643: My mother feeds him sliced apples when she remembers to. He has diarrhoea and my father doesn't want to know anything about it. I hate him. He looks at me and then tells me to clean up my brother. I don't want to: it makes me feel sick. My mother tells me to do something. I don't want to and she pushes me against the radiator.

DR CONROY: We've already documented the bad treatment he received. Let's find out what makes him see the images he sees when he takes the Rorschach. This one in particular concerns me.

FANABARZRA: Let's go back to the fire escape. Sit there. Tell me what you're feeling.

No. 3643: Fresh air. The metal beneath my feet. I can smell the Jewish food from the store in front.

FANABARZRA: Now I want you to picture something. A large black blotch, very big. It fills up all the space in front of you. In the lower part of the blotch there is a small white oval. Does that look like something to you?

No 3643: The darkness. All alone in the closet.

DR CONROY: Pay attention. I think we have something here.

FANABARZRA: What did you do in the closet?

No. 3643: They shut me in there. I'm alone.

DR FOWLER: For God's sake, Conroy, look at his face. He's in pain.

DR CONROY: Shut up. We're getting where we need to be. Fanabarzra, I am going to write further questions on this blackboard. Read them just as they are written – are we agreed?

FANABARZRA: Victor, do you remember what happened before they shut you up in the closet?

No. 3643: Many things. Emil died.

FANABARZRA: How did Emil die?

No. 3643: They've locked me up. I'm alone.

FANABARZRA: I know that, Victor. Tell me how Emil died.

No. 3643: He was in our room. Papa was watching the television; Mama was out. I was sitting on the fire escape when I heard a noise.

FANABARZRA: What kind of noise?

No. 3643: Like a balloon when all the air flies out. I stuck my head into the room. Emil was very pale. I spoke to my father and he threw a beer can at me.

FANABARZRA: He hit you?

No. 3643: On the head. I'm bleeding and crying. My father stands up and raises his arm. I tell him about Emil. He gets really angry; he says it's my fault. That I should have been taking care of him. That I deserve to be punished. And he starts doing it again.

FANABARZRA: The same punishment as always? He touches you there?

No. 3643: He hurts me. I'm bleeding on my head and in my bottom. But he stops.

FANABARZRA: Why does he stop?

NO. 3643: I hear Mama's voice. She's shouting terrible things at Papa – things I don't understand. Papa says she knew already. My mother screams and calls out to Emil as loud as she can. I know Emil can't hear her and I'm very happy. Then she grabs me by the neck and throws me into the closet. I shout. I'm afraid. I bang on the door for a long time. She opens it and shows me a knife. She says if I open my mouth, she'll stab me with it.

FANABARZRA: So what do you do?

NO. 3643: I keep quiet. I'm alone. I hear voices outside. Voices I don't recognise. They are there for hours. I stay in the closet.

DR CONROY: Must have been the voices of the ambulance service taking the body of his brother away.

FANABARZRA: How long are you inside the closet?

NO. 3643: A long time. I'm alone. My mother opens the door. She says that I've been very bad. That God doesn't like bad little boys who make trouble for their parents. That I am going to learn God's punishment for those who misbehave. She gives me an old plastic container and tells me to do my business in there. In the morning she gives me a glass of water, bread and some cheese.

FANABARZRA: How many days were you there?

NO. 3643: A long time went by.

FANABARZRA: You didn't have a watch? You couldn't count the time?

NO. 3643: I try to keep count, but it's too long. If I press my ear hard against the wall, I can hear Mrs Berger's transistor radio. She's a little deaf. Sometimes she listens to baseball.

FANABARZRA: How many games did you listen to?

NO. 3643: I don't know – forty, maybe fifty. I lost count.

DR FOWLER: My God, the child was locked in the closet for almost two months.

FANABARZRA: You never went out?

NO. 3643: Once.

FANABARZRA: Why did you go out?

NO. 3643: I made a mistake. I kick the container with my foot and it turns over. The closet smells like death. I throw up. When Mama comes back, she's angry. She rubs my face in the dirt. Then she drags me out of the closet so she can clean it.

FANABARZRA: You don't try to escape?

No. 3643: I don't have anywhere to go. Mama does it for my own good.

FANABARZRA: And when does she let you leave?

No. 3643: One day. She runs a bath for me. She says she hopes that I've learned my lesson. She says that the closet is Hell and that's where I'll go if I'm not good, except that then I won't be able to leave. She puts on my clothes. She says that I should have been born a girl and that there's still time to change that. She touches my little packages. She says it's all pointless, that I'm going to Hell in any case. That there's no way out for me.

FANABARZRA: And your father?

No. 3643: Papa isn't around. He took off.

DR FOWLER: Conroy, stop this right now. Look at his face. The patient is very ill.

No. 3643: He's gone, gone, gone ...

DR FOWLER: Conroy!

DR CONROY: That's enough. Fanabarzra; stop the recording and take the patient out of the trance.

CHURCH OF SANTA MARIA IN TRASPONTINA

VIA DELLA CONCILIAZIONE, 14

Wednesday, 6 April 2005, 3.21 p.m.

For the second time that week the Crime Scene Analysis team passed through the doors of Santa Maria in Traspontina. They went about their business as unobtrusively as possible, dressed in street clothes so that the pilgrims wouldn't notice them. Inside, Inspector Dicanti barked out orders, jumping back and forth between her mobile phone and the walkie-talkie.

Fowler approached one of the UACV investigators. 'Finished with the murder scene yet?'

'Yes, *padre*. We're about to remove the body and start examining the sacristy.'

Fowler looked at Dicanti apprehensively. 'I'll go down with you,' she said.

'Are you sure?'

'I don't want to miss anything. What is that?'

In his right hand the priest held a small, black case.

'It contains holy oils. We use them to give extreme unction.'

'Is that going to help in any way?'

'Not in the investigation, no. But for Pontiero, yes. He was a devout Catholic, wasn't he?'

'He was. And little good it did him.'

'With all due respect, that's not for you to say.'

The two of them started down the steps cautiously, taking pains to step around the inscription at the entrance to the crypt. They quickly moved along the short hallway and found themselves standing at the edge of the chamber. UACV technicians had installed two electric generators, with powerful lights that lit up the whole room.

Pontiero's inert body, nude from the waist up, hung between the two truncated columns. Karosky had fastened his arms to the stone with duct tape, evidently the same tape as he had used on Robayra. The eyes and tongue had been torn out and the face was horribly disfigured, while strips of bloody flesh hung from his thorax like macabre decorations.

Paola lowered her head while the priest administered the last rites. Fowler's black shoes, shined to a high polish, stood deep in a pool of congealing blood. Paola swallowed hard and closed her eyes.

'Dicanti.'

She opened her eyes again. Dante had joined them in the underground chamber. Fowler had finished and was tactfully preparing to leave.

'Where are you going, *padre*?'

'Upstairs. I don't want to get in the way.'

'You aren't in the way. If half of what they say about you is true, you are a very intelligent man. You've been sent to help us, haven't you? Well, help us.'

'With pleasure, ispettore.'

She swallowed hard and began. 'It looks as if Pontiero entered by the door to the sacristy. He would have knocked on the door and our false friar would have opened it for him. Nothing unusual there. Pontiero then spoke to Karosky and was attacked by him.'

'But where?'

'It must have been down here. If it wasn't, there would be blood upstairs.'

'Why did he do it? Perhaps Pontiero was suspicious?'

'I doubt it,' Fowler said. 'I think that Karosky simply saw an opportunity and seized it. I'm inclined to think he showed Pontiero the way into the crypt and that Pontiero came down here of his own accord, with Karosky following right behind him.'

'That sounds about right. Pontiero had probably ruled out Brother Francesco immediately – not only because he looked like an old man who had trouble moving around ...'

'But because he was a priest. Pontiero would never suspect a friar – am I right? Poor fool,' Dante said sadly.

'Please, Dante.'

Fowler glared at Dante but the Vatican agent avoided his look.

'I'm sorry. Go on, Dicanti.'

'Once they were down here, Karosky struck him with a blunt object. We think it was a bronze candelabrum. The boys at UACV have already taken it away for testing. It was left sitting on the floor close to the body. He then tied him up and ... Well, you can see what happened next. What Pontiero must have gone through ...' Paola's voice broke.

The two men pretended not to notice the criminologist's moment of weakness. Paola coughed, to conceal her emotions and give herself time to recover before speaking again.

'A dark room – extremely dark. Is he repeating the trauma of his early childhood, the time he spent locked up in the closet?'

'Could be. Have they found any deliberate clues?'

'We think the only message is the one upstairs: "*Vexilla regis prodeunt inferni*".'

'The banners of the King of Hell are drawing closer,' the priest translated again.

'But what does that mean, Fowler?' Dante asked.

'You ought to know.'

'If you're trying to make me look like a fool, you're not going to succeed.'

Fowler gave a sad smile. 'Nothing could be further from my mind. I was referring to a quotation from one of your ancestors, Dante Alighieri.'

'He isn't my ancestor. It's my surname, and it was his first name, but we're not connected at all.'

'I apologise. I thought every Italian always declared himself a descendant either of Dante or of Julius Caesar.'

'At least we know who we're descended from.'

Fowler and Dante stood their ground, glaring at each other. Paola broke in: 'If you two are quite finished with the xenophobic backstabbing, we can proceed.'

Fowler cleared his throat. 'As I was saying, "*Vexilla regis prodeunt inferni*" is a quote from the *Divine Comedy*, from the moment when Dante and Virgil are about to enter Hell. It's a paraphrase of a prayer in the Christian liturgy, except that it's dedicated to Satan instead of God. Many people want to read heresy into the declaration, but in reality the only thing that Dante was trying to do was scare his audience.'

'That's what he wants to do? – scare us?'

'He's telling us that Hell is close at hand. I don't believe that Karosky's interpretation goes any further than that. He's not a very cultured man, although he likes to pretend he is. There aren't any other messages?'

'Not on the body,' answered Paola. 'He realised we were coming and he panicked. And it's my fault he knew, because I kept trying to call Pontiero's mobile.'

'Any luck pinpointing the phone now?'

'We contacted the phone company. The tracking system indicates that the telephone is turned off or it's out of range. The last call recorded in this area was from the top of the Hotel Atlante, barely a thousand feet from where we stand,' Paola replied.

'Which is exactly where I'm staying,' Fowler pointed out.

'Wow. And I thought they were putting you up in a hostel for priests. You know – something a little more modest.'

Fowler brushed the comment aside. 'Dante, my friend, at my age one learns to enjoy the good things in life. Especially when Uncle Sam is paying. I've already pitched my tent in plenty of places that reek of death.'

'I'm sure of that, *padre*, absolutely sure.'

'What are you referring to? Whatever you're insinuating, why don't you just spit it out.'

'I'm not insinuating anything other than that you've slept in worse places because of your … ministry.'

Dante was even more full of bile than usual, and it was Fowler's presence that seemed to be bringing it out. Paola didn't understand what he was up to, but she realised that it was something the two of them had to resolve alone, face to face.

'Enough. Let's get out of here and breathe some fresh air.'

The two men followed Dicanti back through the church. She was busy giving the nurses instructions on the removal of Pontiero's body when one of the UACV investigators approached her and began to tell her about some evidence they had found. Paola nodded her head.

She turned to Fowler. 'Could we concentrate, *padre*?'

'Of course.'

'Dante?'

'Why not?'

'All right, so this is what we've found. In the rectory there was a professional make-up kit and a heap of ashes on a table, which in our opinion are the remains of a passport. He poured a fair amount of alcohol on it after he lit the fire, so there's not much left. The UACV team has taken the ashes to see if they can find anything. The only prints found in the rectory aren't Karosky's, which means we'll have to find out who they belong to. Dante, here's your job for the afternoon. Find out who Padre Francesco was and how much time he spent here. Talk to the church's regular parishioners.'

'OK, I'll immerse myself in the senior citizen set.'

'Forget the jokes. Karosky has played a game with us, but he'll be nervous. He's run into the shadows, and we'll not hear from him for a while. If in the next few hours we can manage to find out where he's been, then perhaps we can find out where he's headed.'

Paola secretly crossed her fingers in her coat pocket, trying to make herself believe what she was saying. The two men put on stony faces, while they too pretended that the possibility was more than just a remote dream.

Dante came back two hours later. With him was a middle-aged woman who repeated her story to Dicanti. Brother Francesco had shown up when the previous parish priest, Brother Darío, had died. That had been three years ago, give or take. From that day on, the lady had been helping him clean the church and the rectory. According to her, Brother Francesco Toma had been a model of humility and Christian faith. He had taken thorough care of the parish. No one had had a bad word to say about him.

It was, taken all together, a sufficiently frustrating statement, but at least it made one fact clear. The Franciscan Darío Bassano had died in November 2001, which therefore gave a date for Karosky entering the country.

'Dante, do me a favour. Find out what the Carmelites know about Francesco Toma.'

'I'll make some calls. But I suspect we won't come up with much.'

Dante went out the front entrance, heading towards his office at the Vigilanza.

Fowler was also on his way out. 'I'm going to my hotel to change. See you later.'

'I'll be at the morgue.'

'You don't have to do it.'

'Yes, I do.'

They stood there uncomfortably, not saying a word to each other, their silence underscored by a hymn one of the pilgrims was singing. In the vast, turbulent crowd of people, one after another slowly joined in the chorus. The sun slipped behind the hills and Rome slowly sank into long afternoon shadows; yet nothing tempered the electric atmosphere in the streets.

'A song like that was probably the last thing Pontiero heard.'

Paola didn't respond. Fowler had witnessed what the profiler was going through too many times before, the process that takes place after the death of a close companion: at the outset, a kind of intoxication, mixed with the desire for vengeance. Little by little the person would descend into exhaustion and sadness, as they came to terms with what had happened and the shock took on the character of a physical wound. She would finally be left with a dull grief, a mixture of anger, blame and resentment, which would only resolve itself once Karosky was behind bars, or dead. And perhaps not even then.

The priest was about to put his hand on Dicanti's shoulder but stopped himself. Even if she hadn't seen him, he was standing directly behind her and she must have felt something, because she turned around and looked at Fowler, a worried expression on her face.

'Careful, *padre*. He now knows you're here, and that could change everything. Not only that, but we don't really know what he looks like. He's taken pains to be very clever at disguising himself.'

'How much can he have changed in five years?'

'I've looked at the photograph that you showed me of Karosky, and I've seen Brother Francesco with my own eyes. They don't resemble each other in the slightest.'

'The church was exceedingly dark and you hardly paid any attention to the old Carmelite.'

'Trust me: I'm good at faces. He might be wearing a beard covering half his face, and he'll look like an authentic old man. He knows how to conceal himself, and by now he could be an entirely different person.'

'All well and good. But I've seen him up close. If he crosses my path, I'll recognise him. Subterfuge will only get him so far.'

'It's not just subterfuge. He's got his hands on a nine-millimetre now, with thirty bullets to spare. Pontiero's pistol and his bullet clip are missing.'

Municipal Morgue

She had attended the autopsy encased in stone. All the adrenaline of the first minutes dissolved and she began to feel steadily more depressed. Watching as the coroner's scalpel dissected her partner was almost more than she could bear, but she managed to make it through. The coroner announced that Pontiero had been struck forty-three times with a blunt object, in all likelihood the candela-brum that had been recovered, coated with blood, at the scene of the crime. As to what had caused the cuts on his body, including the slit across his throat, the coroner was reserving judgement until the laboratory personnel furnished him with moulds of the incisions.

Paola listened to the report through a sensory fog that failed to attenuate her suffering in the slightest. She stood there watching for hours, enduring a self-imposed punishment. Dante stopped by the autopsy room, asked a few questions and quickly went on his way. Troi stuck his head in too, but it was only a symbolic gesture. He left immediately, stunned, muttering in passing that he had been speaking with Pontiero just a few hours before.

When the coroner had finished, he left the body on the metal table. He was about to lift the sheet over the dead man's face when Paola spoke up.

'Don't.'

The coroner understood and exited the room without saying a word.

The body was clean, but it exuded a faint coppery scent. Under the harsh, unrelenting light, her small friend seemed to be minuscule.

Bruises covered his body like medals of pain and his wounds, gaping open like huge, obscene mouths, still gave off the rusty odour of blood.

Paola looked around for the envelope with the contents of Pontiero's pockets. A rosary, a few keys, his wallet; a ballpoint pen, a lighter, a newly opened packet of cigarettes. When she saw that last item and realised that no one was ever going to smoke those cigarettes, she felt very sad, and alone. She began to accept the fact that her partner and friend was dead. In a gesture of defiance she shook one of the cigarettes out of the pack. The lighter's dancing flame broke the heavy silence in the autopsy room.

Paola had given cigarettes up after the death of her father. She repressed the urge to cough and took a heavy drag. Imitating Pontiero, she blew the smoke straight at the 'No Smoking' sign. Then she began to say goodbye.

Shit, Pontiero. Fuck. Shit, shit, shit. How could you have been so clumsy? This is all your fault. Look at yourself. We haven't even let your wife see your body. He did a good job on you – fuck, he really did. She wouldn't have been able to take it, she couldn't have seen you like this. It's shameful. Does it seem normal to you that I'm probably the last person in the world who will see you naked? I promise you, this isn't the kind of intimacy I wanted to share with you. No, of all the police in the world, you were the last one to want a closed coffin and now you've gone and got one. Everything for you. Pontiero, you lummox, you jerk. Why didn't you see it coming? What the hell were you doing in that tunnel? I can't believe it. You've always been chasing lung cancer, just like my goddamned father. Jesus Christ, you've no idea the things I think about every time I see you smoking one of these pieces of shit. I see my father in the hospital bed again, coughing his lungs out on to the sheets. And me, studying there every afternoon. In the morning, school, then every afternoon spent cramming the assignments into my head to the sound of his coughing. I always thought I'd end up at the foot of your bed too, holding your hand while you went to the other side, accompanied by Hail Marys and Our Fathers and you with your eye on the nurse's behind. That's what was on the cards for you, but you've gone and checked out early. Couldn't you have called me, you jerk? Shit, you look like you're smiling at me as if you're apologising. Or do you think it's my fault? Your wife and

children don't think so now, but they will when someone tells them
the whole story. But no, Pontiero, it's not my fault. It's your fault
and yours alone, you imbecile. Worse than an imbecile. Why the hell
did you go down into that tunnel? And screw your damned faith in
anything wearing a robe. That bastard Karosky, he really played us.
Well, he played me and you're the one who paid for it. That beard,
that nose. He wore those glasses right in front of us like he was giving
us the finger, just to make us look like fools. The bastard. He looked
me straight in the eye, but I couldn't see his eyes past the two bottle
tops perched on his nose. That beard, that nose. Can you believe that
I don't know if I would recognise him if I saw him again? I already
know what you're thinking. Take a look at the pictures of Robayra's
murder to see if he's there somewhere in the background. And I'm
going to do it, for God's sake. I'm going to do it. So stop being a wise
ass. And stop smiling, you son of a bitch, stop smiling. I know it's
just rigor mortis, for the love of God. Even though you're dead you
want to keep foisting the blame on me. Don't trust anyone, you kept
telling me. Watch your step, you'd say. Is it possible to know why
you gave me all that damned advice if you weren't going to follow it
yourself? God, Pontiero, what a mess you've left me with. Because of
your damned clumsiness I've got to face this monster alone. Fuck, if
we're on the trail of a priest, then robes automatically become suspect,
Pontiero. Don't come at me with that. Don't let yourself off the hook
with the argument that Francesco looked like a homeless, crippled old
man. Christ, he really did a good job on you. Shit, shit. How I hate
you, Pontiero. Do you know what your wife said when she was told
that you'd died? She said, 'He can't die. He likes jazz.' She didn't say,
'He has two kids,' or 'He's my husband and I love him.' No, she said
that you like jazz. As if Duke Ellington or Diana Krall were a fucking
bullet-proof vest. Shit, she senses your presence, she feels you as if you
were still alive, she hears your gravelly voice and the music you listen
to. She can still smell the cigarettes you smoke. That you smoked.
How I hate you, you pious little turd ... What good did all those
prayers do you? The people you trusted turned their backs on you.
Now I remember that day we ate pastrami in the middle of Piazza
Colonna. You said that priests were simply men with a calling, not
angels, and that the Church didn't realise that. And I swear to you
that I'll say that to the next one who stands on the balcony of Saint

Peter's, I swear I'll write it on a poster so big that he'll see it even if he's blind. Pontiero, you goddamned idiot. This wasn't our battle. Oh shit, I'm afraid, I'm very afraid. I don't want to end up like you. That table looks as cold as ice. And what if Karosky follows me to my home? Pontiero, you idiot, this isn't our battle. It's a battle between the priests and their church. And don't tell me it's mine, too. I don't believe in God any more. Or I should say, I do, but I don't believe he's a good person. My love for Him left me stranded at the feet of a dead man who should have lived another thirty years. He took off faster than a cheap deodorant, Pontiero. And now all that's left is the stench of the dead, of every dead body we've seen over the last few years. Bodies that stink to high heaven before their time because God didn't know how to care for some of his creatures. And your body is the one that will smell the worst of any of them. Don't look at me like that. Don't tell me that God believes in me. A decent God doesn't let things like this happen, he doesn't let one of his own be transformed into a wolf among sheep. You heard what Fowler said. That head-case they left with his lower half in knots after all the shit they threw at him is now looking for something even more powerful than raping little boys. And what do you have to say for yourself? What kind of God lets them stick a straight arrow like you in a fucking freezer with wounds big enough for your co-worker to slip her hand into? Shit, it wasn't my battle before, even before I got so carried away with Troi, to catch one of these degenerates. But you can see I'm useless. No, shut up. Don't say a word. Stop protecting me. I'm not a child. Yes, I've been useless. Is that so terrible to admit? I haven't been thinking clearly enough. It´s obvious that this situation has overwhelmed me, but there it is. It's over. Fuck, it wasn't my battle, but it is now. Now it's personal, Pontiero. Now I couldn't give a shit about the pressure from the Vatican, from Cirin, from Troi or from the bitch who gave birth to every single one of them. Now I'm going to go all out, and it doesn't matter to me if heads roll along the way. I'm going to catch him, Pontiero – for you and for me. For your wife who's waiting out-side and for your two brats. But above all for you, because you're in the deep freeze and already your face doesn't look like your face any more. God, he really fucked you over. How fucked over he left you and how alone I feel. I hate you, Pontiero and I'll miss you even more.

Paola went out into the hallway. Fowler was there waiting for her, sitting on a wooden bench and staring at the wall. As soon as he saw her, he stood up.

'Doctor, I—'

'It's OK.'

'No, it's not OK. I know what you're going through. You can't be in good shape.'

'I'm definitely not in good shape. But for Christ's sake, I'm not about to fall into your arms a second time like some damsel reeling from the pain. That only happens in films.'

She was about to leave when Troi appeared in the hallway.

'Dicanti, we have to talk. I'm very worried about you.'

'You too? What a novelty. Sorry, I don't have time for a chat.'

Troi stepped into her path. Dicanti's head came up to her boss's chest.

'You don't understand, Dicanti. I'm taking you off the case. There's too much at stake now.'

Paola looked up. She stared into his eyes and spoke very, very slowly, her voice cold and controlled. 'Listen to me, Carlo, listen carefully, because I'm only going to say it once. I'm going to capture the man who did this to Pontiero. Neither you nor anyone else has any say in the matter. Do I make myself clear?'

'What doesn't seem to be clear is who's in charge here, Dicanti.'

'Maybe so. But what I am clear about is what I have to do. So please – out of my way.'

Troi opened his mouth to say something but thought better of it, and stepped aside. Paola stormed off towards the exit.

Fowler laughed.

'What's so amusing, *padre*?'

'You, of course. You don't fool me. You didn't think of taking her off the case for a second, did you?'

The director of the UACV pretended to be shocked. 'Paola's a strong, independent woman, but she needs to centre herself. All the anger she's feeling must be focused, channeled.'

'Words, words, words. I'm not hearing the truth.'

'OK, yes, I fear for her. I'm nervous about her. I needed to know that she has the strength to keep going. Any other answer than the one she gave me, and I would have thrown her off the case immediately. We're not up against somebody who plays by the rules.'

'Now you're levelling with me.'

Fowler intuited that behind the cynical politician and administrator there lurked a human being. The priest saw what kind of man Troi was at that early morning hour, his clothes all crumpled and his soul rubbed raw by the death of one of his subordinates. Maybe Troi spent a good deal of time on self-promotion, but he'd almost always covered Paola's back. And he was still very attracted to her – that was obvious.

'Fowler, I have a favour to ask you.'

'No.'

'What do you mean by that?' Troi was bewildered.

'You don't have to ask me. I'll take care of the doctor, in spite of herself. For better or worse, there are only three of us on this case: Fabio Dante, Dicanti and myself. We'll have to present a united front.'

Uacv Headquarters

Thursday, 7 April 2005, 8.15 a.m.

'Don't trust Fowler, Dicanti. He's a killer.'

Paola looked up from the Karosky dossier with puffy eyes. She'd only had a few hours' sleep before returning to her desk at daybreak. It wasn't the way she usually did things: Paola liked to enjoy a long breakfast followed by a stroll to work, ready to soldier on well into the night. Pontiero had always pestered her about it: *You are letting the glorious Roman morning pass you by.* And here she was, at her desk, not exactly enjoying the dawn, but paying respect to her friend in her own fashion. In fact, from where she sat, the dawn was indeed beautiful: the sun sliding over the Roman hills at a leisurely pace, the rays of sunlight lingering on each building and cornice, saluting the art and beauty of the Eternal City. Each of the day's shapes and colours made its appearance with such delicacy they seemed to be knocking at the door to ask permission to come in. Then who should walk into Dicanti's office without even asking, with an unnerving accusation on his lips, but Fabio Dante. The superintendent had turned up half an hour before the agreed time – with a Manilla envelope in his hand and a mouth full of serpents.

'Dante, have you been drinking?'

'Nothing of the sort. I'm telling you he's a killer. Remember I told you not to trust him? His name set off alarm bells in my head – a memory lodged somewhere at the back of my mind. So I did a little investigating about our supposed military man.'

Paola took a sip of coffee but it was nearly cold. She was intrigued. 'He isn't in the military?'

'Of course he is: a military chaplain. But he's not in the Air Force; he's in the CIA.'

'The CIA? You're joking.'

'No, Dicanti. Your Fowler isn't a man to be taken lightly. Listen to this. He was born in 1951, into a wealthy family. His father owned a pharmaceutical company or something like that. He studied psychology at Princeton. He finished his degree at twenty years old, *magna cum laude*.'

'*Magna cum laude*. The best grade possible. So he lied to me. He told me he wasn't an especially brilliant student.'

'He lied to you about that and many other things. He didn't pick up his university degree. It seems he argued with his father and enlisted in 1971. A volunteer, smack in the middle of the Vietnam War. Five months of basic training in Virginia and ten months in Vietnam, with the rank of lieutenant.'

'Wasn't he a little young to be a lieutenant?'

'Are you joking? A volunteer with a university degree? I'm sure they were planning on making him a general. I don't know what was going on in his head during those years, but he didn't return to the United States after the war. He studied in a seminary in West Germany, and was ordained as a priest in 1977. Later on he left traces of his presence everywhere: Cambodia, Afghanistan, Romania. We know that he went to China for a visit, but then he had to leave at top speed.'

'All of this doesn't prove he's a CIA agent.'

'Dicanti, it's all here.' While he was talking, Dante started showing Paola photographs, most of them in black and white. She saw a curiously young Fowler progressively losing his hair as the pictures came closer to the present day; Fowler sitting on top of a pile of sandbags, surrounded by soldiers, wearing a lieutenant's stripes; Fowler in a hospital with a smiling soldier; and, on the day of his ordination, receiving the sacrament in Rome from none other than Paul VI; Fowler on an enormous runway, with planes in the background, dressed in his clergyman's garb, surrounded by younger soldiers ...

'When is this one from?'

Dante consulted his notes. 'Nineteen seventy-seven. After his ordination Fowler returned to Germany, to the air base at Spangdahlem. As a military chaplain.'

'Then his story is correct.'

'Almost – but not in every respect. A report that shouldn't be in the file, but is, says that "John Anthony Fowler, son of Marcus and Daphne Fowler, lieutenant in the United States Air Force, received a raise in rank and salary after successfully completing field training in counter-espionage." In East Germany. Right in the middle of the Cold War.'

Paola shrugged. She still couldn't picture it.

'Wait, Dicanti; that's not everything. As I said before, he travelled extensively. In 1983 he disappeared for several months. The last person who saw him was a priest in Virginia.'

Paola began to lose heart. A military man who disappears for several months in Virginia has only one place to go: CIA head-quarters in Langley.

'Go on, Dante.'

'In 1984 Fowler turns up again, briefly, in Boston. His mother and father are killed in a car accident in July. He attends the reading of the will, where he instructs the lawyers to divide all his money and possessions among various charities. He signs the necessary papers and takes off. According to his lawyer, the sum total from his parents' properties and the pharmaceutical company was in excess of eighty million dollars.'

Dicanti let out a whistle of pure astonishment. 'That's a lot of money, even more so in 1984.'

'Well, he gave everything away. A pity you didn't know him back then, eh, Dicanti?'

'What are you insinuating?'

'Nothing, nothing. All right then, to finish it off: Fowler takes off from Mexico and from there he goes to Honduras. He's appointed as chaplain at the military base in El Aguacate, now with the rank of major. And that's where he became a killer.'

Paola looked at the next group of photographs and froze: rows of human bodies in dusty common graves; workers with pitchforks and face masks that failed to hide the horror on their faces; disinterred bodies, rotting in the sun; men, women and children.

'My God, what is this?'

'How much do you know about history? I'm terrible myself. I had to poke around on the Internet to find out what the whole damned thing was about. It seems that in Nicaragua the Sandinistas had a revolution. The counter-revolution, called the Nicaraguan Contra, wanted to put a right-wing government back in power. Ronald Reagan's government supported the rebel guerrillas under the table – guerrillas who in many cases would have been better classed as terrorists.'

Paola was starting to connect the dots.

'According to the *Washington Post*, El Aguacate was "a clandestine centre for detention and torture, more like a concentration camp than a military base in a democratic country". Those lovely, graphic photos I showed you were taken ten years ago. There were one hundred and eighty-five men, women and children in those unmarked graves. And it is believed that there are still an indeterminate number of bodies – as many as three hundred – buried out in the mountains.'

'Jesus, this is terrible beyond belief.' Nevertheless, the photos didn't stop Paola from giving Fowler the benefit of the doubt. 'But it doesn't prove anything.'

'He was there. He was the chaplain at a torture camp, for God's sake! Who do you think attended to the condemned prisoners before they died? How could he not have known?'

Dicanti looked at Dante without saying a word.

'All right, ispettore, you want more? Here's the material from the envelope: a report from the Sant'Uffizio, the Holy Office. In 1993 Fowler was called to Rome to give testimony regarding the assassination of thirty-two nuns seven years earlier. They had fled from Nicaragua and ended up at El Aguacate. They were raped, taken for a ride in a helicopter and, then ka-blam! – nun pancake. In the process he also testified about twelve Catholic missionaries who had disappeared. The root of the accusation was that he knew exactly what was going on but never denounced these flagrant cases of the violation of human rights – in which case he was as guilty as if he had piloted the helicopter himself. Something which, by the way, he does in fact know how to do.'

'And what did the Holy Office decide?'

'Well, there wasn't sufficient proof to charge him, so he got off by the skin of his teeth and left the CIA of his own free will, I'm pretty sure. For a while he was at a loose end, and then he turned up at the Saint Matthew Institute.'

Paola spent a good while looking at the pictures.

'Dante, I am going to ask you a very serious question. As a citizen of the Vatican, would you say that the Holy Office is a careless institution?'

'No.'

'Could it be said that it maintains its independence?'

Dante nodded reluctantly. Now he saw where Paola was headed.

'Taking all of that into account, the most rigorous institution in the Vatican has been unable to find proof of Fowler's guilt, and you come into my office shouting that he's a killer, and advising me not to trust him in the slightest?'

Dante leapt to his feet, furious. He leaned over Dicanti's desk. 'You listen to me, my pretty little girl. Don't think for an instant I don't see the way you're looking at that pseudo-priest. Because of an unfortunate twist of fate we're obliged to hunt for a fucking monster under his orders, and I don't want you thinking with your skirt. You've already lost one co-worker, and I don't want that American covering my back when we're face to face with Karosky. Then you'll see how he reacts. From all appearances, he's very loyal to his country and, when it comes down to it, he might even take the side of a fellow American.'

Paola stood up and, without losing her composure, smacked Dante across the face twice. Two slaps, absolutely on target, the kind that set the ears ringing. Dante just stood there, so completely surprised and humiliated he didn't know how to react. He was transfixed, his mouth hanging open and his cheeks on fire.

'It's your turn to listen to me, Dante. If the three of us are joined at the hip for this fucking investigation, it's because your church doesn't want anyone to find out about this monster, a man who raped children and who was then castrated in one of its secret backwaters, a man who is now killing cardinals only ten days before they elect the next big shot. That and that alone is the reason why Pontiero is dead. I remind you that it was your people who came to ask for our help. It seems that your organisation functions enormously well when it has to get its hands on information about a priest working in a Third World jungle, but it doesn't quite measure up when it comes to controlling a sexual delinquent who relapses dozens of times over the course of ten years, in full view of his superiors, in a democratic country. Since that's the case, get your pathetic little mug out of here before I start to think that your problem is that you're jealous of Fowler. And don't come back until you're ready to work as a team. Is that understood?'

Dante recovered his composure long enough to take a deep breath and turn around. Fowler walked into the office at exactly the same moment, and the Vatican superintendent let out his frustration by flinging the photographs in his hand at the priest's face. Dante was so furious he stormed away without even remembering to slam the door behind him.

But Dicanti actually felt better, for two reasons: first, for having had the chance to do what she had imagined doing so many times; and second, for having done it in private. If the identical situation had presented itself when someone else had been present, or in the middle of the street, Dante would never have forgotten being smacked down in public. No man would. There were still ways of getting the situation back on track and creating a semblance of harmony. She glanced up at Fowler. He stood in the doorway, mesmerised by the photographs littering the floor of the office.

Paola sat down, took a sip of coffee and, without raising her head from the Karosky dossier, said, 'I think you have some explaining to do, *padre*.'

THE SAINT MATTHEW INSTITUTE

SACHEM PIKE, MARYLAND

April 1997

Transcript of Interview Number 11 between Patient Number 3643 and Doctor Fowler

DR FOWLER: Good afternoon, Father Karosky.

NO. 3643: Come in, come in.

DR FOWLER: I've come to see you because you have refused to speak to Father Conroy.

NO. 3643: His attitude was insulting. In fact, I asked him to leave.

DR FOWLER: What exactly was insulting about his attitude?

NO. 3643: Father Conroy questions certain unchanging truths of our faith.

DR FOWLER: Such as …?

NO. 3643: He says that the Devil is an overvalued concept! It will be very amusing to watch when this concept sticks its pitchfork into his rear end.

DR FOWLER: Do you think you'll be there to see it?

NO. 3643: In a manner of speaking.

DR FOWLER: You believe in Hell, yes?

NO. 3643: With every bone in my body.

DR FOWLER: Do you think you deserve to go there?

NO. 3643: I am a soldier of Christ.

DR FOWLER: That doesn't tell me anything.

NO. 3643: Why is that?

DR FOWLER: Because there's no guarantee whether a soldier of Christ will go to Heaven or Hell.

No. 3643: If he is a good soldier, he'll go to Heaven.

DR FOWLER: Father, I want to give you a book that I believe will be a great help to you. It was written by Saint Augustine. It is a book that speaks about humility and our inner struggle.

No. 3643: I'll be happy to read it.

DR FOWLER: You believe that you'll go to heaven when you die?

No. 3643: I'm sure of it.

DR FOWLER: Well, then you know more than I do.

No. 3643: ...

DR FOWLER: Let me give you a hypothesis. Let's assume we meet at the Pearly Gates. God weighs your good acts and your bad acts, and the scale is evenly balanced. And so he asks you to call on anyone you like to help him settle the question. Who would you call on?

No. 3643: I'm not sure.

DR FOWLER: Let me suggest a few names: Ryan, Jamie, Lewis, Arthur ...

No. 3643: Those names don't mean anything to me.

DR FOWLER: Harry, Michael, John, Grant ...

No. 3643: Shut up!

DR FOWLER: Paul, Sammy, Patrick ...

No. 3643: Shut up! I'm warning you!

DR FOWLER: Jonathan, Aaron, Samuel ...

No. 3643: Enough!

[*The sound of a brief, confused struggle between the two men can be heard on tape.*]

DR FOWLER: The part of your body I'm squeezing between my thumb and forefinger is your trachea, Father Karosky. It goes without saying that it will be even more painful if you don't calm down. Signal with your left hand if you understand me. Good. Do it again when you've calmed down a little. We can wait as long as necessary. Already? Good. Here, take a drink of water.

No. 3643: Thank you.

DR FOWLER: Sit down, please.

No. 3643: I'm better now. I don't know what came over me.

DR FOWLER: Both of us know what just happened – just as both of

us know that the young boys on the list I read will not exactly tes-
tify to your good character when you stand before the Almighty.

No. 3643: ...

DR FOWLER: You're not going to reply?

No. 3643: You don't know anything about Hell.

DR FOWLER: You think so? You are wrong: I have seen it with my
own eyes. I'm going to turn off the tape recorder now and tell you
something that I'm sure will interest you.

𝒰ACV ℋEADQUARTERS

Thursday, 7 April 2005, 8.32 a.m.

Fowler finally raised his eyes from the photographs lying scattered on the floor. Making no effort to pick them up, he merely glided over them. Paola asked herself if that represented an implicit response to Dante's accusations. Many times over the course of the next few days Paola felt that she was standing in front of a man who was as unreadable as he was polite, as ambiguous as he was intelligent. Fowler was a walking contradiction, an indecipherable hieroglyph; but at that moment the only thing she felt was another emotion, blind anger, which the tremor in her lips could not conceal.

The priest sat down in front of Paola, resting his worn black briefcase against the side of her desk. In his left hand he carried a paper bag with three coffees in it. He offered one to Dicanti.

'Cappuccino?'

'I hate cappuccino. It reminds me of a dog I once had whose vomit was exactly that colour. But all right.' She took one of the cups.

For several minutes Fowler didn't say a word. Paola gave up the pretence of reading the Karosky dossier and decided to confront him. She had to know.

'And so? You're not going to –' She stopped in her tracks. Paola hadn't really looked at Fowler since he'd walked into her office; but when she did, she discovered that he was miles away. The hands that lifted the coffee cup to his lips were shaking. The room was cool enough, yet tiny drops of sweat sat like pearls on the crown of his bald head; and it was clear from the look in his green eyes that the indelible horrors he had witnessed over the years were playing themselves out once more in his mind's eye.

Paola remained silent because she realised that the apparent ease with which Fowler had passed over the photographs was purely a façade. She waited. The priest took several minutes to recover, and when he was ready, his voice seemed faraway, lifeless.

'It's hard. You think that you're over it, but then it turns up again, like a cork you're trying to sink in a bathtub. You hold it down but it always pops back up to the surface.'

'Maybe talking about it would help.'

'Take my word for it: it won't. It's never helped in the past. There are some problems that can't be resolved by talking.'

'That's a curious thing for a priest to say. Unbelievable for a psychologist. But appropriate for an agent of the CIA who was trained to kill.'

Fowler repressed a grimace. 'They didn't train me to kill – no more than any other soldier. I was trained in counter-espionage. God gave me the gift of perfect aim – that much is true; but I didn't go looking for it. And, to anticipate your next question, I haven't killed anyone since 1972. I killed eleven Vietcong soldiers – at least, that I know of. But all of them were killed in combat.'

'You enlisted voluntarily.'

'Before you judge me, let me tell you my story. I've never told anyone what I'm going to tell you, so please, I only ask that you hear me out. Not that you believe or trust me, because that's too much to ask at this moment. Simply, listen to what I have to say.'

Paola nodded in assent.

'I suppose that all this information has arrived courtesy of our friend in the Vatican. If you've seen the Sant'Uffizio's report, it will have given you a very approximate idea of my history. I enlisted voluntarily in 1971, owing to certain … disagreements with my father. I don't want to blow you away with a horror story about what the war did to me, because words could never describe it. Have you seen *Apocalypse Now*?'

'Yes. Some time ago. I was surprised by how crude it was.'

'A superficial farce. That film was a shadow on the wall compared to what I am trying to describe. I saw enough pain and cruelty to fill several lives. But that's where I discovered my vocation. It didn't come to me in a foxhole in the middle of the night, with enemy fire whistling around my head. It didn't come looking at the face of a ten-year-old kid wearing a necklace of human ears. It happened behind the lines, on a quiet afternoon spent with the regiment's chaplain. I knew there and then that I wanted to dedicate my life to God and his creatures. And that is what I have done.'

'And the CIA?'

'Don't jump so far ahead. I didn't want to return to the United States, as I'd have to face my parents. So I went as far away as I could, right to the edge of the Iron Curtain. I learned many things there but some of them – you're only thirty-four years old, you wouldn't know how to make sense of them. For you to understand what Communism meant for a German Catholic in the 1970s you would have had to live through it. We inhaled the threat of nuclear war on a daily basis. The hatred that existed between the various groups was a religion unto itself. It seemed that every day we came a little closer to someone – either them or us – blowing the whole place sky-high. And that would have been the end of everything, I'm sure of it. Sooner or later, someone would have pushed the button.'

Fowler paused briefly to sip his coffee. Paola lit one of Pontiero's cigarettes. Fowler was reaching across the desk for the packet when Paola slid it a few inches further away.

'They're mine. I have to smoke them all by myself.'

'Don't worry about it. I wasn't going to take one; I just wondered if you'd suddenly picked up the habit again.'

'It doesn't matter. I'd rather you continue your story than we talk about that.'

Fowler intuited the pain behind her words and went back to his story. 'Of course. I wanted to continue to be part of the military. I love the companionship, the discipline, the feeling of a military life. If you think about it, it's conceptually not so very different from the priesthood: it's a question of giving your life to others. Armies aren't bad things in themselves; it's war that's evil. I asked to be sent to an American base as a chaplain, and as I was a diocesan, my bishop gave in to the request.'

'I'm a little vague about the meaning of diocesan.'

'More or less it means I'm a free agent. I'm not tied to a particular congregation. If I want, I can petition my bishop to assign me to a parish. But if I think it's a better idea, I can undertake my pastoral labour wherever I feel it's needed, but always with the bishop's blessing, understood as formal permission.'

'I follow.'

'At the base I worked alongside various members of the agency who were giving special instruction in counter-espionage to military personnel who did not belong to the CIA. They invited me to join them, four hours a day, five days a week over the course of two years. It wasn't incompatible with my pastoral work, although it did cost me a few hours sleep. So I accepted. And it turns out that I was a good student. One night, after class, one of the instructors pulled me aside and proposed that I join the company – that's how the agency was known in its inner circles. I told him that I was a priest – that it would be impossible. I already had a tremendous job ahead of me with the hundreds of young Catholics at the base. Their superiors dedicated many hours each day to teaching them how to hate Communists. I dedicated one hour each week to reminding them that we are all children of God.'

'A lost cause.'

'Almost always. The priesthood is a career for long-distance runners.'

'I think I read those words in one of the interviews with Karosky.'

'It's possible. We limit ourselves to scoring small points, gaining small victories. Every once in a while we achieve something a little more grand, but those incidents are few and far between. We plant small seeds, with the hope that at least some of the crop will flourish. Usually the person who plants doesn't get to harvest, which can be demoralising.'

'Yes, that must be really annoying.'

'Once upon a time a king was strolling through the forest and he saw an old man, a poor man, bent over a furrow. He walked up to him and saw that he was planting seeds for chestnut trees. He asked the old man why he was doing it and the old man replied, "I love the taste of chestnuts." The king responded, "Old man, stop punishing your back bent over a hole in the ground. Do you really not know that by the time even one of these trees has grown tall enough to bear nuts, you may not be around to gather them?" And the old man answered, "Your Majesty, if my ancestors had thought the way you do, I would never have tasted chestnuts.""

Paola smiled, surprised by the fable's undeniable truth.

'Do you know what that anecdote teaches us?' – Fowler paused before he went on – 'that you can always get ahead with goodwill, love of God and a good strong shot of Johnnie Walker.'

Paola was a little abashed. She hadn't imagined the upright, polite priest with a bottle of whisky in his hand, but it was clear he had been alone for most of his life.

'When the instructor told me that another priest could help the young men on the base but that the thousands of young people behind the Iron Curtain had no one to aid them, I knew that what he was saying wasn't far from the truth. Thousands of Christians languished under Communism, praying in bathrooms and listening to mass in dark basements. They could serve the interests of my country and those of my church at the same time, in the spaces where those two coincided. At that time, I really did believe there was more common ground between the two.'

'And what do you think now? After all, you've returned to active service.'

'I'll get to that shortly. Back then, they offered to let me be a free agent, accepting only those missions I believed to be just. I travelled everywhere. In some missions I went as a priest, in others as a normal citizen. My life was in danger many times, but it was almost always worth the risk. I helped people who needed my assistance in one form or another. At times that assistance took the form of a timely warning, an envelope, a letter. On other occasions I organised a chain of communication, or helped to get someone out of a tight spot. I learned languages, and I even felt strong enough to go back to the United States. That was until what happened in Honduras.'

'Hold on. You've skipped an important event: your parents' funeral.'

Fowler's face twisted in a look of extreme discomfort. 'I didn't take part. I merely dealt with a few pending legal matters.'

'You surprise me, Padre Fowler. Eighty million dollars is hardly a legal matter.'

'Ah, so you know about that as well. All right, yes, I relinquished control of the money. But I didn't give it away, as many people think. I used it to create a non-profit foundation that works in various fields of social endeavour, inside and outside the United States. It bears the name of Howard Eisner, the chaplain who inspired me in Vietnam.'

'You set up the Eisner Foundation?' Paola brightened. 'In that case, you really have been around.'

'I didn't create it. I just gave it a push – gave it financial backing. In reality, it was my parents' lawyers who did most of the work – much to their dismay, I might add.'

'Fair enough. But tell me about Honduras. Take all the time you want.'

The priest regarded Dicanti with curiosity. Her attitude had quickly changed in a subtle but important respect: she now seemed inclined to believe what he said. He asked himself what had provoked the change.

'I don't want to bore you with the details. The history of El Aguacate would fill an entire book, but I'll give you the essentials. The CIA's objective was to help the revolution. Mine was to help Catholics who were oppressed by the Sandinista regime. A volunteer army was formed, and trained to undertake guerrilla warfare in order to destabilise the government. The soldiers were recruited from among the poorest Nicaraguans. An old ally of the United States government sold them weapons, a man few people expected to turn out as he did: Osama bin Laden. And the command of the Contras fell into the hands of a high-school graduate by the name of Bernie Salazar – a fanatic, as we later learned. During the months of training I went with Salazar across the border, on incursions that became more risky each time. I helped to get some religious figures whose safety had been compromised out of the country, but I found myself progressively more at odds with Salazar with each raid. He started seeing Communists here, there and everywhere. Under every stone there was a Communist, as far as he was concerned.'

'According to an article I read in an old psychiatric manual, fanatical leaders develop a heightened sense of paranoia very quickly.'

'Well this was a textbook case then. I suffered an accident, which I didn't know until much later had been planned in advance. I broke a leg and that meant I couldn't go on any further border crossings. The guerrillas started to come back later every time. They weren't sleeping in the barracks but in clearings in the jungle, in bivouacs. At night they were supposedly doing target practice, but we later found out they were carrying out summary executions. I was laid up in bed, but the night that Salazar captured the nuns and accused them of being Communists, someone warned me. He was a good kid, like many of those who threw their lot in with Salazar, but he was a little less fearful than the others – only a little less, because he told me what was going on in the secrecy of confession. He knew that I therefore wouldn't tell anyone else, but that I would do everything I could to help the nuns. We did what we could ...'

Fowler's face was deathly pale. He stopped long enough to swallow, gazing at a spot beyond Paola, outside the window.

'... But it wasn't enough. Today Salazar, like his young recruits, is dead, and the whole world knows that the Contras seized the helicopter and threw the nuns out over a Sandinista village. They needed three trips to complete the job.'

'Why did they do it?'

'The message was stark; you couldn't miss it: "We will kill anyone suspected of working with the Sandinistas. Whoever they are."'

Paola sat for a moment, reflecting on what she'd heard. 'And you blame yourself ... It's true, isn't it?'

'It would be difficult not to. I wasn't able to save those nuns. And I didn't take very good care of those young boys either. They ended up killing their own people. My desire to do good was what dragged me there, but that wasn't what I achieved. I was just one more cog in a monstrous machine. And my country has become so used to it that it no longer bats an eyelid when someone we've trained, helped and protected turns against us.'

Although the sunlight was now full on his face, Fowler didn't blink. He merely squinted, his eyes becoming two green slits as he gazed somewhere beyond the rooftops. 'The first time I saw the pictures of the common graves,' the priest went on, 'I was struck by the memory of the gunfire we used to hear during those tropical nights. So-called "target practice". I'd grown accustomed to the noise. Then one night, half asleep, I thought I heard people crying out between the rounds, but I dismissed it and went back to sleep. The next morning I told myself it had just been my imagination. If, at that moment, I had talked to the base commander, and we had investigated Salazar more thoroughly, we would have saved many lives. For that reason I am responsible for many of those deaths; for that reason I left the CIA, and for that reason I was called before the Sant'Uffizio.'

'*Padre*, I don't believe in God any more. Now I'm sure that, when we die, it's all over. I think we go back into the earth, after taking a brief trip through the intestines of a worm. But if you need absolution, I'm offering you mine. You saved the priests that you could before the rebels laid that trap for you.'

A fleeting smile crossed Fowler's face.

'Thank you. You don't know how important your words are to me, even though I lament the profound rupture that lies behind such an affirmation from a former Catholic.'

'But you still haven't told me why you decided to return to this work.'

'It's very simple. A friend asked me. And I don't like to let my friends down.'

'So that is what you are now, God's spy?'

Fowler smiled. 'You could call me that, I suppose.'

Dicanti stood up and walked over to the shelves near her desk. '*Padre*, this goes against my principles but, as my mother likes to say, you only live once.'

She pulled a thick volume of forensic analysis from the shelf and handed it to Fowler. He opened it. The first page had a signed dedication: 'I hope this gift helps you to keep the faith. Maurizio.' The pages of the book were cut out, creating three empty spaces, conveniently occupied by a half-litre of Dewar's and two small glasses.

'It's barely nine a.m.'

'Are you going to do the honours or do we wait for sunset, *padre*? I'd be proud to have a drink with the man who set up the Eisner Foundation – among other reasons, because that foundation provided the scholarship that enabled me to study in Quantico.'

This time it was Fowler's turn to be astonished. He poured two whiskys and raised his glass. 'What are we toasting?'

'Those who are no longer with us.'

'All right. To those who are no longer with us.'

Both of them drained their glasses. The liquid swirled down her throat and for Paola, who almost never drank, it was like swallowing nails soaked in ammonia. She knew her stomach would be throwing a tantrum all day, but she felt proud to have raised a glass with this man. There were some things you just had to do.

'The thing we should worry about now is getting Dante back on the team. As you guessed, you owe this unexpected gift to him,' Paola said as she gestured towards the photographs. 'I'm wondering why he did it. What does he have against you?'

Fowler broke out into laughter. It surprised Paola that such a joyful sound could also seem wistful and sad. 'Don't tell me you haven't noticed.'

'I'm sorry, I don't follow.'

'Dottoressa, for someone so versed in applying reverse psychology to other people's actions, you are showing a surprising lack of judgement in the case before us now. It's quite clear that Dante has taken a romantic interest in you. And for whatever absurd reason, he believes that I'm his competition.'

Paola froze, her mouth half open. She could feel her cheeks turning a suspicious colour, and it wasn't on account of the whisky. It was the second time this man had managed to make her blush. She wasn't completely sure how he'd done it, but she wanted to feel it again, like a child with a weak stomach who insists on getting back on the Ferris wheel a second time.

As luck would have it, the telephone rang at exactly that moment. Dicanti grabbed it, pleased to have escaped an embarrassing situation.

Her eyes filled with emotion. 'I'll be right down.'

Fowler raised his eyebrows quizzically.

'Let's get a move on. Among the photos that the UACV developed from the Robayra crime scene, there's one with our Brother Francesco. Maybe we have something.'

UACV HEADQUARTERS

VIA LAMARMORA, 3

Thursday, 7 April 2005; 9.15 a.m.

It was only a blur on the computer screen. The photographer had captured the interior of the chapel and there in the background was Karosky, disguised as Brother Francesco. The investigator had enlarged that part of the image 160 times, but it was still hard to make out anything specific.

'Not a whole lot there,' Fowler interjected.

'Slow down, *padre*.' Troi barged into the room, his arms full of papers. 'Angelo is our forensic sculptor. He's an expert in image-upgrade and I'm sure he'll find a way to give us a different perspective. Am I right, Angelo?'

Angelo Biffi, one of the UACV's technical experts, rarely got up from his computer. He looked to be somewhere in his thirties and his thick glasses were crowned by a mop of greasy hair. He cloistered himself at a large, poorly lit desk that reeked of half-eaten pizza, cut-rate cologne and singed plastic. A dozen of the most up-to-date monitors took the place of windows. Glancing around, Fowler decided that Angelo probably preferred to sleep next to his computers than to go home. He looked as if he'd been a lab rat his whole life, but even so, he had a pleasant face and always wore a timid smile.

'You see, *padre*, what I mean is – we, the department, or really I ...'

'Spit it out, Angelo. Here, have a coffee,' Paola said, leaning forward with the cappuccino that Fowler had brought for Dante half an hour earlier.

'Thanks, *dottoressa*. But it's cold!'

'Don't complain; it will soon be hot outside. In fact, when you grow up you'll look back and say, "This April is hot, but it's nowhere near as hot as the year Pope John Paul died." Just you wait and see.'

Taken aback, Fowler stared at Dicanti, whose hand was resting gently on Angelo's shoulder. Even if she was going to pieces inside, Dicanti was trying to camouflage it by making a joke. She had barely had any sleep; the bags under her eyes were larger than a raccoon's, and her emotions were torn between confusion, sadness and anger all at the same time. You didn't have to be a psychologist or a priest to see it. And in spite of everything, here she was, trying to help that kid feel more comfortable around a priest who slightly intimidated him. At that moment Fowler loved her for it, but he quickly suppressed the thought. He couldn't forget the shame she had made him feel just a short time earlier in her office.

'Explain to Padre Fowler how you work,' Paola said. 'I'm sure he'll find it interesting.'

When he heard that, the young man's eyes lit up.

'Take a look at the screen. We have – OK, *I* have designed special software for the interpolation of images. As you know, every image is composed of coloured dots called pixels. If a normal image contains roughly 2,500 by 1,750 pixels but we are only interested in a tiny corner of the photo, we'll end up with a few pointless splotches of colour. Making it bigger simply turns it into the blurred image you see now. Normally when a conventional program tries to enlarge an image, it uses the bicubic method, which means it takes into account the colour of the eight pixels adjacent to the one you want to enlarge. So at the end you get the same splotch, but magnified. But with my program ...'

Paola looked sideways at Fowler as he leaned toward the monitor, staring hard. The priest was trying to pay attention to Angelo's explanation in spite of the ordeal he'd just gone through moments before. Seeing those photos from his past had been very difficult and had left him feeling deeply upset – it was obvious to anyone who cared to look; and in spite of all that he was forcing himself to be pleasant towards a timid young man he would never see again. Dicanti loved him for it, but she rapidly pushed the thought aside.

The embarrassment she'd felt in her office that morning still played on her mind.

'... and taking into account the variables in the points of light, let's consider what a three-dimensional information program could bring to the project. It's based on a complex algorithm that takes several hours to work itself out.'

'Damn it, Angelo, you brought us down here to tell us that?'

'But this – you'll see ...'

'Don't worry, Angelo. Dicanti, I suspect that what this intelligent young man is trying to tell us is that the program has already been working for several hours and is about to give us its conclusions.'

'Correct. In fact, it's coming out of the printer right now.'

The laser printer directly in front of Dicanti hummed as it produced a single piece of paper with an old man's face on it, his eyes shaded, but all in all, a much more focused image than the original.

'Nice work, Angelo. Not quite clear enough to identify the man, but it's a starting point. Take a look, *padre*.'

Fowler examined the features in the photograph carefully. Troi, Dicanti and Angelo watched and waited.

'I'd say it was him but it's hard without seeing the eyes. The shape of the eye sockets and something else – something indefinable – tells me it's him. But if this man had walked by me in the street, I wouldn't have given him a second glance.'

'So it's another dead end?'

'Not necessarily,' Angelo suggested. 'I have a program that can make a three-dimensional image out of a few pieces of information. I think we can infer enough with what we have. I've been working with a photo of the engineer.'

'The engineer?' Paola was puzzled.

'Yes, the photo of engineer Karosky – the one who's passing himself off as a Carmelite. You should see the look on your face, Dicanti ...'

Troi went on full alert, making unmistakable gestures of alarm behind Angelo's back. It finally dawned on Paola that Angelo had been left in the dark. Paola knew that the director hadn't let the four investigators looking for clues at the Robayra and Pontiero crime scenes go home. What he had done was give them permission to call their families to explain, and then put them in quarantine in one of the rooms where people usually took their coffee breaks. Troi could be tough when he wanted to be, but he was also fair: he paid overtime at three times the hourly rate.

'Ah yes, what was I thinking? Go on, Angelo.'

Troi was no doubt divvying up the information at every level so that no one had all the pieces of the puzzle. He didn't want anyone to know that they were investigating the deaths of two cardinals. Still, this obviously made Paola's work more difficult, besides which it gave her serious doubts that even she had all the pieces in play.

'As I was saying, I've been working on the photo of the engineer. I think that in about thirty minutes we'll have a three-dimensional image of his photo from 1995, which we can compare with the three-dimensional image we're putting together in 2005. If you come back in a little while, I'll have something more definite.'

'Perfect. If it's OK with you, padre, ispettore, I'd like to go over everything in the conference room. Angelo, we'll see you in a short while.'

'Right.'

The three headed up to the conference room, two floors above. No sooner had Dicanti walked in than she was overwhelmed by the terrible realisation that the last time she'd been in the room was in Pontiero's company.

'May I inquire what the two of you have done to Superintendent Dante?'

Paola and Fowler exchanged quick glances. They shook their heads in unison.

'Absolutely nothing.'

'Good. I hope I didn't see him storm by in a fury because of something you did. I hope he was just pissed off about Sunday's football scores, because I don't want Cirin all over me, or the Minister of the Interior.'

'I don't think you need worry. Dante is an integral member of the team,' Paola lied.

'So why don't I believe you? Last night that guy saved your neck, Dicanti. Want to tell me where he is now?'

Paola didn't say a word. She couldn't talk to Troi about the group's internal problems. She was just about to open her mouth when a familiar voice got there first.

'I went out for cigarettes.'

Dante, wearing his leather jacket and ironic smile, stood in the doorway to the conference room.

Troi studied him sceptically. 'It's one of the very worst vices, Dante.'

'We all have to die of something.'

Paola's eyes followed Dante as he took a seat next to Fowler, acting as if nothing had come between them, although two fleeting, hostile glances were enough to convince Paola that things were not as smooth as they seemed. But as long as the two of them behaved in a civil manner towards each other over the next few days, everything would be OK. What she didn't understand was how her Vatican colleague had recovered from his anger so quickly. Something had happened.

'All right, then,' said Troi. 'This bloody case gets more complicated by the minute. Yesterday, in full daylight, we lost one of the best officers I've known in a long time, and nobody has a clue what will happen next. We can't even hold a public funeral – at least, not until we come up with a reasonable explanation for his death. That's why I want us to put our heads together. Tell me what you know, Paola.'

'Since when?'

'Since the beginning. A quick overview of the case so far.'

Paola stood up and walked over to the blackboard. She could think much more clearly on her feet.

'Let's see. Victor Karosky, a priest with a history of sexual abuse, escapes from a private, low-security institution where he was subjected to excessive quantities of a drug that chemically castrated him while raising his levels of aggression. From June 2000 until the end of 2001 there's no trace of his whereabouts. In 2001, under a false name, he surreptitiously assumes the identity of a Carmelite friar, using as a front the Church of Santa Maria in Traspontina only a few feet from Saint Peter's Square.'

Paola drew a few lines on the blackboard and began to construct a calendar.

'Friday, the first of April, twenty-four hours before the death of

John Paul the Second: Karosky takes the Italian cardinal Enrico Portini hostage in the Madre Pie residence. Have we confirmed that traces of blood from both cardinals were found in the crypt?'

Troi nodded yes.

'Karosky takes Portini to Santa Maria, tortures him and brings him back to the last place he was seen alive: the chapel in the residence. Saturday, the second of April: Portini's body is discovered the same night as the death of the Pope, although the Vatican Vigilanza decides to "clean up" the evidence, believing it to be the isolated act of a madman. Purely by luck, word does not get out, in good measure thanks to the staff of the residence. Sunday, the third of April: Argentine cardinal Emilio Robayra arrives in Rome on a one-way ticket. Our theory is that someone met him at the airport or en route to the Saint Ambrogio residence, where he was expected on Sunday evening. We know he never arrived. Do we have anything useful from the airport's surveillance cameras?'

'No one has checked. We don't have enough personnel,' Troi said, by way of excuse.

'We have more than enough.'

'I can't bring in any other detectives. The important thing is to keep a lid on this case, in accordance with the wishes of the Holy See. Let's play it by ear, Paola. I'll ask for the tapes myself.'

Dicanti pulled a face, but it was the response she'd expected.

'Back to Sunday. Karosky kidnaps Robayra and takes him to the crypt. There, he tortures the cardinal for more than a day, leaving messages on his body and then also at the crime scene. The sentence that was left on the body is from the Gospels: "And I will give unto thee the keys of the kingdom of heaven," referring to the moment when the first Supreme Pontiff of the Catholic Church was chosen. This and the message written in blood on the ground, added to the mutilation of the body, leads us to believe that the assassin has his eyes on the Conclave.

'Monday, the fourth of April: the suspect drags the body to one of the chapels in the church and calmly calls the police in his role as brother Francesco Toma. To mock us even further, he wears Cardinal Robayra's glasses the whole time we're there. Vatican agents call the UACV and Troi calls Camilo Cirin.'

Paola paused briefly and looked directly at Troi.

'When you picked up the phone to call him, I think Cirin knew who the criminal was, although he never suspected that he was a serial killer. I've given it a good deal of thought and I believe Cirin already knew the name of Portini's killer by Sunday night. He probably had access to VICAP's database, and the entry "severed hands" wouldn't have pulled up many cases. His network of contacts put him in touch with Major Fowler, who arrived here on the night of the fifth. Probably the original plan was not include us, Director Troi. It was Karosky who brought us into the game, deliberately. Why is the real question.'

Paola drew the final line.

'Wednesday the sixth of April: while Dante, Fowler and myself track down leads about the victims, Detective Maurizio Pontiero is beaten to death by Victor Karosky in the crypt of Santa Maria in Traspontina.'

'We have the murder weapon?' asked Dante.

'Without fingerprints but, yes, we have it,' Troi responded. 'Karosky made several wounds with what could be a very sharp kitchen knife and he beat his victim repeatedly with a candelabrum found at the scene. But I don't have high hopes for this line of investigation.'

'May I ask why?'

'Because it's not our normal procedure, Dante. Our job is to find out *who* the killer is. Typically, when we're sure of who he is, our work is over. But now we have to apply our knowledge to discern *where* the killer is, and knowing his name is just a point of departure. For that reason, Dicanti's contribution is more important than ever.'

'And I'd like to congratulate her. That was a brilliant chronology, Dicante,' said Fowler.

'Extraordinary,' Dante added, mocking all the way.

Paola could feel the resentment in his words, but she decided that it would be better to ignore him – for now.

'Good summary, Dicanti,' Troi congratulated her. 'What's the next step? Have you found your way into Karosky's head yet? Does the case bear any similarities to anything you've studied before?'

The profiler thought for a few seconds before she answered. 'All sane people are alike, but every one of these bastards is unhinged in their own particular way.'

'And what does that tell us, apart from the fact that you've read Tolstoi?' asked Troi.

'Well, we'd be committing a terrible blunder if we believed that one serial killer is exactly like another. You can try to search for certain rules of thumb, find equivalents, draw conclusions from similarities between cases, but in the end every one of these pieces of shit is a very solitary mind living millions of light years away from the rest of humanity. There's nobody home. They're not human beings. They don't feel empathy. Their emotions are switched off. The thing that makes them kill, that leads them to believe their egotism is more important than anyone else's, the reasons they use to excuse their insanity – none of that matters to me. I don't try to understand them any further than is strictly necessary in order to catch them.'

'Which is why we have to know what his next step will be.'

'Clearly, he's going to kill again. Most likely he'll invent a new identity for himself or he's already chosen one. But it won't be as well rehearsed as that of Brother Francesco, because he worked on that for several years. Maybe Father Fowler can lend us a hand here?'

The priest nodded his head, preoccupied. 'Everything I know is in the file I gave you, dottoressa. But there is something I want to show you.'

A pitcher of water sat on a side table along with some glasses. Fowler filled one of them halfway up and dropped his pencil into it.

'It's a tremendous effort for me to think like he does. Look at this glass. It's as clear as the water, but when I drop an apparently straight pencil into it, the pencil looks like it's broken in two. In the same way, his monolithic attitude shifts at crucial moments, like a straight line that splits off and ends up somewhere unknown.'

'The point where it splits off is the key.'

'Perhaps. I don't envy your work, Dicanti. Karosky is a man who rails against iniquity one minute, only to commit greater iniquities himself the next. What I do know is that we should search for him wherever the cardinals are. He'll try to kill again, and he won't wait long. The Conclave is getting closer and closer.'

The group headed back down to Angelo's laboratory in a somewhat confused state. The young technician was introduced to Dante, who ignored him. Paola couldn't help but notice his rudeness. Dante was a very attractive man but, at heart, he was rotten. His bitter jokes didn't conceal a thing; they were simply the best thing about him.

Angelo was waiting with the promised results. He hit the keyboard and three-dimensional images, conjured out of thin green threads on a black background, popped up on two screens.

'How about fleshing them out?'

'Certainly. Now they'll have skin – rudimentary, but skin.'

The monitor on the left displayed a three-dimensional model of Karosky's head as it had been in 1995, the screen on the right the upper half of the head as photographed at Santa Maria in Traspontina.

'I haven't modelled the lower half because it's impossible with the beard. You can't see the eyes too well either. In the photo they gave me he was walking with his shoulders stooped.'

'Can you copy the jaw from the first model and impose it on the new head?'

Angelo responded with a rapid flurry of keystrokes and clicks. In less than two minutes Fowler's request had been carried out.

'Tell me, Angelo: how faithful do you judge this second model to be?' the priest asked.

The young technician was momentarily flustered. 'Well, you see … without assessing whether there was adequate lighting at the place—'

'We've already covered that, Angelo,' Troi interjected.

Paola spoke slowly and calmly. 'Listen, Angelo, nobody here is judging whether or not you've made a good model. We only want to know to what degree we can trust it.'

'Well, it's somewhere between seventy-five and eighty-five per cent faithful – no more.'

Fowler looked at the screen carefully. The two faces were very different. Too different. The nose was wider, the cheekbones stronger. But were they the subject's natural features or only make-up?

'Angelo, could you rotate both images on a horizontal plane and make a measurement of the cheekbones. Like that. Yes, that's it … That's what I was afraid of.'

The other four looked at him, holding their breath.

'What is it?'

'That isn't the face of Victor Karosky. An amateur applying make-up couldn't come up with differences like that in the size of the cheekbones. Maybe a Hollywood professional could pull it off with latex moulds, but it would be completely obvious to anyone who saw him close up. He wouldn't be able to maintain the deception for very long.'

'Which means ...?'

'There's only one explanation: Karosky has been treated by a surgeon and undergone a complete facial reconstruction. The man we're looking for is a ghost.'

THE SAINT MATTHEW INSTITUTE

SACHEM PIKE, MARYLAND

May 1998

Transcript of Interview Number 14 between Patient Number 3643 and Doctor Fowler

DR FOWLER: Good afternoon, Father Karosky. May I enter?

No. 3643: Come in, Father Fowler.

DR FOWLER: Did you enjoy the book I lent you?

No. 3643: Yes, of course. *The Confessions of Saint Augustine.* I've already finished it. A very interesting book. It's unbelievable just how far innate optimism can take you.

DR FOWLER: I don't understand.

No. 3643: But you're the only person in this whole place who is capable of understanding me. The only person who doesn't call me by my first name in an attempt to achieve a vulgar, unnecessary familiarity that denigrates the dignity of both parties.

DR FOWLER: You are speaking of Father Conroy.

No. 3643: Yes, that man. The one who maintains, time after time, that I am a normal patient in need of a cure. I am a priest just as he is, yet he seems to forget this constantly, when he insists I call him doctor.

DR FOWLER: I believe that point was already clarified for you last week, Father Karosky. It's better that your relationship with Conroy remains that of doctor and patient, and nothing else. You need help in overcoming a number of psychological problems that stem from the suffering you endured in the past.

No. 3643: I suffered? I suffered at whose hands? Perhaps you too want to put my love for my saintly mother to the test? I beg you not to follow the same route as Father Conroy. He even announced that he would make me listen to some recordings that would leave me in no doubt.

DR FOWLER: Some recordings.

No. 3643: That's what he said.

DR FOWLER: I don't think you should hear those tapes, Father Karosky. It wouldn't be good for you. I'll speak to Father Conroy about it.

No. 3643: As you see fit. But I'm not afraid.

DR FOWLER: Listen, father: I want us to get as much out of this session as possible, and there's something you said a little earlier that interests me very much. About Saint Augustine's optimism in *The Confessions*. What were you referring to?

No. 3643: 'And even if I appear laughable in your sight, you will come back to me full of mercy.'

DR FOWLER: I don't understand what strikes you as optimistic in that passage. Don't you believe in the goodness and infinite mercy of God?

No. 3643: The merciful God is an invention of the twentieth century, Father Fowler.

DR FOWLER: Saint Augustine lived in the fourth century.

No. 3643: Saint Augustine was horrified by his own sinful past, and set out to write a string of optimistic lies.

DR FOWLER: But father, it's the basis of our faith! – that God pardons us.

No. 3643: Not always. Some people go to confession like they go to wash their cars … Pah! They make me sick.

DR FOWLER: That's what you feel when you administer confession? – nauseated?

No. 3643: I feel repugnance. Many times I vomited inside the confessional, from the bile the person on the other side of the screen stirred up in me. Lies. Fornication. Adultery. Pornography. Violence. Theft. All of them, sneaking into this small space, contaminating it with their filth. They pour it all out until I'm drowning in it.

DR FOWLER: But, father, they aren't confessing their sins to us. They are confessing them to God. We are merely the transmitters.

When we put on the priest's stole, we represent Christ.

No. 3643: They throw everything at us. They arrive filthy and believe that they leave clean. 'Bless me, father, for I have sinned: I've stolen ten thousand dollars from my business partner.' 'Bless me, father, for I have sinned: I raped my younger sister.' 'Bless me, father, for I have sinned: I took photos of my son and posted them on the Internet.' 'Bless me, father, for I have sinned: I put bleach in my husband's food so he'll stop bothering me about his conjugal rights because I'm sick of the way he reeks of onions and sweat.' Just like that, day after day.

DR FOWLER: But confession is a marvellous thing, Father Karosky, when there is true repentance and an honest attempt to change one's behaviour.

No. 3643: Something that never happens. They always, always pile their sins on my shoulders. They abandon me, leave me alone before God's impassive face. I am the only one standing between their iniquities and God's vengeance.

DR FOWLER: Do you really see God as a vengeful being?

No. 3643: 'His heart is as firm as a stone; yea, as hard as a piece of the nether millstone. The sword of him that layeth at him cannot hold: the spear, the dart, nor the harbergeon. He maketh the deep to boil like a pot: he maketh the sea like a pot of ointment. He surveys all with pride; he rules over the fierce!'

DR FOWLER: I have to admit that your intimacy with the Bible, particularly the Old Testament, always impresses me. But the Book of Job was rendered obsolete by the truth that Jesus gives us in the scriptures.

No. 3643: Jesus Christ is merely the Son; it is the Father who renders judgement. And the Father has a face of stone.

DR FOWLER: I'm very sorry to see that you climb so high in the tower of your convictions. The fall from such a perch could be fatal, Father Karosky. And if you listen to Father Conroy's tapes, there's no question that that's what will happen.

ℋOTEL ℛAPHAEL

Thursday, 7 April 2005, 2.45 p.m.

'Saint Ambrogio Residence.'

'Good afternoon. I'd like to speak with Cardinal Robayra,' said the young journalist in her very worst Italian.

The voice on the other end of the phone was slightly flustered. 'May I ask to whom I'm speaking?'

It wasn't much – the speaker's tone hardly changed; but it was enough to send a signal to the journalist.

Andrea Otero had spent four years working at *El Globo* – four years in which she'd blazed a trail through third-rate press rooms, interviewed C-list celebrities and written stories for the back page. She'd been twenty-four years old when she joined *El Globo*, and she'd only got there because of her connections. She had started off working for the culture pages, but the editor there had never taken her seriously. She had moved on to the society pages, whose editor had never trusted her. Now she'd taken up residence in the international pages, whose editor didn't think she was up to the job. But she was. It wasn't all about grades, or the courses you'd taken. There was also common sense, intuition, the journalist's nose for a story; and if Andrea Otero had even a tenth of what she thought she had in terms of these qualities, she'd be a journalist worthy of a Pulitzer. She didn't lack confidence in herself, in her five foot eight inches of height, in her angelic features, her blonde hair or her blue eyes. Behind these features was a woman of resolve and intelligence. So when her colleague who was to cover the death of the Pope tripped on the stairs of her apartment building – on the way out to the cab that was supposed to take her to the airport – and ended up with a broken leg, Andrea hadn't baulked at her boss's proposal that she go instead. She'd caught the plane with only moments to spare, a laptop her only luggage.

Happily the streets around her hotel in the Piazza Navona were full of little stores selling the basic necessities. So Andrea Otero purchased several serviceable outfits and some underwear, along with a mobile phone, all of which she naturally charged to the newspaper. The last item was what she was using to call the Saint Ambrogio Residence in order to set up an interview with papal candidate Cardinal Robayra.

'This is Andrea Otero, of *El Globo*. The cardinal promised me an interview today, but he's not answering his mobile phone. Would you be so kind as to put me through to his room, please.'

'Signorina Otero, I'm sorry to say we cannot put you through to his room because the cardinal hasn't arrived.'

'And when will he arrive?'

'He isn't coming.'

'He's staying somewhere else?'

'I don't think so. I mean, I suppose he will.'

'And to whom am I speaking?'

'I have to go.'

The dialling tone on the other end of the line told her two things: the conversation was over, and the person she had spoken with was exceptionally nervous. Also, she had been lying – Andrea was sure of that. She was too much of a liar herself not to recognise someone in her own class.

There was no time to lose. It didn't take her more than ten minutes to get hold of the telephone number of the cardinal's private office in Buenos Aires. It was almost ten in the morning there, a good time to call. She smiled at the thought of the phone bill the newspaper was going to receive. They were paying her the absolute minimum, so at least she'd screwed them with expenses.

The telephone rang for a minute and then the line went dead. Strange that no one was there. She tried the line again.

Nothing.

She tried the number of the main office. A woman's voice answered immediately. 'Archbishop's office, good morning.'

'I'd like to speak with Cardinal Robayra, please.'

'I'm sorry, he's already left.'

'Left for where?'

'He's gone to the Conclave, miss – to Rome.'

'Do you now where he's staying?'

'No, señorita. I'll connect you to Father Serafín, his secretary.'

'Thank you.'

The Beatles played while she was on hold. How appropriate. Andrea decided to lie a bit just to keep things interesting. The cardinal had family in Spain. She wanted to see if she could pull it off.

'Hello?'

'Hi, I'd like to speak to the cardinal. It's his niece Asunción – the one from Spain.'

'Asunción, it's a pleasure. I'm Father Serafín, the cardinal's secretary. His Eminence never told me about you. Are you Angustia's daughter, or Remedios's?'

She sensed a trap. Andrea crossed her fingers. A fifty per cent chance of making a false move. She was an expert in false moves, too: she had a long history of putting her foot in her mouth.

'Remedios.'

'Of course, how stupid of me. Angustia doesn't have any children – I remember that now. I'm sorry, but the cardinal isn't here.'

'When can I speak to him?'

Silence. The priest's voice became cautious. Andrea could almost see him on the other end of the line, gripping the receiver and twisting the cord around his index finger.

'What did you want to speak to him about?'

'Well, I've been living in Rome for years, and he promised me that the next time he was here he would visit me.'

The voice on the other end became even more apprehensive. He was speaking slowly, as if he were afraid of making a mistake. 'He has gone to Cordoba to take care of pressing matters in the diocese there. He won't be able to attend the Conclave.'

'But the main office told me that the Cardinal had already left for Rome.'

'Ah, yes, there's a new girl there, and she's still unacquainted with how the archbishopric works,' Serafín fired back. He'd obviously made that one up on the spot. 'Please forgive me.'

'You're forgiven. Will you tell my uncle that I called?'

'Of course. Could you give me your telephone number, Asunción? I want to put it on the cardinal's agenda. We might have to get in touch with you.'

'He already has it. I'm sorry, but my husband is on the other line. Goodbye.'

She hung up on the secretary before he'd even finished speaking. Now she was sure that something wasn't right. But she had to confirm it. Luckily for her there was an Internet connection in the hotel. It took her all of six minutes to find the phone number for the three main Argentine airlines. She struck gold first time.

'Aerolineas Argentinas.'

She made an effort to give her Madrid accent a passable Argentine stamp. It wasn't so bad. Her Italian was much worse.

'*Buenos días.* I'm calling you from the archbishopric of Buenos Aires. With whom am I speaking?'

'My name is Verona.'

'Verona, my name is Asunción. I am calling to confirm Cardinal Robayra's return flight to Buenos Aires.'

'On what date?'

'He'll be returning on the nineteenth of the coming month.'

'His full name?'

'Emilio Robayra.'

'Please wait while I check.'

Andrea chewed the end of her ballpoint pen nervously, checked the state of her hair in the mirror, threw herself on to the bed and wiggled her toes.

'Hello? My colleagues have advised me that you bought only a one-way ticket. The cardinal has already travelled, but you can buy a ticket for the return flight at ten per cent off. It's a special price for April. Do you have his frequent-flyer number handy?'

'One moment, let me check.'

She hung up, barely containing her laughter. But the hilarity quickly changed into a euphoric feeling of triumph. Cardinal Robayra had indeed got on a plane headed for Rome. But he hadn't made an appearance at his guest house. He could have decided to stay somewhere else. Yet, if that were the case, why had Saint Ambrogio and the Cardinal's office lied to her?

'Either I'm crazy, or there's a good story here – a fucking brilliant story,' she said to her reflection in the mirror.

The selection of the next man to sit on the throne of Saint Peter was only a few days away. And the great candidate of the poor, the champion of the Third World, the man who openly flirted with Liberation Theology, had disappeared.

Domus Sanctae Marthae

Thursday, 7 April 2005, 4.14 p.m.

Paola stood at the entrance to the building with a look of surprise on her face. On the far side of the piazza a long queue of cars waited at a petrol station. Dante explained to her that, since the Vatican didn't charge taxes, prices were thirty per cent lower than in Italy. You had to have a special permit to fill your tank at one of the city's seven stations, but even so the queues were never-ending.

Paola, Dante and Fowler were waiting outside while the Swiss Guards who watched over the front door of the Domus Sanctae Marthae informed someone inside of their presence. Paola had a few moments to chew over everything that had happened that morning. Two hours earlier, at the UACV headquarters, she had pulled Dante aside the moment they had escaped from Troi.

'I'd like a word with you.'

Dante avoided Paola's eyes but followed her to her office.

'I know what you are going to say to me, Dicanti – that we're all together in this. Right?'

'That I already know. And I've also noticed that, like Troi, you call me inspector and not doctor. Because it's a lower rank than your own. I don't mind your inferiority complex as long as it doesn't interfere with me doing my job. Like your little performance earlier this morning with the photographs.'

Dante turned red. 'I just wanted to let you know. It's nothing personal.'

'You wanted to warn me about Fowler? Well you've done that. Is my position clear, or must I be even more concrete?'

'I've had enough of your clarity already, ispettore.' Dante dragged out the word, sounding almost like a guilty child and rubbing his cheek. 'You knocked my fucking fillings out. What I don't understand is why you didn't break a bone in your hand.'

'Nor I, because you have a very hard face.'

'I'm a hard man in more ways than one.'

'I don't have the slightest interest. And don't forget that.'

'Is that a woman's no, ispettore?'

He was making Paola angry again. 'What exactly is a woman's no?'

'The kind that's spelt Y-E-S.'

'It's a no that's spelt N-O, you chauvinist bastard.'

'Calm down. No need to get excited, hot pants.'

Dicanti silently cursed him. She was falling into Dante's trap, letting him play with her emotions. But everything was OK. She would adopt a more formal tone, make her disdain for him impossible to miss. She decided to imitate Troi, since he always came out of this type of confrontation smelling like roses.

'OK, now that we've clarified that, I have to tell you that I've spoken with our American counterpart. I have expressed my fears concerning his past. Fowler gave me a very convincing explanation, which, in my judgement, is sufficient for me to trust him. I want to thank you for the trouble you took to dig up the information on Fowler. It's a point in your favour.'

Dante was surprised by Paola's icy tone. He had lost the match and he knew it.

'As the person in charge of the investigation, I have to formally ask you if you are ready to give your full support in capturing Victor Karosky.'

'Of course, ispettore.' Dante spat the words out like red-hot nails.

'All that's left is to ask you why you came back so quickly.'

'I called my superiors to complain, but they were no help. They ordered me to rise above personal animosity.'

Paola's ear pricked up at that last phrase. Fowler denied that Dante had anything personal against him, but the superintendent's words seemed to indicate otherwise. Dicanti had already sensed once before that the two of them knew each other from some earlier time, in spite of the way they acted to the contrary. She decided she would ask Dante directly.

'Had you met Anthony Fowler before?'

'No, ispettore,' Dante said. His voice was firm, unhesitating.

'His case file showed up very quickly.'

'The Corpi di Vigilanza is very well organised.'

Paola decided to drop it.

As she was ready to leave, Dante said something that pleased her immensely. 'Just one thing: if you ever feel the need to call me to order again, I prefer the slapping method. I really don't care for formality.'

Paola asked Dante to show them round the building where the cardinals were going to reside. And there they were: the Domus Sanctae Marthae, Saint Martha's House. Located to the west of the basilica, inside the walls of the Vatican.

From outside its appearance was austere. Straight, elegant lines, without mouldings, adornment or statues. Compared to the marvels that surrounded it, the Domus was as unobtrusive as a golf ball in a barrel of snow. It would have been difficult for the occasional tourist – who wasn't allowed into that restricted area of the Vatican in any case – to give the building any more than a cursory glance.

But when the authorisation arrived and the Swiss Guards let them pass through the entrance, Paola discovered that the inside was completely different from the exterior. Here was what looked like a fashionable hotel, complete with marble floors and tropical hardwood furniture. Traces of lavender wafted through the air. While they were waiting in the vestibule, Dicanti looked around. There were paintings on every wall, and Paola recognised the style of the great Dutch and Italian masters of the sixteenth century; and not one of them appeared to be a reproduction.

'Holy shit.' Paola was trying to limit her outbursts, but she was astounded.

'I know what you mean,' Fowler said.

Dicanti recalled that Fowler's personal circumstances had hardly been pleasant during his stay at the Domus.

'It's a complete contrast with the rest of the buildings in the Vatican – at least, the ones I'm familiar with. The new and the old.'

'Do you know anything about the history of this place? You'll probably remember that in 1978 there were two conclaves, one right after the other, only two months apart.'

'I was a little girl, but I still have a few pictures in my mind of those days.' For a short while Paola let herself sink into the past.

Ice cream in Saint Peter's Square. Mamma and Papa have lemon flavour, I have chocolate-and-strawberry. The pilgrims are singing; there is happiness in the air. Daddy's hand, strong, with deep grooves in his palm. I love to hold on to his fingers and stroll around while morning turns into afternoon. We look up towards the chimney and we see the white smoke. Papa lifts me on to his shoulders. His smile is the best thing in the world. I drop my ice cream and I cry, but Papa just laughs again and promises me that he'll buy me another one. 'We'll eat to the health of the Bishop of Rome,' he says.

'Two Popes were elected within a short space of time, since the successor to Paul IV, John Paul I, died suddenly only thirty-three days after he came to power. There was a second conclave in which John Paul II was chosen. In those days the cardinals resided in tiny cells near the Sistine Chapel. With no home comforts and no air-conditioning, and with the heat of the Roman summer as heavy as lead, a few of the oldest cardinals went through a real Calvary. More than one had to seek emergency treatment. Once he had put on the fisherman's sandals, Wojtyla personally decided that he would do the groundwork so that, when he died, none of this would happen again. The result is this building. Dicanti, are you listening to me?'

Paola emerged from her daydream with a guilty look. 'Sorry, I was lost in thought. Won't happen again.'

At that moment Dante came back. He had gone ahead in order to talk to the person responsible for security at the Domus. Paola noticed that he was avoiding the American priest, possibly just to avoid a confrontation. Both of them were forcing themselves to speak normally, but Paola doubted that Fowler had been entirely honest with her when he had suggested their rivalry could be ascribed to Dante's jealousy. For now, even though the team was fastened together with safety pins, the best she could do was to maintain the farce and ignore the problem – something that Paola had never been very good at.

Dante returned in the company of a tiny nun, who was laughing and sweating inside her black habit. Introduced as Sister Helena Tobina, from Poland, she was Saint Martha's director. She proceeded to give them a thorough report on all the improvements that had been made in the building. The works had been carried out in several stages, the last in 2003. The group walked up a wide staircase, every step of which was polished to a sheen. The building consisted of several floors with large hallways, thick carpets, and doors to the individual rooms on either side.

'There are one hundred and six suites, and twenty-two individual rooms. All of the furniture dates back several centuries and consists of valuable pieces donated by German and Italian families.'

The nun opened the door to one of them. It was a large room, some two hundred feet square, with parquet floors and a beautiful rug. The bed frame was made of wood, with an exquisite carved headboard. A built-in wardrobe, a desk and a bathroom made up the rest of the room.

'This room belongs to one of the six cardinals who has yet to arrive. The other hundred and nine have already taken theirs.'

Dicanti mused that at least two of those who were absent weren't ever going to show up.

'Are the cardinals safe here, Sister Helena?' Paola asked cautiously. She wasn't sure to what extent the nun knew about the current threat to the men in red robes.

'Very safe, my child, very safe. The building has only one entrance, with Swiss Guards on duty twenty-four hours a day. All the telephones have been taken out of the rooms, and the televisions, too.'

Paola found the precautions strange.

'The cardinals must remain incommunicado during the Conclave. No telephones, no mobile phones, no radios, no televisions, no magazines, no Internet. No contact whatsoever with the outside world under pain of being excommunicated.' Fowler cleared things up for Paola. 'Orders of John Paul II, just before he died.'

'But it can't be easy to isolate them completely. What do you think, Dante?'

The superintendent stuck out his chest. It gave him great pleasure to enumerate his organisation's heroic undertakings, as if he were carrying them out personally.

'You'll be happy to know, ispettore, that we are using the most up-to-date technology in signal inhibitors.'

'I'm not really familiar with spy jargon. Mind explaining?'

'We have at our disposal electronic equipment that has created two electromagnetic fields. One here and the other in the Sistine Chapel. In practice, they operate like two invisible umbrellas. Underneath them no appliance that requires contact with the outside world can function – neither a directional microphone nor any kind of spyware. Give your cellphone a try.'

Paola picked it up and saw that it had no coverage. They went outside to the hallway. No signal at all.

'And what about the food?'

'It is prepared here, in our kitchens,' Sister Helena said proudly. 'The kitchen staff is composed of ten nuns, who perform the different services provided here at Saint Martha's throughout the day. At night, the only staff present are the people at the front desk, just in case some emergency should take place. No one else is authorised to set foot inside the Domus, except for the cardinals.'

Paola opened her mouth to ask a question, but it stuck in her throat because just as she was about to speak, a terrible scream reached them from the floor above.

Domus Sanctae Marthae

PIAZZA SANTA MARTA, 1

Thursday, 7 April, 4.31 p.m.

Gaining the man's confidence to get into his room had been easy. The cardinal now had plenty of time to regret his mistake. His error was slowly being spelled out in painful letters as Karosky made each new cut into the cardinal's exposed chest.

'Calm down, Your Eminence. It's not much longer now.'

The victim fought back but his strength was waning. The blood, which had soaked the bedspread and was falling in thick drops on to the Persian rug, carried his strength away with it. Yet he didn't lose consciousness for a second. He felt every blow Karosky dealt him, every cut of the blade.

Karosky finished his handiwork on the cardinal's chest and proudly contemplated what he had written. He held the camera with a firm grip and captured the moment: after all, he couldn't leave without a memento. Sadly, he couldn't use a digital video camera here, but this disposable camera served his purpose admirably. He mocked Cardinal Cardoso as he wound the film on with his thumb.

'Say hello to the camera, Your Eminence. Oh, but of course you can't, because I'm just about to remove your tongue. I need your gift for languages.'

Karosky was the only one laughing at his macabre joke. He put the camera down and brought the knife right up to the cardinal's face, sticking his own tongue out in a mocking gesture. And then he made his first mistake. He started to untie the gag. The man lying on the bed was terrified, but he wasn't as far gone as the other victims had been. He pulled together the little strength he had left and let out a loud scream that resounded through the hallways of the Domus Sanctae Marthae.

Domus Sanctae Marthae

Thursday, 7 April 2005, 4.31 p.m.

Paola reacted immediately when she heard the scream. She gestured to the nun to stay right where she was and then took the stairs three at a time, her pistol drawn. Fowler and Dante followed, one step behind. Their thighs nearly cramped with the exertion of racing up the steps at such speed. Arriving on the floor above they came to a stop, disoriented. They stood in the middle of a long hallway full of doors.

'Where did it come from?' said Fowler.

'I wish I knew,' said Paola. 'Let's stay together. It could be him, and he's a dangerous son of a bitch.'

Paola chose to begin with the left side, across from the lift. She thought she heard a noise in Room 56. Her ear was pressed against the wooden door when Dante motioned to her to move away. The stocky Vatican officer gestured to Fowler; the two of them smashed against the door, and it gave way easily. Both of them went in, Dante going ahead and Paola covering the sides. Fowler stayed in the doorway, his hands at chest level.

Lying on the bed was a cardinal. He was very pale and scared to death but he was in one piece. He eyed the two policemen fearfully, and raised his hands.

'Don't hurt me, please.'

Dante looked around the room and lowered his gun.

'Where did the noise come from?'

'The next room over, I think,' the man said, pointing with a finger, his hands still aloft.

They ran back out to the hallway. Paola stood to one side of Room 57 while Dante and Fowler served as a human battering ram a second time. Their shoulders hit the door hard but at first it didn't budge. The second time, it gave way with a tremendous crash.

A cardinal was lying on the bed. He was very pale and very dead but otherwise the room was empty. Dante crossed the space in two quick strides and looked into the bathroom. He shook his head. And then there was another shout.

'Help me! Help me, please!'

All three ran out of the room. At the end of the hallway, next to the lift, a man lay on the ground, his red robes spread in an oval shape around him. Paola got there first and knelt at his side, but the cardinal was already getting up.

'Cardinal Casey!' Fowler exclaimed, recognising his compatriot.

'I'm OK, I'm OK. He only pushed past me. He ran that way,' the cardinal said, pointing at a metal door that was distinct from the wooden ones to the rooms.

'Stay here with him, *padre*.'

'Don't worry, I'm OK. Just catch that man,' said the cardinal.

'Go back to your room and close the door,' Fowler told him.

The three rushed through the door at the end of the hallway and down the service stairs. The cramped space reeked of damp and a smell of rot seemed to seep from beneath the paint on the walls. The passageway was also badly lit.

Perfect for an ambush, Paola thought. Karosky already has Pontiero's gun. He could be waiting for us at any turn in the stairs, ready to blow off our heads before we even know about it.

In spite of this, they flew down the steps as quickly as they could, tripping up more than once. They followed the stairs to the basement, one level below the street. The door there was closed with a heavy lock.

'He couldn't have got out this way.'

They started back up again. Noises were coming from the first floor. They opened the door and walked directly into the kitchen. Dante walked ahead of Paola, his finger on the trigger, the barrel of his gun pointing straight ahead. Three nuns were rummaging about among the frying pans. They froze in their tracks, staring at the police officers, their eyes like saucers.

'Did anyone come through here?' Paola shouted at them.

The nuns didn't answer. They simply stared with a bovine look on their faces. One of them ignored Paola completely and began slicing green beans and tossing them into a cooking pot.

'Did anyone come through here? A friar!' Paola repeated.

The nuns shrugged their shoulders.

Fowler put his hand on Paola's arm. 'Let them be. They don't speak Italian.'

Dante walked all the way through the kitchen until he came upon a very solid looking metal door six feet across. He tried to open it, but with no success. He looked at one of the nuns and gestured to the door, holding up his Vatican ID. She came over and slipped a key into a concealed lock. The door made a buzzing noise as it opened on to a side street off the Piazza Santa Marta. The Palace of Saint Charles was directly in front of them.

'Shit! Didn't the nun say there was only one exit in and out of the Domus?'

'Well, see for yourself. There are two,' said Dante.

'Let's retrace our steps.'

They ran back up the emergency stairs, from the vestibule to the top floor. There they found that the stairway led to the roof. But at the top, the door was bolted and barred.

'No one escaped through here.'

Out of breath, they sat down in the dirt and dust of the narrow passageway, their lungs pumping like bellows.

'Do you think he's hiding in one of the rooms?' Fowler asked.

'I don't think so. I'm fairly sure he slipped away,' said Dante.

'But how?'

'Probably through the kitchen, when the nuns weren't looking. There's no other explanation. The other doors have locks or they're guarded like the front entrance. Impossible to exit by the windows: it would be too risky. Agents of the Vigilanza make their rounds every few minutes. And it's the middle of the day, for crying out loud.'

Paola was furious. If she hadn't been so out of breath after running up and down the flights of stairs, she would have been banging the wall with her fists.

'I need your help, Dante. Get them to cordon off the piazza.'

Dante shook his head emphatically. His forehead was soaked with dark beads of sweat that rained down on to his leather jacket, and his hair, usually so well combed, was a mess.

'How do you want me to call them, my dearest? Nothing works in this fucking building. There are no cameras in the hallways, and telephones, mobiles, walkie-talkies – nothing works here. Nothing more complex than a light bulb, nothing that requires waves or zeros and ones in order to function. Let's hire a carrier pigeon – how about that?'

'And by the time it gets there, he'll be far away. No one is going to notice one more friar in the Vatican, Dicanti,' said Fowler.

'Can someone please explain to me how that fucker got out of this building then? It has three floors, the windows are locked and we had to break down the damn door. All the entrances to the building are guarded or locked,' Dicanti said, banging on the door to the roof again and again. It answered her with a loud echo and a cloud of dust.

'We were so close,' said Dante.

'Fuck, fuck, fuck, and fuck. We had him!'

It was Fowler who stated the terrible truth, and his words reverberated in Paola's ears like a shovel scraping against stone: 'What we have now, Dicanti, is another dead body.'

Domus Sanctae Marthae

Thursday, 7 April 2005, 5.15 p.m.

'We have to take care of our business discreetly,' said Dante.

Paola was livid. If she had had Cirin himself in front of her at that moment, she wouldn't have been able to control herself. She found herself thinking that this was the third time she'd wanted to knock the bastard's front teeth out, just to see if he'd still maintain his calm air and that monotone voice.

After they'd run into the obstacle at the top of the stairs, they'd turned round and gone back down again, all of them crestfallen. Dante had to walk over to the other side of the piazza to get his phone to work, and he spoke with Cirin about reinforcements and requested an analysis of the crime scene. Cirin's response was that he could only allow access to one investigator from the UACV, and that this person had to be wearing plain clothes. Whatever equipment they needed had to be brought in an ordinary suitcase.

'We can't allow this to go any further. You understand, Dicanti?'

'I don't understand any of this bullshit. We're trying to capture a killer. We must empty the building, find out how he got in, collect evidence ...'

Dante looked at her as if she'd gone mad. Fowler shook his head, not wanting to interfere. Paola knew she was letting the case slip through an unguarded part of her soul, poisoning her sense of well-being. She tried to be as rational as she could, since she knew her own sensitivities well. When something got under her skin, dedication often turned into obsession. At that instant she felt her anger corroding her spirit like a drop of acid falling every few seconds on to a slab of raw meat.

They stood in the third-floor hallway, the same hallway where everything had happened. Room 56 was empty. Its occupant, the man who had told them to look in Room 57, was the Belgian Cardinal Petfried Haneels, 73 years old. He was very much affected by what had happened. The building's doctor was tending to him on the floor above, where he would be staying for the time being.

'Luckily, most of the cardinals were in the chapel, participating in afternoon meditations. Only five heard the shouts, and they've already been told that a mentally ill person somehow managed to get in and went about screaming through the hallways,' said Dante.

'And that's it? That's your damage limitation?' Paola was breathing fire. 'To make sure that none of the cardinals realise that one of their own has been killed?'

'That's easy. We'll say that he was indisposed and was taken to Gemelli with gastroenteritis.'

'And with that everything's been resolved,' Dicanti replied with venom.

'Well, there's one more thing. You can't speak to any of the cardinals without my authorisation, and the crime scene has been limited to Room 57.'

'You can't be serious. We have to look for fingerprints in the doorway, the points of access, in the hallways. You can't really mean that.'

'Just what do you want, bambina? – a whole set of squad cars? thousands of cameras flashing away? Bellowing it to the four winds is a sure way to catch your degenerate,' Dante said, as arrogantly as he could. 'Or are you only looking to wave your degree from the FBI in front of the cameras? If you're so good at what you do, why don't you prove it.'

Paola refused to let him provoke her. Dante completely supported the theory that gave priority to secrecy above all else. She had to choose: either to lose time banging her head against a two-thousand-year-old granite wall, or to give in and try to move as quickly as possible to maximise the few resources at her disposal.

'Call Cirin. Tell him to have Troi send his best investigator.

And put his men on alert for a Carmelite monk in or around the Vatican.'

Fowler cleared his throat to get Paola's attention. He took her aside and spoke to her in a quiet voice, his mouth close to her ear. Paola couldn't help it: his closeness gave her goose bumps, and she was glad that she had worn a jacket, so no one else would notice. She still remembered his strong, unwavering hold on her the day before, when she had thrown herself into the crowd like a madwoman and he had held her back. His good sense had anchored her. She wanted him to hold her again, but in the situation they were in her longing was completely out of place. Things were complicated enough already.

'Those orders will already have been given and I'm sure they are being carried out as we speak. Forget about standard police procedure, because in the Vatican that's never going to happen. We'll have to play with the cards we've been dealt, however weak they may be.' Then his tone changed. 'All of this puts me in mind of something we say in the US: "In the country of the blind, the one-eyed man is king."'

'We have a Roman version of that one. You're right: I shouldn't have argued … and for the first time in this case we have a witness. At least that's something.'

Fowler lowered his voice even further. 'Talk to Dante. Be diplomatic for once. Tell him to let us have a free hand in speaking to Casey. Maybe we can get a description.'

'But without a forensic artist—'

'That comes later. If Cardinal Casey saw him, we should be able to come up with a portrait, a quick sketch of the killer. The most important thing is to have access to his testimony.'

'His name rings a bell. Is Casey the cardinal who appears in the report on Karosky?'

'The same. He's tough and intelligent. Let's hope he can help us with the description. But don't mention the name of our suspect. Let's see if he recognised him.'

Paola went back to join Dante.

'What, are you two love birds already done trading secrets?'

Dicanti decided to ignore the running commentary. 'Fowler has advised me to remain calm, and I think I'm going to follow his advice.'

Dante looked at her with distrust, thrown off balance by her attitude. He had no idea what to make of this woman. 'Very wise of you, ispettore.'

'"*Noi abbiamo dato nella croce.*" Right, Dante? "We've run smack into the Church."'

'That's one way of looking at it. Another way would be to say that you've been invited into a country that isn't your own. This morning we did things your way. Now we'll do it ours. It's nothing personal.'

Paola took a deep breath. 'Fine. I need to speak with Cardinal Casey.'

'He's in his room, recovering from his ordeal. Denied.'

'Dante – do the right thing, for once. If you do, maybe we'll catch our killer.'

The policeman stretched his thick neck, first to the left and then to the right. A few of his bones made a creaking noise. He was thinking things over.

'OK. But with one condition.'

'Which is …?'

'You say the magic words.'

'Go to hell.'

Paola turned around, only to walk straight into Fowler's disapproving glare. He had been following the conversation from a short way off. She spun back around to face Dante.

'Please.'

'Please what?'

The fat pig was enjoying her humiliation. All right then, here it was. 'Please, Superintendent Dante, may I have your permission to speak to Cardinal Casey?'

Dante broke into a smile. She had passed with flying colours. Then he suddenly turned serious. 'Five minutes, five questions. No more. I can play at this too, Dicanti.'

Two members of the Vigilanza, both wearing black suit and tie, exited the lift and took up positions on each side of the door to Room 57, inside which lay the body of Karosky's latest victim. They would guard the entrance until the specialist from the UACV arrived. Dicanti decided to make use of the down time to interview her witness then and there.

'Which one is Casey's room?'

It was on the same floor. Dante led them to Room 42, the room next to the door leading to the service stairs. He knocked softly.

Sister Helena opened the door. She wasn't smiling now but, on seeing who it was, a look of relief appeared on her face. 'Ah, at least you're all right. I heard that they chased the lunatic downstairs. Were they able to catch him?'

'Sadly, no, sister,' Paola answered her. 'We believe he escaped through the kitchen.'

'Oh Lord! Through the delivery door? Blessed Virgin of the Olives, what a disaster.'

'Sister, didn't you tell us that there was only one entrance?'

'There is only one entrance: the main door at the front. That one's not an entrance; it's just for delivery trucks to pull up to. It's a heavy door, with a special lock.'

Paola was beginning to realise that sister Helena wasn't speaking the same Italian as everyone else. She took her nouns very much to heart.

'The kill— I mean the assailant, could have got in through there, though,' Paola said.

The nun shook her head. 'The only two people with a key are the head of the kitchen and myself. And she only speaks Polish, as do many of the sisters who work here.'

Dicanti deduced that the head of the kitchen must have been the woman who opened the door for Dante. Only two copies of the key. The mystery deepened.

'May we come in to see the cardinal?'

Sister Helena shook her head energetically. No, again.

'Impossible. He is – how do you say – *zdenerwowany*. In a nervous state.'

'Just be for a moment,' said Dante.

The nun's face took on an even more serious look. '*Zaden*. No, and no again.'

It seemed that she preferred to take refuge in her native tongue when replying in the negative. The door was already half-closed when Fowler stuck his foot in the jamb, preventing her from closing it all the way. And then he spoke, a little hesitantly, chewing his words. '*Sprawiać przyjemność, potrzebujemy żeby widzieć kardynalny Casey, siostra Helena.*'

The nun's eyes widened in surprise. '*Wasz język polski nie jest dobry.*'

'I know. I ought to visit your beautiful country more often. Haven't been there since the early days of Solidarity.'

The nun shook her head and wrinkled her brow, but it was clear that Fowler had gained her confidence. She reluctantly opened the door and moved out of the way.

'How do you know Polish?' Paola whispered as they were going in.

'I only know a few phrases. Travel broadens the mind, as the saying goes.'

Paola glanced admiringly at Fowler before giving her attention to the man stretched out on the bed. The room was dark, the blinds nearly all the way down. Cardinal Casey lay there with a handkerchief – or perhaps it was a wet towel – across his forehead; there was so little light it was hard to tell. When they drew close to the foot of the bed, the cardinal propped himself up on one elbow and sighed. The towel slid off his forehead. He was a heavy set man with sharp features. His hair was completely white and was matted into a clump where the towel had soaked it.

'Forgive me, I …'

Dante bent over to kiss the cardinal's ring but the cardinal stopped him.

'No, please. Not now.'

The Vatican officer took a step back, a little unnerved. He had to clear his throat before continuing.

'Cardinal Casey, we apologise for the intrusion, but we need to ask you a few questions. Do you feel well enough to respond?'

'Certainly, my children. I was just resting a moment. What a terrible thing to be assaulted here, in this holy place. And the fact is, I have a meeting about several important issues in just a few minutes. So please be brief.'

Dante looked at Sister Helena and then at Casey. The cardinal understood: no witnesses.

'Sister Helena, please tell Cardinal Pauljic that I am running a bit late. If you would be so kind.'

The nun exited the room, grumbling unpleasant words on her way out – certainly things that were inappropriate for a nun.

'Can you tell us what happened?' asked Dante.

'I had gone up to my room for my breviary when I heard a terrible scream. For a second I was frozen in my tracks; I suppose I was trying to figure out if it was all just a product of my imagination. I thought I heard the sound of people racing up the stairway, and then a crash. I went out to the hallway, very much alarmed. In the doorway of the lift was a Carmelite friar. He was trying to hide in the small recess there. I looked at him and he looked at me too. At that instant there was another crash and the Carmelite attacked me. I fell to the ground and cried out. You know the rest.'

'Did you get a good look at his face?' Paola broke in.

'It was almost completely covered by a thick beard. I don't remember anything specific.'

'Could you describe his face and his complexion?'

'I don't think so: I only saw him for a second and my eyesight isn't what it used to be. All the same, I do remember that his hair was a greyish white. I knew right away that he wasn't a real friar.'

'What made you think that, Your Eminence?' Fowler inquired.

'The way he was acting, of course. Standing there pressed up against the lift door, he didn't look much like a servant of God. Absolutely not.'

Sister Helena came back into the room, clearing her throat nervously. 'Cardinal Casey, Cardinal Pauljic says that as soon as it's convenient the commission is waiting for you to begin organising the novendial masses. I've set up the meeting room on the first floor for you.'

'Thank you, sister. Go ahead with Antun, because I am going to need a few things. Tell him that I will join you there in five minutes.'

Dante took that to mean that their meeting with Casey was over. 'Thank you for everything, Your Eminence. We must leave you now.'

'You don't know how sorry I am. The novena masses will be celebrated in churches all over Rome and in thousands of others throughout the world they will be praying for the soul of our Holy Father. It's an immense undertaking and I am not going to step back from it just because somebody pushed me.'

Paola was about to say something, but Fowler discreetly pinched her elbow and she swallowed her question. She too said goodbye to the cardinal, but, just as they were leaving his room, the cardinal asked them a very compromising question.

'Does this man have anything to do with the disappearances?'

Dante turned around very slowly to respond to the cardinal's query, ladling thick syrup on to every syllable. 'Absolutely not, Your Eminence. It's nothing more than a provocateur. Probably one of those young people caught up in the anti-globalisation movement. They frequently dress up to attract more attention, as you know.'

The cardinal sat up a little more, until he was almost upright on the bed. He directed his words to the nun.

'There's a rumour doing the rounds among some of my brother cardinals that two of the most eminent figures of the Curia are not going to participate in the Conclave. I hope that both of them are OK.'

'Where did you hear this, Your Eminence?'

Paola was surprised. In her lifetime she had heard only one voice that was as smooth, as sweet and as humble as the one Dante employed in his question to the cardinal.

'Ah, my child, at my age one forgets many things – like who whispered what to you over coffee and dessert. But I can assure you that I am not the only one who knows it.'

'Your Eminence, it is most assuredly only a baseless rumour. Now, if you will forgive us, we must continue looking for this agitator.'

'I hope you find him quickly. Too many disturbances have taken place in the Vatican already; perhaps it is time for a change of direction in our security policy.'

Casey's veiled threat, as well concealed under a sugary glaze as was Dante's question, did not pass unnoticed. It froze the blood in Paola's veins, even though she detested every member of the Vigilanza she'd met.

Sister Helena left the room with the others and continued down the hallway ahead of them. A heavy-set cardinal was waiting for her by the stairway – it must have been Pauljic – and the two of them walked down to the next floor together.

As soon as Paola saw Sister Helena's back disappear, she turned to face Dante, a sardonic look on her face. 'It seems your damage control isn't working quite as well as you thought.'

'I swear to you I don't understand it.' Dante had a weary expression. 'At least we can hope they don't know the real reason. But still, it doesn't seem possible. As things stand, even Casey could be the next man to wear the red sandals.'

'At the very least, the cardinals know that something strange is going on. In all sincerity, nothing would make me happier than if the whole bloody mess blew up in your face so we could just do our job the way it should be done.'

Dante was about to tear into her when someone came up the marble stairway. Carlo Troi had decided to send the one man he considered the best and most discreet of UACV's personnel.

'Good afternoon, everyone.'

'Good afternoon, Director Troi.'

The time had come to take a close look at Karosky's latest piece of theatre.

ℱBI 𝒜CADEMY

22 *August 1999*

'Come in, come in. I suppose you know who I am, yes?'

For Paola, meeting Robert Weber made her feel the same way an Egyptologist would have felt if Rameses II had invited them to tea. She walked into the conference room, where the famous criminologist was handing out grades to the four students who had taken the course. He had been retired for ten years, but his firm footsteps still inspired a reverential respect in the hallways of the FBI. He was the man who had revolutionised forensic science by creating a new method of tracking down criminals: the psychological profile. In the highly selective course that the FBI offered, whose purpose was to develop new talent in various parts of the world, he was always in charge of giving student assessments. He made a tremendous impression on students, who were honoured to sit face to face with someone they greatly admired.

'Of course I know you, sir. I have to tell you—'

'Yes, I know already. It's an honour to know me. Blah blah blah. If I had a dollar for every time I heard that phrase, I'd be a rich man.'

The criminologist's nose was buried in a heavy file. Paola stuck a hand in her trouser pocket and took out a crumpled note, which she handed to Weber.

'It's an honour to meet you.'

Weber looked at the note and started to laugh. It was a one-dollar bill. Weber smoothed it out and put it into his coat pocket.

'Don't crumple the bills, Ms Dicanti. They're property of the United States Treasury.' But he smiled, pleased by the young woman's quickwitted response.

'I'll remember that, sir.'

Weber's face became serious, strict. It was the moment of truth, and every word that followed was like a hammer blow to his young student.

'You're weak, Ms Dicanti. You only just scraped by in the physical tests and target practice. You have no character. You fall apart too quickly. You give in right away. You put up roadblocks against adversity all too easily.'

Paola was shocked. That a living legend has managed to knock the stuffing out of you in less than a minute is a very difficult thing to accept. It's even worse when his hard-nosed tone reveals that he lacks even the faintest sympathy for you.

'You don't reason. That's OK, but you've got to make use of what you have inside. And to do that, you've got to invent. Make things up, Ms Dicanti. Don't follow the manuals to the letter. Improvise, and you'll see. And be more diplomatic. Here are your final evaluations. Open them after you leave the room.'

Paola took the envelope from Weber with trembling hands and opened the door, grateful to get out of there.

'One more thing, Ms Dicanti. What's the serial killer's real motive?'

'His hunger to kill, which he cannot control.'

The old criminologist shook his head. 'You'll find out what it is when you get to the place where you ought to be. You're not there yet. You're thinking just like the books again, young lady. Can you fathom the torment that makes a person commit murder?'

'No, sir.'

'Sometimes you have to forget all about psychiatric treatises. The true motive is the body. If you want to know the artist, analyse his work. The first thing you do when you enter a crime scene is get inside his head.'

Dicanti ran back to her apartment and threw herself into the bathtub. When she had summoned sufficient peace of mind, she opened the envelope. It took her a little while to comprehend what she read.

She had received the highest score possible on all parts of the coursework. And a valuable lesson, too: nothing is what it seems.

Domus Sanctae Marthae

PIAZZA SANTA MARTA, 1

Thursday, 7 April 2005, 5.49 p.m.

It was just over an hour since the killer had escaped, but Paola could still feel his presence in the room, like someone inhaling fumes, metallic and invisible. When she was speaking to other people about serial killers she was always utterly rational. That was easy – voicing her opinions from a comfortable, carpeted office. And that is where she spent most of her time.

It was a different thing altogether to walk into a room, taking care not to step in the blood on the floor. Not just to avoid contaminating the crime scene: her principal motive for not stomping in carelessly was that the damned blood would ruin a good pair of shoes for ever. And the soul with it.

It had been nearly three years since Director Troi had personally performed the work at a crime scene. Paola suspected he was coming to a degree of involvement where he needed to score points with the Vatican authorities. He really had nothing to gain with his Italian superiors, especially as the whole damn business had to be kept under wraps.

He walked in first, followed by Paola. The others remained behind in the hallway, staring into space and ill at ease. Dicanti heard Dante and Fowler exchange a few words – more than a few of them, she thought, and not exactly civil in tone – but she made every effort to keep her attention focused on what was inside the room and not what she had left outside.

Paola stood by the door, letting Troi go through his routine. First the forensic photographs: one from each corner of the room, from above the body, from every possible side and, finally, one of every element the investigator might consider relevant. When all was said and done, more than seventy bursts of light illuminated the scene in sudden, intermittent flashes that lent the place a blanched, unreal quality.

She took a deep breath, and tried to ignore the smell of blood and the aftertaste it left on your tongue. She closed her eyes and counted from one hundred back to one in her head, very slowly, trying to match the rhythm of the decreasing numbers to the beating of her heart. The frantic gallop at one hundred slowed to a smooth trot by fifty and an easy, steady walk by the time she got to zero.

She opened her eyes.

Cardinal Geraldo Cardoso, 71 years old, was stretched out on the bed. Cardoso was tied to the ornamental headboard with two tightly knotted towels. His cardinal's cap, still on his head, was tipped to one side, giving him a perversely comical look.

Paola recited Weber's mantra slowly: 'If you want to know the artist, analyse his work.' She repeated it to herself over and over, moving her lips silently until the words had lost all meaning, engraving themselves in her mind as if she were dipping a seal into ink and stamping it on a piece of paper again and again until all the ink was gone.

'Let's get started,' Paola said in a loud voice. She took a tape recorder out of her bag.

Troi didn't bother to look at her. He was busy collecting evidence and studying the shape of the various pools of blood.

The criminologist began to dictate into her tape recorder in exactly the manner she had been taught at Quantico: make an observation and an immediate deduction. The results of her conclusions would more or less resemble a reconstruction of how events had unfolded.

OBSERVATION: The deceased's body is tied at the hands in his own room, no signs of violence to furniture or other objects.
INFERENCE: Karosky used some kind of subterfuge to gain access to the room, and then quickly and silently restrained the victim.

OBSERVATION: A blood-soaked towel on the floor. Looks crumpled.

INFERENCE: Karosky likely put the towel in the victim's mouth to stop him from shouting out, and then removed it so that he could continue with his modus operandi: cutting out the tongue.

OBSERVATION: We heard a cry of alarm.

INFERENCE: What most likely happened is that, once the towel was removed, Cardoso found a way to scream. Therefore the tongue is almost the last thing that Karosky cuts, before moving on to the eyes.

OBSERVATION: The victim still possesses both eyes, his tongue is cut into strips. The cutting looks as if it was done under pressure; there is blood all round it. Victim's hands are still in place.

INFERENCE: Karosky's modus operandi begins with the torture of the body, followed by the ritual dissection. Cut out the tongue, pull out the eyes, cut off the hands.

Paola opened the door of the room and asked Fowler to join her for a moment. The priest's face recoiled when he saw the macabre spectacle, but he didn't turn away. The criminologist rewound the tape on her recorder and they listened to the last point together.

'Do you think there is anything special in the order he chooses?'

'I don't know. The ability to speak is the most important thing for a priest: he administers the sacraments with his voice. The eyes have no overwhelming importance in a priest's ministry, since they don't participate in any critical manner in the fulfilment of his duties. But the hands do fulfil a crucial role: a priest's hands are sacred, always, no matter what he is doing with them.'

'What do you mean?'

'Even a monster like Karosky – his hands are still sacred. His capacity to administer the sacraments is the same as the holiest, purest priest. Doesn't make sense, but it's true.'

Paola shuddered. The idea that someone so degraded could be in direct contact with God struck her as repugnant, terrible. She tried to remind herself that this was one of the reasons why she had rejected God's existence, imagining Him to be an unbearable tyrant in a cotton-soft heaven. Yet thinking more deeply about the horror, the depravity of those who, like Karosky, were supposed to be doing His work, produced a very different effect in her. She felt the same betrayal He must have felt and for a few seconds put herself in His position. More than ever she missed Maurizio, mourning that he wasn't there to give some meaning to this wretched insanity.

'Good Lord.'

Fowler shrugged his shoulders, not knowing what to say. He walked out of the room again and Paola turned the tape recorder back on.

OBSERVATION: The victim is wearing a full-length robe, completely open. Underneath, a cotton undershirt and boxer shorts. The undershirt has been torn, most likely with a sharpened instrument. There are a number of cuts on the chest that spell out the words *EGO TE ABSOLVO*.

INFERENCE: In this instance, Karosky's ritual began with torturing the body, then continued with the mutilation. Cut out the tongue, pull out the eyes, cut off the hands. The words *EGO TE ABSOLVO* were also found at the Portini crime scene – according to the photographs Dante gave us – and at Robayra's. The variation in this case is unusual.

OBSERVATION: There are bloodstains everywhere, splashes of blood on the walls. A partial footprint stamped on the floor, next to the bed. Looks like blood.

INFERENCE: Everything at this crime scene is very strange. No way to deduce whether his style has changed or he's adapted himself to a new environment. His modus operandi is anarchic, and –

Dicanti pushed the stop button on the recorder. There was something that didn't fit, something terribly wrong.

'How's it going, boss?'

'From bad to worse. I've taken prints from the door, from the night table, from the headboard of the bed, but there's not much else. There are plenty of partial prints but only one, I think, that might be Karosky's.'

He pressed a piece of plastic on to the headboard as he spoke, making a halfway decent print of an index finger. He then compared the transparency with the digital impression on the ID card that Karosky had had at the Saint Matthew.

'It's only a preliminary impression, but there are various similari-ties. At least I think there are. This ascendant line is characteristic enough, and this deltic ...' Troi said, more to himself than to Paola.

Paola knew that when Troi recognised a fingerprint as a match, that's what it was. He was famous – an expert in the field. Watching him at work, in his element, Dicanti deplored the slow ruination that had turned a forensic specialist into a bureaucrat.

'Nothing else, doctor?'

'Nothing else. No hairs, no fibres, nothing. This man really is a ghost. If they wore gloves, I'd say Cardoso was killed by a spirit.'

'There's nothing spiritual about that severed trachea.'

Troi looked at the cadaver uneasily, perhaps reflecting on the words of his subordinate or extracting his own conclusions.

'No, not much. That's true.'

Paola left Troi to complete his work. But she knew that he wasn't going to come up with anything. Karosky had been thoroughly prepared and, in spite of the pressure, he hadn't left anything be-hind. A disturbing suspicion kept niggling away at the back of her mind. She looked around. Camilo Cirin had arrived, accompanied by another man who was small and terribly skinny, almost fragile in appearance, and who seemed to have a very sharp way of look-ing at people. Cirin walked up to Paola and introduced Magistrate Gianluigi Varone, Vatican City's only judge. As far as Paola was concerned, he didn't seem very pleasant: he looked like a skinny, yellow vulture in a jacket.

The judge signed a form allowing for the removal of the body – something that would be carried out with complete secrecy. The two agents of the Vigilanza who had been standing guard at the door had changed clothes. They were wearing black overalls now, and latex gloves. They would take care of cleaning and sealing the room after Troi and his team had left. Fowler was seated on a small bench at the other end of the hallway, calmly reading his breviary. When Paola managed to extricate herself from Cirin and the magis-trate, she went over to the priest and sat down next to him. Fowler couldn't avoid a sense of déjà vu.

'Very well, Dicanti. Now you know a few more cardinals up close and personal.'

Paola smiled, saddened. So many things had changed since the two of them had waited together outside the chamberlain's office. And yet they weren't even a step closer to capturing Karosky.

'I thought that macabre jokes were Dante's territory.'

'Well, they are. I'm just visiting.'

Paola opened her mouth but closed it again. She wanted to talk to Fowler about something that was disturbing her in terms of Karosky's ritual, but she still couldn't put her finger on what it was that was bothering her so much. She decided to wait until she'd had more time to give it serious thought.

As Paola would have occasion to confirm later on – and bitterly so – that decision was a terrible mistake.

Domus Sanctae Marthae

Thursday, 7 April 2005, 4.31 p.m.

Dante and Paola stepped into Troi's car, which was sitting outside Saint Martha's. He was going to drop them off at the morgue before heading on to the UACV offices, to work on determining the weapon of choice in each of the murder scenes. Fowler had just opened the door to the car when he heard someone calling his name.

'Father Fowler!'

The priest turned round. It was Cardinal Casey who was waving him over. Fowler retraced his steps.

'Your Eminence, I hope you feel better now.'

The cardinal forced a smile. 'We have no choice but to accept the trials the Lord sends us. My dear Fowler, I wanted to take the opportunity to thank you personally for your timely rescue.'

'Your Eminence, you were already safe by the time we arrived.'

'Who knows? Who knows what might have happened if that lunatic decided to pay me another visit? You have my whole-hearted appreciation. I will personally see to it that the Curia learns of your actions.'

'It really isn't necessary, Your Eminence.'

'My son, you never know when you are going to need a favour, or when troubles may beset you. It's important to have money in the bank, as they say.'

Fowler looked him, inscrutable.

'Of course,' Casey went on, 'the Curia's gratitude could go even further. It is possible that we may request your presence here at the Vatican. Camilo Cirin seems to be losing his lustre. Perhaps someone who could ensure that this scandal is utterly erased could fill his shoes. Someone who can make sure it all just disappears.'

Fowler was beginning to catch his drift. 'Your Eminence, are you asking me to see to it that a certain dossier is lost?'

The cardinal smiled and shrugged his shoulders in a childish gesture that was completely incongruous, given the subject under discussion. He was close to getting what he wanted, or so he thought.

'Precisely, my son: "A dead body revenges not injuries."'

Fowler smiled maliciously. 'Well, well. A quotation from Blake. I never thought I'd hear a cardinal reciting the Proverbs of Hell!'

Casey stiffened and his voice became more abrupt. He didn't care for the priest's tone. 'The ways of the Lord are mysterious.'

'The ways of the Lord are contrary to those of the Adversary, Your Eminence. I learned that in school as a child, and it hasn't lost its validity.'

'A surgeon's tools will sometimes be stained with blood. And you are a very sharp scalpel, my son. Let's just say that I am aware that you represent more than one interest in this case.'

'I'm a humble priest – nothing more,' said Fowler, attempting to look stunned.

'I don't doubt it. But in certain circles they speak of your ... abilities.'

'And in those circles do they not also speak of my problem with authority, Your Eminence?'

'Yes, that too. But I don't doubt that, when the moment comes, you'll behave as you ought. You won't let the good name of the Church be dragged through the press, my son.'

The priest responded with a cold, hostile silence. The cardinal gave him a few paternal slaps on the shoulder, and then lowered his voice to a whisper. 'In times like these, who doesn't have a secret or two? Who knows? – your name might turn up on other pieces of paper. For example, in the summons of the Sant'Uffizio. Once again.' And without another word, the Cardinal turned and walked back into Saint Martha's.

Fowler got into the car where his friends were waiting for him. The motor was running.

'Are you all right, *padre*?' Dicanti asked, '– you look upset.'

'I'm perfectly fine.'

Paola studied him closely. It was a patent lie: Fowler was as white as a sheet. He looked as if he'd aged ten years in the space of a minute.

'What did Cardinal Casey want?'

Fowler gave Paola an unconvincing smile, which only made things worse. 'His Eminence? Nothing. He merely sent his regards to a mutual friend.'

Municipal Morgue

'I'm getting used to throwing open the doors for you in the middle of the night, Dicanti.'

Paola's response was a compromise between courtesy and shock. Fowler, Dante and the coroner stood to one side of the autopsy table, while Dicanti faced them from the other. All four donned the mortuary's blue masks and latex gloves. Finding herself there for the third time in so few days made her remember something she had read when she was young, something about being sent back to Hell, and about how that consisted in doing the same thing over and over again. Maybe Hell wasn't directly stretched out in front of her, but she was getting a close look at the proof of its existence.

On the autopsy table Cardoso's body looked even more horrific than it had earlier. Just a few hours before, his body had been awash with blood; now it resembled a pale doll festooned with ugly, raw scars. The cardinal was on the svelte side and, drained of blood, his face seemed like a mask – sunken and accusatory.

'What do we know about him, Dante?' asked Dicanti.

The superintendent carried a small notebook in his jacket pocket at all times. He took it out and began reading. 'Geraldo Claudio Cardoso, born 1934, cardinal since 2001. Well known as a defender of the working class, always on the side of the poor and the homeless. Before being named cardinal, he established his reputation in the diocese of San José. The largest factories in Latin America are found in that region, and Cardoso frequently acted as an intermediary between the workers and the owners. The workers loved him, called him the "union bishop". He was a member of various congregations in the Roman Curia.'

This time even the coroner was quiet. He had cut up Robayra with a smile on his face, mocked Pontiero's inability to stomach the sight of blood. A few hours later the man he had made fun of had been stretched out on his table. And the following day, another cardinal – a man who, on paper at least, had done a great deal of good in the world. He asked himself if the official version and the unofficial were in agreement, but it was Fowler who finally put the question to Dante.

'Is there anything more besides the press clippings?'

'Don't make the mistake, Fowler, of thinking that everyone in Our Holy Mother Church leads a double life.'

'I'll try to remember that.' Fowler's face was implacable. 'And now, how about answering my question?'

Dante pretended to think, stretching his neck again, first left then right. Paola was sure he already knew the answer or at least was ready for the question.

'I made a few calls. Almost everyone confirms the official story. He had two unimportant run-ins, but nothing of note. Played around with marijuana as a young man, before he became a priest. Dubious political affiliations at university, and that's it. Since he became a cardinal he's had a few confrontations with colleagues in the Curia, owing to his defence of a group the Curia doesn't care for: the Charismatics. The big picture is that he was a decent man.'

'As were the other two,' Fowler said.

'So it seems.'

'Anything new on the murder weapon, doctor?' Paola managed to get a word in edgewise.

The coroner pointed to the victim's neck and the cuts on his chest. 'A short, smooth blade, probably a small kitchen knife, but very sharp. In the previous cases, I reserved my opinion, but now that I've seen the moulds of the incisions, I believe he used the same instrument on all three occasions.'

Paola made a mental note.

'Dicanti,' asked Fowler, 'what do you think the chances are that Karosky will try something during John Paul's funeral?'

'Christ, I don't know. No doubt the security around Saint Martha's has been reinforced by now.'

'Of course it has,' Dante crowed. 'They're locked up so tight, they can't even tell if it's daytime without looking at a clock.'

'Though the security had already been stepped up, and that didn't help us much. Karosky has shown us his ability to adapt and his unbelievable sangfroid. Truthfully, I don't have the slightest idea. I don't know if he's going to try something then, although I doubt it. In this last incident, he wasn't able to complete his ritual or leave us a message written in blood, as he did on the first two occasions.'

'Which means we've lost another clue,' Fowler grumbled.

'Yes, but at the same time, it should make him feel nervous and even a little vulnerable. Though with a son of a bitch like this, you never know.'

'We'll have to pay close attention to protecting the cardinals,' said Dante.

'Not only protecting them, but looking for him. Even if he doesn't try anything, he'll be there, watching us and laughing. I'd stake my neck on that.'

Saint Peter's Square

VATICAN CITY

Friday, 8 April 2005, 10.15 a.m.

John Paul II's funeral took place with tedious normality. Everything was as ordinary as it could be at the funeral of the religious leader of more than a billion people that was attended by royalty and some of the world's most powerful heads of state. But they were not the only ones who took part. Hundreds of thousands of people flowed in and around Saint Peter's Square, and every face told a story that burned behind its eyes like flames in a fireplace.

One of those faces belonged to Andrea Otero. She couldn't see Robayra anywhere, but the journalist did notice three things as she stood on the rooftop terrace alongside colleagues from a German television team. One, that looking through binoculars for half an hour gives you a splitting headache. Two, that the backs of the necks of the assembled cardinals all looked alike. And three, that there were only one hundred and twelve red robes seated on those chairs. She counted them several times. And the printed list pressed against her knees clearly stated that there should have been one hundred and fifteen.

Camilo Cirin wouldn't have felt in the least bit comfortable if he had known what Andrea Otero was thinking, but he had his own problems to deal with. Victor Karosky, the serial killer who specialised in cardinals, was one of them. But while Karosky didn't cause Cirin any trouble during the funeral, an unidentified plane that invaded Vatican air space in the middle of the funeral did. The anguish that overwhelmed Cirin during those moments as he recalled the 11 September terrorist attacks was no less than that of the three pilots who set off after the plane. Luckily for everyone, the situation resolved itself within a few minutes, when it became clear that the pilot of the unidentified plane was a Macedonian who had simply flown off course. The episode stretched Cirin's nerves to the limit. A subordinate standing nearby later commented that it was the first time in fifteen years he had ever heard Cirin raise his voice to give orders.

Another of Cirin's subordinates, Fabio Dante, was mingling in the crowd. He cursed his luck as people pressed in close in order to see John Paul's casket as it was carried by, and many of them shouted, 'Santo subito!' – 'Sainthood now!' – right in his ears. Dante desperately tried to see over the tops of their heads and past the signs they were carrying; he kept searching for a Carmelite friar with a bushy beard. He didn't lead the celebrations when the funeral was finally over, but he was next in line.

Anthony Fowler was one of many priests giving communion to the assembled crowd, and more than once he thought he saw Karosky's face in that of the person who was about to receive the body of Christ from his hands. While hundreds of people filed up to him, Fowler prayed for two things: one concerned the reason he had come to Rome, and the other was that the All Powerful should give him the strength and illumination to face what he had found in the Eternal City.

Ignorant of the fact that Fowler was seeking the Creator's help, in large part because of her, Paola scrutinised the faces on the steps of Saint Peter's. She had taken up position in a corner of the square. She didn't pray; she never did. Nor did she give the people parading past her any special attention, because their faces very quickly blurred into one. She spent her time contemplating what motivated a monster.

Carlo Troi sat behind a desk full of television monitors with Angelo, the UACV's forensic sculptor. They were getting their feed directly from the RAI cameras in the square, before they went on the air. From this vantage point they staged their own hunt, for which they were rewarded with headaches almost as intense as Andrea Otero's. Of the 'engineer', as Angelo continued to call him, they saw not so much as a trace.

On the esplanade, the secret-service agents attached to George

Bush came to blows with agents of the Vigilanza when they were denied permission to enter Saint Peter's Square. For those familiar with the way the American secret service operates, if only through hearsay, what happened that day was remarkable. Nowhere before had they been denied entrance, yet the Vigilanza would not let them in. And no matter how much they insisted, outside they stayed.

Victor Karosky took part in John Paul's funeral, devoutly praying aloud. He sang with a beautiful, deep voice at the appropriate moments. He shed a sincere tear and made plans for the future.

No one paid any attention to him.

Vatican Press Room

Andrea Otero arrived at the press conference with her tongue hanging out. Not just on account of the heat, but because she had left her press card in the hotel and had had to yell at the dumbfounded taxi driver to make a U-turn in the middle of traffic to go back for it. Her carelessness wasn't disastrous, as she'd left an hour early. She had wanted to arrive ahead of time so she could have a word with the Vatican spokesman, Joaquin Balcells, about Cardinal Robayra's 'evaporation'. She'd tried to track him down earlier, but without success.

The press room was an annexe to the large auditorium built during John Paul II's papacy. Extremely modern, with room for more than six thousand, the latter was always filled to overflowing on Wednesdays, when the Holy Father gave his audiences. The door from the press room led directly on to the street, right next to the palace of the Sant'Uffizio.

The press room itself had room for 185 people. Andrea thought she'd get a good seat if she arrived fifteen minutes before the hour, but it was obvious that more than three hundred journalists had had the same thought. And it wasn't so surprising that the press room was filled to capacity: 3,042 accredited media outlets from ninety countries were there to cover the funeral and the Conclave. More than two billion human beings, half of them Catholic, had said farewell to the deceased Pope from the comfort of their living rooms that very morning. 'And here I am: me – Andrea Otero.' If only her professors at Journalism School could see her now.

Fine, she was at the press conference where they were going to explain how the Conclave worked, but she didn't have a seat. She leaned against the wall near the entrance. It was the only way in, so when Balcells arrived, she would be able to make contact.

She calmly went over her notes on the spokesman: a doctor who'd taken up journalism; a member of Opus Dei; born in Cartagena, Spain; according to all reports, deadly serious and something of a cold fish. He was nearly 70 years old, and from what an unofficial source had told her – a source who'd never failed her yet – he was one of the most powerful men in the Vatican. For years he'd heard news directly from John Paul's lips before passing it on to the wider public. If he decided that something was secret, secret it stayed. There were no leaks with Balcells. His CV was impressive. Andrea read the list of prizes and medals he had been awarded: Knight of this order, Prince of that, Member of the Holy Cross of something or other. His achievements took up two full pages, a different award on every line. He'd be a tough bone to gnaw on.

'But I have sharp teeth, damn it.'

She was trying to hear herself think over the increasing murmur of voices when the press room suddenly exploded. First one sounded – the initial raindrop that signals the downpour; then three or four. Finally, a great cacophony of ringing as dozens of mobile phones seemed to go off at the same time. The noise lasted some forty seconds. The journalists all grabbed their handsets and tilted their heads. Now and then a loud complaint was heard.

'OK, we're on hold. Fifteen minutes' delay, which leaves us exactly no time to edit the story.'

Andrea heard a voice speaking Spanish a few feet away from her. She elbowed her way over and saw that it was a woman journalist with brown skin and delicate features. Her accent led Andrea to believe she was from Mexico.

'Hello, I'm Andrea Otero, from *El Globo*. Listen, can you tell me why all the mobile phones started ringing at once?'

'It's a message from the Vatican Press Office. They send us an SMS whenever there's important news. It's the latest innovation, the hassle being the noise when we're all in the same place. The news that Balcells is going to be delayed is what just came in.'

Andrea was impressed. Getting information out to thousands of journalists couldn't be easy.

'Don't tell me you haven't signed up for the phone service?' The Mexican journalist was surprised.

'Well no, not yet. Nobody told me anything about it.'

'Don't worry. See that girl over there?'

'The blonde?'

'No, the one in the grey jacket, carrying the file. Go over to her and tell her you want to register for their phone service. In less than half an hour they'll have you on their database.'

Andrea went over to the woman and mumbled all the pertinent information in Italian. The girl asked her for her press card and typed her mobile phone number into a handheld device. 'This connects to the main data bank.' The young woman was proud of the technology but her smile was tired. 'In which language would you like to receive your communications from the Vatican?'

'Spanish.'

'Castilian Spanish or a variant?'

'Oh, just the everyday sort.'

'*Scusi?*' the woman responded haughtily.

'I'm sorry. Castilian, please.'

'In about fifty minutes you will be registered on the service. I just need you to sign this form, if you would be so kind, authorising us to send you the information.'

The journalist scrawled her name at the bottom of the page without looking at any of the small print. She then thanked the girl and said goodbye.

Otero went back to where she'd been standing and tried to read more about Balcells, but then a buzz went round the room that he was about to arrive. Andrea focused on the main door, but the spokesman had slipped in using a door hidden behind the stage. He calmly pretended to be organising his notes, which gave the cameramen a second to frame their shots and the journalists time to sit down.

Andrea cursed her luck and once again elbowed her way to the front, this time as far as the stage, where the Vatican spokesman stood behind a dais. It wasn't easy, but while everyone else was taking their seat, Andrea managed to get close to Balcells.

'Mr Balcells, I'm Andrea Otero from the paper *El Globo*. I've been trying to get in touch with you all week but—'

'Later.' The spokesman didn't even look at her.

'But, Mr Balcells, you don't understand. I need to verify some information—'

'Miss, I've already told you: later. OK, let's get started.'

Andrea was dumbstruck. He hadn't even looked at her once, which infuriated her. She was used to getting men to do what she wanted, usually with just a flash of her blue eyes.

'But, Mr Balcells, I represent an important Spanish newspaper ...' She was trying to gain traction by mentioning that she represented the Spanish media, but it didn't work. Balcells shot her an icy look.

'What did you say your name was?'

'Andrea Otero.'

'From which paper?'

'*El Globo*.'

'And where is Paloma?'

Paloma, the regular correspondent for Vatican assignments; the woman who had had the extremely unfortunate mishap of falling and breaking her leg, thereby giving Andrea her place. It wasn't a good sign that Balcells had asked after her – not good at all.

'She couldn't come; she had a problem ...'

Balcells furrowed his brow as only a lifelong member of Opus Dei could. Andrea was caught off guard and took a short step backwards.

'Young lady, please take a look at the people behind you, if you would,' Balcells said, gesturing to the packed rows of seats. 'These are your colleagues from CNN, the BBC, Reuters ... Some of them were already accredited journalists here at the Vatican before you were born. And all of them would like this press conference to get under way. Please do us all the favour of taking your seat, now.'

Andrea spun around, feeling ashamed and flustered. The journalists in the front row chuckled at her expense. A few of them did look almost as old as Bernini's damn colonnade. As she pushed her way to the back of the room, to the spot where she had left her bag and her laptop, she overheard Balcells joking in Italian with the ancient scribblers in the front row. Hollow guffaws echoed behind her back.

She had no doubt that the joke was on her. More people turned around to look at her, and Andrea went red right up to her ears. She felt as if she was swimming through an ocean of bodies as she made her way, her head down and her arms extended, through the narrow passage to the door. The woman who'd taken all her information walked over and put a hand on her arm.

'Just remember: if you go, you won't be able to come back in until after the press conference. The door is locked. That's how it works.'

'Like a theatre,' Andrea thought to herself. 'Just like a theatre.'

She slipped out of the woman's grasp and exited the press room. The door swung closed behind her, slamming in a way that did nothing to diminish her embarrassment.

She felt a little better now that she was outside. She desperately needed a smoke, so she rummaged through all her jacket pockets until her fingers found a packet of mints – her consolation in the absence of her old friend nicotine.

'What a fucking time to give up.'

She opened the mints and popped three into her mouth. They didn't really taste any better than vomit, but at least they kept her mouth busy. Even so, they didn't help much with the withdrawal.

Andrea Otero would recall this moment many times in the future. She would remember standing in that doorway, leaning against the stones framing the entrance; she would remember trying to calm herself down and cursing herself for having been so stupid, for having embarrassed herself like a child.

But none of this was the reason why she would remember it. She'd remember it on account of the terrible discovery that nearly cost her her life, and which finally put her in touch with the man who would change that life, whom she ran into thanks to the fact that she decided to wait for the mints to dissolve in her mouth before she hurried away – just so she could calm down a bit. How long does it take for a mint to dissolve? Not very long. For Andrea it seemed an eternity. Every inch of her body was begging to go back to the hotel and slide as far under the bedsheets as possible. Yet she forced herself to stay where she was, if only because she didn't want to watch herself flee through the streets like a beaten dog.

There was just a little bit left of one of the mints, a thin sliver perched on her tongue, when a messenger came barging around the corner. He was wearing a bright-orange boilersuit and a baseball cap, and had a large bag slung over his shoulder. He was in a hurry and walked right up to Andrea.

'Excuse me, but is this where they hold the press conferences?'

'It is.'

'I have an urgent package for the following: Michael Williams of CNN, Bertie Hegrend of RTL—'

Andrea interrupted him. She didn't want to listen to all those names. 'Don't kill yourself, buddy. The press conference has already started and you're going to have to wait at least an hour.'

The messenger looked at her, crestfallen. 'No way. They told me that—'

The journalist found a kind of malign satisfaction in taking her problems out on someone else. 'You understand. That's the way it works.'

The messenger rubbed his hand across his face. He really was desperate. 'You don't understand, signora. I've already missed a few deadlines this month. The urgent deliveries have to get to their destination within one hour, or we don't get paid. There are ten Manilla envelopes here at thirty euros each. If I'm late with this job, my agency's going to lose the Vatican route and I'll get kicked out on my backside – no doubt about that.'

Andrea softened. She was a decent person. Impulsive, thoughtless and capricious, yes, and at times she used lies – with a heavy dose of luck – to get what she wanted; but she was a good person. She read the messenger's name printed on the ID card hanging from a pocket of his suit. Another of Andrea's traits: she always called people by their names.

'Listen, Giuseppe, I'm sorry but you couldn't open that door even if you wanted to. It only opens from the inside. See for yourself. There's no lock and no door handle.'

The messenger grunted in despair. He put his hands on his hips either side of a prominent belly that was visible even through his work clothes: he was trying to think. He stared down at Andrea. She was sure he was stealing a look at her breasts – she'd gone through this disagreeable experience almost every day since puberty; but then she saw that his eyes were concentrating on the press badge dangling from her neck.

'Listen, I've got an idea. I'll leave the envelopes with you and we're done.'

Her badge had the Vatican shield on it and he must have thought she worked there.

'Look, Giuseppe—'

'Enough with the Giuseppe. Call me Beppo,' the messenger said, rooting around in his bag.

'Beppo, I really can't—'

'Look, please just do me this one favour. Don't worry about signing. I'll sign the delivery slips with a different squiggle on each line and that's it. You just have to promise you'll deliver the envelopes as soon as they open the door.'

'It's just that—'

But Beppo had already handed her the ten envelopes in question. 'Each one has the name of the journalist it's going to. The client was sure they'd all be here, so don't worry. OK, I'm off. I've just got one more delivery to make at the Corpo di Vigilanza, and another on Via Lamarmora. *Ciao bella*, and thank you.'

Before Andrea could say a word, this strange individual had turned on his heels and taken off. Andrea was left standing there, staring at the ten envelopes. She was a little confused. They were addressed to the ten most important media companies in the world. Andrea knew four of the journalists by reputation and had recognised at least two of them inside the press room.

The envelopes were half the size of a normal page and all of them were identical except for the addressee. The thing that awakened her journalist's instinct, and set alarm bells ringing, was the phrase that appeared on all of them. In the upper left corner, written by hand:

'EXCLUSIVE – OPEN IMMEDIATELY'.

Andrea's moral dilemma lasted all of five seconds. She resolved it with a new mint. She looked to the left and to the right. The street was deserted: no sign of any witnesses to possible postal fraud. She picked one of the envelopes at random and then opened it as carefully as she could.

'Simple curiosity.'

There were two items inside the envelope. One was a Blusensbrand DVD with the same phrase as on the envelope written in magic marker on the sleeve. The other was a note, written in English:

'*The content of this disk is of the utmost importance. It is likely to be the most important news of the year, perhaps of the century. Someone will try to cover it up. Watch this disk and disseminate its content as soon as possible. Father Victor Karosky*'.

Andrea acknowledged the possibility that it was a joke, but there was only one way to find out. She slipped her laptop out of her bag, turned it on and pushed in the disk. She cursed the operating system in every language she knew – Spanish, English and bad Italian – until it finally booted up. She saw that her DVD was a film.

Forty seconds into the film she was overwhelmed by the urgent need to vomit.

UACV Headquarters

Saturday, 9 April 2005, 1.05 a.m.

Paola had been looking everywhere for Fowler. Still, it was hardly a surprise when she found him in the basement, a pistol in his hand, his dark jacket neatly folded over a chair, his clergyman's collar hanging from a peg on the wall and his sleeves rolled up. He was wearing headphones to protect his hearing, so Paola waited for him to finish a round before walking up to him. His utter concentration fascinated her – the way his body assumed the firing position so completely. His hands were strong, in spite of the fact that he was 50 years old. The barrel of the gun pointed straight ahead without wavering so much as an inch.

She watched him empty not one, but three, rounds. He took his time firing, didn't hurry in the slightest, his eyes bearing down, his head tilted just so to the side. He finally noticed her presence in the training room, which consisted of five booths separated by heavy wood, from which the cables holding the targets extended. The targets could be set at a maximum distance of forty yards through a system of pulleys.

'Good evening, *dottoressa*.'

'Kind of a strange hour for target practice, isn't it?'

'I didn't want to go back to my hotel. I knew I wasn't going to get any sleep.'

Paola understood him perfectly. Being on their feet without doing anything throughout the funeral was bad enough, but the night was guaranteed to give them no rest. Paola was going crazy trying to think of something useful to do.

'Where's my beloved superintendent?'

'Oh, he got an urgent call. We were going over the report on Cardoso's autopsy when he ran out, leaving me right in the middle of a sentence.'

'How very like him.'

'Of course. But let's not talk about that. Let's see what the army taught you.'

Paola pressed the button to bring the paper target – the silhouette of a man outlined in black – closer to her. The crude image had a white circle in the centre of his chest. It took a while for the target to come back to them; Fowler had moved it as far away as possible. She wasn't in the least surprised to see that almost all the holes he'd made were inside the circle. What surprised her was that the last one had missed. She felt disappointed that he hadn't managed to get them all neatly inside the target, like the protagonists in action films.

But he's not an action hero, he's flesh and bone. Sharp-witted, cultured and a damn good shot. In some ways, the one shot he missed makes him more human, she thought to herself.

Fowler laughed when he saw the target, amused by his own failure. 'I'm a little out of practice, but I still like to shoot. It's an unusual sport.'

'As long as it remains a sport.'

'You still don't trust me?'

Paola didn't respond. She liked watching Fowler, without his collar, dressed only in his shirt with the sleeves rolled up and his black trousers. But the photos Dante had shown her of El Aguacate were still whirling round inside her head, splashing about like drunken monkeys in a bathtub.

'No, *padre*. Not completely. But I want to. Is that enough for you?'

'It will have to do.'

'Where did you get the gun? The depository is closed at this hour.'

'Troi lent me his. He told me he hadn't used it in a while.'

'Sadly enough, that's true. You should have seen him three years ago. A real pro, the best sort of analyst. He still is, but back then his eyes were full of curiosity. Now that look has gone and all that's left is the anxiety of a paper-pusher.'

'Is that bitterness or nostalgia in your voice, *dottoressa*?'

'A little of both.'

'Did it take you long to get over him?'

Paola acted as if she didn't know what he was talking about. 'What did you say?'

'Forget it. I didn't mean to offend you. I've seen the way he creates walls of solid air between the two of you. Troi is an expert at keeping his distance.'

'Unfortunately it's something he does very well.'

Dicanti hesitated a moment before she went on. She felt that emptiness in the pit of her stomach again that looking at Fowler sometimes gave her – the feeling that she was on top of a Ferris wheel. Should she trust him? She thought, with a sad, fleeting irony, that when all was said and done he was a priest, and he was accustomed to seeing people at their worst. As was she.

'Troi and I had an affair. It was brief. I don't know if he stopped liking me or if his mania about being promoted got the upper hand.'

'But you prefer the second choice.'

'I like to fool myself – in that and other things. I always say to myself that I live with my mother in order to protect her, but in reality I'm the one who needs protection. I suppose that's why I'm attracted to strong but unsuitable types – men I will never actually share my life with.'

Fowler didn't respond. She had made herself very clear. They were standing close, looking at each other. The minutes ticked by in silence.

Paola was absorbed in Fowler's green eyes, knowing his intimate thoughts. Somewhere in the background she thought she could hear a quiet hum, a persistent noise, but she ignored it.

It was Fowler who said, 'You'd better answer your phone.'

Paola realised it was her mobile that was ringing, and it was starting to increase in volume. She picked it up and for a second was furious. She hung up without saying goodbye.

'Let's go, *padre*. That was the laboratory. This afternoon someone sent us a package by messenger service. And it was supposedly sent in Maurizio's name.'

Uacv Headquarters

Saturday, 9 April 2005, 1:25 a.m.

'The envelope arrived almost four hours ago. Can anyone tell me why we didn't find out what was in it until now?'

Troi looked at her, patient but burned out. It was very late in the day to put up with a subordinate's nonsense. Nevertheless, he kept a tight grip on himself as he put the pistol that Fowler had borrowed back into its drawer.

'The envelope arrived with your name on it, Paola, and when it arrived you were at the morgue. The girl in reception put it in with my mail and I only saw it later. When I realised who had supposedly sent it, I set things in motion, but at this hour of the night that takes time. The first people I called were the bomb squad. Nothing suspicious in the envelope, as far as they were concerned. When I found out what was in there, I called both you and Dante. We haven't seen hide nor hair of him, and Cirin hasn't been answering his phone.'

'They'll be sleeping. It's the middle of the night.'

They were sitting in the fingerprint lab, a narrow space replete with lamps and bulbs. The smell of the powder used to recover prints was everywhere. There were technicians who claimed to love the smell – one even swore he sniffed it before going to see his girlfriend because it was an aphrodisiac – but Paola found it distinctly off-putting. The smell made her want to sneeze, and the dust stuck to her dark clothes and was hard to wash off.

'All right, do we know for sure that Karosky sent this message?'

Fowler was studying the script of the person who'd written the address. He held the envelope up, his arms slightly extended. Paola suspected he didn't see well close-up. He must need glasses when he reads fine print, she thought. She wondered how he would look with them on.

'This is his handwriting – that's certain. And the macabre joke of putting Pontiero's name as the sender – that's Karosky too.'

Paola took the envelope out of Fowler's hands, placing it on top of the large table that took up most of the space in the room: a sheet of glass for a surface, lit from below. Spread over the top of the table were the contents of the envelope, in transparent plastic bags.

Troi pointed at the first one. 'His fingerprints are on the note. Take a look at it, Dicanti.'

Paola lifted the plastic bag with the note written in Italian and gave it a closer look. Looking through the plastic, she read the message out loud.

Dear Paola,
    I miss you so much! I'm in MK 9, 48. It's warm here and it suits me fine. I hope you can come and say hello sometime soon. In the meantime, I've sent you a video of my vacation.
    Kisses,
    Maurizio

Paola recoiled from a mixture of anger and horror. She tried to hold back the tears, forcing them to stay inside; she wasn't going to cry in front of Troi. Maybe in front of Fowler, but not Troi. In front of him, never.

'Father Fowler?'

'Mark, chapter 9, verse 48 : "Where their worm dieth not and the fire is not quenched."'

'Hell.'

'Exactly.'

'Fucking bastard.'

'There's no mention of his having to flee the scene a few hours ago. It's possible that the note was written before that. The disk was cut yesterday morning, according to the dates on the files.'

'Do we know the model of the camera or computer with which it was recorded?'

'With the program he used, those details aren't on the disk. No series numbers, no codes – nothing that could help us identify the equipment he used.'

'Fingerprints?'

'Two partials, both Karosky's. But I didn't need them to know it was him. Seeing the contents would have been enough.'

'So what are you waiting for? Put the DVD in, Troi.'

'Father Fowler, could you excuse us a minute?'

The priest understood the situation instinctively. He looked Paola in the eye. She gestured to him slightly, telling him that everything was OK.

'Why not. Coffee for three, Dicanti?'

'Two spoonfuls of sugar in mine, please.'

Troi waited for Fowler to exit the room before taking Paola's hand in his. She flinched at the contact: his palms were too fleshy and moist. Yet how many times had she sighed, wanting those hands to touch her again? She'd hated their owner for his disdain and his indifference. Now there wasn't even a spark left from the fire that used to burn between them. It had been extinguished in a green ocean only a few minutes before. All she had left was her pride, and it was something she had in abundance. She definitely wasn't going to give in to his emotional blackmail. She withdrew her hand and Troi let his drop.

'Paola, I just want to warn you. What you are about to see is going to hit you very hard.'

Dicanti gave a hard, humourless smile and crossed her arms. She wanted to keep her hands as far away from him as possible. Just in case. 'I'm used to looking at dead bodies.'

'Not of your friends.'

The smile on Paola's lips trembled like a leaf in the wind, but her spirit didn't waver. 'Let's see the video, Troi.'

'Is this the way you want things to be? It could be very different.'

'I'm not a little doll you can treat any way you like. You rejected me because it was dangerous for your career. You preferred to return to your wife and the comfortable misery of your marriage. Well I prefer my own misery now, thank you very much.'

'Why now, Paola? Why now, after all this time?'

'Because before I wasn't strong enough. But now I am.'

Troi ran his fingers through his hair. He was getting the picture.

'You'll never be with him, Paola. Even if that's what he wanted.'

'You might be right. But it's my decision. You made yours some time ago. At this point, I'd rather give in to Dante's lechery.'

Troi was disgusted by the comparison. Paola relished seeing him look so uncomfortable; her angry outburst had penetrated her boss's ego. She'd been a little hard on him, but he deserved it for the many months he'd treated his conquest like a piece of shit.

'As you wish, Dottoressa Dicanti. I will go back to being the ironic boss, and you, the pretty novelist.'

'Believe me, Carlo. It's for the best.'

Troi's smile was sad and defeated. 'All right then. Let's see the disk.'

As if he had a sixth sense, Fowler came in with a tray of something that could have passed for coffee if given to someone who'd never tasted the real thing.

'Here you go: venom from the caffeine machine. May I presume that the meeting is about to get under way again?'

'It is indeed, *padre*,' Troi responded.

Fowler observed them closely, unobtrusively. Troi seemed the sadder of the two, but there was something in his voice. Relief? Paola was obviously stronger, less insecure.

The director pulled on a pair of latex gloves and removed the disk from its sleeve. Technicians from the laboratory had rolled a small table in from the conference room. Sitting on top were a 27-inch TV and a cheap DVD player. Troi wanted to watch the film in here because the walls in the conference room were glass, and anyone walking down the hallway could have got a good look at Karosky's film. By now, rumours about the case Troi and Dicanti were working on had circulated around the building, even though not one of them came close to the truth.

The disk began to play. The film started immediately, without titles or any preliminary material. The style was utterly crude; the camera was jumping about hysterically and the lighting was atrocious. Troi turned the brightness on the TV all the way up.

'Good evening, souls of this world.'

Paola cringed when she heard Karosky's voice, the same voice as had tormented her over the phone after Pontiero had been murdered. But the screen was still blank.

'This film depicts the process by which I am going to eliminate the holiest men in the Church from the face of the earth, fulfilling the work of the shadows. My name is Victor Karosky, a renegade priest of the Roman religion. Over the course of many years I abused children, protected by the stupidity and complicity of my former superiors. For these good deeds I have been chosen by Lucifer himself for the task, at exactly the moment in which our enemy the Carpenter selects his chosen one to rule on this ball of mud.'

The screen changed from complete darkness to a series of shadows. A man appeared, soaked in blood, his head hanging down on to his chest, tied up to what looked to be the columns in the crypt at Santa Maria de Traspontina. Dicanti barely recognised him as Cardinal Portini, the first victim – the one whose dead body she had never seen because the Vigilanza had cremated it. Portini uttered a few quiet groans. Karosky was only visible in the tip of a knife that poked the flesh of the cardinal's left arm.

'This is Cardinal Portini; he is too exhausted to protest. Portini did more than his share of good in the world, which is why my master detests his stinking flesh. Now you will see how I put an end to his miserable existence.'

The knife was pressed against the cardinal's throat. Karosky then slit it with a single cut. The screen went blank again, and then a new picture appeared, with a new victim tied up in the same place. It was Robayra, looking extremely afraid.

'This is Cardinal Robayra, quaking with fear. He carried a great light within him. It's time to return that light to its Creator.'

This time Paola had to look away. The camera showed the knife as it attacked Robayra's eye sockets. A single drop of blood splashed on to the camera lens. It was the most awful spectacle Dicanti had ever seen, and she felt as if her stomach was only one image away from heaving up everything she'd eaten. And then the film had a new subject, the one she'd feared the most.

'This is Detective Pontiero, one of the followers of the Fisherman. They put him on my trail but he was powerless against the Prince of Darkness. The detective is slowly beginning to bleed.'

Pontiero looked straight into the camera, but the face wasn't his. His teeth were clenched but the life in his eyes had not been extinguished. The knife slit his throat agonisingly slowly. Paola looked away.

'This is Cardinal Cardoso, friend to the disinherited of the world, the bedbugs and the parasites. His love was as repugnant to my Master as the stinking entrails of a goat. He too has died.'

There was something wrong. In place of the filmed images, they were looking at photographs of Cardinal Cardoso on his deathbed. Three photos in all, all of them a dull shade of green. The blood was unnaturally dark too. The three photos were on the screen for fifteen seconds, five seconds each.

'Now I am going to kill another saintly man, the most saintly of all. People will try to stop me, but they will end up in exactly the same position as those you have seen die before your very eyes. The cowardly Church has hidden it all from you, but it can no longer continue to do so. Good night, souls of this world.'

The DVD showed nothing more than static now so Troi switched it off. Paola had turned white. Fowler clenched his teeth, furious. The three of them sat there for a few minutes without saying a word. They had to gather their wits. Paola, the one most affected by the film, was nevertheless the first to speak.

'The photographs. Why photographs? Why not video?'

'Because he couldn't.' Fowler said. 'Video cameras don't work inside Saint Martha's, remember? "Nothing more complex than a light bulb" works in there, according to Dante.'

'And Karosky knew it.'

'What do you think of the little game about diabolic possession?'

Once again Dicanti had the feeling that something didn't fit. The video seemed to throw her in totally different directions. She needed a good night's sleep in a quiet place where she could think. Karosky's words, the clues left on the corpses – all of it had a connecting thread. When she found it, she would be able to unravel the ball. Until then, she was short on time.

Of course, my good night's sleep has just been blown to shit, she thought to herself.

'Karosky's crazed histrionics about the Devil aren't what's bothering me,' Troi interjected, anticipating Paola's thoughts. 'The most serious thing is that he's challenging us to stop him before he finishes off another cardinal. And time is passing us by.'

'What can we do?' Fowler asked. 'He didn't show any signs of life during John Paul's funeral. There's more security around the cardinals than ever before. Saint Martha's is sealed up tight, as is the Vatican.'

Dicanti bit her lip. She was tired of playing by some psychopath's rules – because now Karosky had committed a new error: he had left a trail that they could follow.

'Who brought this to our offices?'

'I've put two boys in charge of following the trail. It arrived by messenger service – Tevere Express: a local company that operates in the Vatican. We haven't managed to get hold of the person who's responsible for that route, but the cameras on the exterior of the building took a picture of him driving up on his bike. The licence plate is registered under the name of Giuseppe Bastina, 43 years old. He lives in Castro Pretorio, on Via Palestra. Number 31.'

'No phone?'

'Motor Vehicles has no number for him, and there's no listing in the Yellow Pages.'

'Maybe it's under his wife's name,' Fowler said.

'Maybe. But for now it's our best piece of evidence, which means we ought to take a walk. Coming, *padre*?'

'After you, *dottoressa*.'

BASTINA FAMILY RESIDENCE

VIA PALESTRA, 31

Saturday, 9 April 2005, 2.02 a.m.

'Giuseppe Bastina?'

'Yeah, that's me.' Giuseppe Bastina cut a curious figure, standing in the doorway in his underwear, a nine-month-old baby in his arms. At that hour of the morning it wasn't surprising that the doorbell had woken the kid up.

'I'm Inspector Paola Dicanti and this is Father Fowler. Don't worry, you're not in any trouble and nothing has happened to anyone in your family. We just want to ask you a few urgent questions.'

They were standing in the foyer of a modest but well-kept house. Someone had put out a doormat with a smiling frog, welcoming visitors to the house. Paola hazarded a guess that the welcome didn't extend to them, and she was right: Bastina was fairly annoyed by their presence.

'No way this can wait till the morning? The baby has to eat and sleep at certain times, and we're trying to keep her to a schedule.'

Paola shook her head. 'This will only take a moment. You made a delivery this afternoon, didn't you? An envelope. To Via Lamarmora?'

'I remember that. What do you think? I've an excellent memory,' Bastina said, touching the side of his forehead with his right index finger. His left arm was still full of baby, who had, for the moment at least, calmed down.

'Could you tell us where you picked up this envelope? It's very important; it's related to an investigation into a series of murders.'

'The client called the agency, just like always. They asked me to

209

swing by the Vatican post office, and said that I'd find some envelopes on the desk in the porter's office.'

Paola was taken aback. 'More than one envelope?'

'Yeah, there were twelve. The client asked us to deliver the first ten envelopes to the Vatican press room. Then one to the Corpo di Vigilanza, and the last one to you.'

'Nobody handed you the envelopes? You just picked them up?' Fowler was irritated by the man.

'At that time of day there isn't anybody at the post office. They leave the outside door open until nine, for anyone who wants to drop letters in the international box.'

'So how did they pay?'

'They left a small envelope on top of the others. The small one had three hundred and seventy euros in it, three-sixty for the express service and ten euros tip.'

Paola raised her eyes to the ceiling in despair. Karosky had thought of everything. Another fucking dead-end street.

'So you didn't see anybody?'

'Nobody.'

'And what did you do then?'

'What do you think I did? I made the run to the Press Room and then delivered the envelope to the Vigilanza.'

'Who was supposed to receive the envelopes at the Press Room?'

'They were addressed to different journalists. Foreigners.'

'And you handed them out to their recipients?'

'What's with all the questions? I take my job seriously. I hope all this isn't because I screwed up. I need the work, I really do, so please – my kid has to eat and my wife has another bun in the oven.'

'Look, this has nothing to do with you but it's no joke either. Tell us what happened and we're gone. If not, then I'll see to it that every traffic officer in Rome can recite your licence plate from memory. OK, Mr Bastina?'

Bastina was cornered. The baby started to wail, frightened by Paola's tone.

'All right. You don't need to talk like that; you've scared the baby. Don't you have a heart?'

Dicanti was very tired and irritable. She hadn't wanted to speak to the man like that, in his own house, but she just couldn't handle any more obstacles in the investigation. 'I'm sorry. So please, help us here. It's life or death at this point. Take my word for it.'

With his free hand the messenger scratched the stubble on his chin and he gently rocked the baby in his arms. Little by little the baby calmed down and stopped crying.

'I gave the envelopes to the lady in charge of the Press Room, OK? The doors to the room were already closed and to deliver them by hand I would have had to wait another hour. Special deliveries have to be taken care of within the hour following pick-up or you don't get paid. I've had a few problems on the job lately, you see? If anyone finds out I did this, I'll lose the job.'

'Nobody's going to find out from us, Mr Bastina – trust me.'

Bastina looked at her and nodded. 'I'll try to believe it.'

'Do you know the name of the woman in charge?'

'No. She was wearing an ID card with the Vatican coat of arms and a blue band on top. It said, "Press".'

Fowler stepped a few feet into the hallway with Paola and started whispering in her ear again. She tried to concentrate on his words and not on the way being close to him made her feel. It wasn't easy.

'The card this man is describing doesn't belong to someone who works for the Vatican. It's an ordinary press pass. The disks never reached their destinations. Do you know why?'

Paola tried to think like a journalist for a second. She pictured herself receiving an envelope while she was sitting in the middle of the press room, surrounded by all her rivals in the media.

'They never arrived at their destinations, because if they had, their contents would already be splashed over every newspaper and television in the world. If all of those envelopes had arrived at the same time, the journalists would have had everything they needed sitting right in their laps. They'd have corralled the Vatican spokesman there and then.'

'Definitely. Karosky tried to send a message of his own to the press but it backfired on him, thanks to the fact that this man was in such a hurry and someone obviously had no qualms about swiping the envelopes. Unless I'm wrong, this woman will have opened one of the envelopes and then taken all of them. Why should she share this great piece of luck that fell into her lap?'

'Right now, somewhere in Rome, that woman is typing out the story of the century.'

'And we've got to find out who she is. As soon as possible.'

Paola took the urgency in Fowler's words to heart. They turned around and walked back to Bastina, who was still standing in the doorway.

'Mr Bastina, tell us about the person who took the envelopes.'

'Sure. She was a pretty girl with blonde hair down to her shoulders, twenty-something. Blue eyes. A light-coloured jacket, beige trousers.'

'I can see you've got a good memory.'

'For the good-looking girls.' Bastina was a child of the streets and he was slightly offended, as if they'd questioned his worth. 'I'm from Milan originally, ispettore. It's a good thing my wife is in bed right now. If she heard me talking like this … There's a just a month to go before the next baby is born, and the doctor says she's got to take it easy.'

'Do you remember anything else that could help us to identify the young girl?'

'Yeah. She was Spanish, I'm certain of it. My sister's husband is Spanish, and you can always pick them out, trying to imitate the Italian accent. You get the picture.'

Paola got the picture. She also knew it was time to take off.

'We're sorry we bothered you.'

'Don't worry about it. The only thing I don't like is answering the same questions twice.'

Paola spun around. She went on red alert, and had to restrain herself from yelling at the man. 'Somebody's already asked you these questions? Who? What did they look like?'

The baby was crying again.

'Get lost, both of you! You're upsetting my kid!'

'Tell us and we'll leave,' said Fowler, trying to calm everyone down.

'It was one of your colleagues. He flashed the Corpo di Vigilanza badge at me. At least he had some identification. A short guy, thick shoulders. Leather jacket. Left here an hour ago, OK? Now get out and don't come back.'

Dicanti and Fowler looked at each other nervously. They sped towards the lift, trying to make sense of this new revelation.

'You thinking what I'm thinking?'

'Exactly. Dante disappeared about eight o'clock this evening, with some lame excuse.'

'After getting a call.'

'Because over at Vigilanza they'd already opened the package. And what they saw disturbed them. Why didn't we put two and two together before? Fuck, the Vatican takes a record of every vehicle that goes in and out of the city. Standard procedure. And if Tevere Express works with them on a regular basis, it's clear that they'd be able to pinpoint all of the employees, including Bastina, by his licence plate.'

'They followed the trail of the envelopes.'

'If the journalists had opened their packages at the same time, in the Press Room, a few of them would have slipped the disk into their laptops and the place would have exploded. There'd have been no way for anybody to contain it. Ten well-known journalists ...'

'But this way just one journalist gets the scoop.'

'Exactly.'

'One is a manageable number.'

Stories flashed through Paola's mind – a whole raft of them, the kind that officers on the street passed quietly among themselves, usually when they were hitting the third round at a bar: dark tales of disappearances and accidents.

'You think it's possible they ...'

'I don't know. Anything's possible. It would depend on the journalist's flexibility.'

'*Padre*, do you have to keep dancing around the subject? What you're saying to me is: they'll pay her off if she hands over the disk.'

Fowler didn't say a word. His silence was eloquent.

'Well, then, we'd better get there first, for her own good.' Paola gestured to him to get in the car. 'We've got to get back to the UACV as soon as possible. Let's start by looking in the hotels, check the airline companies.'

'No, *dottoressa*, there's somewhere else we need to go.' And he handed her an address.

'That's on the other side of town. What's—'

'A friend. He can help us out.'

An Apartment Somewhere in Rome

Saturday, 9 April 2005, 2.48 a.m.

Paola drove towards the address Fowler had given her without knowing exactly where she was headed. It was a long row of apartments and they waited outside while Fowler's finger pressed insistently on the buzzer.

'So this friend of yours … How exactly do you know him?'

'Let's just say it was the last mission I did for my old employer. The kid was fourteen years old back then, a real rebel. Since then I've been something of a – how shall I say? – spiritual guide to him. We've never fallen out of touch.'

'And now, does he work for your *business, padre*?'

'*Dottoressa*, if you stop asking me tricky questions, I can stop telling you plausible lies.'

Five minutes later Fowler's young friend finally got up to let them in. He turned out to be another priest, and a young one at that. He led them into a small studio apartment full of cheap furniture. It was very clean. There were two windows, both with the blinds lowered all the way down. On one side of the room was a table some six feet long, with five hard drives and five flat screens sitting on top. Under the table, dozens of lights flickered manically, like an out-of-control forest of Christmas trees. On the other side of the room was an unmade bed. It was clear that its occupant had only got up a few minutes before.

'Albert, I want to introduce you to Doctor Paola Dicanti. We're working on something together.'

'Father Albert,' said Paola.

'Please, just Albert.' The young curate's smile was pleasant, very nearly a grin. 'Sorry about the mess. Anthony, what the hell are you doing here at this hour of the morning? I don't feel like playing chess right now. And you could have told me you were coming to Rome. I heard you were back in action last week, but I would have preferred to hear it from you.'

'Albert was ordained last year,' Fowler told Dicanti. 'He's an impulsive kid, but he's also a wizard with computers. And I'm sure he'll do us a favour.'

'What kind of mess have you got into this time, you old lunatic?'

'Albert, please. Try to show a little respect. There are ladies present,' Fowler said, pretending to be offended. 'We want you to supply us with a list.'

'What sort of list?'

'The list of every accredited reporter working at the Vatican.'

Albert looked serious. 'Not so easy to do.'

'Come on, Albert. You're in and out of the Pentagon's computers the way some guys go to the bathroom.'

'Baseless rumours,' Albert said, but his smile betrayed him. 'Even if it were true, you can't compare the two. The Vatican's information system is like Mordor – it's impregnable.'

'Then let's get going, *Frodo26*. I'm sure you've already been there before.'

'Ssssh. Don't say my handle out loud, ever.'

'Sorry.'

The young priest became serious. He scratched his chin, then turned around to face Fowler. 'Is it really vital? You know I'm not authorised to do this, Anthony. It goes against all the rules.'

Paola resisted the temptation to ask who exactly gave permission for something like this.

'Someone's life is in danger, Albert. And we've never exactly been men who play by the rules.' Fowler shot Paola a look that said, *Help me out here.*

'Could you give us a hand, Albert? You've managed to get in before?'

'Yes, Dottoressa Dicanti, I've been there before – once; but I didn't get very far. And I swear I've never been so scared shitless in my whole life. Excuse the language.'

'Relax. I've heard the phrase before. What happened?'

'They caught me trespassing, which automatically activated a program that sent two guard dogs nipping at my heels.'

'What do you mean? Remember, you're talking to someone who doesn't have a clue about computers.'

Albert lit up. He loved talking about his job. 'There are two hidden servers which are just waiting for someone to slip past their defences. The moment I entered, they sent the cavalry out to find me. One of the servers went all out to locate my home base, while the other started to put clips on me.'

'Clips?'

'Imagine you're on a trail that crosses a gully. Your route is a series of rocks that surface above the water. What the computer does is to delete the rock I'm about to put my foot on and put spurious information in its place.'

The young man pulled over a chair and a small side table for his guests to sit on. Clearly he didn't have visitors very often. He then took a seat in front of the computer.

'Like a virus?'

'A very powerful one. If I had taken just one more step, its lines of code would have erased my hard drive and I would have been completely in his hands. It's the only time I've ever used the panic button.' The young priest pointed to a harmless-looking red button that sat to one side of the largest monitor. The button had a cable that descended into the thickets of wire below.

'What is it?'

'It cuts the electricity to the whole floor of this building. Ten minutes later, the power comes back on.'

Paola asked him why he had to cut the power for everyone on his floor, and not just unplug the computer from the socket. But Albert wasn't listening: his gaze was directed at the monitor, while his fingers flew over the keyboard.

Fowler answered for him. 'Information is transmitted in seconds. The time Albert loses in getting to his knees and unplugging the machine could be crucial.'

Paola half understood what the men were talking about, but she wasn't that interested. What did matter to her at that moment was finding the young Spanish journalist, and if this was how they did it, then so much the better. The two priests had obviously been in situations like this before.

'What's he going to do now?'

'He'll pull up a screen. I don't know exactly how he does it but he routes his computer through hundreds of others, in a sequence that eventually ends up in the Vatican network. The more complex and more widely spread the camouflage, the longer it will take them to find him, but there is a buffer zone that should never be crossed. Each computer only knows the name of the computer before it, the one that asked permission to connect. And it only knows that name while the connection lasts. In that way, if the connection is interrupted before they get to him, they won't be able to find him.'

The rhythmic clicking of the keyboard went on for about a quarter of an hour. Every minute or so a small red dot appeared on a map of the world that filled one of the monitors. There were hundreds of dots, covering the greater part of Europe, the north of Africa, the USA, Canada and Japan. Paola noticed that there was a greater density of red dots in the wealthier countries, and only one or two in Africa, with a dozen or so in Latin America.

'Each one of the points you see on that monitor corresponds to a computer Albert is going to connect to, in sequence, in order to penetrate the Vatican's system. It could be the computer of a young man working at a university; it could be one in a bank or law firm. It could be in Beijing, Austria or Manhattan. The more extensive the geographical nexus, the more efficient the sequence.'

'How does he know that one of those computers won't accidentally be turned off, interrupting the entire process?'

'I keep records on each computer.' Albert's voice was distant and he didn't stop typing. 'I try to use computers that usually aren't turned off. These days, with all the programs for file-sharing, many people leave their computers on day and night, downloading music or porn. That type of computer system is ideal for use as a link in the chain. One of my favourites is —' He mentioned a well-known figure in European politics. 'The old fart likes pictures of young girls with horses. Every once in a while I substitute them with a photo of some golfers. The Lord forbids that kind of perversion.'

'Aren't you afraid you're merely substituting one kind of sin for another?'

The young man laughed at Fowler's joke without taking his eyes off the instructions and commands his hands were bringing to life on the monitor. Finally, he took a breather.

'We're almost there. But let me warn you: we can't copy anything. I'm using a system in which one of the computers is doing the work for me, but it erases the information copied to this computer as soon as a certain number of kilobytes have been used up. So you'd better have good memories. From the moment they detect us, we have sixty seconds.'

Fowler and Dicanti nodded.

'There it is. We're in.'

'Go to the Press Office, Albert,' said Fowler.

'We're there.'

'Hunt around for a list of accredited journalists.'

Barely two miles away, in the basement of a Vatican building, Archangel, one of the Vatican's security computers, sprang into action. One of the many routines it performed automatically had detected the presence of an external agent in its system. It immediately activated its location program. The first computer activated another, this one named Saint Michael. Both were Cray supercomputers, able to undertake billions of operations per second, and valued at well over 200,000 euros apiece. Both began to run through their calculation cycles, searching for the intruder.

An alert appeared on the main monitor. Albert pursed his lips.

'Shit. Here they come. We've got less than a minute. I can't find a list of accredited press.'

Paola tensed. She watched as the red dots on the map of the world started to go out, one by one. To begin with, there had been several hundred, but now they were disappearing at an alarming rate.

'Press passes.'

'Nothing. Fuck. Forty seconds.'

'Media?' Paola suggested.

'We've got it. Here's a file. Thirty seconds.'

A list appeared on the screen. A database.

'Shit, it has more than three thousand entries.'

'Arrange it by nationality and pull up Spain.'

'There. Twenty seconds.'

'Damn it, there aren't any photographs. How many names are there?'

'More than fifty. Fifteen seconds.'

There were only thirty red dots left on the map of the world.

'Eliminate the men and arrange the women by age.'

'Done. Ten seconds.'

Paola's hands were balled into fists. Albert took one hand off the keyboard and placed it on top of the panic button. Large drops of sweat fell from his brow as he typed with one hand.

'Here you are! At last! Five seconds, Anthony!'

Fowler and Dicanti memorised the names on the screen as fast as they could. They still hadn't finished when Albert hit the panic button. The screen and the whole apartment went pitch black.

'Albert,' Fowler said in the depths of the darkness.

'Yes, Anthony?'

'You don't by any chance have candles, do you?'

'You ought to know I never use analogue systems, Anthony.'

Hotel Raphael

Saturday, 9 April 2005, 3.17 a.m.

Andrea Otero was very, very frightened.

'No, sir, I'm not afraid, I am fucking terrified.'

The first thing she had done when she got to the hotel was to buy three packets of cigarettes. The first shot of nicotine had been a blessing. Now that she was on to the second packet, the contours of reality had begun to stabilise. She felt a slightly comforting dizziness, something like a lullaby.

She was sitting on the floor of the room, her back against the wall, her arms clutching her legs while she smoked non-stop. Her laptop computer was on the other side of the room. It was turned off.

Considering the circumstances, she had acted correctly. Once she'd seen the first forty seconds of Victor Karosky's film – if that was his real name – she'd been ready to throw up. Andrea had never been the kind of person who could hold things back, so she'd looked for the nearest bin and then coughed up macaroni and cheese, her breakfast croissant and probably yesterday's dinner as well. She asked herself if it was a sacrilege to vomit into a bin belonging to the Vatican.

When the world had finally stopped spinning around her, she'd walked back to the Press Room door thinking that she had made such an awful racket that somebody would certainly have heard her. No doubt, by now, two Swiss Guards were on their way to arrest her for postal fraud, or whatever it was they called opening an envelope that obviously hadn't been addressed to you – because none of these envelopes was.

'OK, officer, so I thought it might be a bomb, and I acted as bravely as I could. I'll wait here while you go for my medal.'

That wouldn't be very believable. Decidedly unbelievable. But the journalist didn't need an explanation for her captors because they never came. Andrea collected her things and left the Vatican as calmly as she could, giving a flirtatious smile to the Swiss Guards at the Arch of the Bells, the entrance journalists used, and then crossed Saint Peter's Square, which was finally clear of people after so many days. She stopped feeling the Swiss Guards' eyes clamped on her when she got out of the taxi at her hotel. She stopped believing that they were following her about half an hour after that.

And no, no one had followed her and no one suspected a thing. In the Piazza Navona she had thrown the nine unopened envelopes into a bin. Better to have only one bit of evidence on her. Back at the hotel she'd gone directly to her room, though she did make a stop at a kiosk to buy some nicotine.

When she felt sufficiently at ease – after inspecting the pot of dried flowers in her room for the third time without finding any hidden microphones – she loaded the disk into her laptop and tried to watch the film again.

The first time, she managed to last sixty seconds. The second, she watched almost the entire thing. She made it all the way through the third time, but had to race to the bathroom. The fourth time, she managed to stay calm enough to convince herself that it was very real, that it wasn't a tape of something like *The Blair Witch Project*.

Andrea was a very intelligent journalist, which was both her great advantage and her major downfall. Her intuition had already told her from the very first viewing that the film was genuine. Perhaps some other journalist would have dismissed the disk almost immediately, thinking that it was a fake. But Andrea had spent days looking for Cardinal Robayra, and she suspected that other cardinals were missing as well. Hearing his name on the film dispelled any remaining doubts she had in an instant.

She'd watched the film a fifth time, just to get used to the images. And then a sixth time, to take notes – barely more than a few disconnected squiggles. She'd shut down her laptop, sat as far away from it as possible in a sliver of space between the desk and the air-conditioning unit. And then she'd surrendered to the lure of nicotine.

'Definitely a bad time to give up smoking.'

Those images were a nightmare. At first, the disgust they had filled her with, the dirty way they had made her feel, was so intense that she was unable to react for a couple of hours. When the shock finally wore off and she was able to think, she began to take stock of what she had on her hands. She took out her notebook and wrote down three points which would serve as the basis for her article.

1. A satanic killer is murdering cardinals in the Catholic Church.
2. The Catholic Church, most likely in collaboration with the Italian police, is keeping this hidden from us.
3. The Conclave, where those cardinals would have played a key role, is taking place within the next nine days.

She typed in a nine and then replaced it with an eight: it was now very early on Saturday morning.

She had to compose an impressive piece of reporting. A full report, three pages long, with summaries, quotes, sidebars and a killer headline. She wouldn't send any images to the newspaper beforehand, because she knew they'd take her off the story without a second's delay. The editor would no doubt drag Paloma out of her hospital bed so that the article would have the weight it deserved. Maybe they would let her have a byline on one of the sidebars. But if she sent the completed story to the paper, laid out and ready to send to the printers, then not even the editor-in-chief would have the gall to take her name off it. It wouldn't happen, because if it did, Andrea would also send a fax to the *Nation* and another to the *ABC* with the complete text and photographs for the article before it was published. And to hell with the exclusive – and her job, for that matter.

'As my brother Michael would say, "Either we all get a fuck, or we'll dump the whore in the river."'

It wasn't exactly a simile appropriate for a young lady like Andrea Otero, but nobody butted in to insist that she was a young lady. It wasn't proper for young ladies to steal other people's correspondence as she had done, but she'd be damned if it mattered to her. She could already see herself writing the bestseller *I Caught the Cardinal*

Killer. Hundreds of thousands of books with her name on the cover, interviews all over the world, conferences held about her work. Shameless robbery had definitely been worth the trouble.

'Though, of course, sometimes you have to be careful who you rob.'

Because the film hadn't been sent by the senior executives of a newspaper. It had been sent by a heartless killer who was probably counting the hours until his message would be broadcast all over the world.

She considered her options. Today was Saturday. Certainly whoever had sent the DVD wouldn't find out that it hadn't reached its destination until the following morning. If the messenger service was open on Saturday, which she doubted, they'd be on her trail within a few hours, perhaps by ten or eleven. But she doubted that the messenger had read the name on her press badge – he'd seemed more preoccupied by what lay inside her shirt. Best-case scenario: if the service didn't open until Monday, she had two days. Worst case: she had a few hours.

It was true that Andrea had learned that the most sensible thing to do was always to act as if the worst case was the most likely. So she would put the story together right away. As soon as the editor-in-chief and the newspaper's director in Madrid sent the article to press, she'd have to dye her hair, hide behind her sunglasses, and fly out of the hotel like a bee.

She got to her feet, told herself to be strong. She switched on the laptop and opened the newspaper's paste-up program. She started writing straight into the template. She felt much better when she saw how her words would look in the text.

It took her three-quarters of an hour to prepare the three-page mock up. She was almost finished when her mobile phone rang.

'Who the hell is calling me at three in the morning?'

Only the newspaper had that number; she hadn't given it to anyone else, not even to her family. So it had to be someone from Editorial with an emergency. She got up and searched around in her bag until she found it. She looked at the screen, expecting to see the long display of numbers that appeared when there was a call from Spain, but what she saw instead was a blank. The screen didn't even say 'Caller Unknown'.

She took the call anyway. 'Hello?'

The only reply was an engaged signal.

She hung up.

'Must have been a wrong number.'

But something inside told her that the call was important, and she'd better hurry up. She went back to the keyboard, writing faster than ever. The errors she let stand – she'd always been good at spelling – and never went back to correct them. They could do that at the newspaper. She was suddenly in a tremendous rush to finish.

It took her four hours to complete the rest of the article – hours spent searching for profiles and photos of the cardinals, biographies, snippets of information and, of course, writing about their deaths. The article included several images she'd taken directly from Karosky's video, some of them so shocking they made her blush. What the hell. Let Editorial censor them if they wanted to.

She was right in the middle of the closing lines when there was a knock at the door.

ℋOTEL ℛAPHAEL

LARGO FEBO, 2

Saturday, 9 April 2005, 7.58 a.m.

Andrea looked at the door as if she'd never seen one before in her life. She took the DVD out of her computer and jammed it back into its plastic slipcover before burying it inside the waste-paper basket in the bathroom. She walked back to her room, her heart balled like a fist, wishing that whoever it was on the other side of the door would just go away. But the knocks continued, courteous but insistent. It couldn't be housekeeping. It was barely eight in the morning.

'Who is it?'

'Signorina Otero? It's breakfast, courtesy of the hotel.'

Andrea opened the door. She was surprised. 'I didn't order any—'

The man on the other side of the door didn't let her finish her sentence. There wasn't the slightest chance he was one of the hotel's elegant porters or waiters. Short and stocky but clearly fit, he wore a leather jacket and black trousers, and he hadn't shaved for a day or so. He was sporting a broad smile.

'Miss Otero? I'm Fabio Dante, superintendent of the Vatican Corpo di Vigilanza. I'd like to ask you a few questions.'

In his left hand he held an ID card. Andrea looked at the photo intently. It appeared to be authentic.

'As you can see, I'm very tired and I need to get some rest. Please come back later.'

She tried to shut the door abruptly, but the man had his foot wedged in the gap like an encyclopedia salesman with a large family to support. Andrea was forced to remain where she was.

'Didn't you understand me? I need to get some sleep.'

'It seems that you are the one who doesn't understand me. I need to speak with you urgently. I'm investigating a robbery.'

'Oh Christ,' she thought to herself. 'How did they find me so quickly?'

There wasn't a twitch on Andrea's face, but inside, her nervous system switched from 'alarm' to 'total crisis'. She'd have to bluff her way out. Her nails digging into her palms, she opened the door wide so the superintendent could enter.

'I can't give you much time. I have to send an article to my paper.'

'A little early to be sending an article, wouldn't you say? The printers won't even have shown up for work yet.'

'Right, but I like to have time to spare.'

'Are we talking about a special story, perhaps?' Dante asked, taking a step in the direction of Andrea's laptop. She stood in front of him, blocking his way.

'No, nothing special. Just the usual conjectures about who's going to be the next Supreme Pontiff.'

'Of course. A question of great importance, no?'

'Of great importance. But there's not much in the way of news at the moment. You know how it goes: the usual human-interest stories. Not much else.'

'And we'd like it to stay that way, Signorina Otero.'

'Except, of course, for this robbery you were talking about. What exactly was stolen?'

'Nothing extraordinary. Just a few envelopes.'

'What's in them? Must be something very valuable. The cardinals' payroll?'

'What makes you think the contents were valuable?'

'Well, why else would they put their best sniffer dog on the trail? Maybe it's a collection of Vatican stamps. I've heard that collectors would kill to get their hands on them.'

'Actually, it wasn't stamps. Mind if I smoke?'

'You ought to take up mints.'

The superintendent breathed in the air around him. 'Advice which you don't seem to be following yourself.'

'It's been a long night. Smoke, if you can find an empty ashtray.'

Dante lit up a cigarette and exhaled. 'As I was telling you, Miss

Otero, the envelopes don't contain stamps. It's a matter of some extremely confidential information that mustn't fall into the wrong hands.'

'For example ...?'

'I don't follow. For example what?'

'Whose hands would be the wrong ones?'

'Someone who has no idea what's good for them.'

Dante looked around in vain for an empty ashtray. He resolved the question by flicking the ash on to the floor.

Andrea swallowed hard: if what he'd just said wasn't a threat, she was a nun in a convent.

'And what kind of information is it?'

'The confidential kind.'

'Valuable?'

'It could be. I expect that when I find the person who took the envelopes, it will be someone who knows how to negotiate.'

'You're prepared to offer money for it?'

'No. I'm prepared to let the person keep their own teeth.'

Dante's words didn't frighten Andrea, but his tone did. He spoke with a smile and used the same tone as he would have done to order a decaffeinated coffee. And that was dangerous. Andrea was suddenly very sorry she'd let him into the room. She had one card left.

'Fine, it's been interesting talking to you, but now I'll have to ask you to leave. My boyfriend is due back any minute and he's the jealous kind.'

Dante burst out laughing. Not Andrea, though – not at all: Dante had drawn his gun and was aiming it at her chest.

'Game's over, pretty one. There's no boyfriend. Give me the disks, or we'll get a look at the state of your lungs.'

Andrea glared at the pistol. 'You're not going to shoot me. We're in a hotel. The police would be here in thirty seconds, and then you'd never find what you're looking for, whatever it is.'

Dante wavered for a few seconds. 'You know what? – you're right. I'm not going to fire.'

He landed a left hook with terrible force. Andrea saw coloured lights and a solid wall in front of her. It took her some time before she realised the punch had knocked her legs out from under her and she was staring at the ceiling.

'I won't take much more of your time, Miss Otero. Just enough for me to get what I need.'

Dante walked over to the computer. He pushed the letters on the keyboard until the screensaver disappeared and Andrea's article materialised in its place.

'First prize!'

She staggered to her feet, one hand massaging her left eyebrow. The bastard had split it and now blood was pouring out all over the place. She couldn't see a thing out of that eye.

'I don't get it. How did you find me?'

'Signorina, you gave us the authorisation yourself when you handed over the number of your mobile phone and signed the waiver.'

Dante took two objects out of his jacket pocket as he was speaking: a screwdriver and a small, shiny, metal cylinder. He shut down the laptop, turned it over and used the screwdriver to get into the hard drive. He passed the cylinder over the drive several times, at which point Andrea worked out what it was: a powerful magnet that would completely erase the article and all the information stored in her hard drive.

'If you had read the small print of the form you signed, you would have noted that one of its provisions authorises us to locate your mobile phone by satellite, "in case of danger to your personal security" – a clause put there should a terrorist infiltrate the press, but one which has turned out to be very useful in your case too. Just be happy it was me you met up with, and not Karosky.'

'Oh yes, I'm jumping for joy.'

Andrea kneeled down again. With her right hand she felt around for the heavy crystal ashtray that she had been planning to take home as a souvenir from the hotel. It was sitting on the floor next to the wall, where she'd sat smoking like a demon. Dante brushed past her and then sat down on her bed.

'It must be said that we do owe you a debt of thanks. If it wasn't for your petty theft, the vile actions of that psychopath would be front-page news all over the world by now. You wanted to take advantage of the situation, but I'm afraid you haven't pulled it off. That's a fact. Be good, and we'll leave things as they are. You won't get your exclusive, but you will save face. What do you say?'

'The disks ...' Andrea mumbled a few unintelligible words.

Dante leaned down until his nose was almost touching hers. 'What were you saying, my petal?'

'I said you can shove it up your ass, you bastard,' said Andrea.

She brought the ashtray down hard on his ear. The crystal collided with Dante's head and the ashes flew in all directions. He cried out in pain, his hand over his ear. Andrea sprang to her feet and pushed him over, then tried to hit him with the ashtray a second time. But he was faster than she was. He grabbed her arm when the ashtray was a mere inch from his face.

'Well, well. So the little whore has claws.'

Dante squeezed her wrist and twisted her arm until she dropped the ashtray. And then a straight punch to her stomach. Andrea hit the floor a second time, the air knocked out of her, feeling as if a heavy lead ball was pressing down on her chest. Dante massaged his ear as a thin thread of blood ran down the side of his neck. He looked at himself in the mirror: his left eye was half-closed, he was covered with ashes, and there were cigarette butts in his hair. He walked back over to the girl and dragged her to her feet. He was going to punch her in the chest. Had he done it, he would have broken a few ribs. But Andrea was ready for him. Just as Dante was pulling his fist back, she kicked him hard in the ankle. Dante lost his balance and fell to the floor, giving her just enough time to run into the bathroom. She slammed the door.

Dante got up, limping.

'Open up, you *bitch*.'

'Go fuck yourself, asshole.' She said it more for herself than for him. She noticed she was crying and thought about praying, but then she remembered who Dante worked for and decided that maybe it wasn't such a good idea. She leaned against the door, but it didn't do much good. It flew open, pushing Andrea against the wall as Dante burst into the room, his face red and overwhelmed by rage. Andrea put up her fists. Dante countered by grabbing her hair and dragging her across the room. He was a brute, using every ounce of his strength to hold her down. All she could do was tear at his face and his hands, trying to free herself from his grasp. She managed to scratch him twice on the face, making him bleed, and this enraged him even more.

'Where are they?'

'Go fuck—'

'Tell me ...'

'—yourself!'

'... where they are!'

He pressed her face against the bathroom mirror, then pulled her head back and slammed it against the glass. A spider spread its web over the mirror, with a glob of blood in the middle that quickly dripped down into the sink.

Dante forced her to look at her reflection in what was left of the mirror. 'Want to keep going?'

Andrea quickly decided she'd had enough. 'In the waste-paper basket,' she said in a weak voice.

'Good. Bend down and get it with your left hand. And no more tricks, or I'll cut off your nipples and shove them down your throat.'

Andrea followed his instructions and handed Dante the disk. He examined it carefully: it appeared to be identical to the one sent to the Vigilanza.

'Very good. And the other nine?'

Andrea swallowed hard. 'I threw them away.'

'More bullshit.'

Andrea felt as if she were flying and in fact she was, as Dante hurled her back into the main room and she landed on the carpet.

'I don't have them, for fuck's sake. I don't have them! Go look in the damn bins in the Piazza Navona, you fucking pig!'

Dante approached her, smiling. She stayed on the floor, her breath coming in short, rapid gasps.

'You don't get it, do you, bitch? All you had to do was hand me the shitty disks and then you would've been on your way home with a nice big strawberry on your face. But no, you think you're brighter than me, so now we have to get serious. Your chance of getting out of this alive has gone.'

Dante put one leg on either side of the journalist, took out his gun and pointed it at her head. Andrea was terrified but she looked straight at him. This bastard was capable of just about anything.

'You won't shoot. You'd make too much noise.' She said it with less conviction this time.

'You know what, you little cunt? You're right again.'

He took a silencer out of his pocket and screwed it on to the barrel of his gun. Andrea was now face to face with certain death. But this time, it would be a little less noisy.

'Drop it, Fabio.'

Dante spun around, an astonished look on his face. Dicanti and Fowler were standing in the doorway. Paola was holding a gun and Fowler the electronic pass with which they'd got into the room. Dicanti's badge and Fowler's collar had played a crucial part in obtaining it. It had taken them a while to get to the hotel because first they had tried one of the other four journalists on their list. They'd arranged them by age, beginning with the youngest, who'd turned out to be a gofer for a television crew, with brown hair, as the talkative receptionist at the front desk had informed them. As talkative as the receptionist at Andrea Otero's hotel.

Dante stared at Dicanti's pistol, dumbstruck. His body was turned towards Dicanti and Fowler, but his gun was still pointing at Andrea's head.

'Come on, Dicanti, you won't do it.'

'You're attacking a civilian on Italian soil, Dante. I'm a police officer. You're not about to tell me what I can or can't do. Drop the gun or I'll be forced to shoot.'

'Dicanti, you don't understand. This woman's a criminal. She stole confidential information, property of the Vatican. She won't listen to reason and she might ruin everything. It's nothing personal.'

'You've said that to me before. And I've noticed how deeply you're involved in quite a few assignments that "aren't personal".'

This was more than Dante could take, and it showed. He changed tactics.

'You're right. Let me take the girl to the Vatican, so we can find out what she did with the envelopes. I will make myself personally responsible for her safety.'

But Andrea knew what that meant and she didn't want to spend another minute with this cretin. She started to move her legs very slowly, getting them into position.

'No way,' said Paola.

Dante's voice took on a steely edge. He directed his words to Fowler. 'Anthony, you can't let this happen. We can't let her bring everything out into the open. For the cross and the sword.'

The priest stared back at Dante. 'Those aren't my symbols any more, Dante. Even less so if you tarnish them with innocent blood.'

'But she's not innocent. She stole the envelopes.'

Dante was still talking when Andrea finally managed to get into position. She chose her moment and kicked out with her foot. She didn't use all her strength – not because she didn't want to, but because she wanted to make sure she hit her target. She wanted to hit that son of a bitch right in the balls. And she did.

Three things happened at once.

Dante let go of the disk as he grabbed his crotch with his left hand. With his right hand he cocked the pistol, his finger pressing against the trigger. His mouth was open, like a fish out of water.

Dicanti jumped across the room in three bounds and rammed her fist into Dante's stomach.

Fowler reacted a half-second after Paola – either because his reflexes were slower or because he was sizing up the situation – and beat a quick path to the pistol, which was still pointing at Andrea. He grabbed Dante's right wrist at almost the same time as Dicanti's shoulder barrelled into Dante's chest. The pistol fired at the ceiling.

The three of them fell together in a confused heap beneath a rain of falling plaster. Fowler, without letting go of Dante's wrist, pressed both thumbs down on the wrist joint, forcing Dante to release the pistol. He still managed to butt Dicanti in the face with his knee. She rolled over, out cold.

Fowler and Dante stood up. Fowler held the gun by the barrel in his left hand. With his right hand he undid the latch and let the clip fall out. It made a loud noise as it bounced on to the floor. With the other hand he took a bullet out of the firing chamber. Two more rapid movements, and the firing pin was in his hand. He threw it across the room, where it came to rest at Dante's feet.

'Not good for much now.'

Dante smiled, flexing his shoulders and lowering his head. 'You're not much good for anything either, grandpa.'

'Try me.'

Dante threw himself at the priest. Fowler took one step to the side and threw a punch at the superintendent. It just missed his face, hitting him on the arm. Dante threw a hard left, and Fowler tried to dodge it, only to run into Dante's fist between his ribs. He fell down, gritting his teeth, out of breath.

'You're a little rusty, old man.'

Dante picked up what was left of the pistol and the clip of bullets. He didn't have time to put it back in and find the trigger, but he wasn't going to leave the weapon behind. Moving quickly, he forgot that Dicanti had a gun too, one that he could use. It was, at that moment, concealed between the rug on the floor and her body, but she was still unconscious.

Dante looked around the room, in the bathroom and the wardrobe. Andrea Otero wasn't in any of them; nor was the disk that had been tossed out of his hand during the tussle. A drop of blood on the window ledge stopped him in his tracks, and for a second he considered the possibility that the journalist could walk on air as Christ had walked on water. Or, more likely, crawl like a cat on all fours.

He soon realised that the room was at the same height as the roof of the building next to it, which sheltered the beautiful cloister of the convent of Santa Maria de la Paz – a beautiful building, built by Bramante.

Andrea had no idea who had built the cloister; but she raced along the roof like a cat, over the red tiles glowing in the morning sun, trying as hard as she could not to draw the attention of the cloister's early-morning tourists. She wanted to get across to the other side, where an open window held the promise of salvation. She was already halfway there. The cloister had two high peaks, and the roof tilted at a dangerous angle above the stone courtyard, thirty feet below.

Dante's testicles were howling in pain, but he ignored them. He raised the window and climbed out after the journalist. She looked back, saw him land on the roof and took off, trying to go even faster.

Dante's voice stopped her. 'Don't move.'

Andrea turned around. Dante was pointing his gun at her – a gun incapable of firing bullets, but she didn't know that. She wondered if this bastard was so insane he'd be willing to fire his gun in broad daylight in front of witnesses. Because by now the tourists had noticed him, and they were standing transfixed by the scene unfolding above their heads, their numbers steadily growing. A pity Dicanti was still out cold, because she was missing a vivid demonstration of what is, in forensic psychology, called the Bystander Effect – a many-times-proven theory, which states that, as the number of bystanders watching a person in danger grows, the probability that anyone will help the victim diminishes, while the number of people pointing and telling others to watch increases.

Dante took a few short steps towards the journalist. As he got closer, he could see that she had only one disk in her hand. She must have been telling him the truth, but it had been a dumb mistake to throw the other ones away. That disk was now more important than ever.

'Give me the disk and I'll go. I swear. I don't want to hurt you,' Dante lied.

Andrea was scared to death, but she put on a show of being brave. 'What shit! Get lost or I'll throw it away.'

Dante stood in the middle of the roof, paralysed. Andrea's arm was extended, her wrist bending back and forth. A simple flick and the disk would take off like a frisbee. Maybe it would break when it hit the ground, or maybe it would ride on a light morning breeze and one of the spectators would grab it, and then it would evaporate long before he got down to the cloister. And with that, so long and farewell.

Way too risky.

Checkmate. What could he do? Distract the enemy until the scales were balanced in his favour.

'Signorina,' Dante said in a loud voice, 'don't jump. I don't know what's driven you to this, but life is very beautiful. If you think about it, you'll see you have many reasons to go on living.'

That's the way to do it, Dante thought: get close enough to help the madwoman with the face bathed in blood who'd jumped on to the roof and was threatening suicide; try to hold her down without anyone noticing as I snatch the disk, and then as we're rolling around on the roof, she slips. I can't save her. A tragedy. The people in charge will take care of Dicanti and Fowler. They'll know how to apply the pressure.

'Don't jump. Think about your family.'

'What are you bellowing about, you prick?' Andrea looked at him wide-eyed. 'I'm not going to jump!'

The spectators down below were pointing at her. No one had called the police. There were a few scattered shouts of 'Don't jump, don't jump'. No one seemed to think it strange that her rescuer was waving a gun. Perhaps they couldn't make out what her intrepid saviour was holding in his right hand.

Dante silently rejoiced. He was getting closer and closer to the young reporter. 'Don't be afraid. I'm an officer of the law!'

Andrea only now realised what her pursuer was up to. He was less than six feet away.

'Don't come any closer, you creep. I'll throw it!'

The spectators below thought they heard her say she was going to throw herself off the roof and there were more cries of 'No, No!'

Dante's outstretched hand brushed Andrea's heel. She stepped back, slipping a few inches down the roof. The crowd – there were about fifty people standing in the cloister now and hotel guests had begun to stick their heads out the windows of their rooms – held their breath.

Suddenly someone shouted, 'Look, a priest!'

Dante turned round. Fowler had both feet on the roof, a roof tile in each hand.

'Not here, Anthony!' Dante yelled.

Fowler acted as if he hadn't heard. He hurled one of the tiles, with devilishly good aim. Dante was lucky. There was just enough time to cover his face. If he hadn't, the crunch he heard when the tile struck his arm might have been the sound of his skull cracking. He lost his balance, fell, and started to slide towards the edge of the roof. By some miracle he was able to grab hold of the gutter that jutted out from the edge. He was now dangling ten feet above the ground, his legs wrapped around one of Bramante's priceless columns. Three people left the crowd of spectators to help Dante, more of a broken puppet than a man, slide the rest of the way down to the ground. He was busy thanking them as he lost consciousness.

Fowler stood facing Andrea on the roof.

'Signorina Otero, please do us the favour of climbing back into your room before you hurt yourself.'

Hotel Raphael

Saturday, 9 April 2005, 9.14 a.m.

Paola came back to the land of the living in the midst of a small miracle: Anthony Fowler was attentively placing a cold, wet towel across her forehead. But the bliss was short-lived and in a second she was sorry her body didn't end at the shoulders as her head was pounding like a jackhammer. She pulled herself together just in time to deal with the two police officers who'd finally showed up at the hotel room, telling them they could go back outside, she had everything under control. Dicanti swore to them that no one had tried to commit suicide, and that the whole thing was nothing more than a big mistake. The two officers nosed around the carnage of the hotel room with wary looks, but did as they were told.

Fowler was trying to put Andrea's forehead back together after her run-in with the mirror. Dicanti stuck her head into the bathroom just as Fowler was telling the journalist she was going to need stitches.

'At least four on your forehead and two on the brow. But right now you don't have time for that. I'll tell what you need to do: you're going to take a cab to Bolonia right away. It will take you four hours to get there. A doctor friend of mine will be waiting for you. He'll stitch your forehead and then make sure you get to the airport. You can fly to Madrid via Milán. You'll be safe there. See if you can avoid Italy for a few years.'

'Wouldn't it be faster for her to catch a plane out of Naples?'

Fowler scrutinised Dicanti, his face serious. '*Dottoressa*, should you ever need to get out of these people's clutches, don't run in the direction of Naples whatever you do. The town is crawling with informants.'

'I'd say they have eyes just about everywhere.'

'You've got that right. And I fear that crossing the Vigilanza will have unpleasant consequences for both of us.'

'Let's go and see Troi. He'll take our side.'

At first, Fowler didn't respond. Then: 'He might. Nevertheless, our priority right now is to get Miss Otero out of Rome.'

The conversation that Andrea was listening to did nothing to take the pained look off her face. The cuts on her forehead were still throbbing, even if, thanks to Fowler, they were bleeding a good deal less. Ten minutes before, she'd witnessed Dante plunge over the edge of the roof and had felt an overwhelming surge of relief. She'd run towards Fowler and put her arms around his neck, running the risk of making them both tumble over the edge. Fowler had quickly filled her in on the situation: a very powerful element in the Vatican hierarchy didn't want this incident to come to light, which was why her life was under threat. The priest had glossed over the minor detail of her deplorable theft of the envelopes, something for which she was grateful. But now he was imposing his conditions, and the journalist wasn't pleased. She was thankful for her opportune rescue at the hands of the priest and the inspector, but she wasn't disposed to give in to blackmail.

'I'm not thinking of going anywhere. I am an accredited journalist, and my paper trusts me to deliver news of the Conclave. And I want them to know that I have uncovered a conspiracy, operating at the highest levels, to hide the death of three cardinals and an Italian police officer. *El Globo*, and possibly several other papers, are going to publish this information, alongside some powerful photos, and all of it is going to carry my name.'

Fowler listened patiently before he answered: 'Miss Otero, I admire your courage. You have more of it than many of the soldiers I've known. But in this game, you need a good deal more than courage.'

Andrea pressed the bandage that covered her forehead with her hand and gritted her teeth. 'Once the report is published, they wouldn't dare touch me.'

'Maybe yes, and maybe no. But I don't want them to publish the report either. It's not helpful right now.'

Andrea looked at him, stupefied. 'What did you just say?'

'Let's make it simple: give me the disk.'

Andrea got to her feet unsteadily. She was indignant, and held the disk tightly against her chest. 'I didn't realise that you were one of those fanatics, too – ready to kill to preserve their secrets. I'm getting out of here.'

Fowler pushed her back down on to the toilet.

'Personally, for me, the most illuminating phrase in the Gospels is, "The truth shall make you free." And if it were up to me, you could take off and tell everyone that a priest with a long history of abusing young boys had gone mad and was walking around knifing cardinals. Perhaps then the Church would realise once and for all that priests are, always and only, men. But that has little to do with you or me. I don't want this to get out because Karosky *wants* it to get out. When a little time has gone by and he sees no results, he'll make a move. Then we can catch him, and in the process save lives.'

Andrea crumbled. It was a combination of exhaustion, pain, stress and a feeling she found absolutely impossible to put into words – a sentiment composed of equal parts of fragility and self-pity that welled up in her from time to time, when she realised just how small she was in relation to the larger universe. She handed the disk to Fowler and cradled her head. She started to cry.

'I'll lose my job.'

The priest took pity on her. 'No you won't. I'll see to that personally.'

Three hours later, the US ambassador to Italy called the editor-in-chief of *El Globo*. He sent his apologies for the accident that had taken place between one of the embassy's official cars and the newspaper's special correspondent in Rome. As he told it, the accident had taken place the day before when his car had been en route to the airport. Luckily, the driver had slammed on the brakes in time to avoid a catastrophe, and except for the journalist's small wound to the head, everyone was all right. It seemed that the journalist had insisted repeatedly that she had to continue with her work, but the doctors at the embassy had ordered two weeks of rest, and they were offering to send her to Madrid on the embassy's tab. Of course, because of the great professional injury she had suffered, they were disposed to compensate her. One of the people in the car had taken an interest in her and wanted to arrange an interview. They would get in touch in two weeks' time to finalise the details.

El Globo's editor-in-chief was a bit perplexed after he hung up. He had no idea how that rebellious, difficult young reporter had managed to snag what was probably the most difficult interview on the planet to get for their paper. He attributed it to a tremendous piece of luck. He felt a pang of jealousy and wanted to crawl back into his skin.

He'd always wanted to visit the Oval Office.

Uacv Headquarters

Saturday, 9 April 2005, 1.25 p.m.

Paola burst into Troi's office without knocking, but she didn't like what she saw, or rather who she saw when she got there. Cirin sat facing the UACV's director and as Paola came in, he stood up and walked out of the office, without even giving Dicanti so much as a glance. She did her best to block his exit.

'Listen, Cirin –'

The chief of the Vatican Vigilanza deftly stepped around her and disappeared down the hall.

'Sit down, Dicanti,' Troi said, still seated at his desk.

'But I want to tell that man about the criminal actions of one of his subordinates—'

'Enough, ispettore. The inspector general has already given me a useful summary of the events that transpired at the Hotel Raphael.'

Paola's jaw dropped. As soon as she and Fowler had put the Spanish journalist into a taxi headed for Bolonia, they'd gone directly to the UACV headquarters to give their side of the story to Troi. The situation was no doubt complicated, but Paola still believed that Troi would back them up over the rescue of the journalist. She'd decided to talk to him alone, though naturally the last thing she'd expected was that her boss wouldn't want to hear her version of the story.

'He must have told you that Dante attacked an unarmed journalist.'

'What he told me was that there was a difference of opinion, which has been resolved to everyone's satisfaction. It seems that Inspector Dante was trying to reassure a potential witness who was a bit nervous when you two attacked him. Dante is in hospital as we speak.'

'That's absurd! It's not what happened at all.'

'Cirin also informed me that he was no longer going to work with us on this case.' Troi raised his voice several notches. 'He was very disappointed by your attitude, which was hostile and aggressive towards Dante and towards the sovereignty of our neighbouring country – something which I have witnessed myself, albeit in passing. You will go back to your usual assignments, and Fowler will return to Washington. From this moment on, the Corpo di Vigilanza will be solely responsible for protecting the cardinals. We must hand over the disk that Karosky sent us immediately, as well as the one we recovered from the journalist, to the Vatican. And then we will forget it ever existed.'

'And Pontiero – what about him? I still remember the look on your face during the autopsy. Was that faked too? Who'll see that justice is done for him?'

'That's no longer our responsibility.'

Dicanti was so disappointed, so disgusted, that she felt physically sick. She couldn't recognise the man sitting in front of her, and whatever small ties of affection she might have felt for him were long gone. She asked herself, with some sadness, if this was why he had withdrawn his support so quickly. Perhaps it was the bitter finale to last night's confrontation.

'It's because of me, isn't it, Carlo?'

'Sorry?

'Because of what happened last night. But I never thought you'd be capable of this.'

'Please, ispettore, don't give yourself delusions of grandeur. My only interest in this case is in collaborating with the Vatican as efficiently as possible – something I've observed you seem to be unable to do.'

Thirty-four years of life so far, and Paola had never witnessed such a discrepancy between a person's words and the look on their face. She couldn't hold back.

'You're a useless pig, Carlo. Seriously. It doesn't surprise me that everyone laughs at you behind your back. How did you end up like this?'

Troi turned red to the tips of his ears, but he managed to repress an explosion of anger. Instead, he abruptly channelled his rage into a cold, measured verbal slap.

'At least I ended up somewhere, ispettore. Be so kind as to leave your badge and your gun on my desk. You are suspended from duty for one month, until I've had the opportunity to review your case. Go home.'

Paola opened her mouth, but nothing came out. In films, the hero always responds with a crushing phrase that foreshadows their triumphant return when they are stripped of the symbols of their authority by a tyrannical boss. But in real life, Paola didn't say a word. She dropped her badge and her pistol on the desk and stormed out of Troi's office without looking back.

Fowler was waiting for her in the hallway. He had escorts: two policemen. Paola guessed he had already received his fateful phone call.

'So this is how it ends,' Dicanti said.

A smile lit up the priest's face. 'It's been a pleasure knowing you, *dottoressa*. Unfortunately, these gentleman have the duty of accompanying me to my hotel so I can collect my belongings before heading out to the airport.'

Paola grabbed his arm, her fingers pressing the sleeve. '*Padre*, can't you call someone? At least get them to delay this?'

'I'm afraid not.' Fowler shook his head. 'But I hope that one day I can take you out for a good cup of coffee.'

Without saying another word, he got up and walked down the hallway, followed by the two policemen.

Paola didn't cry until she reached her apartment.

THE SAINT MATTHEW INSTITUTE

SACHEM PIKE, MARYLAND

December 1999

Transcript of Interview Number 115 between Patient Number 3643 and Doctor Canice Conroy

DR CONROY: I see you've brought a book with you. *Enigmas and Curiosities.* Any tricky ones?

No. 3643: They're very easy.

DR CONROY: All right, then. Tell me one.

No. 3643: They're too simple, really. I don't think you'll like them.

DR CONROY: But I like riddles.

No. 3643: OK. If a man digs a hole in one hour and two men dig two holes in two hours, how long will it take a man to dig half a hole?

DR CONROY: That's easy. Half an hour.

No. 3643: [*Laughs.*]

DR CONROY: What are you laughing at? It's half an hour. One hour, one hole. Half an hour, half a hole.

No. 3643: Doctor, there's no such things as half a hole. A hole is always a hole. [*Laughs again.*]

DR CONROY: Are you trying to tell me something, Victor?

No. 3643: Of course, doctor. Of course.

DR CONROY: You're not a hole, Victor. You aren't irredeemably condemned to being the way you are.

No. 3643: But I am, Doctor Conroy. And I have you to thank for showing me the way.

DR CONROY: What way?

No. 3643: I've fought for so long to resist being who I am, trying to be something I'm not. But thanks to you, I've become who I really am. Isn't that what you wanted?

DR CONROY: It's not possible. I couldn't have gone so wrong with you.

No. 3643: Doctor, you weren't wrong. You made me see the light. You made me understand that to open a heavy door, you need a strong hand.

DR CONROY: Is that you? The strong hand?

No. 3643: [*More laughter.*] No, doctor. I'm the key.

DICANTI FAMILY APARTMENT

VIA DELLA CROCE, 12

Saturday, 9 April 2005, 11.46 p.m.

For a long time the door to her room was shut. Paola was inside, completely distraught. Her mother was away, visiting friends in Ostia for the weekend, a small piece of luck about which Paola was greatly relieved. She was at her lowest, and wouldn't be able to hide it from her mother. If she saw the condition her daughter was in, Signora Dicanti would try to cheer her up, which would only make matters worse. Paola needed to be alone, to plunge into the failure and desperation she felt inside.

She lay down on the bed, not bothering to remove her clothes. Noise from the street below and the faint light of an April afternoon filtered into her room as she endlessly relived her conversation with Troi and the events of the last few days. Finally, she drifted off to sleep. Nearly nine hours after she had collapsed with exhaustion on to her bed, the unique aroma of fresh coffee invaded her dream, forcing her to open her eyes.

'Mamma, you're back early ...'

'You're right, I did come back quickly.' The voice was firm, polite, speaking a tuneful but slightly hesitant Italian: the voice of Anthony Fowler.

Paola's eyes shot open and, without realising what she was doing, she threw both her arms around his neck.

'Careful, careful. You'll spill the coffee.'

Paola unwillingly let go of him. Fowler was sitting on the edge of her bed, looking at her with a mischievous smile. In one hand he held a cup he had taken from the kitchen.

'How did you get in? And how did you manage to escape from the police? They were putting you on a plane to Washington ...'

'Calm down. One question at a time,' Fowler laughed. 'As to how I managed to slip out of the hands of two fat, poorly trained public servants, I simply ask you not to insult my intelligence. As to how I got into your apartment, the answer is easy: I picked the lock.'

'I see. CIA basic training – right?'

'More or less. Sorry for the intrusion, but I knocked several times and nobody answered. I thought you might be in danger. When I saw you sleeping so peacefully, I decided to make good on my promise about the coffee.'

Paola stood up, lifting the cup out of Fowler's hand. The only light in the bedroom came from the lamps on the street, which threw long shadows across the high ceiling. Fowler looked around the room. On one wall hung Paola's diplomas: school, university, the FBI Academy; swimming medals, too, and even a few oil paintings that must have been done at least thirteen years ago. Once more Fowler felt just how vulnerable this intelligent, energetic woman was – a woman who moved into the future burdened by her past; a woman who, in large part, had never abandoned her earliest childhood. Fowler glanced over the walls around the bed, trying to ascertain the line of sight of the person who slept there. At the end of the imaginary line he drew from the pillow to the wall was a framed photograph of Paola sitting on a hospital bed with her father.

'It's good coffee. My mother's coffee is terrible.'

'Just a question of an even flame, *dottoressa*.'

'So why did you come back?'

'Various reasons. Because I didn't want to leave you stranded. To stop that lunatic from going about his business. And because I suspect that there's much more to this case than meets the eye. I feel like we've been used by everybody, you and I. What's more, I suspect you have very personal reasons for wanting to see it through.'

Paola frowned. 'You're right. Pontiero was a friend and a colleague. Right now, what I really want is to bring his killer to justice, but I really don't think we can. Without my badge and everything that comes with it, we're like two tiny clouds. The slightest breeze and we'll be blown away. And besides, they're probably looking for you.'

'Quite possible. I gave the two officers the slip in Fiumicino. But I doubt Troi would go so far as to issue an order for my capture and arrest. With all the hullabaloo going on in the city right now, it wouldn't do him any good, and how could he justify it? My guess is he's going let it go.'

'And your bosses, *padre*?'

'Officially, I'm in Langley. Unofficially, they haven't objected to me sticking around here for a while longer.'

'At last some good news.'

'What's going to be difficult for us now is getting into the Vatican, because Cirin will be on the lookout.'

'I don't see how we can protect the cardinals if they're on the inside and we're not.'

'I think we ought to start at the beginning. Go back over the whole chain of events from the outset, because it's clear that something has sailed right over our heads.'

'How are we going to do that? I don't have the necessary information. The Karosky file is sitting in the UACV.'

Fowler's lips curled into a roguish smile. 'God sometimes grants us small miracles.'

His hand pointed in the direction of Paola's desk, at the other end of the room. Paola turned on the small lamp, which cast its glow over the unwieldy pile of Manilla envelopes that made up the Karosky dossier.

'Let me propose a joint venture. You concentrate on what you do best: a psychological profile of the killer – a definitive one, with all the facts we now have at our disposal. I, meanwhile, will ensure the supply of fresh coffee.'

Paola finished the first cup. She wanted to take a closer look at the priest's face, but he was sitting outside the cone of light cast by the lamp. Suddenly, she was struck by the niggling feeling that had overcome her in the hallway at Saint Martha's, a premonition she'd ignored, putting it off until a later date. Now, after the long list of events that had followed the death of Cardoso, she was more than ever convinced that her intuition had been correct. She turned her computer on, picked up a blank profile from among the papers on her desk and started to fill it out, consulting the dossier from time to time.

'Let's have another pot of coffee, *padre*. I want to see if a theory of mine holds up.'

Psychological Profile of a Serial Killer

Patient: KAROSKY, Victor
Profile created by Doctor Paola Dicanti.
Current location of patient: *In absentia*
Date of entry: 10 April 2005
Age: 44
Height: 6 feet
Weight: 187 lbs
Description: Brown hair, grey eyes, healthy complexion, highly intelligent (IQ of 125)

Family history: Victor Karosky was born into a lower-middle-class family of immigrants ruled over by a domineering mother who had profound problems relating to reality, owing to the influence of religion. The family emigrated from Poland, and from early on this lack of stability is evident in all family members. The father presents a typical portrait of irregular work history, alcoholism and bad behaviour, to which can be added repeated, periodic sexual abuse (intended as punishment) of his son when the subject reaches adolescence. The mother seems to have been aware of the abuse and incest committed by her husband, while acting as if she wasn't. An older brother ran away from the family household on account of the sexual abuse. A younger brother was left to die, after a long illness brought on by meningitis. The subject was locked into a closet, incommunicado, for long periods of time, after the 'discovery' by his mother of the father's sexual abuse. By the time he was freed, the father had abandoned the household, and it was the mother who imposed her personality, in this case impressing upon the subject a Catholic fear of damnation, the inevitable result of his 'sexual excess', as defined by the mother. She dressed him in her clothes and even went so far as to threaten him with castration. This produced a grave distortion of reality in the subject, as well as a serious disorder in terms of an unintegrated sexuality. The first signs of rage and antisocial behaviour began to appear. He attacked a schoolmate, and was sent to a reformatory. Upon leaving, his record was wiped clean, and at nineteen years old he decided to enter a seminary. They did no checks on his psychological profile, and accepted his application.

Adult history: Indications of unintegrated sexual disorder are confirmed at nineteen years old, shortly after the death of his mother, when the subject engages a minor in heavy petting, an act which gradually becomes more frequent and extended. The ecclesiastical authorities in the seminary make no punitive response to his sexual aggression, which becomes even more problematic when the subject is responsible for his own congregation. According to his file, there are at least 89 documented cases of sexual aggression against minors, 39 of which consist of sodomy with full penetration, and the remainder, petting or forcing masturbation and/or fellatio. The compendium of interviews with the subject allows us to deduce that, however strange it may seem, he was fully convinced of his vocation in the ministry. In cases of pederasty among priests, it is often possible to identify their sexual drive as the motive for their entrance into the ministry, somewhat like a fox entering the hen house. But in Karosky's case, the motives behind his vows are very different. His mother pushed him in this direction, even going so far as to use force. After an incident in which he attacked a parishioner, the Karosky scandal could no longer be kept under wraps and the subject was at last admitted to the Saint Matthew Institute, a rehabilitation centre for Catholic priests. There we find Karosky closely identifying with the Bible, especially the Old Testament. An episode of sudden violence against an employee of the institute takes place just a few days after his arrival. From this incident we are able to deduce an overwhelming cognitive dissonance between the subject's sexual compulsion and his religious convictions. When the two collide, they produce a violent crisis, as in the case of the attack on the laboratory technician.

Recent history: The subject presents a portrait of rage, reflected in his displaced aggression. He has committed various crimes, in which elevated levels of sexual sadism are manifest, including ritual symbols and insertional necrophilia.

Profile of notable characteristics manifest in his actions:
　　Agreeable personality, medium-to-high intelligence
　　Frequent lies
　　Total absence of guilt or feelings towards his victims
　　Complete egocentricity
　　Personal, affective disconnect
　　An impersonal and impulsive sexuality, harnessed to the satisfaction of egocentric needs
　　Antisocial
　　High levels of obedience

INCOHERENCIES!!!!!
　　Irrational thought integrated into his actions
　　Multiple neuroses
　　Criminal behaviour understood as a means not an end
　　Suicidal tendencies
　　Mission oriented

Dicanti Family Apartment

VIA DELLA CROCE, 12

Sunday, 10 April 2005, 1.45 a.m.

Fowler finished reading the report Dicanti had handed to him. He wasn't sure what to make of it.

'I hope you don't mind me saying this, but the report seems incomplete. You've simply written a résumé of everything we already knew. In all sincerity, this isn't going to get us very far.'

Dicanti stood up.

'You're couldn't be more wrong. Karosky presents a very complex clinical portrait, from which we can deduce that the increase in his aggression turned a sexual predator who'd been clinically castrated into a multiple killer.'

'Which is the basis of our theory.'

'And it's as worthless as a voting booth in Florida. Look closely at the characteristics in the profile, and the end of the report. The first eight would define a serial killer.'

Fowler went down the list, nodding his head.

'There are two types of serial killers: disorganised and organised. It's not a perfect classification, but it works. The first type corresponds to killers who commit spontaneous, impulsive crimes, with a high probability that they will leave evidence at the scene. They often know their victims, and tend to live in the same geographical area. They use whatever weapons happen to be convenient: a chair, a belt – whatever they can get their hands on. Sexual sadism appears post-mortem.'

Fowler rubbed his eyes. He was very tired and had only a few hours sleep. 'Sorry. Go on.'

'The other kind, the organised, is someone who has great freedom of movement and who captures his victims before using force. The victim is usually a stranger who corresponds to a specific criterion. The weapons and restraints employed match a preconceived plan, and the killer never leaves them behind. The body is abandoned in a neutral spot, in exactly the manner the killer intends. OK, so to which of the two groups does Karosky belong?'

'The second, obviously.'

'That is what any observer could deduce. But we can go further. We have the dossier. We know who he is, where he comes from, what he's thinking. Forget everything that's happened in the last few days and concentrate on the Karosky who entered the institute.'

'An impulsive character, who, in certain situations, exploded like a keg of dynamite.'

'And after five years of therapy?'

'A different creature entirely.'

'Would you say that this change occurred gradually, or all at once?'

'It was pretty sudden. I would pinpoint the change to the moment when Conroy forced him to listen to the tapes of his regression therapy.'

Paola took a deep breath before she went on. '*Padre*, I don't mean to offend you, but after reading dozens of the interviews between Karosky, Conroy and yourself, I think you could be wrong. And that mistake has sent us off in the wrong direction.'

Fowler leaned forward. 'No offence taken. I have a degree in psychology, as you know, but I was only at the institute as a kind of punishment. My real expertise lies elsewhere. You're the expert criminologist and I'm lucky to have your insight. But I don't understand where you're taking this.'

'Take a second look at the profile,' Paola said, pointing towards it. 'Under the heading, "Incoherencies" I have noted five characteristics which make it impossible for us to conclude that our subject is an organised serial killer. Criminology textbook in hand, any expert would say that Karosky is an organised anomaly, evolving from a trauma – in this case the confrontation with his past. Are you familiar with the term cognitive dissonance?'

'It's the state of mind in which the actions and intimate beliefs of a person are at extreme odds with each other. Karosky suffered from extreme cognitive dissonance: he believed himself to be an exemplary priest, while his eighty-nine victims would have asserted that he was a pederast.'

'Exactly. So then, according to you, the subject – a committed Catholic, neurotic, impervious to all intrusion from the outside world – is, in the space of a few months, transformed into a serial killer, cold and calculating, without a trace of neurosis. And all of this after listening to a few tapes in which he comprehends for the first time that he was mistreated as a child?'

'Looking at it from that perspective … It does seem a bit far-fetched.' Fowler was hesitant.

'Or impossible. There's no doubt that Conroy's irresponsible action did harm Karosky, but it couldn't have provoked such a disproportionate change. The fanatical priest who covers his ears, infuriated when you read the names of his victims to him out loud, could not transform himself into an organised serial killer in the space of a few months. And let's remember that his first two ritual crimes took place at the institute itself: the mutilation of one priest and the murder of another.'

'But *dottoressa*, the cardinals died at Karosky's hands. He himself confessed; his fingerprints were found at all three of the crime scenes.'

'That is true. I don't dispute that Karosky murdered those men. It's more than certain that he did. What I'm trying to say is that the motive that made him commit those crimes isn't what we thought it was. The most important detail in his profile – the thing that led him to become a priest in spite of his tortured soul – is the same thing as has conditioned him to commit these terrible acts.'

Fowler finally understood. Overcome by shock, he had to sit down on Paola's bed to keep from losing his balance. 'Obedience.'

'Correct. Karosky isn't a serial killer at all. He's a hired assassin.'

The Saint Matthew Institute

SACHEM PIKE, MARYLAND

August 1999

There wasn't a single noise in solitary confinement – which was why the urgent, demanding voice that kept whispering his name filled Karosky's ears like an incoming tide.

'Victor.'

Karosky jumped out of bed, like a child. There he was, once again. He'd come to help Victor, to guide him, to light the way; to give him a reason for and to help him channel his strength and his needs. Now he was able to endure the cruel interference of Doctor Conroy, who examined him as he would a butterfly pinned under a microscope. There he was on the other side of the iron bars; but it felt almost as if he were sitting with Victor in his cell. Victor could respect this man; he could follow him. And he in turn could understood Victor, and give him direction. They had spoken for hours about what he should do. About how he should do it. About how he should act, how he should respond to Conroy's repetitive, bothersome interference.

During the night-time he thought about his role and waited for the man's arrival. He only came once a week, but Victor waited for him impatiently, counting the hours and even the minutes one after another. As he went over it in his head, he patiently sharpened the knife, trying not to make any noise. The visitor had brought it to Victor. He could have given him a sharp knife, or even a gun, but he wanted to temper his courage and his strength. And Victor had done what he asked. He had given proof of his loyalty and devotion. First he had mutilated the sodomite and then, a few weeks later, he had killed the pederast – both priests. If he pulled out the weeds the way the man had asked him to, he would receive his reward – the reward he wanted more than anything in the world. He would give it to Victor because no one else could. No one.

'Victor.'

He was demanding his presence. Victor crossed the cell with hurried steps and bowed down in front of the door, listening to the voice that spoke to him of the future; of a mission, far away; in the very heart of Christianity.

DICANTI FAMILY APARTMENT

VIA DELLA CROCE, 12

Sunday, 10 April 2005, 2.14 a.m.

Silence followed Dicanti's words like a dark shadow. Fowler looked around, his hands gripping his face, caught between astonishment and despair.

'How could I have been so blind? He kills because he's been told to. Jesus Christ. And the messages, the ritual?'

'If you think about it carefully, they don't make any sense: the *"Ego te absolvo"* written first on the ground and then on the victim's chest; the hands washed clean, the tongue cut out: it's the exact equivalent of the Sicilian practice of putting money in the victim's mouth.'

'The Mafia ritual that indicates the victim talked too much – is that it?'

'Exactly. At first I thought Karosky was condemning the cardinals for some crime, something done to him or some affront to their position as priests. But the clues left on the crumpled pieces of paper don't add up. In my opinion, they were his personal contribution, his own finishing touch to a scheme dictated by someone else.'

'But why kill them in such a dramatic way then? Why not just get rid of them?'

'The mutilations are nothing more than an absurd disguise to cover up one crucial fact: someone wanted them dead. Just look at this.'

Paola pointed at the flexible lamp on her desk. Its beam was directed on to Karosky's dossier. Everything that didn't fall inside its cone of light was in darkness.

'Now I get it. They forced us to look at what they wanted us to see.

OK, but who would want to do something like this?'

'The essential question when you want to find out who's committed a crime is: who benefits? A serial killer erases that question with one swipe because he does it for his own benefit. His motive is the body. But in this case the killer's motive is his mission. If he had wanted to give free rein to his frustration, his hatred for the cardinals, supposing that he feels these things, he could have done it at some other time when the cardinals were much more visible. And much less protected. So why now? What's different now?'

'Because someone wants to influence the Conclave.'

'So now you must ask yourself who does want to influence the Conclave. And to answer that it's essential to look at who they killed.'

'The cardinals who died were eminent figures in the Church – men of great standing.'

'With a simple connection between them. Our job is to work out what that is.'

Fowler stood up. He began pacing around the room, his hands clenched behind his back. '*Dottoressa*, I have an idea about who might be prepared to eliminate the cardinals in this way. There's one clue we've conveniently ignored: Karosky underwent a complete facial reconstruction, as Angelo Biffi took the trouble to show us. It's an expensive operation and requires a long convalescence. If done well, especially with the necessary discretion and anonymity, it could cost more than one hundred thousand dollars. That's not the kind of money that a poor priest like Karosky would have lying around. Nor would it be easy for him to come to Italy, or to pay his expenses after he got here. We've relegated these questions to the back burner the whole time, but they're crucial now.'

'And they reinforce the theory that there's an unseen hand behind the assassinations.'

'Correct.'

'*Padre*, I'm not in your league when it comes to knowledge of the Catholic Church, or the way the Curia works. In your opinion, what is the common denominator between the three dead cardinals?'

The priest mulled it over. 'There could be a link – something that would have been much more obvious if they'd simply disappeared or been executed. They were all ideological liberals. They were part of – how should I describe it? – the liberal wing of the Holy Spirit. If you'd asked me for the names of the five cardinals who were most in support of Vatican Council II, those three names would have been on the list.'

'I need more detail.'

'OK. With the arrival of John XXIII to the papacy in 1958, it was obvious to everyone that the Church had to change course. John XXIII convoked the second Vatican Council, a call to bishops all over the world to come to Rome to debate with the Pope about the state of the Church. Two thousand bishops responded to the call. John XXIII died before the council finished but his successor, Paul VI, completed the job. Unfortunately, the initial reforms that the council planned didn't go nearly as far as John XXIII had hoped.'

'What are you referring to?'

'There were enormous changes inside the church. It was probably one of the landmarks of the twentieth century. You won't remember it because you're very young, but until the end of the sixties it was considered a sin for a woman to smoke or even wear trousers in public. And those aren't the only examples. Suffice to say that, although the changes were extensive, they were by no means far-reaching enough. John XXIII wanted to throw open the doors of the Church to the reviving air of the Holy Spirit. They were only opened a crack. Paul VI turned out to be a very conservative pope. John Paul I, his successor, was barely in the job for a month; and John Paul II was an apostolic pope, strong and media-savvy, who certainly did a great deal of good on humanitarian issues but was extremely conservative when it came to normal Church politics.'

'So the great reform of the Church still hasn't happened?'

'There's a lot of work to be done – there really is. When the results of Vatican Two were published, the most conservative sectors of the Church were up in arms. And the council still has enemies – people who believe that anyone who isn't a Catholic will go straight to Hell, that women don't have the right to vote, and other, even worse, ideas. Even the clergy expects this Conclave to give us a forceful, idealistic pope, a pope who will dare to open the Church up to the world. And the perfect man for the job would no doubt have been Cardinal Portini, a hard-core liberal. But he'd never get the votes of the ultraconservative wing. Robayra would have been something else: a man of the people but a brilliant one. Cardoso had similar backing. Both were defenders of the poor.'

'And now they're both dead.'

Fowler's expression darkened. 'Paola, what I'm going to tell you now has to remain a secret at all costs. I'm risking my life and yours and, take my word for it, I'm scared. This line of reasoning points in a direction I really don't want to look at too closely, much less follow.' Fowler paused briefly to take in some air. 'Ever heard of the Santa Alianza – the Holy Alliance?'

Once more, Dicanti's head filled with stories of spies and assassinations, just as it had when they were visiting the messenger. She'd always thought that they were the sort of tall tales told only by drunks, but at that late hour, sitting in her room with a man whose background was, to say the least, unusual, the possibility that such stories were real acquired a new dimension.

'It's supposedly the Vatican's Secret Service, or so they say – a network of spies and secret agents who won't hesitate to kill. But it's just an old wives' tale, used to scare rookie officers who've just joined the force. Nobody takes the rumours seriously.'

'Doctor Dicanti, you should take the Santa Alianza very seriously indeed, because it does exist. It has existed for the last four hundred years, and it's the right hand of the Vatican for assignments that even the Pope himself doesn't know about.'

'I find that very difficult to believe.'

'The motto of the Holy Alliance is: "The cross and the sword".'

Paola had a flashback of Dante in the Hotel Raphael, his pistol pointed at the journalist. Those had been his exact words when he'd asked for Fowler's help, and now she understood.

'Oh, good Lord. So you're ...'

'I was, a long time ago. I served two flags: those of my country and my religion. I had to let one of them go.'

'What happened?'

'I can't tell you, so don't ask.'

Paola didn't want to push the point. This was part of the darker side of the priest, the cold pain that clutched at his soul. She suspected there was a great deal more to this than he was letting on.

'Now I understand why Dante loathed you so much. It has something to do with that part of your life, doesn't it?'

Fowler didn't respond. Paola had to make a quick decision because they were short on time. There was no room for doubt. She finally let her heart speak. She knew she was in love with the priest – with each and every part of him, from the dry warmth of his hands to the afflictions of his soul. She wanted to be able to rid him of all that, to give him back the open smile of a child. She knew that what she wanted was impossible: there were oceans of bitterness inside him and they'd been there for a long time. It wasn't only the unsurmountable wall of his priesthood: anyone who wanted to get near him would have to cross those oceans, and they would most probably drown. At that moment she realised that she would never be with him; but she also knew that he would risk his own life before letting anyone do her harm.

'It's OK, *padre*. I trust you,' she said in a whisper. 'Go on.'

Fowler sat back down; and he began to unfold a long and chilling story.

'They've existed since 1566. In those dark times, Pius V was fearful of the rise of the Anglicans and heretics. As head of the Inquisition, he was tough, inflexible, pragmatic. The attitude in the Vatican was much more territorial then than it is now, though it enjoys more power today. The Holy Alliance was created to recruit young priests and *uomos di fiducia* – trustworthy lay persons of proven faith. Their mission was to defend the Vatican as a country and the Church as a spiritual entity, and their numbers grew with the passing of time. By the nineteenth century the number of members had reached the thousands. Some were mere informants, dreamers, sleepy-heads …Others – around five hundred men – formed the elite: the Hand of Saint Michael. This was a group of special agents who were posted throughout the world and could execute an order precisely and at speed. They'd invest money in a revolutionary group when necessary, trade influence, fabricate crucial information that would change the course of a war. They would silence, deceive, and at the furthest extreme, kill. Every member of the Hand of Saint Michael was trained in weapons and tactics – originally, also in population control, codes, disguise and hand-to-hand combat. A Hand was capable of splitting a grape in two with a knife from fifteen paces. He could speak four languages. He could decapitate a cow, throw its decaying body into a well full of pure water and place the blame on a rival group. The Hands trained for years in a monastery on an island in the Mediterranean, whose name I won't reveal. With the arrival of the twentieth century, the training evolved, only to have the Hand of Saint Michael nearly pulled out by its roots during the Second World War. It was a time bathed in blood, a time when many men perished, some of them defending noble causes but others far less so.'

Fowler paused to take a sip of coffee. The shadows in the room had grown darker and longer, and Paola shivered.

'In 1958 John XXIII, the Pope who initiated Vatican Two, decided that the time for the Holy Alliance had passed and its services were no longer required. Right in the middle of the Cold War he dismantled the lines of communication between the various informants, absolutely prohibiting members of the alliance from carrying out any action without his prior approval. And for four years it stayed like that. There were only twelve of fifty-two Hands left in 1939, and several of them were getting on in years. The Pope ordered them to return to Rome. The secret location where they trained mysteriously went up in flames in 1960. And the head of the Hand of Saint Michael, the leader of the Holy Alliance, died in a car accident.'

'Who was he?'

'I can't say – not because I don't want to, but because I don't know. The identity of the head is always a mystery. It could be anybody: a bishop, a cardinal, an *uomo di fiducia*, a simple priest. It has to be a man, and he must be more than forty-five years old. That's all. From 1566 until today only the name of one head has ever been discovered: the parish priest Sogredo, an Italian, originally from Spain, who fought Napoleon tooth and nail. And that piece of information is only available in very limited circles.'

'It's not exactly strange that the Vatican wouldn't recognise the existence of a secret service, if it uses methods such as those you describe.'

'That was one of the reasons why John XXIII wanted to have done with the alliance. He said it was never right to kill, even in the name of God; and I agree. I know that a few of the campaigns undertaken by the Hand of Saint Michael hit the Nazis very hard. One of their attacks saved hundreds of lives. But there was one faction, albeit a very small one, that operated completely on its own and committed terrible atrocities. I don't want to go into that now, especially not at this hour.'

Fowler waved one of his hands in front of him, as if he was trying to chase away ghosts. In someone like him, whose economy of movement seemed almost supernatural, the gesture betrayed tremendous anxiety. Paola realised he wanted to be done with this particular story.

'You don't have to go on. Just tell me what you think I need to know.'

Fowler smiled gratefully. 'But that, as I guess you might imagine, wasn't the end of the Holy Alliance. The arrival of Paul VI on the throne of Saint Peter in 1963 came amidst the most fraught international situation the world had ever seen. Less than a year before, the world had been only a few inches away from nuclear war. And a few months later, Kennedy, the first Catholic president, was assassinated. When Paul VI learned the news, he ordered the Holy Alliance back into action. The network of spies, although diminished by time, regrouped. The tricky part was recreating the Hand of Saint Michael. Of the twelve Hands who had been recalled to Rome in fifty-eight, only seven were fit for service in 1963. One of them was put in charge of rebuilding the organisational structure to train new agents. The job took about fifteen years, but they succeeded in training a core of thirty agents. Some of these men had absolutely no prior experience, and some came from other secret services.'

'Like yourself: a double agent.'

'In reality, I was considered as a potential agent. That's someone who normally works for two allied organisations, but the first is unaware that the second adds to or modifies the directives in each mission. It was my job to use my knowledge in order to save lives, not to take other people's. Almost every mission they sent me on involved getting people out: saving endangered priests in complicated positions.'

'Almost every mission.'

Fowler nodded. 'We had a complex job where things got bent out of shape. I stopped being a Hand that very day. It didn't make things easy for me, but here I am. I thought I would be a psychologist for the rest of my life, and look where one of my patients has led me.'

'Dante is one of the Hands, no?'

'Years after I resigned, there was another crisis. Once again there were very few agents, and all of them were far away, involved in missions it wouldn't have been easy to get out of. The only man available was Dante, and he wasn't known for his scruples. In reality, he was probably a perfect fit for the job, if my suspicions are right.'

'So Cirin is the Head?'

Fowler looked straight ahead, unperturbed. After a minute Paola decided he wasn't going to answer, so she asked him another question. 'But why would the Holy Alliance want to make a mess like this …?'

'The world is changing. Democratic ideals are taking root all over the world, including among some flexible members of the Curia. The Holy Alliance needs a pope who will steadfastly support them or they'll disappear. But the alliance is a divisive issue. What the three cardinals had in common was that they were all determined liberals – as liberal as a cardinal could be, when all is said and done. Any one of them would have dismantled the secret service, maybe for good.'

'Take them out of the picture, and that threat is gone.'

'And in doing so you increase the need for security. If the cardinals had just disappeared, there would be a lot of questions. And they wouldn't have been able to make it look like an accident either: the Pontificate is naturally paranoid. But if you have something certain ..'

'A killer in a disguise. Jesus, this is making me sick. I'm glad I distanced myself from the Church.'

Fowler moved closer to her and knelt down in front of the chair, taking both her hands in his. 'Don't make that mistake. Behind this Church, made out of the blood and bricks you see before you, there is another Church, infinite and invisible, whose flags are raised towards Heaven. This Church lives in the hearts of the millions of faithful who love Christ and his message. It will be reborn from its ashes and fill the world. The Gates of Hell shall have no dominion.'

Paola's eyes bored into the priest. 'You really believe all that?'

'I do believe it, Paola.'

Both of them stood up. He kissed her tenderly and slowly, and she accepted him as he was, with all of his scars. Her anguish flowed into his pain and came undone there, and over the course of the small hours of the morning they discovered what it was to be happy.

Dicanti Family Apartment

VIA DELLA CROCE, 12

Sunday, 10 April 2005, 8.41 a.m.

This time it was Fowler who woke up to the aroma of fresh coffee.

'Here you are, *padre*.'

He glanced at her, puzzled by the formal address. She looked at him unwaveringly, and he understood. Hope had given way to the clear light of morning, which already filled the room. He didn't say anything more and she wasn't expecting him to; he couldn't offer her anything except pain. Even so he felt a little better, comforted by the certainty that they had both gained something from the experience, taking strength from each other's weakness. It would have been easy to think that Fowler had strayed from his calling in those early hours of the morning, but that would have been wrong. The truth was that he was grateful to her for taming his demons, even if only for a short time.

She was happy he understood. She sat on the edge of the bed, a smile on her face; and it wasn't a cheerless smile, because in the last few hours she felt that she had overcome something. She wasn't any more sure of herself that morning than she'd been before, but at least her confusion had dissipated. Perhaps she was keeping her distance from him just to be on the safe side, to steer clear of any new pain. But it wasn't true: she understood Fowler, knew that he kept his promises and wasn't about to give up his personal crusade.

'*Dottoressa*, I have something to tell you, and it won't be easy to take.'

'Go ahead, *padre*.'

'If you ever leave your career as a criminal psychiatrist, don't open a café,' he said, grimacing in the direction of the coffee she'd brought him.

They both laughed, and for a brief moment everything was perfect.

Half an hour later, showered and refreshed, the two went over the details of the case: Fowler standing by the window in Paola's room; Paola sitting at her desk.

'You know what? In the light of day, our theory that Karosky is an assassin following orders from the Holy Alliance seems strange and unreal.'

'Very possibly. Nevertheless, in the light of day, the mutilations he's carried out are still very real; and if we're right, we're the only two people who can stop him.'

Those words were enough to take the sheen off the morning. Paola felt her soul become as tense as a tightrope. She was more aware than ever that it was their responsibility to catch this monster – for Pontiero's sake, for Fowler and for herself; and when she'd caught up with him, she wanted to ask him who exactly was on the other end of his leash. In the mood she was in, she could barely contain herself.

'The Vigilanza is compromised – I understand that much. But the Swiss Guard?'

'Beautiful uniforms, but they're quite useless. They probably don't even know that three cardinals have been murdered. I can't take them seriously: they're just traffic police.'

Paola rubbed her neck. She was perplexed. 'So what do we do now?'

'I'm not sure. We don't have a clue where Karosky is going to attack next, and since yesterday he's going to find it easier to kill.'

'What do you mean?'

'The cardinals have begun the novendial masses for the Pope's soul. They are celebrated during the nine-day period after the death of a pope.'

'You're not telling me ...'

'I am. The masses will be held all over Rome, at San Giovanni in Lateranor, Santa Maria Maggiore, San Pietro, San Paolo fuori le Mura ... The cardinals say mass, in groups of two, in the fifty most important churches in Rome. It's the tradition and I don't think they'll change it for anything in the world. If the Holy Alliance is mixed up in all of this, it would be the perfect opportunity for an assassination. The story still hasn't got out and, as it stands, the cardinals would rebel if Cirin tried to stop them from celebrating the novenas. No, the masses will take place, come what may. And damn it, another cardinal could already have been murdered and we wouldn't even know about it.'

'Christ, I need a cigarette.'

Paola looked all over her desk and felt inside her coat for Pontiero's packet of cigarettes. She put her hand in the breast pocket. Her fingers touched something tiny and hard.

'What's this?' She pulled out a card a few inches long, with the image of the Virgin of Carmen printed on one side: the card that Brother Francesco Toma had given her when she was about to leave Santa Maria in Traspontina – the false Carmelite, Karosky the killer. She was wearing the same black jacket she had worn last Tuesday morning and the card was still there.

'How could I have forgotten this? It's evidence.'

Fowler walked over, his interest piqued. 'It's a devotional card. The Virgin of Carmen. There's something written on the back.'

Fowler read the text out loud. It was in English:

'If your very own brother, or your son or your daughter, or the wife you love, or your closest friend secretly entices you, do not yield to him or listen to him. Show him no pity. Do not spare him or shield him. You must certainly put him to death. Then all Israel will hear and be afraid, and no one among you will do such an evil thing again.'

Paola translated it into Italian. She was livid.

'I believe it's from Deuteronomy. Chapter 13, verses 7 to 11.'

'Shit!' Paola said between clenched teeth. 'It was in my pocket the whole time. It should have set off alarm bells when I saw it was written in English.'

'Stop beating yourself up. A friar handed you a card. Considering your lack of faith, it's no wonder you didn't give it a second look.'

'Maybe so, but we found out who this friar was a short time later.

I should have remembered he gave me something. I was too busy trying to remember what I saw of his face in the dark. Even if ...'

'*I tried to preach the word to you, do you remember?*'

Paola held her breath. Fowler turned around with the card in his hand.

'Look, Paola, it's just an everyday card. He stuck a piece of adhesive paper on the back –'

'*Santa Maria del Carmen.*'

'– which is very helpful in locating the text. Deuteronomy is –'

'*Take it with you wherever you go.*'

'– a pretty unusual source for a quotation on a card, wouldn't you say? I think that –'

'*It will show you the way in these uncertain times.*'

'– if I tug a little on the corner, I can lift it off—'

'Don't touch it!' Paola grabbed Fowler by the arm.

Fowler blinked, taken aback. He didn't move a muscle as she took the card out of his hand.

'I'm sorry I screamed at you,' Paola said, trying to calm down. 'I just remembered that Karosky told me the card would show me the way in uncertain times. I think it's a message, and he put it there to mock us.'

'Maybe. Or maybe it's another of his attempts to throw us off track.'

'The only thing we know for sure is that we are very far from having all the pieces to the puzzle. Maybe there's a clue here.'

She turned the card over, held it up to the light, sniffed the paper.

Nothing.

'The quote from the Bible could be a message. But what was he trying to say?'

'I don't know, but I think there's something else here – something you can't see at first glance. I think I've got the perfect instrument for a case like this.'

Dicanti rummaged around in a nearby wardrobe. After a few minutes she pulled out a box, laden with dust. She put the box down carefully on her desk.

'I haven't used this since I studied at the institute. It was a gift from my father.'

She opened the box slowly, reverently. She still remembered the advertisement for the device, how expensive it was and how careful you had to be with it. She took it out and sat it upright on the desk. A standard microscope: Paola had worked with equipment a thousand times more expensive when she was at college, but she hadn't treated any of it with the respect she showed this piece. She liked feeling that way: the microscope was a connection to her father, and a rare one at that, especially for someone who'd mourned ever since the day she'd lost him. She fleetingly asked herself if it wouldn't be better to treasure the glittering memories she had rather than holding on to the idea that they had been snatched away from her too soon.

The wrapping paper and plastic had protected the instrument from dust. She put the card under the lens and adjusted the focus. With her left hand she moved the multicoloured card around, slowly inspecting every speck of the image of the Virgin. Nothing remarkable. She turned the card over.

'Hold on … There's something here.'

Paola let Fowler look through the eyepiece. Fifteen times their normal size, the letters on the card were like enormous black chess pieces. There was a minuscule white circle around one of them.

'Looks like a perforation.'

Paola took the microscope back from Fowler. 'I'd say it was done with a pin and it appears to have been done intentionally. It's too perfect.'

'Where does the first mark appear?'

'In the "f" of "if".'

'Keep looking. Check to see if there are perforations around other letters.'

Paola checked each letter in the first line of text. 'There's another here.'

'Go on.'

After eight minutes of looking, Paola had successfully identified eleven perforated letters:

'If your very own brother, or your son or your daughter, or the wife you love, or your closest friend secretly entices you, do not yield to him or listen to him. Show him no pity. Do not spare him or shield

269

him. You must certainly put him to death. Then all Israel will hear and be afraid, and no one among you will do such an evil thing again.'

When she had checked that there were no more perforated letters, Paola wrote them out in the order they appeared. What they read shocked them. And then Paola put the pieces together.

If you very own brother tries to seduce you in secret: the psychiatric sessions.

Do not spare him or shield him: the letters to the families of the victims of Karosky's sexual depredation.

You must certainly put him to death.

She recalled the one name that figured in all of it.

Francis Casey.

Reuters News Feed, 10 April 2005, 08.12 GMT

CARDINAL CASEY WILL CONDUCT THE NOVENDIAL MASS IN SAINT PETER'S TODAY

ROMA (Associated Press) – Cardinal Francis Casey will officiate today at the midday novendial mass at Saint Peter's Basilica in Rome. The American cardinal will enjoy the honour of directing the ceremony on this, the second day of the nine-day mourning period for the soul of John Paul II.

Some organisations in the US have not looked upon Casey's participation in the ceremony favourably. Specifically, the SNAP (Survivor's Network for those Abused by Priests) has sent two of its members to Rome to formally protest the fact that Casey has been allowed to officiate at the most important church in Christendom. 'There are only two of us, and we will protest in a peaceful, orderly fashion and tell our stories to the press,' said Barbara Payne, president of SNAP.

The organisation is the principal group representing the victims of sexual abuse by Catholic priests, and it has more than 4,500 members. Its chief activity is to locate and support victims, which it does via group therapy sessions that help victims to acknowledge what happened to them. Many of its members only join SNAP once they have reached adulthood, after years of shame and silence.

Cardinal Casey, at present Prefect of the Congregation for the Clergy, was involved in the sexual-abuse scandal that exploded in the United States in the late 1990s. Casey, cardinal for the Boston archdiocese, was the most important figure in the North American Church at the time and, many say, the strongest candidate to succeed John Paul II.

His career suffered a severe setback when it was discovered that, for years, he'd kept more than three hundred cases of sexual abuse in his jurisdiction out of the public spotlight. He frequently moved priests accused of crimes of this nature from one parish to the next, hoping to avoid scandal. In almost every instance he limited himself to recommending only 'fresh air' to those charged with abuse. Only when the cases were of the most serious kind did he send the priest in question to an institution where he could receive treatment.

As the first serious charges began to surface, Casey agreed to settlements with the families of the victims – settlements whose financial remuneration was accompanied by a vow of silence. After a period of time the scandals became common knowledge throughout the country, and 'highly placed Vatican authorities' found themselves forced to replace Casey. He was transferred to Rome, where he was named Prefect for the Congregation of the Clergy, a position of some importance but one which would seem to be the last chapter in his career.

There are nevertheless some who continue to regard Casey as a saintly man who used all of his strength to defend the Church. 'He has suffered persecution and calumnies for defending the faith,' his personal secretary, Father Miller, said. But in the media's eternal betting over who will become the next Pope, Casey's chances are not rated. The Catholic clergy is in general cautious and no friend to extravagance. Casey can count on some supporters, but, short of a miracle, it seems likely he will receive very few votes.

04/10/2005/08:12 (AP)

SACRISTY OF THE VATICAN

Sunday, 10 April 2005, 11.08 a.m.

The priests who would celebrate the mass with Cardinal Casey were helping each other with their vestments in the auxiliary sacristy near the entrance to Saint Peter's. They were to wait there, along with the altar boys, until five minutes before the ceremony began, when they would be joined by the cardinal himself.

Until that moment, the museum was deserted except for the two nuns who served under Casey and the other cardinal who would be celebrating the mass, Cardinal Pauljic. There was also a Swiss Guard, who stood in the doorway to the sacristy.

Karosky felt the comforting bulge of his knife and pistol nestled inside his clothing. He calculated his options.

At last, he was about to carry off the prize.

The moment was at hand.

$\mathscr{S}$AINT $\mathscr{P}$ETER'S $\mathscr{S}$QUARE

Sunday, 10 April 2005, 11.16 a.m.

'We'll never get in through the Santa Ana gate. It's heavily guarded and the only people they're letting in are those authorised by the Vatican.'

Dicanti and Fowler had reconnoitred the entrances to the Vatican from a discreet distance, always staying separate so as not to attract attention. In fifty minutes or less the novendial mass in Saint Peter's would get under way.

A mere thirty minutes before, the revelation of Francis Casey's name on the devotional card of the Virgin del Carmen had led to a frantic search on the Internet. From the press-agency postings, Dicanti and Fowler were able to glean the time and the place where Casey would next appear, in full view of anyone who wanted to read it.

And there they were, in Saint Peter's Square.

'We'll have to go in by the main door.'

'Won't happen. It's a classic funnel trap. Security has been tightened everywhere except for the main door, which is open to the public, so that's exactly where they'll be waiting for us. And even if we did manage to get in, we'd never get close to the altar. Casey and whoever is celebrating the mass with him will enter from the Saint Peter's Sacristy. It's easy to get to the basilica from there. And they won't use the main altar, as its reserved for the Pope alone. They'll use one of the secondary altars, and even so, there will be at least eight hundred people attending the ceremony.'

'Do you think Karosky would really dare to act in front of so many people?' Paola asked.

'Our problem is that we don't know who's playing which role in this drama. If the Holy Alliance wants to see Casey dead, they won't let us stop him celebrating the mass. And if they're intent on catching Karosky, they won't let us warn the cardinal either. He's their bait. I'm convinced that, come what may, we're nearing the end of this particular play.'

'Well, by this stage there's no longer any role for us. It's already a quarter past eleven.'

'Not true. We can still find a way into the basilica, dodge Cirin's agents and slip into the sacristy. We have to stop Casey from celebrating his mass.'

'And how are we going to do that, *padre*?'

'We'll take a route that Cirin could never have imagined.'

Four minutes later they stood at the front door of a sober five-storey building. Paola knew Fowler was right. Never in a million years would Cirin have imagined Fowler knocking, of his own free will, on the front door of the Palace of the Holy Office – the Sant'Uffizio.

One of the entrances to Saint Peter's is located between the building that houses the Sant'Uffizio and Bernini's colonnade. It consists of a roadblock and a guard station and there are usually only two Swiss Guards on duty. On this particular Sunday there were five, joined by a single Vatican police officer. He was carrying a file in his hand, inside which were Fowler's and Dicanti's photos, a fact of which both were ignorant. The officer, a member of the Vigilanza, watched as a couple who seemed to match their descriptions crossed the open space in front of him. He saw them only for an instant before they disappeared, and he wasn't absolutely sure it was them. He wasn't authorised to leave his post, so he didn't set off in pursuit. His orders were to report back if the individuals concerned tried to enter the Vatican and to detain them, by force if necessary. It was clear to him that these two were important, so he pushed the button on his walkie-talkie and gave a description of what he had seen.

Just short of the corner with Porta Cavalleggerri, and a mere sixty feet from the guard station where the officer was taking orders via his walkie-talkie, stood the entrance to the Palace of the Sant'Uffizio. The door was locked, but there was a bell. Fowler kept his finger glued to the buzzer until he heard the sound of locks being opened on the other side. The face of an aged priest squinted through a crack in the doorway.

'What do you want?' he asked, his tone unpleasant.

'We're here to see Bishop Hanër.'

'Who are you?'

'Father Fowler.'

'I'm not familiar with the name.'

'I'm an old friend.'

'Bishop Hanër is resting. Today is Sunday and the palazzo is closed. Good day,' he said, brushing them away as if he were swatting at flies.

'Would you please tell me which hospital or cemetery I can find the bishop in then?'

The old priest was taken aback.

'Excuse me?'

'Bishop Hanër told me he wouldn't rest until he'd made me pay for my sins, so he must be either sick or dead. There's no other explanation.'

The look on the priest's face changed a little, from hostile disinterest to slight irritation.

'It appears you do know Bishop Hanër. Please wait outside.' The priest shut the door in their faces.

'How did you know that this Hanër would be there?'

'Bishop Hanër hasn't taken a single Sunday off in his entire life. It would have been a sad coincidence if he'd done so today.'

'He's a friend of yours?'

Fowler cleared his throat. 'Actually, he hates me more than anyone in the world. Gonthas Hanër oversees the day-to-day working of the clergy. He's an old German Jesuit who reins in the Holy Alliance when its overseas missions get out of hand – an ecclesiastical version of Internal Affairs. He's the one who put me on trial. He has a real aversion to me because I wouldn't say a single word about the missions they sent me on.'

'But you were absolved?'

'Barely. He told me that he had an anathema with my name on it, and sooner or later the Pope would sign it.'

'An anathema?'

'A decree of final excommunication. Hanër knows it's the one thing I really fear in this world: that the Church I've given my life to will prevent me from entering Heaven when I die.'

Dicanti gave him a troubled look. 'And so, *padre*, why exactly are we here?'

'I've come to make a full confession.'

$\mathcal{S}$ACRISTY IN $\mathcal{S}$AINT $\mathcal{P}$ETER'S $\mathcal{B}$ASILICA

Sunday, 10 April 2005, 11.31 a.m.

The Swiss Guard tumbled to the floor as gracelessly as a drunk on the street; the only sound was that of his ornate pike clattering on to the marble floor. His throat was slit from one side to the other, completely severing his trachea.

One of the nuns came out of the sacristy when she heard the noise. She didn't even get the chance to scream. Karosky struck her on the face as hard as he could. The nun fell to the floor face down. She was out cold. The killer took his time, searching around for the right spot beneath her black garments with his right foot. He was looking for her neck. He chose the spot he wanted and put all of his weight on the ball of his foot. Her neck made a dry cracking sound.

A second nun stuck her head out from the sacristy. She didn't sense any danger. She just needed some help from her sister.

Karosky sank his knife deep into her right eye. He threw her to the floor and, as he dragged her over to the short hallway leading to the sacristy, he was already dragging a corpse.

He surveyed the three bodies, and then glanced at the door to the sacristy. He checked his watch.

He still had five minutes left to put the finishing touches to his work.

Just Outside the Door of the Sant'Uffizio

Sunday, 10 April 2005, 11.31 a.m.

What Fowler had said made Paola's jaw drop, but before she could get a word out, the front door of the Sant'Uffizio swung open with a great flourish. Instead of the elderly priest who'd greeted them earlier, a bishop now stood before them. Slender in build, with immaculate blond beard and hair, he looked to be about 50 years old. His heavy German accent dripped with disdain as he spoke to Fowler.

'Well, well. Look who's turned up on my doorstep after all these years. To what do I owe this unexpected honour?'

'Bishop Hanër, I need to ask a favour of you.'

'I'm afraid, Father Fowler, that you aren't in a position to ask me for anything. Some twelve years ago I made a request to you, and you didn't say a single word for days. Days! The commission may have found you innocent, but I did not. Please be on your way.'

His index finger pointed in the direction of the Porta Cavalleggeri. To Paola, his finger seemed so straight and inflexible, she could imagine Fowler hanging from it. Instead Fowler offered up his own noose.

'You haven't heard what I have to offer you in exchange.'

The bishop crossed his arms. 'Go on, Fowler.'

'There's a strong possibility that there will be a murder inside the basilica in the next half-hour. Ispettore Dicanti and I are trying to stop it, but, sadly, we can't get in. Camilo Cirin has denied us access. I ask your permission to pass through the palazzo as far as the car park so that we can enter the basilica without being seen.'

'And in exchange ...?'

'I will answer all of your questions about El Aguacate. Tomorrow.'

Hanër turned to Paola. 'Show me some identification.'

Paola couldn't take out her police badge as Troi had made her surrender it, but luckily she still had the ID card that enabled her to pass in and out of UACV headquarters. She held it authoritatively in the bishop's face, praying that it would pass muster.

Hanër took the card from Dicanti's hand. He studied her face and the photograph on the card, the UACV emblem and even the magnetic band.

'So, you are telling the truth – though I'm inclined to believe, Fowler, that you've added concupiscence to your other sins.'

Paola turned away so that Hanër wouldn't see the smile that was spreading across her face. She was relieved that Fowler managed to hold the bishop's gaze with the same serious expression. Hanër cleared his throat, making no attempt to mask his contempt.

'Fowler, where you're going is surrounded by blood and death. My feelings towards you haven't changed in the slightest. I have no desire to let you in.'

The priest was about to respond, but the bishop cut him off. 'Even so, I know that you're a man of your word so I will accept your petition. Today I will let both of you enter the basilica, but tomorrow, Fowler, you must come and meet me, and you will tell me the truth.'

With these words the bishop stepped aside. Fowler and Dicanti entered the building. The cream-coloured entrance hall was elegant but bare of mouldings or adornment of any kind. The whole building was filled with a Sunday silence, and Paola suspected that the only person who remained there was the tense and wiry man beside them. The bishop seemed to regard himself as the direct agent of God's justice. She shivered just thinking about what such an obsessed mind might have done had he lived four hundred years earlier.

'I'll see you tomorrow, Padre Fowler. And I'll have the pleasure of showing you a document I've been keeping for you.'

The priest led Paola down a hallway on the ground floor without looking back. He was perhaps afraid that he'd find Hanër still standing next to the door, waiting for him to come back the following morning.

'Very unusual, *padre*. People normally *leave* the Church via the Sant'Uffizio rather than enter it,' Paola said.

Fowler's expression showed a combination of irony and sadness. 'I hope that, in capturing Karosky, we aren't saving the life of someone who will eventually reward me with excommunication.'

They came to the emergency exit. A nearby window looked out into the car park. Fowler pressed the bar in the middle of the door and stuck his head out. One hundred feet away the Swiss Guards were watching the street. He closed the door.

'We'll have to make it quick. We've got to get to Casey and explain the situation to him before Karosky finishes him off.'

'How are we going to get there?'

'We'll go out into the car park and continue walking in single file, staying as close to the wall of the building as possible. We'll arrive almost immediately at the building where the Pope holds his public audiences. We'll keep going, hugging the wall, until we get to the corner. Then we'll have to cross on the diagonal as quickly as we can. Keep your face turned to the right, because we don't know if anyone will be looking out for us there. I'll go first, agreed?'

Paola nodded her head and they set off, walking quickly. They made it to the sacristy without any problems. It was an imposing edifice, attached to the side of the basilica. The latter was open all year round to tourists and pilgrims and its public spaces functioned as a museum containing some of Christianity's most beautiful treasures.

Fowler reached out to the door.

It was already half-open.

Sacristy of Saint Peter's Basilica

'A bad sign,' Fowler said as quietly as he could.

Dicanti's hand moved towards her waist, and she pulled out her revolver, a thirty-eight.

'Let's go in,' she said.

'I thought Troi had taken your pistol.'

'He made me give up my automatic; it's standard issue for every officer. This little toy is only for emergencies.'

They crossed the threshold. The museum was deserted, the lights in the display cases turned off. The marble lining the walls and the floors reflected the minuscule amount of sunlight that filtered through a handful of windows; although it was midday, the galleries were practically in darkness. Fowler led the way without a word, silently cursing the noise his shoes made on the floor. They passed straight through four of the museum's galleries without looking to either side. But in the sixth gallery Fowler stopped in mid-step. On the ground a mere twenty inches in front of him, partially hidden in the shadows of the corridor he was about to enter, was an extraordinary sight: a white-gloved hand and an arm arrayed in vivid yellows, blues and reds.

Rounding the corner, they discovered that the arm was connected to a Swiss Guard. He still clutched his staff with his left hand, but what had been eyes were now just two empty sockets drained of blood. A little further along the corridor Paola found two nuns in black habits and wimples, united in a last embrace.

Their eyes were missing too.

Paola cocked her gun. She and Fowler looked at each other.

'He's here.'

They stood in the short hallway that led to the Vatican's central sacristy, which was usually roped off, its double doors left open so that the public could satisfy its curiosity by staring into the room where the Holy Father put on his robes before celebrating mass.

The doors were closed.

'I hope for God's sake that we're not too late,' Paola said, her eyes staring at the bodies on the floor.

The Swiss Guards and the two nuns brought the total of Karosky's victims to at least eight. Paola swore to herself that these would be the last. She didn't need to think twice. She ran along the corridor to the door, stepping around the bodies. She threw open one side of the door with her left hand, her pistol raised and ready in the right. She crossed the threshold.

Inside was an octagonal room with ceilings some thirty-six feet high, suffused with a golden light. Directly in front of her was an altar standing between columns, with an oil painting hanging above it: the descent from the cross. Standing against the sublime, highly polished marble walls were ten armoires fashioned out of teak and myrtle, inside which hung the sacred vestments. If Paola had glanced up to the ceiling she would have seen a cupola adorned with beautiful frescos, through whose windows streamed the light that flooded the space. But Paola's eyes were fixed on the two men standing on the other side of the room.

She recognised Cardinal Casey first. The second was also a cardinal and he looked vaguely familiar. At last she recognised him: Cardinal Pauljic.

The men were standing together at the altar. Pauljic, behind Casey, was making a few final adjustments to Casey's robes when Dicanti barged in, her pistol pointed directly at them.

'Where is he?' she shouted, her voice echoing in circles around the cupola. 'Have you seen him?'

His eyes riveted on Dicanti's pistol, the American cardinal spoke very slowly. 'Where is who, miss?'

'Karosky – the man who slaughtered the Swiss Guard and the two nuns.'

She hadn't finished speaking when Fowler entered the sacristy.

He stood next to Paola. He looked at Casey, and then, for the first time, he and Pauljic exchanged glances.

There was fire, and recognition too, in those eyes.

'Hello, Victor,' said the priest, his voice deep and hoarse.

Cardinal Pauljic, better known as Victor Karosky, put his left arm around Cardinal Casey's neck. With his right hand he took out Maurizio Pontiero's pistol and placed it against the cardinal's temple.

'Don't move!' Dicanti shouted, her voice reverberating around the room.

'Don't *you* move a muscle, Miss Dicanti, or we'll get a good look at the inside of the cardinal's head.'

The killer's voice hit Paola with the force of all the anger, fear and adrenaline that pulsed through her veins. She remembered how angry she had been when the monster had called her on the phone, right after she'd seen Pontiero's body.

She took aim carefully.

Karosky was more than thirty feet away and only part of his head and his forearms were visible as he stood behind Cardinal Casey, his human shield.

Even with her skill and a revolver, it was an impossible shot.

'Put the gun down on the floor, or I'll kill him right here.'

Paola bit her lower lip to keep herself from screaming. She had the killer right in front of her, yet she couldn't do a thing.

'Don't do it, *dottoressa*. He'd never hurt the cardinal. Isn't that right, Victor?'

Karosky tightened his grip around Casey's neck. 'Of course I would. Put the gun on the ground, Dicanti. Put it down!'

'Please, do as he asks,' Casey groaned in a quavering voice.

'Excellent acting, Victor.' Fowler's voice was shaking with rage. 'Remember how we thought it was impossible that the killer could have got out of Cardoso's room, because it was locked up tight? Damn, that part was easy. He never left.'

'What?' Paola didn't know what to make of Fowler's words.

'We broke down the door. We didn't see anyone. And then there was a very opportune cry for help about some mad attack taking place by the service lift? Victor was in the room, there's no doubt about it. Were you under the bed? Hiding in the closet?'

'Very astute, *padre*. Now put the gun down, ispettore.'

'But this cry for help and the description of what the attacker looked like came from a trustworthy source, a man of faith. A cardinal. The killer's accomplice.'

'Shut up, Fowler!'

'What did he promise you if you'd take his competitors out of the picture, Victor? – if you helped him in his quest for a glory he stopped deserving a very long time ago.'

'That's enough!' Karosky looked like a madman with his face drenched in sweat and one of the fake eyebrows he'd glued in place dangling precariously over one eye.

'Did he come to see you at the institute, Victor? He's the one who sent you there – isn't that so?'

'Enough of these absurd allegations, Fowler. Tell the woman to put the gun down, or this madman is going to kill me,' Casey commanded. He was clearly desperate.

'Tell us His Eminence's plan, Victor,' Fowler said, ignoring Casey. 'You had to pretend to attack him right in the middle of Saint Peter's? And he would dissuade you from carrying out the attack, right in front of all of God's people and the television cameras?'

'You keep talking, and I'll kill him! I'll kill him!'

'You would have been the one who ended up dead. And he'd be the hero. What did he promise you in exchange for the keys to the kingdom, Victor?'

'Heaven, you fucking son of a bitch! Eternal life!'

Karosky lifted the gun from Casey's temple, aimed it at Dicanti and fired.

Fowler shoved Paola forward and the pistol slipped out of her hand. Karosky's shot just missed Dicanti's head and destroyed Fowler's left shoulder.

Karosky let Casey go and the cardinal scurried off to hide between two of the armoires. Paola, with no time to look for her gun, threw herself headlong at Karosky, her hands balled into fists. Her right shoulder smashed into his stomach, knocking him against the wall, but she didn't manage to wind him, as he was protected by the extra padding he wore beneath his flowing robes in order to look fatter. Even so, Pontiero's pistol clattered to the ground with a hollow metallic echo.

Karosky beat Dicanti on the back and she howled in pain but managed to get to her feet and smashed Karosky in the face. He looked dazed and almost lost his balance.

Then Paola made her only mistake. She looked around for the pistol. Karosky seized the moment to hit her in the face, the stomach, the kidneys. He grabbed her round the neck, just as he had done with Casey. But this time he was holding a short object with which he caressed Paola's face: a common fish knife, but a very sharp one.

'Ah, Paola, you have no idea how much I'm going to enjoy this,' he whispered into her ear.

'Victor!'

Karosky turned around. Fowler was sitting up, one knee positioned on the marble floor, his left shoulder shattered, his blood-soaked arm dangling inertly towards the floor. His right hand held Paola's revolver and he aimed directly at Karosky's forehead.

'You won't shoot, Fowler.' Karosky was breathing heavily. 'We're not so very different. The two of us have shared the very same hell. And you swore in your vows that you would never again take a life.'

Making a tremendous effort, his face flushed with pain, Fowler managed to lift his left hand to his priest's collar. With a single gesture, he tore it off and threw it into the air between Karosky and himself. It spun in circles, the starched cloth an immaculate white save for one red stain, where Fowler had pressed his thumb and torn it loose. Karosky watched it, hypnotised, but he didn't see it hit the ground.

Fowler fired once – a single, deadly accurate shot that hit Karosky straight between the eyes.

The killer fell to the ground. From far away he heard the voices of his parents calling out to him. And he went to join them.

Paola ran towards Fowler, who looked deathly pale. As she crossed the room, she tore off her jacket to use as a tourniquet for Fowler's wound.

'Lie down.'

'It's a good thing you got here, my friends,' said Cardinal Casey, slowly recovering enough to get back on his feet. 'That monster had taken me hostage.'

'Don't just stand there, cardinal. Go and get someone ...' Paola began, as she tried to help Fowler stretch out on the floor. And then she suddenly realised exactly where Casey was headed: to the spot next to Karosky's body, where Pontiero's pistol had fallen to the ground. It struck her that she and Fowler were two very dangerous witnesses. She felt around for her revolver.

'Good afternoon,' said Inspector Camilo Cirin as he walked into the room with three agents of the Vigilanza in tow. He hastened over to the cardinal, who was leaning over to grab the pistol from the floor. He immediately straightened up again.

'I was beginning to think you were never going to show up, inspector general. You must arrest these two immediately,' Casey said, pointing at Fowler and Dicanti.

'Forgive me, Your Eminence. I'll be with you in a moment.'

Camilo Cirin looked down. He walked over to Karosky, picking up Pontiero's pistol along the way. He poked the tip of his shoe at Karosky's face.

'It's him?'

'That's right,' said Fowler.

'Fuck, Cirin, a fake cardinal,' Paola said. 'How did that happen?'

'He had very good references.'

Cirin put things together at an incredible speed. Behind his impassive face was a brain operating like a machine. He instantly recalled that Pauljic had been the very last cardinal nominated by John Paul II – only six months ago, at a time when the Pope had rarely got out of bed. He remembered that he had told Samalo and Ratzinger about the nomination of a cardinal *in pectore*, whose name *he had revealed to Casey alone*, so that Casey could announce the papal choice upon his demise. It wasn't very hard to figure out whose lips had breathed Pauljic's name into the stricken Pope's ear, nor who had acompanied the new 'cardinal' to Saint Martha's for the first time, in order to introduce him to his intrigued brethen.

'Cardinal Casey, you've a lot of explaining to do.'

'I don't know what you mean.'

'Cardinal, please.'

Casey looked out of sorts, but he soon began to recover his usual arrogance, his perennial pride, the very thing that had led to his downfall.

'Over the course of many years, John Paul was preparing me to continue his work. You, more than anyone, know what could happen if the control of the Church should fall into the hands of those who lack the necessary discipline. I trust that, in the present instance, you will act in the best interests of the Church, my friend.'

Cirin's eyes arrived at a summary judgement in a split second. 'I will of course do so, Your Eminence. Domenico?'

'Inspector,' said one of the agents who had entered the room with Cirin.

'Cardinal Casey will celebrate the novendial mass in the basilica.' The cardinal smiled.

'Afterwards, you and the other agent will escort him to his new residence: the monastery at Albergradz, high in the Alps, where the cardinal will be able to reflect on his actions in solitude. He will also have the opportunity to improve his mountain-climbing.'

'A dangerous sport, from what I've heard,' said Fowler.

'Most certainly. Plagued with accidents,' Paola added.

Casey didn't respond. His silence revealed exactly how far he had fallen. He hung his head, his chin resting against his chest. He didn't say a word to anyone as he left the sacristy, accompanied by Domenico.

Cirin knelt at Fowler's side. Paola held his head up with one hand, pressing her jacket on to the wound with the other.

'Permit me.' He moved Dicanti's hand away. Her improvised dressing was already soaked and he put his own wrinkled coat in its place. 'You can relax; there's an ambulance on its way. Do you mind telling me how you managed to get into this circus?'

'We avoided your ticket booths, Cirin. We prefer to use those of the Sant'Uffizio.'

Cirin, seemingly imperturbable, raised an eyebrow. Paola understood that this was his way of showing surprise.

'Ah, but of course. Old Gonthas Hanër, a man who never quits. I see that he's relaxed his criteria for admission to the Vatican these days.'

'But his prices are high,' Fowler said, as he thought about the wrenching interview that awaited him the following day.

Cirin nodded. He knew what Fowler was trying to tell him, and he leaned even more heavily on the jacket wrapped around Fowler's wound.

'That could be sorted out, I suppose.'

An emergency medical crew entered the room, carrying a stretcher.

While the two medics attended to the injured man, inside the basilica eight altar boys and two priests carrying censers waited at the door to the sacristy for Cardinals Casey and Pauljic. It was now four minutes past twelve and the mass should already have begun. The more senior of the two priests was tempted to send one of the altar boys into the sacristy to find out what was going on. Perhaps the oblate sisters, in charge of overseeing the sacristy, were having problems with the appropriate vestments. But protocol demanded that he stayed where he was, keeping watch over the participants in the mass.

At the last moment Cardinal Casey appeared by himself at the door that led into the basilica. The altar boys escorted him to the altar of Saint Joseph, where he would lead the mass. The faithful perched closest to the altar during the ceremony talked among themselves, whispering that the cardinal must truly have loved the Pope. Casey was in tears throughout the entire mass.

'Calm down; you're out of danger,' said one of the nurses. 'We'll be on our way to the hospital in a minute. They'll run some tests on you but the haemorrhaging is under control.'

The emergency crew lifted the stretcher, and at that instant it hit Paola: the alienation from his parents, the rejection of his inheritance, the terrible resentment. She stopped the two men carrying the stretcher just as they were loading it into the ambulance.

'Now I get it. The private hell you both shared. You went to Vietnam to kill your father, didn't you?'

Fowler gave her a startled look. 'Sorry?'

'Anger and resentment are what took you to Vietnam.' Paola spoke as quietly as possible in order to keep the others out of the conversation. 'The deep hatred of your father, the cold rejection of your mother. The refusal to accept your inheritance. You wanted to cut every tie you had with your family. And the interview with Victor where you talked about Hell. It's all in the dossier you gave me. It's been right in front of my face the whole time.'

'Where are you going with this?'

'I get it now,' Paola said. She leaned over the stretcher and gently placed her hand on the priest's shoulder. Fowler was in pain and barely repressed a moan. 'I understand why you took the job at the Saint Matthew, and how it made you what you are today. Your father abused you as a child. That's the truth, isn't it? And your mother knew the whole time. Just like Karosky. Which was why he respected you. Because the two of you had been on opposite sides of the same line. You chose to become a man, and he chose to be a monster.'

Fowler didn't reply; it wasn't necessary. The men carrying the stretcher started towards the ambulance again, but Fowler gathered his strength and managed to look at her and smile.

'Take care of yourself, *dottoressa*.'

In the ambulance Fowler fought to maintain consciousness. His eyes closed for a second but a voice he recognised brought him back.

'Hello, Anthony.'

Fowler smiled.

'Well, Fabio. So how's your arm?'

'Pretty well fucked.'

'You were lucky on that roof.'

Dante didn't answer. He and Cirin were sitting on a bench that backed on to the ambulance's cabin. The Vigilanza superintendent tried to fight off his typically cynical expression despite the fact that his left arm was in a cast and his face was covered with bruises. Cirin for his part wore his habitual stony face.

'And so? How do you intend to kill me? Cyanide in the drip? let me bleed to death? or the classic shot to the back of the head? I personally prefer the latter.'

Dante's smile was joyless. 'Don't tempt me. Maybe one day, but not now, Anthony. This is a round trip. There will be a better opportunity.'

Cirin looked straight at Fowler. 'I want to thank you. You've been a great help.'

'I didn't do it for you. Or for your cause.'

'I know.'

'In fact, I was certain you were behind all this.'

'I know that too, and I don't blame you.'

The three said nothing for the next few minutes. Finally, it was Cirin who began to speak.

'Any chance you'll ever work with us again?'

'None whatsoever, Camilo. You tricked me once. I won't let it happen again.'

'One last time. For old times' sake.'

Fowler thought for a few moments.

'On one condition. And you know what that is.'

Cirin nodded. 'You have my word. Nobody goes near her.'

'Nor the other – the Spanish girl.'

'That I can't guarantee. We're still not sure she doesn't have a copy of the disk.'

'I spoke to her. She doesn't have it, and she won't talk.'

'That's good. Without the disk she can't prove a thing.'

This time the silence in the ambulance stretched and was interrupted only by the beeping of the electrocardiogram attached to Fowler's chest. The priest was fading, little by little. Cirin's last words came to him as if through a fog.

'You know what, Anthony? For a while there I was sure that you were going to tell her the truth – the whole truth.'

Fowler didn't hear what he said in response, but it didn't matter. Not every truth will set you free. He knew that even he couldn't live with his truth, much less put its heavy weight on someone else's shoulders.

RATZINGER IS CHOSEN AS THE NEW POPE, ALMOST UNOPPOSED

ANDREA OTERO (special correspondent)

ROME – The Conclave that gathered in order to choose Pope John Paul II's successor came to a close yesterday with the selection of the former Prefect of the Congregation of the Doctrine of the Faith, Joseph Ratzinger. Despite having sworn on the Bible to maintain secrecy, under penalty of excommunication, regarding the election of the Pope, the first reports from Conclave members have already begun to slip out. It appears that the German cardinal was chosen with 105 votes of the possible 115, many more than the 77 he needed to obtain a majority. Vatican sources state that the overwhelming support Ratzinger enjoyed is unprecedented, and even more so in light of the fact that the Conclave took only two days to make its decision.

Experts attributed the unprecedented and swift election of Ratzinger to the lack of any real opposition to this candidate, who was, in the early stages, very far behind in the race. Sources close to the Vatican indicate that Ratzinger's principal rivals (Portini, Robayra, and Cardoso) would never have attracted the necessary votes at any time. These same sources further commented that the aforementioned cardinals seemed 'a little out of it' during the election of Benedict XVI.

El Globo, Wednesday, 20 April 2005, page 8

Epilogue

OFFICE OF POPE BENEDICT XVI

PALAZZO DEL GOVERNATORATO

Wednesday, 20 April 2005, 11.23 a.m.

The man in white robes was the sixth person to greet Paola. Two weeks earlier and one floor below, Paola had waited in a similar hallway, a bundle of nerves, ignorant of the fact that at that very moment her friend was slowly dying. Two weeks later her anxiety about the correct way to behave was gone, and her friend avenged. An enormous number of events had taken place in those past few days, not the least important of which were in Paola's soul.

The criminologist stared at the door still adorned with the red ribbons and wax seals that had been hung there to protect the office between the death of John Paul II and the election of the new Pope. The Supreme Pontiff gestured towards the door.

'I've asked for them to be left there for a while. They'll serve to remind me that this post is only temporary,' he said in a weary voice as Paola kissed his ring.

'Your Holiness.'

'Inspector Dicanti, welcome. I asked you to come so I can personally thank you for the brave things you did.'

'Thank you, Your Holiness. I only did what my job required.'

'No, ispettore, you went far beyond what your job required. Sit down, please,' he said, gesturing towards one of the throne-like chairs in a corner of the office. A gorgeous Tintoretto hung overhead.

'Actually I was hoping I'd meet Father Fowler here, Your Holiness,' Paola said, barely disguising the urgency in her voice. 'I haven't seen him in ten days.'

The Pope took her hand and smiled in a comforting manner.

'Father Fowler is resting in a safe place out of harm's way. I took the opportunity to visit him last night. He asked me to send you his greetings and gave me this message: "Now is the time for both of us, you and I, to let go of the sadness we feel for those we have left behind."'

Those words were enough to provoke an intense emotional catharsis in Paola, and she was no longer able to hold back her tears. She spent another half-hour in the presence of the Holy Father, but whatever conversation may have taken place in his office is known only to the two of them.

A short while later Paola went out for a walk in Saint Peter's Square. It was a little past midday and the sun was a brilliant ball of light. She took out Pontiero's packet of cigarettes and lit the last one. Her face lifted towards the open sky and she let the cigarette smoke escape from between her lips.

'We got him, Maurizio. You were right. And now get a move on – go into the fucking light and leave me in peace. And hey, say hello to my father for me.'

Acknowledgements

The author wishes to express his thanks to Antonia Kerrigan and Tom Colchie, the best agents an author can hope for. At Orion, to Kirsty Dunseath. Her command of Spanish and her passion for detail have helped substantially in making this novel possibly even better than the original. And I can't forget to thank my *mano* James Graham, author of a classic New York novel and translator of the one hundred thousand words you have just read. The efforts of these four people *went far beyond what their job required*.

Various people played key roles in the research for *God's Spy*: Julie Meridian and Alice Nakagawa in New York, and Dobbie and Mike Nelson in Maryland (thanks for letting me sleep on your sofa); masterly psychiatrists Carlos Álvarez and Thomas Hurt, who helped me to make detailed profiles of Victor, Paola and Anthony; and Sor Fermina in Vatican City. To you, and to those who helped and who asked not to be mentioned, many thanks.

And, of course, to Katu and Andrea. For your aid throughout and your unconditional love.